"Although much of the novel takes place at a school for magic, the novel smartly eschews a now-tiresome Hogwarts-ian ethos, instead focusing more on Christa's experiences in elven society. The bigotry directed toward her—both casual and overt—is handled with surprising nuance."

— *Kirkus Reviews*

"In this first book of The Altar Trilogy, Allan C. R. Cornelius combines the best aspects of the genre with fascinating characters in order to tell a fresh, exciting tale . . . a must read for fantasy fans."

— *Carrie Gesner - The Dying of the Golden Day*

"[Cornelius] left no stone unturned in this world. There are no neglected characters or ideas. In his wake, he leaves a rich landscape with a living history and culture."

— *Jason Jack Miller – The Devil and Preston Black*

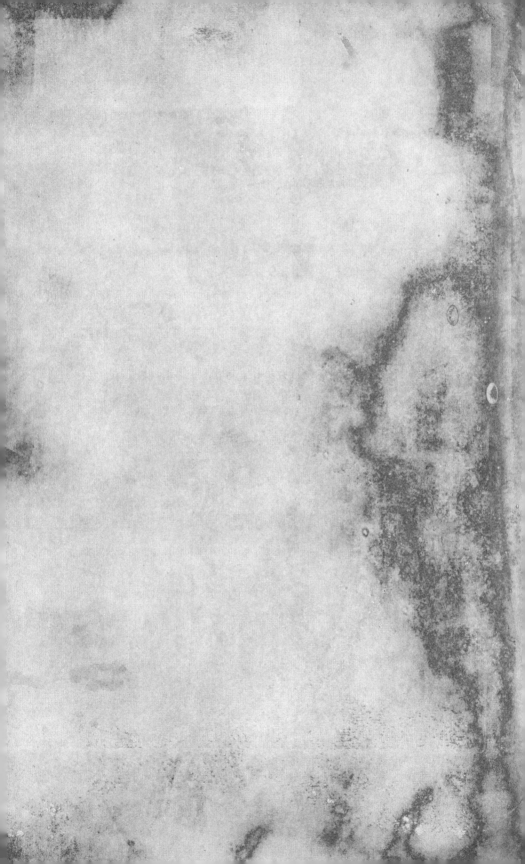

WHISPERS AT THE ALTAR

ALLAN C.R. CORNELIUS

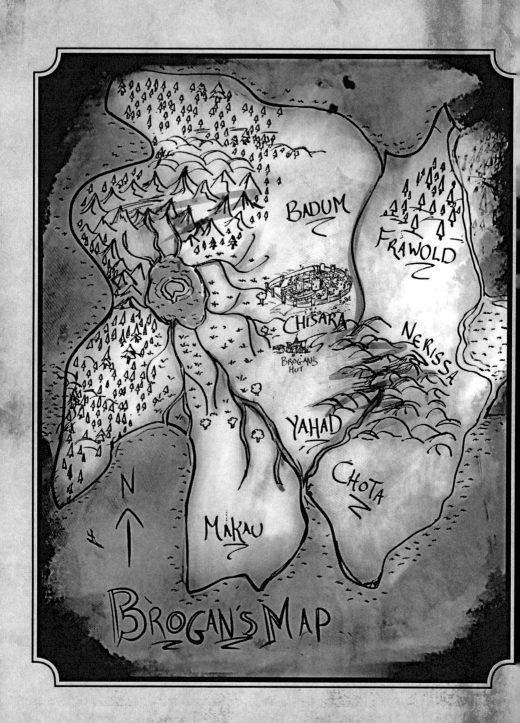

UNEARTHLY
PRESS

Whispers at the Altar is a work of fiction. Names, characters, businesses, places, events and incidents are either the products of the author's imagination or used in a fictitious manner. Any resemblance to actual persons, living or dead, or actual events is purely coincidental.

Copyright © 2017 by Allan C. R. Cornelius

All rights reserved.
Printed in the United States of America

Paperback isbn: 978-0-9990893-0-9
Hardback isbn: 978-0-9990893-1-6

Cover Illustration Copyright © 2017 by Raul Gonzalez
Cover Design by Raul Gonzalez
Maps by Tiffany Munro
Editing by Lisa Rojany, Editorial Services of Los Angeles
Interior Illustrations © 2017 Raul Gonzalez and Annie Fodge
Interior Book Design & Typesetting by Write Dream Repeat Book Design
Author Photo by Teresa Lee Photography

For Moira, Amberly, and Allan,
Who never cease to inspire me to greater things.

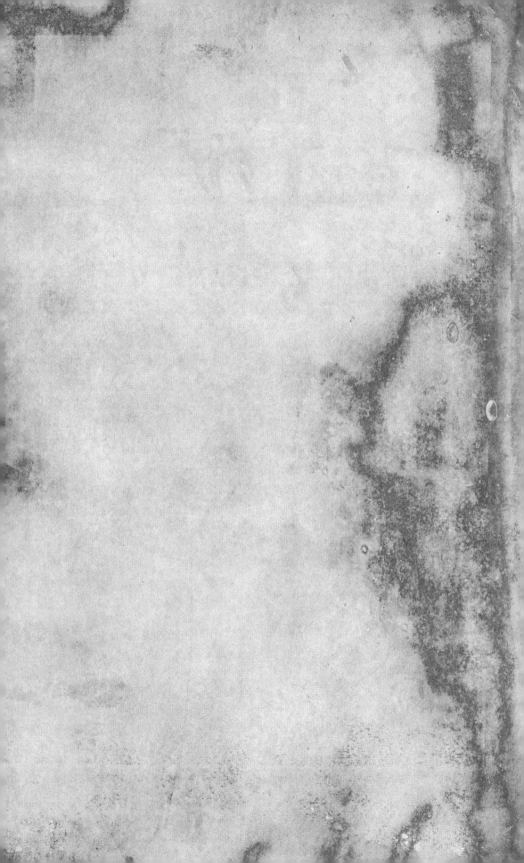

Year 1

*Emily & Zack
Always keep your
friends close
Allen R [signature]*

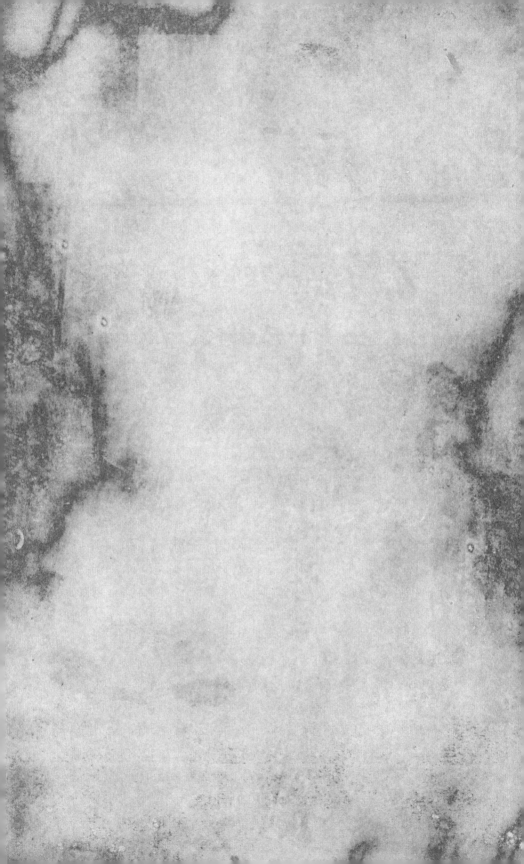

Lost

Steven tried to stretch his shoulders, but the rope binding his hands behind his back allowed for little relief. It was useless, but he couldn't help trying. After all, he didn't have much else to do, except walk. And sweat. At least there was less sweating now. The sun had finally dropped below the highest branches of the dogwoods and willows, providing a blessed bit of shade from time to time. Of course it also shone right in his eyes, forcing him to stare at a point two paces ahead. Right at Mother's mud caked boots.

It probably should have surprised him when he awoke to Mother slipping a rope around his neck and tying his wrists. After all, she hadn't taken him anywhere in his thirteen years. Then again, maybe it shouldn't have. He'd suspected for a few days something was amiss. Mother had been happy. Smiling happy. And smiles were as foreign to her face as warm food was to his bowl. He even caught her humming to herself as she brushed her long fiery red hair, the only thing he figured she loved in the whole of their dirty hovel. She'd been happy for sure, and that didn't mean anything good for him.

A tug on the rope strung from his neck yanked his thoughts back to more immediate problems. She was walking faster now, her legs pumping through the muck of the swamp at a rate he never would have imagined. Mother was no friend of work, not real work anyway. That's what she kept him around for, as she was fond of reminding him.

"Hurry up, *boy*." She spat the word at him as though it were the worst insult she could conjure. Another sign she was in a good mood. If she was really mad she'd use his name.

"Yes, Mother." He couldn't remember the last time he'd said anything else to her, but it satisfied her. She even stopped, though he knew better than to think it was for him.

She squinted ahead as he struggled up the side of an embankment, and the thick odor of rot sank into his brain. Her eyes were wide, searching all around as if seeking some landmark in the marshy maze. The sun shone through the unruly hair that floated about her head, reminding him for a moment of the fall leaves on the tree behind their dilapidated shack.

"Where is it, where is it, where is it?" She muttered. "He said west, and I went west, but I don't see it." She wrung her hands for a moment then patted down her errant hair.

Steven had no idea what she was talking about. No one ever visited them. And she hadn't left the house for months. Whatever she was trying to find, it only existed in her mind.

She started off again with a jerk, just as he was mounting the small, mercifully dry, hillock. Her controlled stumble down the other side jerked him forward, nearly pulling him clean off his feet before he could get them moving to keep pace. He just hoped she tied him off somewhere dry tonight. Maybe even somewhere he could see a few stars.

But stars were not in Steven's immediate future. As the sun dipped below the horizon it set fire to a long low bank of clouds. Which of course meant rain—the only thing that could make this journey through the swamp any worse.

They stopped as the last of the stars winked out and the cold spring rain started. They were in a small clearing of sucking mud that rose past his ankles. Surrounding them, the fetid alders grew thick, as each tried to choke the life out of its neighbors. The clearing was dotted here and there with dark pools that rippled with the impact of each drop of rain. At least he hoped the ripples were rain. Steven didn't want to guess how deep those pools might be, or what might call them home, but he assumed they were the source of the putrid stench filling the space.

He jumped as a frog croaked somewhere nearby, the grating sound soon echoed by a chorus of its brothers. Flies, ever present the entire trek, thought better than to spend their evening here. But Steven wasn't sure he liked the idea of hundreds of frogs any better. At least there weren't any snakes. He hated snakes.

As if on cue, something long and narrow slid over and between his feet.

"Eeeeee!" The scream came out before he could stop it.

"Shut your hole, boy."

Mother was pacing the length of his leash, muttering to herself, her face furious and ecstatic by intervals.

Steven clamped his mouth shut and tried to stop the shaking.

Please. Please, if there is anything good and happy in this world that looks after children. Please, let her give up searching for whatever it is. Please let us go home. He prayed to the same nameless, evidently powerless, *whatever* he always prayed to. It rarely worked, but it was something to do. Anything was better than listening to the infernal croaking and echoed plops of the frogs around him.

Then it all stopped. And the abrupt silence, punctuated only by the steady patter of rain, echoed in his ears louder than a hundred frogs. Mother stopped too, rooted in place as surely as one of the alders around them as her gaze shifted around and a small, excited whine escaped her barely parted lips.

Steven wanted to sit down, to curl up and hide. Something was watching them. He could feel it now, out there in the dark and quiet. The whole diseased swamp watched them. Two intruders into a place no human had a right to be.

He heard them first. Soft hissing spread from the unseen trees around them, first on one side then answered on another. Steven tried to follow them, to recognize them, but it was too dark, and the sounds came from too many directions.

A dull blue flame blossomed in midair, sputtering and hissing in the rain. Steven dropped back a step, squinting against the sudden light. It didn't move. It didn't go out.

Large, sickly green eyes materialized over the flame and Steven stumbled back. His fall jerked the rope out of Mother's limp grasp, and he landed on his butt in the mud. His hands, trapped beneath him, squeezed small slithering things beneath them that wriggled against his palms in a desperate attempt to get free.

He tried to scream, tried to say anything, but the only sound that came out was a soft whimper.

"You've come." The voice whispered through the rain, rasping and spitting as if forming the sounds were a task of monumental effort. "And you brought . . . the boy."

The eyes focused on Steven, and he shuffled back, sliding through rotten plants and squirming insects until his back met something solid.

"Of course I brought the boy," Mother growled back. "Now do it. Give me what I want."

Steven tried to feel behind him. The trees shouldn't be this close.

"The task is not mine to perform," the raspy voice answered.

Steven tore his gaze from those inhuman orbs long enough to risk a glance behind. Legs the size of small tree trunks ran up to a massive barrel chest, all of it covered in scales that glistened in the rain. A low-sloped face with a long, narrow, fang-crowded jaw was angled down, allowing golden eyes to watch him with cold calculation.

A giant leathery foot, the length of nearly three of Steven's, rose. Steven scrabbled to get up, his roughly patched shoes slipping in the mud. His mind held an image of that foot coming down and crushing his skull like an egg.

The image shattered in a thousand points of burning light as the foot collided with his back, shoved him into the muck, and forced the air from his lungs. He heaved only to suck in mud. He tried to retch but couldn't breathe. He could feel the worms crawling in his mouth, eager to get a head start on their inevitable meal. Mercifully, another blow to his side spun him over, flinging the ooze from his mouth.

He lay there groaning, a sharp pain carving into his side with every breath, until Mother's face blocked out the rain. She smiled, the biggest smile he'd ever seen, and for the first time he realized she was beautiful. Her green eyes sparkled with life in the light of the blue fire.

"You'll see now, Steven," she hissed, rainwater flying from her lips. "You'll see why you were born. I didn't even know. Not until *he* told me. *He'll* help me. Help me get what I've always wanted. And all he needs . . . is you."

Strong clawed hands gripped his legs, slicing through skin as they wrapped ropes around his ankles.

"I knew I kept you around for a reason," Mother continued. "And now through my greatest curse I'll receive the ultimate blessing."

She laughed, a horrible tittering sound he never heard her use before. Powerful arms lifted and dragged him across the clearing. Still Mother kept pace, mad eyes glinting in the shifting light.

Steven looked away, past the rippling bulk of the thing carrying him, and ice gripped his sodden skin. The blue flame brightened, revealing an enormous hooded viper. It was as tall and wide as a man, and its sickly yellow and red scales ran down slender arms and over looped coils where legs should be. Its narrow head was split by a lipless mouth from which a forked tongue flicked in restless anticipation.

Steven twisted and squirmed against the claws holding him. "I'm sorry, Mother. I'm sorry! I'll do better! I promise."

Inch by inch, they dragged him forward as the thing whispered unintelligible words in a hoarse guttural language.

The mud answered. Gradually, it heaved up in a mound of rotten detritus, churning as if something boiled just below its surface. Snakes, not the slim fingerlings curling through his toes, but giants thicker than his arms with ridges as sharp as blades, burst from the summit. Up and out they rose, climbing and twisting over each other's fetid black-green bodies in their haste. The pile flattened and the snakes calmed into a writhing table.

No, not a table, Steven realized. An altar.

The giant lizard flung Steven upon this altar, and the snakes immediately twined over his legs and chest to hold him down.

The serpents' ridges sliced across his skin, and his pounding pulse echoed through his brain. He couldn't think. Not of the shifting things under him, nor the reptilian monsters stepping from the black of night around him into the ethereal light that bathed him. Only Mother, standing over him with that manic grin spread across her face, her hair splayed to her skull by the rain, captured his attention. Mother. He knew she loved him.

He tried to speak. Tried to form the words to beg her forgiveness for whatever he had done.

•Whispers at the Altar•

Then he saw the knife. A jagged piece of iron with a handle little more than a cord of leather wrapped around the bottom half. He squinted against the gleam as the blade caught the light of the azure flame above him. There was chanting around him—soft, heavy, inhuman sounds—and the flame shifted and flickered with the methodical beat.

She was going to kill him. Here was his death. And why should he care?

The chanting filled his mind.

She was his mother. She knew better than he when his time was up. And what was life to him? Just an endless series of miseries and suffering.

The rhythm reverberated in his skull.

It was better this way.

The dagger swayed to the chorus.

His life was without meaning. Without purpose. Its end would bring more. Something better. Something he could never under-stand, never comprehend.

His thoughts darkened with each heavy beat.

Yes. It was better this way. He smiled. He wanted to sing, to join the music. To beg for the sweet ending of it all. That his blood would flow out and over this blessed bog and fuel the rise of—

You are not meant for this, Steven. Wake up!

The words pierced through his mind's fog like a shaft of sunlight through the clouds.

His thoughts lurched to a halt. Who? Who would rise? Or . . .what?

Mother raised the knife to the sky, her face beaming with the same ecstatic joy he experienced seconds ago.

"As your blood runs, so will his!" she screamed up into the clouded night sky.

Steven tried to think, tried to push the song out of his head. He needed to escape. But how? Bound to an altar of snakes, hands and feet tied, surrounded by . . . giant lizards?

17

"As your strength fails, his will grow."

He tried shifting on the altar, but the pythons were too strong and all he got were more painful cuts on the arm for his trouble.

"As your life ends, his begins!" Mother looked down, eyes wide with manic rapture, and Steven grasped at the only chance he had.

"I love you, Mother."

The knife stopped mid-stroke. Her eyes dimmed in momentary confusion then filled with hate.

"How dare you." She backhanded him hard across the face. "How dare you say that to me?" Another blow, this one a fist to his chest. "You never loved me. You worthless pile of—" She dropped the knife beside him, needing both hands to wrap around his neck.

Steven knew this anger. He had lived with it all his life. It was comforting after the zealous insanity. And he knew how to endure it. Blocking out the words, he focused on his hands. Again and again he dragged the ropes binding his hands over the serpents' razor-sharp spines.

"You lied to me. You deceived me. You betrayed me! When all I did was love you." Mother's words glided off him, barely heard.

He sawed while the snake twisted, squirmed, and bit. Until one hand snapped free.

"You left me with this thing. This parasite. You left me for dead! But now you'll die, Steven. You!"

He could hardly see. The walls of unconsciousness were closing around him. He scrambled one hand out, groping for the knife, thanking the *whatever* she was too angry to do the job right.

"Stop!" The snake-person-thing croaked, trying to pierce Mother's insane screaming. "You must spill his blood."

He felt her lifted away, struggling against powerful arms. The black receded, but air still refused to pass into his heaving lungs. He had the knife, his fingers inched over its coarse leather handle. He tried to sit up, tried to reach out to cut through the rope around his ankle.

She lunged, wild fury lending her strength.

She landed on top of him, her hands stretched around his neck once more, and went rigid.

Something warm spread over his chest. That warmth slid slowly over his hand and the knife it clutched desperately between him and Mother.

Steven rolled over, barely aware that the constrictors no longer held him. Mother fell onto the table beside him, the knife still protruding from her chest. He touched it, uncertain if he should pull it back out.

"Mother, I'm sorry." He pushed her hair back from her face. "I didn't mean to. I'm sorry."

There was noise around him, loud croaking and guttural shouts, but they hardly registered. Her blood was spilling, running over the snakes beneath them who in turn coiled and churned in increasing desperation to lap it up with their forked tongues.

"What should I do, Mother? I'm sorry. I'm sorry." Her gaze found his, and he tried to let his eyes tell her just how sorry he was.

One of her hands inched up. He thought at first it might try to hold his, but it didn't stop. Not until her fingers curled around his neck, and the last light of hate winked from her eyes.

Steven didn't remember how he got away. He remembered the ecstatic screams of the beasts surrounding him. He remembered the altar of snakes rising, throwing him off in its mad reach for the clouds. Then a thing, a snake-like shadow of black in the darkest night. It towered over him as he crawled away. Taller than trees, taller than the sky for all he knew, with wings to stretch from horizon to horizon. He didn't turn. The glimpses from the corners of his vision were more than enough. He remembered a roar that threatened to split his eardrums as he stumbled away. But the image that would never leave, not even in his dreams, was his mother's body sinking into the bog. Her blood stained the water red around her. Red, like her beautiful hair

THE ROOST

Twenty years had done far more to Janus than it had the creek in front of him or the tall pines that grew on either side. He stood on the rocky bank, transfixed by the flicker of sunrise within the steady movement of the water. Perhaps it was a magic of the elves or some contagious characteristic that made time matter as little to the land as it did to them. But Janus was certain he could have been gone for centuries and this spot would be just as it had been then.

He could replay the entire scene in his mind. At least that much hadn't changed over the decades. He could see her as clearly as the lionpetals waving in the soft spring breeze. They were—had been—Chrysobel's favorite. He bent down, plucked one, and twirled it between two fingers. The yellow petals spun, back and forth, and for a minute he was back in that summer two decades ago. He closed his eyes and for a moment he could feel her beside him again.

But she never would be. He threw the flower into the brook and turned, refusing to watch it float away. He took one step toward the fire he built the night before then stopped as his gaze met Christa's. He barely suppressed the flinch. How long had she been lying there watching him?

"Good morning, sleepyhead." He sat next to her, taking up a stick to poke the fire. Anything to avoid her eyes. Chrysobel's eyes.

Christa stretched next to him then jerked upright. "Is there breakfast? Did you get anything? Would you like me to make something? How about some tea?" She jumped up before he could say a word and rummaged through their mostly empty packs.

Janus let out a long breath and shook his head. It had been like this the entire trip. She was trying to change his mind about taking her. But even now, on the last morning, he couldn't. He loved her, but he could barely look at her. What kind of father did that make him? How could he raise her? For the past fortnight of travel, the memories haunted him. All of Christa's firsts flooded through his mind. They taunted him, teased him, as inevitably they gave way to the image of Chrysobel's crushed and broken body. The reminder of what Christa had done.

"I found some leaves. I'll get some water, and we'll have some tea at least. We can finish off the dried fruit, too. There isn't a lot left." She bit her lip as a cloud of worry passed over her cheerful face. But the smile sprang back resolutely.

She knows the trip is almost over.

"I'll look around and see if I can find—"

"It's fine, Christa," Janus said. He hesitated, then leaned forward, unsure if he meant to pat her shoulder or pull her to him.

It didn't matter, she had already leapt to her feet and started toward the river.

He watched her go, the doubt and pain rolling over each other within him. He didn't think he would eat this morning. He didn't think he could.

Whispers at the Altar

Mama died six months ago.

Six months of quiet mornings, lonely afternoons, and awkward evenings. Six months of Christabel silently crying herself to sleep, only to jerk awake from the nightmares. She shivered but kept the bounce in her step as she walked to the creek. Papa didn't know about the nightmares. Not because she didn't want to tell him. She tried to more than once, while the images still echoed in her mind. But the words refused to come, and in the end she decided he didn't want to hear about them anyway. He didn't even look at her anymore, why would he care about some bad dreams. Especially if they were about Mama.

Their fight before leaving home had only made things worse. She hadn't wanted to argue with him, and she hadn't meant to break the plate, but she didn't understand how he could do it. How could he give her away like this? Still, there had to be something she could do to change his mind about the trip and, more importantly, about her.

She knelt to fill the kettle, trying to ignore the knot in the pit of her stomach. That squirmy feeling had been her second companion all the way here and now it gnawed away like a monster determined to escape. She'd tried to ignore it, and she guessed Papa might be doing the same. Maybe that was why he wouldn't look at her. Maybe he was trying to forget. But she could feel the rift between them growing. The usual awkwardness since Mama died had turned to a painful solitude walking a pace from the only companion she had left.

The trip into Mama's city went much the same as the trip through her country. Ellsabae was *Mama's* nation. It certainly wasn't Christabel's. Mama had been an elf. But Christabel had never set foot over the Ellring River in all her thirteen years, let alone entered the capital. And the stares she, not to mention Papa, received since entering elven lands confirmed what she already knew. She wasn't welcome here. She reached up to touch the slender ring hanging from its chain around her neck. Mama's ring.

Watch over me, Mama. Please.

Christabel sat next to Papa in a large plaza filled with pale elves a foot taller even than he was. She couldn't see much else through their milling figures, but the cries of merchants and the hum of hundreds of conversations echoed off the walls around her. Iridescent towers rose to dizzying heights above her, and bright banners and pennants whipped in the spring breeze like ribbons in girls' hair at festival. It was both breathtaking and overwhelming.

She glanced over to Papa. He stared up at the gate. She had to admit it was impressive. As big as a house in its tall wall of white stone, the silver surface glittered in the rays of the evening sun. Even so, it was odd Papa wouldn't take his gaze from it. But she didn't want to think about why.

The city. She liked the city, despite its cold welcome. She'd never been anywhere so . . . full. Not just of people, but buildings, statues, parks, and wagons. Certainly not the village back home. Even Deliverance Day, when people came from days around, would have fit entirely within the courtyard she sat in now.

Christabel scowled. Thinking of home brought back memories of the other children, their laughter and mockery. Whether it was her hair being too curly, her freakish, pointed ears, or just her desire to sit alone, they needed little reason to torture her. They never tired of it. But only once did they dare say anything about Mama. Christabel had beaten stupid Farlo for it, hitting him with a branch until it broke. Then more with her fists and feet until Papa pulled her off

Whispers at the Altar

him. It had felt good, and she had thought that would end it, but a week later they were right back to their usual sport. They were the one thing she didn't miss, would never miss. She hated them.

But here. Here were so many interesting people, fascinating sights, and delicious smells she didn't know where to begin. It was probably for the best Papa kept her hand in a vice grip or she'd already be off in a vain effort to explore it all. The city frightened and awed her. Made her want to shelter next to Papa and go running through every street at the same time.

So she bounced in her seat next to him and maintained a careful balance. Most people avoided them as though they were diseased. So she took the opportunity to stare, especially at their clothes. She loved dresses. She only owned a few but Mama made them all, and Christabel cherished them like gold. More than gold. But the elven dresses were wondrous creations like she never saw before. They swayed like tall grass in the autumn breeze, or shifted like puffy clouds before the sun as the wearer moved among the merchant stalls. Each was unique, and all were beautiful. She couldn't help brushing at her own dress in a vain effort to rid it of some of the travel dust. She didn't think she could ever bring herself to wear one of those dresses. There was no chance she would ever do them justice.

And the food stalls! Her stomach pulled her attention that way, urged by the sweet smell of strawberry pastries and the smoke of grilling venison. After a month of trying to force down travel rations and small game burned over a campfire, the thought of real food was intoxicating.

Her stomach growled as the sun slipped further to the west. Merchants packed up carts or shuttered up windows, taking their sounds and smells with them, not to mention the crowds. And still Papa waited. As the crowds thinned, she finally saw the entirety of the square rather than only what rose around it.

What fascinated Christabel most was the large fountain in the center. It was the biggest she'd ever seen, three times her height, all

25

tiered waterfalls and steps with what she assumed were elven fish spitting water out of their mouths. She closed her eyes, enjoying the cool spray of the water on her face after the long day's walk.

Papa's shout turned her around. When had she walked to the fountain's edge? When had he walked to the gate? She gave the best curse she knew—she had no idea what it meant but the mean boys at the manor had been fond of it—and hurried back. She started at a run but slowed as she saw an elven man walking with purpose toward Papa.

He was dressed in a long white robe trimmed in gold with sleeves closely cuffed at the wrists. Long, straight, corn-yellow hair complimented his clothes. But the deep-blue eyes were what slowed her. When they glanced in her direction they seemed to pierce through to her soul.

"I see you still remember your way about the city, Janus." The elf sneered Papa's name. Christabel knew that tone well. The devil children back home used it every day.

She came to a stop next to Papa and took his hand, squeezing it tight and leaning into him, just in case he needed a bit of support. She gave the elf her best glare. How dare he talk to Papa like that?

Papa didn't even seem to notice. "Well enough, Namarian. Thank you very much for meeting with me." He sounded tired. Of course, he'd sounded that way for months.

"I am not here for you. I think you know that." The elf shifted his gaze to Christabel.

Her glare faltered under his attention, and within seconds her view was back on Papa. His chestnut eyes were focused on her, filled with love and regret.

It was the same face as when he told her they were coming here. She'd fought for days. He'd made excuses. He said it would be best for her. She could have a better life. Her mother would have wanted it. She'd heard his reasons, but she hadn't listened. It all ended in shouting and crying. Deep down, she knew the real reason.

Then the real silence started.

•Whispers at the Altar•

Papa faced her and reached down to her shoulders. His expression shifted, and she knew what was coming. It was the look he used whenever he tried to get her to do something she didn't want to do, like eat her vegetables. It made her want to smile a little, but she couldn't manage it.

"This is your uncle, the one I told you about." He leaned in close, so only she could hear. "He'll take you to the palace."

"I don't want to go." Her stomach churned. She flicked a glance over Papa's shoulder to her uncle, but his attention was pointedly elsewhere. "Please. I'll be good. I promise. I'll cook dinner every night and do the dishes, and I won't fight with the other kids or lose my temper, and I won't track mud in the house and—"

"Christa." Papa squeezed her shoulder in a failed effort at reassurance. "This is for the best. You belong here and they . . . they can take care of you. Help you. I . . ." He sighed and pulled her in for a crushing hug. "You have an incredible future ahead of you, Christa. You can do so much. I know you can. You have your mother in you."

She squeezed him until it hurt. When he pulled back, there was a wet spot on his cloak from her tears, though she didn't remember shedding them. She wiped her face and noticed Papa doing the same.

"I'll be good, Papa. I promise," she whispered, then, with a deep breath, walked away. She didn't even peek over her shoulder. Papa told her once it was bad luck to look back after saying goodbye. He said you would never see the person again, and she dearly wanted to see Papa again.

Namarian watched her come, impassive. He opened the silver gate before her, one huge door swinging back without a sound. She glanced up as she passed and tried to give her bravest smile. He didn't return it. Instead he faced Papa.

"Wait here. She will be tested, and you will be told whether she can remain."

"What do you mean?" Papa's voice sounded surprised, angry.

She stopped in the doorway. Papa hadn't said anything about her needing to be tested. He'd said he would drop her off, and she would go to the palace. He'd sounded quite certain. She gripped Mama's ring tight through her dress until the points of the claw holding the single red gem poked her fingers.

"You may have lived among us, but you never bothered to learn our ways, Janus." Uncle Namarian's voice shifted to cold anger.

She kept her gaze focused straight ahead as her heart pounded away at her chest.

"She has the right to be tested," he continued, a measure of calm finding his tone again. "But if she fails, she will have no business here."

There was a gentle nudge on her back, but she hesitated, waiting to hear what Papa would say and wanting to hear his voice one last time. There was nothing, and after another firmer nudge she walked through the gate. It closed behind her with a soft thud, and she let out a long breath.

Attempting to coax her stomach back to where it should be, she forced herself to look around. Her steps slowed to a crawl. Meandering walkways wound through slopes of emerald green grass broken by copses of cool shade trees, small gardens rife with spring blossoms, and covered gazebos twined with roses of every color.

All of this led to a single gigantic structure, a massive dome of unbroken ivory stone into which entire farms could be swallowed. Only on the third, impatient, nudge against her back did she notice Uncle Namarian next to her. Annoyed at the interruption, she drifted forward, eyes wide.

From the top of the dome, slender towers capped with golden minarets pierced the heavens, intent upon touching the very stars whose image they held on their fluttering banners. As if to further flaunt gravity, arching bridges and sweeping walkways flung themselves out across the intervening expanses. Like the most intricate spider's

•Whispers at the Altar•

web, they twisted and rose in a dance that left her breathless, even with her feet firmly set upon solid ground.

It reminded her of a great cloud a strong wind might, at any moment, whisk away. Yet the closer she walked, the larger and more intimidating it became. The towers, which at first seemed so delicate, actually ranged from the size of a cottage to larger than any of the mansions she saw in the city below.

Doors, nearly impossible to spot, interrupted the smooth base of the dome at regular intervals, but Uncle kept to the widest path leading to the largest. They were open, and Uncle walked through without a pause. Which was something Christabel couldn't manage.

"But . . . The ceiling is . . ."

"An illusion, yes," he stated. He stopped several steps in and waited for her to follow.

Hurrying to catch up, she blurted, "But . . . it's a forest." A strange forest, but a forest nonetheless. Within the dome, the great trunks of broad trees rose all around. The boles and branches stretched, tier upon tier, into an eternity of dark sapphire sky that perfectly mirrored the setting sun outside. A cool breeze even blew across her cheek, rustling impossible leaves above her.

"The towers start here and rise through the dome. Within it, they have been made to look like trees. The ceiling," he made a sweeping gesture over his head, "has been given the appearance of a sky to complement it." He shrugged. "There is nothing strange about it. Certainly nothing to be afraid of. In fact . . ."

She stopped listening. Silent all the way here and now he decided to lecture her on the impossible? They turned to the left, north she guessed, though her sense of direction was rather distorted in here, and she decided to ignore the trees and the ceiling. Thinking about them made her head hurt. Instead she focused on everything else. There was plenty to see.

There were elves all around. They sat in circles on the grass, under trees, and on benches. Groups, some wearing long cloaks that shifted between dark red and light brown, ambled along paths or stood talking and laughing. She spotted two girls on her left whispering to flowers as they unfolded their petals. Another group farther off on her right tossed a small ball of fire back and forth between one another.

But for all their differences, there was one similarity. They all stopped as she passed and gave her *the look*. The same one she'd received since she crossed the Ellring. That galling mix of curiosity and contempt, as though she were half cockroach, at once fascinating and repulsive. The ratio shifted, but it never failed.

She was so absorbed in ignoring them while still trying to watch them, she didn't notice when Uncle stopped. Not until she heard him clear his throat behind her. She whirled, clenching her skirt in her hands.

"Wait here," he repeated. "I must inform the other directors you have arrived and need to be tested. You may walk about the immediate area, but do not interfere with . . . anything. Do you understand?"

"I'll stay out of trouble. I promise." She gave her most honest face and best curtsy. It was her standard response, as natural as "sir," "ma'am," and "please." He seemed satisfied though, and walked toward another double door set into one of the many large fir trees.

She didn't watch him enter. Instead, she continued to ignore everyone as she tried to decide what to do. She spotted a stone bench not far off and, the day catching up with her at last, skipped over, plopped down, and tucked a foot under her.

A woman passed by on some urgent task, her brisk pace streaming her golden hair behind her. A deep purple cloak rippled over a rosy pink dress that shimmered in waves. Christabel watched her pass with rapt attention. Everything about the woman shouted perfection, and she didn't even notice. She wore it as easily as Christabel wore her tired leather shoes.

•*Whispers at the Altar*•

Christabel looked down at her best blue dress with its little embroidered white flowers, at her stringy tangled brown hair she brushed just this morning, and her nicest, almost-white stockings with only one hole in one heel. How could she ever stay here? How could she ever belong *here* any more than the village? She'd never aspired to be anything more than herself, but sitting there, surrounded by all that beauty, she suddenly felt woefully inadequate—and alone.

THE TEST

Sinna watched from her usual seat under the boughs of the administration tower as the stranger bounced along beside Director Namarian through the palace yard. Even beyond the obvious surplus of energy, the girl was strange. For one, her ears were far too short for her age, although they were beautifully narrow. At the same time, her face was unusually round. Aristocratic, dark hair curled around in adorable but exotic waves that made Sinna tug her own straight, commoner-yellow braid self-consciously. But no aristocrat in their right mind would wear such a simple and threadbare dress to the palace.

She was a mystery, one Sinna couldn't ignore any more than could the dozens of officials, nobles, and Hawks watching the girl's every move. Then it struck Sinna, and she leaned forward a bit. The girl must be a half-human. Sinna had heard of them, but the humans hadn't raided across the river for years. Surely this stranger was too young. And even if she was the product of a raid, what would she be doing on this side of the river? Weren't all half-humans given back to the barbarians?

The director left the girl at the entrance to the Essence tower. She seemed so lost, so alone as she sat on a bench staring into the Winter Fountain. Sinna closed her book and stood. She couldn't resist helping. She knew all too well what it felt like to be different.

Vaniel, the consummate bully, was already eyeing the newcomer like a barn cat watching a mouse, an eager grin wide across her face as her lackeys laughed and pointed. Vaniel was too young to cause Sinna much trouble—that was her brother's job—but this new girl was easy prey.

Sinna quickened her pace. The new girl didn't even notice the attention focused on her. She just stared through the fountain. She even waved, which made Sinna slow, searching for who the girl might be greeting. There was no one there.

Taking a deep breath, Sinna pressed on, determined to intervene before Vaniel could pounce.

"B-B-Beautiful, isn't it?"

Christabel jumped, surprised to see another girl standing close by. She was shorter than the other elves, roughly Christabel's height, and her sky-blue dress perfectly matched the wide eyes that watched Christabel so curiously.

"What is?" Christabel asked. So much was beautiful, she had no idea what the girl meant.

She laughed. "The t-trees, the sky, the grass. Take your pick. I-I know I never get used to it."

Christabel nodded, "I just got here so it's pretty overwhelming. Are you learning magic here? Papa said I would learn to use magic, but my uncle said I had to pass a test first, and if I didn't I wouldn't be able to stay. My name is Christabel by the way, but you can call me Christa, that's what everyone else calls me back home because Christabel is too long, but I do think it's a pretty name." She stopped to take a breath, ready to launch into another discourse.

"You can call me S-S-Sinna." The other girl hurried to say. "My name's pretty long, too." She sat down on the bench beside Christa and arranged her skirt around her. "I do stay at the R-Roost. That's the part of the palace where we learn magic. I hope you'll be able to as well. It is a nice place, if a bit i-i-intimidating."

Christa shifted in her seat to face her new friend. "I like your name, too. The Roost is a funny name for a magic school. Why do they call it that? Are there a lot of people who go there? How long have you been here? Did they teach you how to do things like that?" She pointed over to where a young man determinedly ignored her as he created images of tiny dragons that hovered in the air.

Sinna shook her head. "No, that isn't my talent. There are different kinds of magic and many ways to use it. That's only one. My magic manipulates the e-elements."

Christa just squinted, so Sinna held out a hand. She focused on her palm for a moment, and before Christa's astonished eyes, a flame sprang up, flowering into a small fire cradled in Sinna's palm.

"What will I be able to do?" Christa asked with a mix of wonder and fear.

"I don't know," Sinna answered with a shrug. She closed her hand, and the flames winked into nothing. "Like I said, th-there're many different kinds and ways to use magic. Some create perfect i-illusions, real enough to touch. Others bring themselves so in tune with the Creator and his creation they can m-make trees grow from a desert. S-some can even call on the power of the Creator himself to heal the most grievous injuries. Even death."

Christa's eyes brightened. "I want to do that!"

Sinna's laugh was contagious. "I imagine we'll see soon. Not only will the directors be able to tell if you can use magic, but what kind."

Christa's imagination filled with thoughts of healing people. Of helping the blind see. Helping the crippled walk. Papa would be so proud. People that never had a chance at a healthy life—

I can bring Mama back!

Her head swam with thoughts of holding Mama again. Papa would surely forgive Christa then. He would *love* her again. And they could all live together, like they always had. The images came so fast they made her dizzy.

"W-what is it?" Sinna said

Christa blinked back to the present, frantically trying to remember what they had been talking about.

"I was telling you about the t-test," Sinna said.

"Right." Christa carefully tucked the daydream away. "Does it hurt? Do they have to stick me with anything? Mama taught me to read and write, even in elven, and my numbers, but I never liked tests. They make my head hurt. Sometimes, when Mama would make me write sentences, my hand would start to hurt from holding the quill because I had to concentrate so hard to make the letters how she wanted them."

"I promise it won't hurt. And it isn't that kind of t-test. You don't actually *do* anything. But you will take plenty of written tests if you stay." She glanced around then leaned in closer. "Y-your f-f-father wasn't elven, was he?"

Christa shook her head. She'd expected the question. It was only a matter of time. At least Sinna came out and asked instead of just staring at her.

Sinna patted the air between them. "It's all right, Ch-Ch-Christa." She gave a wide smile. Then furrowed her brow. "How did you survive? I mean, being left on the other side of the river." She stopped. "Wait. How did your mother know elven?"

"What?" Christa squinted in confusion. "Because she was an elf. I grew up with my mama and papa in the village. I wasn't left anywhere." Unless you counted here, of course.

"Oh." She blinked in surprise.

"Why? What's wrong?"

"I've never heard of that. Did your father . . . k-k-kidnap her?" She whispered the last, leaning in very close.

Christa blinked several times. "What? No, they—" She stopped as Uncle walked out of the tree-door accompanied by two women. Whatever Sinna thought about human families, it would have to wait.

The first had brown hair to the back of her knees, and her thin angular face held the most welcoming expression Christa had seen yet, apart from Sinna's. Still, there was something odd about the way she looked at Christa. As if they already knew each other.

The second was an exact opposite. Her thin lips set in a smug, sarcastic grin that made Christa squirm in her seat. The woman's dress was like a shifting night sky full of stars winking in and out of view. Christa found it difficult to pull her attention from it, and when she did, the woman's dark-brown eyes met her own with an air of certain superiority.

"Oh, there are the directors to test you," Sinna said and stood to give a curtsey. Christa hurried to do the same, watching Sinna in case there was some other formality she wasn't aware of. Still she nearly missed the palm to heart motion Sinna made as she dipped and had to rush to compensate.

"Christabel." Uncle Namarian waited for her gaze to meet his. "This is Director Marellel of the Elementalists." He motioned to the friendly face, and Christa curtseyed again, remembering to keep her right hand free to place over her heart this time.

"A pleasure to meet you, Christabel," Marellel said. "I knew your mother. We became very good friends during her time here."

Namarian gave her an exasperated look, then motioned to Miss Sour Face. "And this is Director Elirel of the Mentalists."

She barely inclined her head, but Christa gave her a curtsy anyway. It couldn't hurt to be polite.

"And I am the director of the Divinists. Each of us represents one of the three aspects of magic. We will join our different magics together in a ritual, with you as the center. It will enable us to determine whether you have the gift for any of them. Do you have any questions?"

She had a million and a half questions, but she couldn't find the words to express any of them with those three elves peering down at her. Instead she stood there, fidgeting with her skirt and glancing back and forth from one to the other.

Satisfied, the three directors spread out around her, forming a triangle with her at the center. This made it impossible to watch everyone. So she faced Director Marellel. Better to look at a friendly face.

Nothing happened for a long moment, and it became hard to ignore the dozens of people around the yard staring at her. Then a warmth slid inch by inch down from the top of her head. Not the warmth of a fire or a summer breeze, but a sensation like being submerged, unclad and headfirst, in a hot bath—without getting wet. She gulped for air as it passed over her nose and mouth, then took deep steadying breaths as the line of warmth passed down over her neck and chest. She focused on Director Marellel's cobalt eyes, ignoring the feeling of standing naked in front of her, determined not to let a friend of her mother see her scared.

The line passed her heart, and it skipped a beat. Her gaze bore into Marellel's. There was depth there in those blue orbs, like in that of a great body of water. Christa had heard of the ocean, water as far as one could see, and this was how she imagined it. In those eyes was a steady river and rolling waves. It was both peace and power.

She didn't feel the warmth pass her knees, but her focus jerked back to the yard in a rush as Marellel's eyes widened in fear. The director cried out and stretched out a hand as if to ward off a blow. Startled, Christa backed away several steps. She didn't know what happened but it must be her fault.

Christa glanced to Sinna, then back, as Director Marellel recovered her composure. The director waved away Elirel's help, then brushed off her skirt as she glared at the rest of the yard to go back to their business.

After a moment she looked back to Christa. "I am fine, Christabel. I was just startled."

"She is the same as her mother?" Namarian asked.

"The same," Marellel answered. "What is more, I am certain her talent lies with elemental magic. I have never seen such a fire inside someone." She shook her head, more cautious and considering than before. "Do you understand, Christabel? You are able to use magic. The same magic as myself, your mother, and even Sinna." She motioned to the other girl, standing to the side and nearly forgotten. "You will be able to stay here and learn to use it."

"But I don't want that! I don't want a *fire*! I want to help people." It wasn't fair. The dream of bringing Mama back, of Papa looking at her again like he used to, was so close. She wouldn't let it be destroyed before it even had a chance.

Marellel took a step back, her surprise plain in her eyes as she glanced from Christa to Namarian to Elirel and back. "But you would be helping people, Christabel. You would be able to help the entire elven nation. Isn't that—"

"I think we should leave her to recover from the test," Namarian interrupted. "We need to make our report to Secretary Iyian. Remember, her time here is still not assured."

"W-what do you mean?" Sinna broke in, taking a few steps forward to place herself within the conversation.

"It is not your concern," Elirel snapped, though she, too, gave Director Namarian a curious look.

Namarian nodded. "You will be told in due time what has been decided, Christabel. For now, relax here. If you need anything, Sinnasarel will get it for you." Facing Sinna he continued, "You are excused from classes until someone informs her of the secretary's decision." Then he strode back to the door, Elirel following.

"Christabel," Marellel said as the other directors left, "do you want to stay here? Do you want to learn to use magic? To help people, even if it is not in the way you would have liked? Because if you do, I will do everything I can to make sure that happens.

"But know this. The training here is strenuous and leaves no time for trips home. If you stay, you will not be able to leave the city until you are finished. A process that will take decades. Also, the training here is for a purpose. The knowledge shared is valuable, and the graduates are great assets to the Crown. To put it bluntly, if you stay, you will be sworn to serve the needs of Queen Elisidel and the kingdom from now on." She paused meaningfully before continuing.

"I was very close to your mother. I was her mentor as she was training and would be happy to be yours as well. I know she would want this for you. She would want you to learn, to better yourself. And I think your father would, too, or why bring you?" She stopped and peered into Christa's eyes.

"But if you do not want this—if you think it will be too hard, or you miss your father too much—tell me now and I will make sure you are returned to him. You can go home and forget all of this."

Christa's fear and frustration leaked away as Marellel spoke, replaced by firm determination. Mama would have wanted this. Mama trained here, and Christa owed it to her, to her memory, to do the best she could. She would make Mama proud. She had to. Besides, what was there to go home to?

"I want to stay."

Marellel smiled. "Excellent. Sinna, make sure she gets something to eat. She must be hungry. I will be back as soon as I can." With that she stood and followed the other directors into the tree-tower.

Dalan

Director Dalan watched as the girl was left alone with her little blonde friend. Even from this distance the half-breed reminded him of her mother. Not as beautiful, but the memories she stirred... he shook his head and turned from the hall window. This was not the time to let emotions cloud his judgment. Not like Marellel. He could guess what she was up to. Really, the very idea of letting a half-human train at the Roost. It was ridiculous.

He quickened his pace toward the council chamber. This wasn't a vote he could afford to lose. He pondered the short list of directors. Obviously Marellel, attached as she was to the girl's mother, would vote to admit. Her short-sightedness would see all the elves' secrets handed over to their enemies. Of course, she was only a piece of the problem, a part of a growing movement that considered the humans not just "reformed" in some abstract sense but actually of benefit as allies.

That notion went beyond ridiculous, into the realm of dangerous. Had they forgotten the first overtures toward the barbarians? The deaths of countless diplomats and missionaries? Or the pillaging, rape, and murder they subsequently perpetrated all along the Ellring? Now he was supposed to believe, because a few hundred years had passed, they had changed? Become more civilized? The girl's father was evidence enough of the futility of that thinking.

He took a deep breath and squared his thoughts away again. He needed to focus on the vote. Namarian was the girl's uncle, which might swing his vote in her favor, but he was no human-lover. He still held a proper view of them, especially since his sister's death. Still, Dalan doubted he could depend on his vote.

Director Aerel was traditional, with a good head on her shoulders, but she had sided with Marellel often in the past. What would swing her vote most would be the rules, or at least her interpretation of them. He had seen her twist them to suit her own ends before.

He was confident Elirel was still in his pocket. The impetuous girl *was* becoming annoyingly self-possessed of late. She was young, and he had hoped she would be more impressionable and guidable, but he was sure she would do the right thing—if only for her own career.

That left Director Micanan, the biggest human-lover of them all. Just thinking about the amount of time he spent among the humans being poisoned by their words, by their attitudes . . . Dalan shivered. It was disgusting. That Micanan was even allowed to retain his position as a director baffled Dalan and exemplified the queen's growing lack of judgment. Fortunately, Director Micanan was out on one of his many excursions.

That left a vote of two each, with Namarian the swing. Dalan cursed as he pushed open the door to the council chamber. It galled him not having enough time to prepare. He would prefer to take it slowly, coordinate his allies, and find ways to place pressure on the others. As it stood, everything rested on Director Namarian.

⋆Whispers at the Altar⋆

Dalan paced across the empty room, sinking into one of the seven high-backed chairs set at the table. How much bitterness did Namarian still carry? Dalan could only hope, for the sake of Ellsabae, it was significant.

Elirel and Namarian walked in together, the first smiling ear to ear while the other maintained his ever-impassive mask. Dalan leaned forward on the table, trying to gauge Director Namarian's mood, but it was impossible. Blasted emotionless Divinist. And where was Marellel?

"I assume the girl tested well?" Dalan tried.

Namarian nodded. "Director Marellel feels she is quite adept." He sat, smoothed out his robe, and regarded Dalan.

"'I have never seen such a fire inside someone,'" Elirel imitated in a high voice. She laughed. "Really. When was the last time Marellel tested someone?" Her chair scraped along the stone floor as Elirel dragged it out.

Dalan ignored her. "And how do you feel about her entrance?"

"She qualifies." Namarian said with a shrug.

Dalan scoffed. "That is not the point. You know very well what the humans are capable of. What happens when—?"

Namarian held up one hand. "Please, Director Dalan. Let us leave the arguments for when we are all assembled. I would hate for you to be forced to repeat yourself."

Dalan sighed and leaned back, glaring.

"Don't look so sour, Dalan," Elirel said.

He shifted the glare to the Mentalist. "And you do not forget who put you in that chair." Her face soured, which cheered him up a bit. When this was over, he would need to have a talk with her. Reestablish the rules.

The door opened again, and Marellel walked in along with Director Aerel, who managed to appear stunning even in a plain brown dress. Her jet-black hair was pulled back today in a long braid draped over her shoulder. Dalan greeted each, contemplated a quick overture to

Aerel, then thought better of it. Marellel got to her first. That explained why Marellel hadn't arrived with Namarian. That ship had sailed.

Everyone waited.

Ten minutes of uncomfortable silence were broken by the emphatic swishing of slippers on the marble floor of the hall. Secretary Iyian rounded the corner, narrow face in full scowl. He strode to the largest chair, scarlet robe billowing behind, and dropped into it.

The doors closed with a sharp click, and Dalan leaned forward, focusing his attention on Marellel.

"This council has been summoned by Director Marellel," the secretary said. "What business do you have for us?" He gazed at her with mock curiosity.

Taking a deep breath, Marellel stood and rested her fingertips on the smooth stone of the table. "This afternoon, Directors Namarian, Elirel, and I tested a child brought to the capital by her father. The test proved she is gifted with Essence Magic." She paused, perhaps unsure how best to proceed and choosing her words carefully. "All of us know this would be no cause for a council. However, it has been suggested her acceptance is impossible due to the girl being half-human. My reason for taking your time is to call a vote on whether the child should be allowed to stay and train as a Hawk."

Of course, none of this was news. Word of the girl, her heritage, and her testing had swept through the Roost and the palace.

Her case opened, Marellel sat down and folded her hands. "It is my position that if she is gifted and willing to swear herself in service to the crown than the Roost should be open to her. There is no law to state otherwise."

Dalan jumped in. "So you would see our greatest secrets, the knowledge and power of millennia, given to anyone who shows up at the gate?" He paused just long enough for her to begin to counter. "Apologies. Anyone who is willing to swear an oath and show any form of ability to learn."

•Whispers at the Altar•

"That is not what I mean, and you know it. She is the child of a Hawk. She is of elven blood. There is no reason she should be refused."

"There is every reason!" Dalan slammed his fist on the table. "She is human. If we bring her in, if we teach her, how long do you think she will stay, even if she does take the oath? A year? Five? Ten? How long did her mother stay?"

Marellel shook her head, "I fail to see what that has to do with—"

"And what happens when she leaves? When she takes the knowledge, secrets, and power we gave her back to her own people? The Roost exists to guard and serve the elven people. Allowing our enemies—and make no mistake, they *are* our enemies—access to what she would learn here. That is tantamount to treason, Director."

"You forget something, Dalan," Aerel put in, as Marellel was about to respond. Everyone focused on the Corporalist, straight and regal in her chair. "You are correct to point out her human ancestry and all the dangers it brings. However, you forget she is also half elven. If we are to assume the one half has the power to corrupt, we must also assume her elven half has the power to enlighten, to bring her above the downfalls of her other half. She may indeed use the skills we teach her to do horrible things, but it is equally likely she may use them to better all our lives. No one has the power to see what the future holds for this girl, nor for us. The question is not what she may do, but what we should do."

"True, we cannot guess what she may do," Namarian said. "But as with anything else, we must decide based on the general wisdom of the action. Is it wise to teach this girl, or is it not? And the possibilities of what she might do with the knowledge we give her must be factored into that decision."

Marellel shook her head, "Why? Because of who her father was? We have never let the possibility of future misjudgments guide the entrance of any other candidate. Any of them may have given secrets to the Dwarves or the Anathonians. The fact is, by the rules, she is as eligible to study here as any other prospective trainee has been. More so in some ways. Her innate affinity for magic is greater than any prospective I have ever tested. To deny her based on a feeling of what she may do because of who her father was is ludicrous."

"No more ludicrous than to accept her because of who her mother was," Dalan snapped, drawing all eyes to him. "We all know why you are spearheading this crusade, Marellel. But her mother chose her course. She left the Roost. The Crown trusted Chrysobel's word she would not reveal our secrets to the humans. It will not trust the word of some half-breed."

"Let's vote." Elirel's exasperated tone cut through the tension. "No one is convincing anyone here."

"Very well," the secretary said. "We will now vote on the matter of whether Christabel, daughter of Chrysobel, should be allowed entrance into the Roost."

"Certainly not," Dalan stated.

"Yes," Marellel said at nearly the same time.

Namarian glanced at Marellel and sighed. "No."

Dalan nearly cheered as Marellel sat back in her chair, defeated.

Aerel considered for a long moment before giving a small nod. "Yes."

Which made two for and two against with Elirel left to vote.

Elirel shrugged and was about to vote when a burst of movement by the door drew everyone's gaze. A high squeak turned to a groan of effort, and the tall form of Director Micanan, still brushing small patches of short downy fur from his bare arms and brown tunic, took shape.

Dalan almost screamed. Of all the times for that radical to show up . . .

"I believe the next vote is mine, Elirel, thank you." He took a deep breath and strode to take his seat, giving Marellel a cocky wink.

Dalan ground his teeth. That pretentious, traitorous, uncouth bastard.

The secretary frowned. "I am afraid the door was closed with your seat vacant, Director Micanan. You were not present for the discussion and therefore you may not vote on the issue at hand."

Whispers at the Altar

"Ah, but I was here the whole time, just over there," he motioned to the corner of the room. "I heard Marellel present the girl's case. I heard Dalan spout his racist nonsense. And I thought, for once, here was an issue worth voting on."

The secretary rolled his eyes and waved Micanan to continue.

"Thank you, Secretary." His expression became seriousness. "I vote yes. I also believe one day we will be very grateful we did."

Dalan ground his teeth. Fool. But no matter. Elirel had still to vote and a tie would take the matter to the secretary for a break. Dalan knew which way that would go. He leaned back, relaxed once more.

Elirel's grin was wolfish. Dalan chuckled. Enjoy this moment of power, Elirel. There will be more if you remember your place.

Elirel leaned forward, let the silence hang, then cast her vote.

Waiting

Christa gazed at the doors for a full minute after they closed. What did she just do? As certain as she felt moments ago, she couldn't help the twinges of doubt in the back of her mind. But it was done.

With a deep breath, she tried to let go of as much stress as her nerves would allow. It wouldn't do any good to worry. Besides, as she stood there, a rumbling in her stomach reminded her of something more important. She turned to Sinna. "Food?"

A moment later they were walking across the yard to a tree bigger than ten houses. Christa skipped, determined to cheer herself up. Then a thought came and, flashing a mischievous smile to Sinna, she set off running. In seconds the race was in full swing.

As they neared a door in the massive trunk, both girls put forth their final effort. By the time they saw the door open it was too late.

Christa barely had time to register two young men walk out. Sinna managed to skid to a stop, but Christa wasn't so lucky. She held out one arm before bowling into first one, then the other. They all went down in a tangle of limbs.

Luckily, one of the boys cushioned Christa's fall perfectly. But it still took several moments, and Sinna's help, to untangle herself and stand, all while fighting off a case of the giggles.

"What in the world were you doing?" her cushion asked as he picked himself up and primped his fancy red robes.

The other boy brushed at his plain white shirt with one hand and adjusted the long thin sword at his waist with the other. "What was chasing you? A human horde?"

Christa's laughter stopped. Sinna was tugging on her hand, but she hardly felt it.

Fancy-robe stood there for a moment, an expectant look on his face. "Well? Are you going to apologize?" He seemed to notice Sinna for the first time, and his face dropped into a sneer. "Of course, I suppose we cannot expect manners from a corn-haired farm elf who cannot even manage to speak correctly. She probably does not even know the word." He leaned forward. "It is 'm-m-m-man-n-ners,'" he exaggerated.

Christa reared back a fist to punch him square in his smug face. Sinna grabbed her hand, but she couldn't grab Christa's tongue. "Maybe you shouldn't have popped out of your hole like a jackrabbit in spring if you didn't want people running into you." Christa backed up a step toward the door as Sinna tugged her. "You run into us and then try to make us apologize?" Sinna's tugging became more insistent, but Christa wasn't done yet.

"And you," she rounded on Sword-boy. "How dare you! What do you know about 'human hordes'? Or humans at all? At least they know when to step out of a lady's way, which is more than I can say for your elven 'man-ners.' At least—"

"We're sorry," Sinna broke in. "W-w-we'll be more c-careful." She pulled Christa through the door.

Whispers at the Altar

Christa swung around, grumbling. "Why'd you pull me away?"

"Because, A-A-Adasian is a j-j-jerk." Sinna said as she hurried across the empty floor of the tower. She took a deep breath, and her words slowed. "A jerk whose family is powerful both in the palace and E-Ellsabareth. The last thing you need on your first day here is to make an enemy of him."

"I'm not afraid of him. What can he do?"

Sinna sighed. "Make your life here miserable for one. Trust me." She stopped. "Think ahead, Christa. If you're going to stay here, you must always be thinking ahead. With Adasian's connections, he'll certainly make d-d-director one day. He will always be above you, always able to influence your life in subtle but very painful ways. And his sister, V-Vaniel, is no better. Just stay away from them."

Christa knew all about staying away from bullies. And she knew it never worked. They always found you. But she decided to change the subject. "So why is this place called the Roost?"

"It'll make more sense once we're there," she said with an enigmatic smile as she motioned for Christa to enter one of several floor to ceiling glass tubes set against the wall.

Christa eyed it then her new friend. "What is this?"

Sinna grinned. "It's an elevation shaft. Just step inside and think about going up. When you get where you're going, think about s-stopping. It takes some practice, but it's much faster than the alternative," she gestured to a flight of stairs winding up the wall.

"And where am I going?" Christa didn't like this idea, but she didn't fancy a long slog up the stairs, either. She'd seen how tall some of the towers were from outside the palace.

"Floor twenty," Sinna answered before walking to the next tube in line.

By the time Christa stumbled out of the tube on the twentieth floor a minute later, her stomach was spread somewhere between floors one and forty. Sinna waited, tapping her foot with mock impatience.

51

"Why . . . in the Creator's name . . . would you willingly do that to yourselves?" Christa braced herself against the wall as she tried not to retch over Sinna's feet.

Sinna laughed, but patted Christa on the back. "Like I said, it takes a bit of practice, and the n-nausea does get better."

Christa didn't believe her. But at least Sinna had the decency to wait a few minutes before they headed off down the hall. Christa leaned heavily on the concave wall, her eyes focused on the thankfully motionless floor.

About ten paces later the wall gave way to a window, nearly sending her tumbling out. Christa gripped the sides to keep the vertigo from dropping her to the floor. She stood above the dome but still far below the peak of even the shortest tower. Still, the view stretched past the network of bridges and out over the surrounding countryside. The city was fascinating before. From here, it was breathtaking. The last rays of the setting sun sparkled across a rainbow of roofs and gables.

"This is why we call it the Roost," Sinna whispered as she leaned against the window frame. "None of the school rooms, including the apartments, are any lower than this." She gave a small chuckle. "And it's something of a joke too, I suppose."

Christa shook her head as she pushed off from the sill, continuing in the direction they'd been going. "What do you mean?"

"Well, after you finish your training you're called a H-Hawk. A s-s . . . an agent of the queen. So when the Hawks aren't out on a mission . . ."

"They come here to roost," Christa finished with a shake of her head.

"I never said it was a good joke." Sinna chuckled again and stopped to open a door leading further into the tower. "And here is the dining hall. At least one of them. There are about a dozen places to eat in the palace. This one s-serves the Roost."

Christa walked in and couldn't help but shake her head in amazement. The room was enormous, flanked by tables stocked with every kind of food and drink she could imagine, and even more she couldn't.

Whispers at the Altar

Row upon row of stone tables took up the center of the floor, each carved in a different shape with a kaleidoscope of colorful stones inlaid into their tops. The high ceiling vaulted up to dark rafters carved into twisting vines covered in fruits and berries. Crystal chandeliers cradled small globes of soft light bright enough to illuminate the entire room, yet soft enough to admire.

They made their way between crowded tables to a long board spread with food. Taking up a plate, Sinna helped herself but stopped when Christa didn't join her.

"Is something wrong? Y-you can take whatever you want. They'll bring out more if it runs low."

"I just . . . I don't know where to start."

Sinna chuckled and took up another plate, loading it with a varied and full complement. The selections Sinna made contained nothing Christa recognized. True, there were familiar things like pork, and some kind of sliced potatoes, but the exact recipes were foreign. The meat was mixed with a thin wiggly substance, with a brown sauce whose smell made her nose itch. The potatoes were sliced thin, and yellowed, she guessed from some cheese by the smell. The vegetables seemed safest, even if there were at least three varieties she couldn't name.

Holding both plates, she led Christa to a table in an out-of-the-way corner of the room. Its legs were carved into striding foxes and a swirling pattern of red, yellow, and orange stones swirled across the surface. "This is where I usually sit, along with a few friends. You're w-welcome to sit here whenever you want. Well . . . if they let you stay, I guess." She frowned, setting the plates down across from each other.

"Do people often need to wait to find out if they can stay?" Christa thought she knew the answer, but maybe Sinna could explain why.

"No. Not ordinarily," Sinna answered. "Everyone with the gift is trained to be a Hawk. I don't know why they wouldn't tell you right then that you could stay. It sounded as though they needed the s-secretary's permission."

53

"But the Hawks serve the queen?"

"Yes, but she doesn't have much to do with t-training. She leaves that to the Intelligence Secretary."

"So why would he not want me trained?"

Sinna thought as she chewed. Then her eyes widened, and she hurried to swallow. "I bet it's because you're part human," she whispered.

Christa squinted. "Why would that matter?"

"There's never been a human here before. I doubt they're allowed. Hawks deal with s-sensitive government information."

Christa shook her head. "Sensitive?"

Sinna made a broad gesture with her fork. "You know, secrets. That's why we belong to the q-queen. That's why we're called Hawks. We're her eyes when she needs them. Or her talons, though I don't think we've been used that way for a long time. At least that's how it got s-started. Now we do a lot of other things, too."

Christa didn't know what to say. She could keep secrets. It was easy when you were the only one who knew them, and you didn't like the kids who wanted them.

She started with the vegetables, the better to get them over with, but, two bites later, threw caution to the wind. Everything was delicious—somehow lighter than anything she was used to, with flavors that tingled as they hit her tongue. It didn't take long before she forgot all about debates, the secretary, and even the queen.

The conversation died as they sat and ate. Christa was too absorbed in her food to focus on anything else. She didn't even look up until someone sat down next to her. By that time there wasn't much left on the plate to occupy her, anyway.

"Oh, hello," Sinna said. "Westrel, this is C-Christa. She's new here, just arrived today. Christa, this is Westrel, a good friend of mine. She's a Corporalist." Sinna indicated each with her hand as she completed the introductions. "Is D-D-Darian with you?" she asked, craning her head to peer back toward the food tables as Westrel situated herself.

Whispers at the Altar

"Hello, Christa, a pleasure to meet you." Westrel straightened each piece of silverware to either side of her plate with its neatly divided portions. She then chose a fork before answering. "No, he is still in Cerebral Studies. I believe he is having some trouble and wanted extra help."

Something about Westrel, beyond her fastidious eating habits, struck Christa as unusual, but it was difficult to place. The accent was different, less lilting than Sinna's and more drawn out on the vowels, but that wasn't it. It might have been her apple-red hair. The color didn't appear to be unusual though. In fact, most of the elves she'd seen here and in the city had hair some shade of blond to red. Her hair was cut above the shoulders, far shorter than what seemed to be the prevailing style, but that wasn't it, either.

Then it hit her. It was the clothes. Westrel was the only girl Christa had seen wearing a shirt and pants.

Twisting back to Christa, Westrel inspected her more closely. "You must be a half-human. I did not know any still lived." Her clover green eyes narrowed. "You seem too young? There have been no human raids in at least two centuries."

Christa didn't know how to react. She'd never heard the term "half-human" before, and it was somehow demeaning, even if Westrel's tone was at worst academically curious. "I don't know anything about raids. I was raised across the river in Ardale. Before today, I never saw an elf except my mother, but she wasn't so different from anyone else. Except maybe that she was much nicer than a lot of other people." She tried to keep her tone level, but she couldn't help a bit of indignation creeping in.

Sinna laughed, but Westrel just smiled. "I would be careful who you tell that your mother was just like humans. Some here might take offense. Personally, I have never met a human so I cannot say, but I will take your word for it as a first-hand witness."

55

"I apologize for Westrel," Sinna added. "But you'll get a lot of odd looks and questions if you stay. I doubt any but a handful at the p-palace have even seen a human. So you are the next closest thing."

"Well, they're regular people. I don't see how they're any different from people here. Some are mean, some are nice, and some are just jerks."

"I am sure you are right," Westrel answered. "However, not everyone sees things so clearly. Nor do they wait to know someone before making a decision about them. But enough of that. I am very pleased to meet you, Christa, and I hope we will get to know each other much better over the years."

That gave Christa pause. "Years? So, how long does it take to learn everything here? I know . . ." She searched for the name. "Marellel said it would take decades. But she was exaggerating, right?"

Sinna shook her head. "No, she wasn't. I-I've been here twenty-three years now and won't graduate for at least another five. Even then I'll just be fully t-trained. There's always more to learn."

Christa gaped. "But I'll be so old by then!" she exclaimed, causing them both to break into full laughter Christa couldn't help but join.

"Not as old as you might think," Westrel said, composing herself back to full seriousness. "I can see why you would think so, having grown up among the short-lived humans, but your elven blood will likely give you a much longer life. I do not have any evidence, but I would not be surprised you appeared no older than Sinna or I when you graduate."

"But how old are you now if you've been here for fifteen years?"

"I'm forty-two," Sinna answered. "I think Westrel is thirty-three, though. S-She arrived a few years after me."

"That's amazing," Christa gasped. "Neither of you seem much older than me, and I'm thirteen. I would have guessed eighteen at the oldest."

"We are not even tested for the gift until we are around twenty." Westrel shifted to face Christa. "You could think of it this way. The humans live such a short amount of time, they need to grow up faster, or they would have no time to accomplish anything. We elves live for many centuries, even millennia, so we have more time to grow and still have time to be productive." She shrugged, as though this all should be obvious.

Christa nodded but still had a hard time absorbing it all.

"I can't believe your mother never explained this to you," Sinna said as she stood up, leaving her tray and heading for the doors. "After all, she taught you our language."

Westrel got up to follow. Christa stood next to the table, torn about leaving the dishes sitting there, but eventually followed.

"I think she would have. I'm sure she was waiting until I was older."

Westrel and Sinna exchanged glances, but said nothing.

Christa followed them back into the hallway and around to a door in the outside wall. Sinna opened it, revealing a cloudless night sky and a bridge wide enough for the three of them. It spanned fifty paces to another tower that gleamed in the starlight. Only thin railings running along the side in smooth, twirling vines of glittering metal prevented a fall of over one-hundred and fifty span to the dome below.

Christa stopped. "You have to be kidding."

Already mounting the span, Sinna and Westrel turned back.

"Is something wrong?" Westrel asked.

"Oh. I don't think she likes heights," Sinna answered for her. "But really, Christa, it's p-perfectly safe. And the view is wonderful."

Christa took an unsteady step out, firmly in the center and with her gaze fixed on her friends. What kind of crazy people would come up with such ridiculous ways of getting from one place to another? First tubes that wrenched your stomach all over your body, and now this?

"There you go. See? Nothing to worry about." Sinna came up beside her, while Westrel took the other side.

Allan C.R. Cornelius

"Yeah . . . right." She tried to push the knowledge of what she was doing to the back of her head. "So . . . what's a Corporalist?" She grasped at the first conversation topic that popped into her head.

"One of the six disciplines of magic," Westrel answered immediately. "Corporalist magic is generated within our own bodies, and focused inward, as opposed to the Mentalist who focuses the same magic outward. Our abilities allow us to control our bodies and minds in minute detail to include enhancing speed and strength, healing, and even altering shape."

Sinna shoved her playfully. "Westrel, I don't think she needed a book read to her."

"She asked. Besides—"

Sinna shushed her. "Director M-M-Marellel," she pointed back to the door they came through. The two words were full of meaning Christa well understood. She faced the director and tried her best to stand proud and still, determined to be brave whatever the verdict.

Found

It was the water. That was all Steven could think as he stumbled forward. It was the only thing that could account for the twisting, boiling, and churning in his gut. It couldn't be anything he ate. He'd thrown up all that yesterday. Still, he had to drink something, didn't he? The sun and its oppressive heat were determined to beat him down until he was swallowed by the mud of the swamp.

He shuffled to a stop and reached out a hand to the trunk of a scraggly tree to steady himself. It was farther away than he thought, and the sudden imbalance tossed him on his side instead. He lay there, staring up at a cloudless sky filled with splotches of light that moved with his gaze. At least the sun was still too low on the horizon to join them. If only that made any difference to the heat. But if it was so hot, why wasn't he sweating?

Of course his stomach wouldn't let him rest. It had to pick that moment to upend the few berries he tried eating that morning. Steven rolled over, heaving his meager breakfast over his swollen hands.

The angry red holes of the snake bites stared up at him, contrasted starkly against the white of the swelling around them. He'd tried bandaging them the first day, but he didn't have anything to use but leaves. He didn't know what he was doing anyway. The bandages fell off within hours so he'd stopped trying yesterday. It just didn't seem important anymore.

His stomach empty, Steven looked up to the east. It was all he had. Keep moving east. But he couldn't even guess how far he still had to go. It took three full days to get in as far as Mother took him. And he was hardly keeping the same pace going out. Still, it was something. A purpose.

Taking a deep breath, he pushed himself slowly to his feet. He stood there, trembling, before the black edged into his vision. He reached a shaking hand out to the tree as his vision narrowed, but it was still too far away. He fell. This time the black swallowed him.

The soft buzzing in Steven's ears and the flickering light shining through the dark brought Steven's heart into his throat. They found him! He was back on their altar. He tried to sit up, tried to roll off, but he couldn't move. Something was holding him down. He tried to claw at it with his hands, but he couldn't move his fingers. The buzzing turned harsher. It was right over him. He could almost see it, a blurred silhouette against the dancing red light behind. He tried to push it away. He had to get away!

Then something struck him hard across the face.

"And if you don't stop trying to hit me you'll get another, you ungrateful swamp weasel."

The figure slowly resolved into something man-shaped. Steven blinked against the sting on his face and let his arms fall.

Whispers at the Altar

"That's better. Next time I'll let you scream and pummel yourself like an idiot." The face of a man formed, all valleys and crags like some blasted and weathered landscape capped by thin clouds of white hair. He rubbed a deep tanned hand against one cheek. "Thanks I get for trudging all the way here," he muttered.

"I'm sorry," Steven managed. His throat was parched, and his tongue felt far too big to fit in his mouth.

The old man grunted and leaned back, his clear, hazel eyes watching Steven as if he were a dangerous animal that might attack at any moment. When Steven did not, the old man grunted again and shuffled over to a pot sitting to one side of the fire. He ladled something clear into a cup and shuffled back, reaching it up toward Steven's lips. "You should drink a bit. I gamble you thought it would be a good idea to drink any water you came across that wasn't green, didn't you? Stupid brain didn't think to boil it properly first, did it?"

The water was hot, like liquid fire running over his heavy tongue and down his dry throat. It was the most wonderful thing Steven had ever tasted.

"There now, not so much. Can't expect to almost die and then go drinking whatever you want, can you?" He stood, a chorus of creaks and cracks accompanying the simple movement, and wiped the cup off on his worn but clean brown tunic. In fact, not even the old man's drab, brown pants looked to carry a hint of the mud surrounding them. Even his boots were impossibly clean—impossible to Steven at least, who was still covered nearly head to toe in the muck.

"Who are you?" It was only slightly easier to talk, but he couldn't resist asking.

"Brogan," the old man answered as he ambled back to the fire. He set the cup down next to the water.

"How . . ." Steven swallowed, "how did you find me?"

Brogan threw his hands in the air. "Why couldn't he have stayed unconscious? I told you, I don't like talkers." He turned around. "I found you because I was told where to find you. How else would I

61

find one idiot boy in the whole of this forsaken pit? Do you have any idea what the odds of that are? Do you even know what 'odds' are?" He sighed and eased himself down practically on top of the fire. "Of course not. You didn't even know enough not to drink swamp water."

Steven fell back onto his back and stared up at the stars. At least he spoke more than Mother did. That was something. He closed his eyes, fighting back the flood of images that came whenever he thought of her.

"Fine, fine . . . I'll try," Brogan muttered. Then his voice shifted, taking on a more patient, long-suffering tone as he stared into the fire. "So, what's your name?"

"Steven." It was weird to say it out loud. He'd never had reason to before.

"Parents?"

He shook his head, then realized Brogan wasn't looking at him. "No," he croaked out.

"I see. Well, I don't know why a boy your age would be out in this filth of a place, but I'm not going to ask, either. I figure—"

"There were things in the swamp!" He struggled to sit up but his bandaged hands were like clubs at the ends of his arms.

Brogan turned at the commotion, his wild eyebrows knitting together as he reached out a hand as if to keep Steven down though he was much too far away to do so. "Hold up, boy. Calm down. You'll hurt yourself."

Steven only managed to prop himself on one elbow. "No. There were . . . *things*. Lizard . . . snake . . . THINGS. Bigger than you. They wanted me. There was an altar. And . . . and . . ." He couldn't bring himself to mention Mother. He had killed her. What would this man think if he knew Steven was a murderer? What would he do?

"Of course there are. Did you think no one lived here?" Brogan shook his head. "Now what do you mean they *wanted* you? Did they kidnap you? Where you from some village some fools built too near the swamp?"

"No. I . . ." Steven thought for the right words. It was hard. He wasn't used to talking this much. He never guessed how exhausting it could be. "I was there. There was an altar. They wanted to kill me. I ran. There was a . . ." He gestured wide with his arms, trying somehow to convey the hugeness of it. "A shadow. With wings. It was . . ." he was shaking now, the effort of talking and the fear of remembering sapping the strength from him. He could feel the fever coming back, the darkness closing in around him. He had to fight it.

He gripped his head in his hands as his body curled tight upon itself. Like a snake. Like an enormous snake. He could see it now, behind his eyes, watching him run away. Like a worm.

And then there was a cool hand on his head, and Brogan's rough voice piercing through the dark.

"You're safe, son. It's over. It's just the sickness. I'll keep a watch out. Get some rest. You should be good to walk in a day or so." Brogan sighed. "I've been told to bring you back to my house. You'll stay with me." He didn't sound enthusiastic about the idea.

The next days passed in a blur of dark nightmares filled with Mother's tittering laughter and brief respites of blessed wakefulness and mouthfuls of lukewarm water and weak broth. In truth, Steven had no idea how long it was. It felt like weeks, but he couldn't see how that was possible when he thought about it. Surely the snakes would have found them by then.

Then one afternoon he woke, and the shadow didn't follow him. He squinted in the sunlight, despite the shade of the canopy of branches Brogan must have erected over him at some point. The day was clear, hot, and he was starving. There was a bowl of water next to him, and he drank it greedily as he looked about for Brogan. He was gone.

Steven's heart sank. But he should have expected it. What was he to the old man? What reason would he have to stay? Still, Steven wished he could have done something for him. Kindness was a rare thing. Something Steven had learned to repay profusely when even the faintest hint of it was shown. Brogan had saved his life, cared for him when he was sick. Mother had done that, but with her it was . . . different. Steven wasn't sure how.

"You're looking much better."

Steven nearly jumped out of his skin as Brogan walked into the clearing, a small sack slung over one shoulder.

"I-I feel better," Steven stammered as he stood up.

"Good. About time." Brogan dropped the bag next to the fire pit and stretched. "You can help me get these ready to cook up. We'll be leaving in the morning, and I wouldn't mind having a bit to take along with us for the road."

"Yes, Mo— I mean . . . yes, sir." He hurried forward, crouched on the ground, and opened the bag. A dozen round flat shells slid over each other. Steven stopped and looked up, confused.

"What's the matter? Never seen a turtle?"

Steven could only shake his head. He reached in to take one, then jerked his hand back as a head snapped out of the shell intent on his finger.

Brogan chuckled. "Come on. Dump them out, and I'll show you."

"Who told you to find me?" Steven asked as they hung the turtles from a nearby tree a few minutes later. It was a question that had been nagging at the edges of his thoughts since that first night. Now, with other thoughts sliding back into the darkness at the back of his mind, he couldn't think of much else.

"The only one who matters," Brogan answered.

Steven paused. He didn't want to pry. Didn't want to make him angry. But he couldn't resist the question either. "But . . . who?"

Brogan sighed. "Him." He gestured at the sky and the trees. "I don't know if He has a name, and I've never cared much to give Him one. But He's always taken care of me, guided me. So I've learned to go where He says."

"Where is he?"

"Gracious, you wake up after two days of fever, and all you can do is ask questions. How should I know, boy? All around us, I suppose. Or maybe way up high looking down like we look at the ants. Why does it matter?"

Steven shrugged and went back to his work. He knew when to shut up.

There was a moment's silence, then Brogan's heavy sigh. "Look. I'm sorry. They're good questions. I guess I never tried to explain it before."

Steven hunched over his work. Why was Brogan apologizing? It was his fault. He deserved to be yelled at. The man saved his life and this was how Steven repaid him?

There was another grunt, and the silence folded around them once more. It was better that way, Steven thought. He knew silence. It was familiar, like old worn shoes. He closed his eyes for a second and let himself enjoy it.

"I'll take you back to my place," Brogan said.

Steven nodded. It was only right. He had saved Steven's life after all.

Chorus

The bells for Chorus chimed again, and Christa grunted as Sinna pulled her down the hall, nearly knocking her book out of her hand.

"Hurry up, Christa! You can f-finish your reading after Chorus. If you don't put it down and watch where you're going we'll be late."

"I am relatively certain the book will still be there when you are done," Westrel said.

Christa gave a brief roll of her eyes and tucked the book under her arm.

"I am sure she just thinks she can do both at the same time," Darian said. "Or perhaps she is practicing. It could be a very useful skill to develop."

Christa gave him a big smile. She liked Darian. He was always so kind and polite to her. He was a Mentalist, someone who could read other's minds, and a friend of Westrel's, though Sinna spent more time talking to him than Westrel ever did.

As expected, with no fight given, the conversation rolled on to other topics. Christa did her best to keep up with both the pace and the conversation. But her companions' strides were hard to match, and she ended up in a near jog that kept every other thought out of her mind.

She still wasn't sure why she agreed to go to Chorus. She had a million other things she could be doing right now. But all her friends had asked her at one point or another. Sinna had promised she would love it. Westrel explained that she found it a good break from her studies. In the end it was Silvana cornering her in the yard that convinced her.

Chorus is how we remember who we are, Christa. Where we come from, and what the Creator has done for us.

There had been something in the girl's gaze that made Christa feel a bit guilty she'd avoided it. After all, Mama would have wanted her to go.

They reached the doors just in time to slip through before they closed. The sight gave Christa even more to think about. The Chapel was huge, easily one of the largest single rooms she had seen in the palace. Dark wood beams, too slender to be anything but decorative, caressed a towering vaulted ceiling of alabaster. Walls of pale marble streaked with gold circled her, interrupted by twelve framed alcoves. Exquisitely carved dark wood statues stood in each nearest the door. Christa assumed the same for the others. She could barely make them out through the crowd of elves.

They stood in front of long high-backed benches ranked in rows that radiated from the center of the circular chamber. Some even stood in the aisles or in the back, as Christa and her friends would be doing.

Next to the immense size of the room, the next thing Christa noticed was the intense silence. It wasn't the hushed quiet of anticipation. It was a natural silence, the sort that seemed appropriate and necessary. Glancing at her friends, she found them standing calmly, their eyes focused on the center of the sanctuary.

As soon as the doors clicked closed behind them, the music started. It was impossible for Christa to tell where it came from at first. It came from everywhere. It came from the walls and up out of the tiled floor, before reverberating down from the lofty ceiling. It started so softly, like the hum of a bee or the song of a distant bird, that Christa almost thought she imagined it. Slowly, in no hurry, it gained volume. Time did not exist for the song, and so it did not fear measurement. Christa looked about for the source, determined to at least know this much. But it was her friends who sang it, the voice of every elf that carried it as it filled the chamber who carried it.

Chorus with Mama had never been like this. There had been words to those songs. She gave up on the idea of joining in—how could she?—and listened. The song hummed through her, reverberated in her chest. As she closed her eyes the hum surged through her, filling her thoughts. She could see it in her mind. The music of the song played out before her as naturally as breathing.

At first there was only darkness, a solid palpable black lit by the song that played around the edges. As it rose in volume, Christa became aware of other voices within the song, voices surrounding and accompanying but never overwhelming.

Then, with a crescendo, there was light, and that light became dozens, hundreds, millions more, like stars in a clear night sky. The lights wheeled and danced above and around her. She danced with them, laughing as they twirled in circles that left streaks of light across her mind's eye. The song picked up tempo, the chorus behind it keeping pace in steps of perfect unison. Christa glanced down and was surprised to see grass and a pond reflecting the lights around it. The melody of the song changed, moving from the almost frenetic dance to something slower, contemplative. Christa examined the trees more closely. They appeared old, but she knew they just sprouted moments ago. The forest carried such wild beauty she was sure she should be frightened, but she wasn't.

As she watched, ghostly shapes rose from the water before her, the ground below her, and the trees around her. They joined the dance, twirling and spinning through the air. Slowly they coalesced, taking the shape and form of elves, their faces shining with the carefree abandon of youth. She danced with them, floating from one to the other, laughing as her mind reeled in dizziness. The song faded into the background, a framework for life.

She was reminded of when she was younger. Mama would make crowns of daisies, and they would rule the little garden behind their house. And they would dance. Mama was so beautiful and such a wonderful dancer.

Christa could see her now. The field faded away, and Christa stood once more as she had in that little garden watching Mama sway in slow circles around the little path. Her golden hair flashed in the spring sun as her simple white dress curled and swept across the tips of the grass along the path. She stopped, and the smile that fell on Christa made her heart glow with warmth.

Mama!

She reached out a hand, Christa took it, and they danced together as they always had. Just as Christa longed to do again. And all the while the song of the elves ran over them like a waterfall.

I've missed you so much, Mama.

I know, my little flower. But I am always with you.

The words hummed through Christa's mind. But she knew they weren't true. Mama wasn't here. She never would be again. And it was all Christa's fault.

Don't blame yourself.

But there was no one else to blame. No one else had been there. No one else had done what she did. The song changed, the undercurrent growing stronger, and the melody shifting. She felt Mama slipping away. She tried to hold on tighter.

Mama! No . . . don't go. I need you!

The song taunted as it floated around her. The original comforting voice was gone, replaced by something far more sinister. It laughed at her, a sound like rocks crumbling against each other and glass breaking.

Whispers at the Altar

But you already said, the voice whispered in her heart. *She isn't really here. And you know why.*

The garden vanished, replaced by a broken cliffside, the rocks still clattering as they came to rest at the bottom. Tears fell down her face as her hand reached out, still clutching Mama's ring as if there was any chance to save her.

Christa's ears filled with that broken voice.

You did this. It's your fault.

She'll never forgive you.

He'll never love you.

They'll never accept you.

You're a monster.

Christa had to get away from that horrible laughter. Her lids felt fastened shut, pressing the image of those rocks into her brain. She tried rubbing them. She told herself to open them, to reject what she saw.

Mama's form floated past, a pale specter. She called out to Christa, one hand reaching out, but the mocking laughter drowned out whatever words she had to say.

With a final, brutal effort, Christa's lids snapped open.

She shouldered through the Chapel's giant doors at a run, her eyes so wet she could barely tell if what she saw was real or some remnant of that horrible vision.

She didn't dare close them, even to cry. She was too afraid of what she might find there. So she ran, intent on putting as much distance between her and that music and those visions as possible. By the time she stopped she had no idea where she was, other than somewhere in the Divinist tower. She collapsed into a soft couch under a colorful tapestry she didn't bother to glance at. She let the sobs overtake her then, not caring who might walk by or take notice.

She heard someone stop next to her. Raising her head, she wiped her eyes expecting to see Sinna, or maybe Westrel. She had to blink a few times before she recognized Darian.

"Christabel? Are you well?"

"What was that?" she asked, a sob working its way out despite her best efforts to keep it down.

Darian looked confused but recovered quickly. "That was the Chorus of Beginnings. I have sung it countless times, but never seen someone react that way. What is wrong?"

"What's wrong?" Christa forced a remnant sob into a mere hiccup. "It . . ." She tried to think of how to explain, but she couldn't think of the words. "It changed! It became . . . horrible." The memories of that laugh and of Mama were too much, and the tears came back in full force. She turned her head away, ashamed, burying it into the arm of the couch.

"Just . . . go away," she mumbled.

Either he didn't hear her, or he was as stubborn as she. Either way, he didn't leave. Instead he sat down beside her, a single hand placed awkwardly on her back. After some moments, when the shaking once again subsided to occasional shivers, he spoke again, barely over a whisper.

"I do not pretend to know what you are feeling, Christabel, or what you saw during the song. But . . . will you let me show you something that may cheer you up? It has brought me comfort many times."

Unwilling to stay, but less willing to be alone, even if the company was someone she hardly knew, Christa nodded and pulled herself up off the couch. Darian stood with her and offered his arm, but Christa just hugged herself. Playing off the refusal, Darian turned to go and, as she followed her gaze caught on the arm of the couch. For the first time she noticed the cushions were soft amber, except where her tears had soaked the cloth and turned it a deep russet red like blood dripping down. She shivered, hugging herself tighter as she hurried off after Darian.

He led her in silence out of the Divinist Tower to the central spire, then up the circling stairs that wound inside its walls. Christa had no idea where they were going, but she was sure there must be a faster

Whispers at the Altar

way to get there. But then, the fastest way would be the tubes and, now that she thought about it, she was glad Darian had chosen the stairs.

Soon the walkway left all the rooms and side passages behind as it climbed in ever tightening circles. Only then did Christa turn her attention from the stone beneath her feet to the startlingly close sky above.

In fact, there seemed to be no roof at all. As near as she could tell, the walkway exited onto some rampart or battlement open to the clouds. As she neared the top, however, she could make out faint bends of light like the edges of walls and the lines of a floor. Before she knew it, she was walking up through a floor of clear crystal. That alone boggled her, but she quickly realized the top of the entire tower was made up of it. The floor, walls, even the high peaked roof that soared another fifty span into the air, all was made of a single piece of flawless crystal.

Christa stood there for a moment, afraid to walk out onto that plateau of thin glass. She even tried to step back but bumped into the wall. She spun and the sight made her even more sick to her stomach as she stared down into the forest of towers and the palace dome far below. She reached out for something, anything, to hold on to that would support her and found her arm taken by Darian, his hands steadying her gently.

"I apologize. I should have warned you, but I had forgotten what a shock it can be the first time. Do you need a moment? We are nearly there. We need to cross to the center of the floor. Just over there." He pointed out to the middle of the transparent floor, and Christa paled.

"I . . . I don't know if I can do it. I feel like I'm going to faint."

"I understand. But you will not fall. Trust me. It helps to keep your gaze on the sky as you walk, rather than down toward the ground. And I will be here to help you."

Christa took a deep breath and tried to steady her stomach. She knew she must look immensely silly, clinging to this young man's arm like a frightened bird, but he was asking her to walk on air. Or near enough. Closing her eyes, she willed herself to take a step forward. She didn't fall. Opening them a bit, she focused on the sky above her, imagining she was walking out in the garden back home. The sky was darkening toward night and a scattering of stars were already shining down. Another step, then another, and she forgot all about what might lie below her or how far away that might be. She could feel Darian's arm supporting her on one side but she paid little attention to it, or him, until he spoke again.

"Here we are." He moved behind her, placing a hand on each shoulder. "Now, look around."

Christa lowered her gaze from the stars above and found she was speechless. What small traces of wall and floor there had been were gone. Not only that, but so was the palace below her. All the walls, towers, even the dome were gone. Or rather they were far below her. It was as though she were floating or flying thousands of spans above the city. She could see it all laid out below her, all the streets and parks, shops and mansions were there in miniature. She looked up again and if it had been possible her eyes would have widened even further. The night sky was lit up around her in a way she had never imagined. Stars shone like small fragments of white fire on a sheet of black velvet. She was sure she could reach out and touch each one or scoop whole constellations up in her hands.

"This is the observatory," Darian whispered in her ear. "I think it is used for some astronomy classes, but aside from that not many people come up here. I do occasionally to think. It is nice during the day, but at night . . . Well, you can see."

Christa had no idea what to say. So she just stared.

SILVANA

"Psst. Hey, freak."

Christa closed her eyes for a second, willing the voice away and trying to focus on Instructor Riltan. Elven History was complicated enough without Vaniel and her henchgirls whispering to her from the table behind.

"Hey... freak. I am talking to you."

Christa knew Riltan had to hear it. But either he was waiting to punish Vaniel after class, or he didn't care. Christa was sure she knew which.

"Maybe she is deaf," Crony-girl whispered.

"Obviously. I mean look at her ears," Vaniel answered.

"Yeah, they are so tiny I bet she cannot hear anything," Flunky-girl piped in.

"Poor Freak," Vaniel feigned compassion. "She has such sad ears."

Christa balled her hands into fists and tried to ignore the blood rushing to her ears and the giggling that ensued. She tried to remember what Sinna had said: Vaniel was powerful. She would be around forever. And there was nothing Christa could do. She just had to ignore it.

"Hey, Sad-ears." Crony and Flunky went quiet the instant Vaniel spoke. "I heard you have been hanging out with that peasant, Darian. Maybe he likes you. You should ask him."

Christa squinted at Instructor Riltan in her effort to focus.

"Oh, but Vaniel," Flunky-B admonished, "do you think that is a good idea? I mean with her . . . you know . . ." She made a pretense at lowering her voice. "Her flat ears?"

"Oooh right." Vaniel giggled. "Besides, I hear that stuttering straw-head Sinnasarel has her eyes on him. It is just as well. Not as if any sane elf would like this ugly little freak anyway." The giggling started up again.

With a growl, Christa grabbed her writing board, spun around, and slammed it down on Vaniel's table, right over her delicate little fingers. Her howl was sweet music accompanied by a chorus of high screams from her lackeys.

Christa smiled, a part of her, the part she didn't like, enjoying the moment—until she was rotated, against her will and without a thing touching her, to face Instructor Riltan.

"You owe me an hour, Christabel."

"But I have Arithmetic after this. I'll be late."

"Excellent." His lips formed a thin curve that stayed well away from his hard, beady black eyes. "You can explain to Instructor Faellel why you are late. I am sure she will have some punishment for that as well."

"But she was—"

"And you owe Vaniel an apology."

"What!" Christa tried to stand, would have had she not been pinned by the same force that turned her around. "She should be apologizing to me."

"I do not see her slate marks on your fingers."

Christa glanced sidelong to see Vaniel, her wet eyes twinkling as she grinned victoriously and cradled her wounded fingers. "I'm sorry," Christa muttered.

"For what?" Riltan prompted.

"For hitting your sensitive little hands," Christa said through clenched teeth.

Riltan frowned. "Now apologize to the class for stealing their time with your tantrum, and we will get back to the Destined Expansion."

The invisible grip on her body relaxed. She shivered as it left, then faced forward as the class erupted in titters of laughter.

"Sorry," she muttered as she sank deeper into her chair.

The slate shattered as it hit the side of the palace dome, but somehow the destruction did little to calm Christa's fury. She watched, chest heaving, as the tiny pieces slid down the side. If only that could be Vaniel.

"I think that might get you into more trouble."

Christa jumped back, turning to face a girl about Sinna's age standing not four paces away, the same girl she saw by the fountain that first day. "What?" She hid her hands behind her back, as if that would hide what she'd already done.

The girl just laughed and walked up to lean over the railing of the bridge. Christa had made sure to pick one low enough to not make her queasy but high enough to get the effect she wanted.

"Don't worry, I won't tell anyone." She beckoned Christa over. "I saw what happened. In class."

Christa inched over, not taking her gaze off the girl. There was still something about her. Something familiar. She'd noticed it that first day, too. "I didn't know you were in that class." In fact, the more she thought about it, the more certain she was the girl wasn't.

"Oh, I was passing by in the hall. My name is . . . well, you can call me Silvana. It is what all my friends call me."

Christa nodded once, still staring as Silvana looked out over the city. "Oh. I'm Christabel. Or, Christa, I guess." She couldn't take her eyes off this girl. Maybe it was something in her voice?

"So Christa," Silvana leaned her side against the rail, "do you think Vaniel will try something again?"

"Probably," Christa sighed and dropped down to sit, peering through the swirling vines of the railing as if they were prison bars. "She hates me, and I don't even know why. I never did anything to her."

"I know. It is frustrating. But there will always be people who don't like you. Going around hitting them probably isn't the best solution," Silvana sat down beside Christa.

"So, what am I supposed to do?"

"I guess that depends."

"On what?"

"On what kind of person you want to be." Silvana leaned her head against the metal vines, green eyes appraising Christa without condemnation.

"What do you mean? I . . . I want to be a good person. Just like everyone else does."

"Not everyone holds that goal with the same determination as you might think. But if it is what you want, then listen to that side of you. We all have two sides. Some of us might find it harder to listen to the correct one, but in the end, it is up to us to decide which one we follow. Which one we let in, and which one we shut out."

Christa considered this, remembering how happy she was to hear Vaniel scream. "So . . . I shouldn't hit her in the face with a fire poker?"

Silvana chuckled. "I think you know the answer."

"That isn't really helpful. Can't you just tell me what to do?"

"Sometimes there are no easy answers." She stood, brushing off her skirt. "But in this instance I think you know what you should do. The hard part will be doing it."

Christa squinted up at her. "Thanks. I guess."

She shook her head, the last bits of laughter slipping out. "You are welcome. Be well, Christa."

Then she was walking to the nearest tower, closing the door softly behind her.

Sinna opened the door to the bridge and breathed a sigh of relief. There was Christa, staring at the opposite tower. "T-thank goodness you're still here."

Christa waved. It was an odd gesture but she'd seen Christa do it a lot and deciphered what it meant.

"How did you know I was here?" Christa called.

Sinna waited until she was close enough to have a polite conversation. Christa's manners were rarely what they should be, but Sinna thought that might be part of what made her so fun. She got to live wildly through Christa, doing things Sinna never would have thought of doing otherwise.

"I saw you from farther up." She pointed to the Elemental Library bridge. "What are you d-doing here?" She glanced at the Attendant Tower. "Visiting someone?" Sinna sat down carefully next to Christa, tucking her feet properly under her skirt. If her mother saw her, getting her dress all dirty like this, oh the lecture she'd get. She almost smiled, but stopped as she got a better look at Christa. "What's wrong?"

Christa ran her hands through her unruly hair. "You don't . . . there isn't something wrong with my ears, is there?" she whispered, voice cracking.

Sinna shook her head instantly. "Of course not, Christa. W-why would you think that?"

"Vaniel," she answered and peered out through the bars.

Sinna tried and failed to think of an appropriate yet lady-like epithet. "Your ears are lovely, Christa." She shifted a little closer. "Vaniel's being s-stupid. Like her brother."

There was a short silence, during which Christa leaned into her a bit. Sinna stiffened against the unexpected contact but didn't move. It was likely just another human mannerism.

Christa sniffed. "She said I was an ugly little freak."

Sinna made a mental note to push Vaniel in a pond. She knew she'd never do it, but the image was quite satisfying. "You're not ugly. I only wish I had hair like yours, so dark and full of life. And your ears might be small, but they're slender and d-delicate. If you took care of yourself, brushed your hair occasionally, I bet you'd rival even Director A-Aerel for beauty."

Christa scoffed, whether at the idea of brushing her hair or being beautiful Sinna couldn't tell.

"Anyway, that's probably one reason V-Vaniel doesn't like you. For one, your hair's darker than hers." Sinna chuckled, "I bet that eats her up."

"Why?" Christa turned toward Sinna.

"It's a s-stupid status thing. Darker hair is rare. It's a-a-a . . . it's linked with nobility and royalty. Hair like mine . . ." She sighed and tossed her braid back over her shoulder. "It's common. As in actually do the real work kind of common."

"So that's why Vaniel's family is so powerful?"

"No. Not just that. But I doubt she's ever done a lick of real work in her life. Not like my family. They're f-farmers."

"So she hates me because I'm not noble but still have dark hair? That's dumb. I didn't pick what color hair I have."

Whispers at the Altar

Sinna didn't think she could have said it better herself. "Of course not. The whole thing is d-dumb. They do the same thing with eye color. Everything in the capital, and especially the palace, is all about status. And somehow you look like you have it when she thinks you shouldn't. So, don't let Vaniel or anyone else tell you you're ugly, Christa. They're just j-j-jealous."

Nightmares

Another crack of thunder shook the tower. Christa pulled the sheets tighter and buried her head under the pillow. Clenching her eyes tight, she willed, begged, for sleep to find her. Another flash lit the night through her window, barely visible through the white cloth around her, followed by another low rumble seconds later. With all the magic the elves tossed around, you would think they could regulate the weather around their own palace.

She took a deep breath and tried to ignore the unnerving sound of the rain spattering against the wall and window of her room. A second breath and she could feel herself starting to relax. It would be all right. The tower wouldn't fall.

Another crack echoed like an explosion right outside her window. Christa screamed, unable to help herself, as her heart jumped into her throat. Without thinking, she scrambled off the bed and crawled under it, dragging her sheet and pillow with her. She wrapped herself up again, panting as she curled up against the wall. She tried to channel some of its strength, but it didn't work. She blinked back the tear and took deep breaths, like Papa told her. *Papa. Please take me back. I'm sorry.*

The trees blurred as Christa ran through the forest. She thought she'd left them behind. Had she left them behind? She wanted to slow down, but the trees rushed past. Then she heard them again, and she couldn't go fast enough. They weren't just behind her now, they were all around. She could hear them laughing. The same grinding laughter from Chorus. It hammered against her ears and made her temples ache. A tree branch slapped across her face, but she didn't feel it.

She pressed on, taking furtive glances to each side as she ran. She spotted one to her left, like a misshapen wolf. Then another to the right. They snarled and snapped as they laughed. Instead of tooth-filled maws, they wore the faces of children from the Roost. The tormentors of her new life. Vaniel led them, snapping at her heels, howling the same painful, grinding laugh while her canine tongue streamed out of her elven mouth.

Christa stumbled into a clearing. A little girl sat there, her blue dress with its little white flowers plastered to her by the rain. When did it start raining?

Christa struggled to steady her breathing, but her heart wouldn't stop racing. The little girl was digging in the mud, making a doomed palace with tall slender towers.

Christa crept around, desperate to see the girl's face, but terrified of what she knew she would see.

The girl was her.

"Run!" Christa yelled. But the girl ignored her.

"You have to get away. They're coming!" Christa ran to her younger self, knelt in the mud, and shook her by the shoulders. "Don't you understand? They'll get you." She didn't know what it was they would do when they caught her, either of her, but she knew to be afraid.

The girl didn't listen. She just gazed up with a wide, proud smile. She pointed at her castle.

"I don't care about the castle. It's fine. But you have to run." Christa tried to pull the girl up, but there was no strength in her arms.

The girl giggled, as though it were all a game, and pointed down at the castle again.

Frustration setting in, Christa glanced down.

A cold chill itched down her spine. There wasn't a castle. There was only a hand buried beneath a mound of mud. It reached up from the earth in desperation. Mama's hand. With Mama's silver ring.

Christa screamed, all thought of herself, the rain, and the wolf-children flew from her mind. She took the hand in both of hers and pulled. It was cold, like ice, but she gripped it as hard as she could and pulled. She shivered almost uncontrollably. It wouldn't budge. She stood up and tried to heave all her weight into it, but it was as though her arms were made of air.

Then the ground dropped below her. There was a terrifying feeling of hovering for the briefest second, and she fell into blackness. Still holding her mother's hand.

Christa woke with a start and banged her head against the bottom of the bed. She was soaked in sweat. Her nightgown, as well as the sheet she had wrapped around her, was plastered to her skin, and she was shivering. She crawled out, bumping her head again, and grabbed the blanket from the foot of her bed. She wrapped it around herself as she sat on the floor, knees pulled up to her chest. The wind had died and the only rumble of thunder she heard was low and distant. But her heart still hammered.

The window was open—the wind must have knocked the latch loose—and the floor beneath it was puddled with water. Christa bemoaned yet another chore to do in the morning, but her mind couldn't focus. It was still in the clearing, looking down at her mother's hand. Reaching down, she pulled out the chain that held Mama's ring and gripped it as tight as she could. Then she cried. Shivering on the floor of her room, she buried her head between her knees and let herself miss Mama.

When she had nothing left, she took a deep breath and rubbed her eyes. Morning was hours away, but sleep was unlikely. She stumbled to her closet and pulled out some clothes. She started to change then stopped, remembering she was covered in sweat. A bath then. That might help her mood, too.

An hour later, bathed, changed, and hair brushed, she made her way down to the dining hall. She had considered going to the Yard to stand on some actual ground. But while the idea of being firmly planted appealed to her, the thought of any kind of earth right now made her stomach uneasy.

She was surprised to find any food laid out at this hour. But there it was: a small spread of sweet rolls, biscuits, and numerous fruit preserves. The lingering smell of freshly baked bread made her stomach growl, reminding her of the quick dinner she had between classes. She heaped a plate with as much as it would hold and sat at her usual table. She was halfway done when someone walked up behind her.

"A little early for breakfast." Silvana sat down next to her, swiveling on the bench to face her.

Christa swallowed. "I couldn't sleep." She stared down at her food, praying Silvana wouldn't ask the obvious question.

"Bad dreams?"

She fingered a biscuit, debating how much she should say. Silvana was nice, but not even Sinna knew about Mama. It wasn't something she wanted floating around the Roost. She could only imagine what Vaniel would do with it. "For a while," she said eventually. "But they've been worse since I went to Chorus. This one felt so . . . real."

Silvana nodded, watching her in a way that made Christa nervous. "Do you want to talk about them? Sometimes it helps."

Christa shook her head. That would definitely *not* help.

"Can you tell me what they are about?"

"My mama. She's . . . gone."

"I see."

Christa stared at the table between them, unwilling to meet her eyes.

"There is something else that might help." Silvana's hand rested on hers. "You are not alone. I am here."

Christa looked up and Silvana's gaze seemed to look right through Christa. "Thank you. I guess I'm not used to having people to turn to besides my family."

"Well, you do. Now have you tried writing to your mother?"

"What do you mean? Like a letter?"

"Perhaps. I was thinking like a journal. If you set aside some time to write in it, like you were talking to her, you might find it helps you to feel better. Like she is still with you."

"And that will make the nightmares go away?"

"I didn't say that. But if the nightmares are about your mother . . . One reason might be because you miss her. And this might at least help with that." She shrugged. "It is just an idea."

Christa chuckled. "Thanks. Maybe I will." She didn't think it would help. Mama was gone. And nothing could bring her back.

"Good. I hope it helps. Have a good day, Christa." Silvana stood, waved, and walked away.

If only Christa had the right kind of magic. One thing was certain. No matter what kind of magic she could use, she had to find some way to bring Mama back. That would stop the nightmares. And it was the only way Papa would love her—and take her back—again. Then everyone would be happy.

THE BRIDGE

Christa squeezed her eyes shut and stifled a yawn with her free hand. A late night of studying combined with another nightmare was making this test take far longer than it should have.

Rubbing her eyes, she tried to make them focus on the parchment in front of her, but the words kept blurring together. She glanced up and saw Ilisibel yawn at the table ahead. Then Rollan beside her. And so it went echoing around the room. Christa grinned as she watched. It was like seeing how many times she could skip a stone across the pond.

Four . . . five. A record.

She remembered the test and groaned inwardly. Who cared about how Ellsabareth was founded? Or how cold it had to be for water to freeze? Or the difference between transitive and intransitive verbs? With a sigh she wrote down and labeled all the conjugations for *take*.

It wasn't that she didn't know the answers. None of them were that hard if you paid attention. It was the sheer . . . monotony. She flipped back a page and wrote the word in the only blank she'd left, and then took a moment to pat herself on the back. Returning to the end, she started in on the final essay. She hated essays. Why did they always want you to use ten times as many words as it should take any reasonable person to explain something?

At least Vaniel wasn't here to distract her. Although, if Christa passed this test, that wouldn't be the case any longer. So far she'd only had to put up with Vaniel in Elven History, which Christa gathered wasn't Vaniel's strong suit, but with this advancement test they would be in several training groups together. Lovely.

Christa paused and stared down at the paper. As usual, she was only halfway through the essay and couldn't think of a single thing more to say. How many ways could you describe the genius of the elven professional focus system? What she wanted to write was it was a horrible way for the nobility to keep those they saw as below them in their place, but she didn't think that would win her any points. So back to the old standby. Flattery. It didn't answer the question any better, but she discovered months ago the trainers loved it.

With the essay finished, to the exact required word, she gave the test a final examination for any mistakes, signed her name with a flourish, and stood with a screech of chair legs on marble. She tried to ignore the annoyed looks as she walked up to the front of the room and presented the sheets of parchment to Trainer Cesinel.

Cesinel frowned. "You have thirty minutes more to complete the test. I suggest you review your answers."

"I don't need to." Christa tried her best to sound neither arrogant nor annoyed—even if she felt a bit of the first and a lot of the second. "They're right."

The trainer's frown deepened but she took the pages. Flipping to the last, she read the essay.

Christa watched as she made a few notes, probably spelling mistakes, and tried to suppress another yawn. It wouldn't do to appear bored while her test was being graded.

"Your analysis is passable, though not as in-depth as I would have liked," Cesinel whispered, then spread the sheets over the desk.

There was a brief glow, then the trainer smiled.

"Congratulations, Christabel. Only three answers wrong. You are officially a Second Tier Eyas."

Christa bounced down the hall of the Roost Administration Tower. She couldn't wait to tell Sinna and Westrel. Second tier. In a year. No elf had ever made it that fast. Maybe now the classes would actually be interesting. And second tier meant just one more test before she could start learning magic. She couldn't even express how happy that made her. She twirled in the middle of the hall, dancing the last few paces to the door.

Flinging it open, she took a deep breath of the fresh air. As much as she disliked heights, she'd found the bridges well worth it. Up here the air was cleaner than inside the dome, the sun brighter and warmer than the artificial light below. Neither Sinna nor Westrel understood the difference. But to Christa it was like being truly alive versus only pretending.

She skipped out onto the bridge, her hand gliding over the railing as she gazed out across the city. It was beautiful today. The late afternoon sun struck the rainbow hues of the roofs to make a sea of swirling color below her. She paused in the middle of the bridge and gripped the railing tight with both hands as she watched the flags of the many noble houses flutter lazily in the spring breeze.

Almost a year ago now she had walked through those gates with Papa. She sighed. A year and no word at all from him. She'd tried to write, but he never wrote back. After a few months . . . What was the use of writing someone who didn't want to talk to you?

The slam of a door jerked her back to reality. But when she turned, her heart dove down into her gut. Vaniel stalked across the bridge from the Essence side, two lackeys behind her. Christa spun to leave the way she came, only to find two more hench-girls calmly walking from that direction.

"Here you are, Freak," Vaniel shouted.

Christa sighed. "What do you want, Vaniel?" She expected them to stop a pace away, but they kept coming, forcing her to back up against the rail.

"I heard about your test. Second Tier Eyas Christabel. Did that wild sow Westrel help you cheat? Or maybe it was your dirt-lover friend. What is her name again? She can never spit it out."

"You're just jealous." Christa stood her ground. "Jealous and pathetic. No matter how good your breeding, you can't stand to think you'll never be as good as me."

Vaniel's hand flashed across faster than Christa could react. The slap swung her head around, making her vision fuzzy and her ears ring, as four pairs of hands grabbed her. They pushed her against the rail until it dug against her spine as she leaned back over it. Christa tried to struggle, but her feet were all that moved, sliding forward until she could feel her balance starting to slip.

"You are *not* better than I am, you dirty half-breed," Vaniel hissed, her face an inch away as she leaned over.

Christa caught a whiff of lavender and something like cinnamon. "What are you going to do? Push me over the edge? Right here where anyone passing by can see?"

Vaniel barked a laugh. "You think anyone here cares? Who do you think is going to come running to your rescue? No one wants you here, Freak. You are nothing but a sad-eared half-human pretending at being something else. Like a sow pretending she deserves a seat at the table. Do you know what we do to a pig?"

She reached out a hand, and Christa's feet scrabbled for purchase as she leaned back. Vaniel laughed. "Did you see how she flinched?"

Whispers at the Altar

The cronies all laughed as told.

Vaniel leaned forward until her breath brushed over Christa's ear. "You should be afraid of me." She pulled back and nodded to her cronies. "Let's get this over with."

Christa barely felt the grip tighten on her arms. Her gaze was focused on the knife Vaniel pulled from the pocket of her tunic. Eight hands forced her around until she was gazing once more over the city's rooftops. But now the rainbow was harsh, the colors putrid and stale. Christa wondered if Vaniel would stab her in the back. She screamed, but no one came.

She cried out as a hand yanked her head back by the hair, then watched as a sheaf of brown strands floated down toward the dome below her. She tried to push back, away from the rail, the fight returning as she realized what Vaniel was doing. She had better leverage, but there were too many of them.

Another small cloud of brown.

She looked down and around at the other bridges for help. There were some people on a bridge below. She screamed again. But either they didn't hear, or Vaniel was right, and no one cared. The tugs were coming faster now, more painful as the hair became shorter until the last handful of hair floated away.

"This is a warning, Freak."

Christa could feel Vaniel's breath on her ear, along with the cool wind on her scalp.

"Leave. You don't belong here. Next time it won't be just your hair."

Vaniel leaned, back then paused, reaching out for Mama's ring dangling from Christa's neck on its silver chain.

Christa strained against the hands holding her arms, twisting and squirming, but she couldn't keep Vaniel's hand from curling around the ring. With a vicious yank, she broke the chain.

"Stop! That's my mama's!" Christa could feel heat spreading through her along with the anger. She knew this feeling. Like sparks flying in her chest. Like a fire burning deep inside.

•*Whispers at the Altar*•

"Aww. Is it all you have to remember your human-loving mother? You poor thing." Vaniel sneered.

The fire was roaring in Christa's ears now. She barely registered Vaniel's cronies cry out and retreat. "Give. It. Back!" She roared as she turned to grab for the ring. Only then did she see the flames racing along her arms.

Sinna ran onto the bridge then skidded to a stop in shock. Christa, at least what she knew had to be Christa, stood wreathed in flames before a wide-eyed Vaniel. The bridge railing was already melted and the stone was showing bright hairline cracks radiating out from Christa's feet.

"Christa!" She broke back into a run. She hadn't the slightest idea what she would do, but she had to do something.

Christa's head tilted a fraction toward Sinna, and Vaniel seized the opportunity to run.

"GIVE IT BACK!" Christa bellowed, shaking the slender bridge with the words. Vaniel stumbled, lost her footing, and went down, flinging a small object from her hand across the span and off the edge.

Sinna slid to a stop as near to Christa as she dared. Christa was almost on top of Vaniel now even as the bully scrambled to get away.

"C-C-Christa, stop!"

Christa raised back a burning fist.

"STOP!" Sinna flung out one hand, collected the air together, and Christa's blow fell against an invisible wall. The impact vibrated up through Sinna's arm, numbing it to the shoulder, but Christa turned to look at her, which was all the opportunity Vaniel needed. She ran.

"W-what are you doing?" Sinna yelled at Christa. She was barely recognizable. The dark brown hair that had once fallen to her lower back was a butchered mess, none of it longer than a few inches and all of it stark white. But it was her eyes that made Sinna pause. There was no trace of the girl she knew. Only burning rage.

"It's me, Christa. What . . . what happened?" She took a tentative step forward then back again as Christa wheeled on her. There was no recognition.

"You let her get away!"

Sinna shook her head. "That wasn't the way. Y-you know that. You know it. Whatever she did, we'll fix it. Together. I promise. Please, Christa. J-j-just calm down."

Slowly, the fire faded as the person Sinna knew came back into Christa's eyes. The flames winked out with a final flicker, and Christa sagged to the cracked stones of the bridge. Sinna hurried to her and wrapped her arms around her. Manners be damned.

"Are you all right? Are you h-hurt?" She felt over Christa's body, but there were no burns. Her dress wasn't even singed.

"I'm sorry. I don't know . . . She took Mama's ring and . . ." Christa sniffed back tears. "I just wanted her to give it back. She had no right to take it. Oh, Sinna I almost . . ."

"It's fine, C-Christa. Everything's fine. She wasn't hurt. We'll get the ring back." She left unsaid that it had gone over the edge. There was no telling where it landed outside the palace. But the pit if she wasn't going to search until she found it.

"Can you stand? Let's get you to Director Marellel's office. She'll know what to do. Vaniel can't get away with this. It's . . . it's unheard of. She'll get expelled, I just know it." She helped Christa to her feet as she talked, keeping up a stream of one-sided dialogue more to distract her than anything else.

As they passed back into the tower something about Christa's hair caught Sinna's attention. She had to stare at it for a moment to make sure. But the tips were returning to a light brown. Sinna shook her head and kept walking. Definitely something for Marellel.

Christa fell silent for a few steps then gave a wan smile. "I passed my test."

"She . . . *exploded*?" Dalan repeated, the word dripping with equal parts disbelief and disdain. "You want me to believe this . . . mongrel dog, exploded into flame, and nearly killed you?" He couldn't believe he was having this conversation. The day had gone from bad to worse very quickly. All because of this . . . child.

He turned back to Vaniel who stood before his desk as he paced about the office. "You are a fool. And you can be sure your father will hear about this fiasco."

"But I was only trying to get her to—"

"SILENCE!" The word reverberated through the room, knocking one of his favorite glass sculptures off his desk, but it had the desired effect. She cowered, the color draining from her face.

He took a deep breath and smoothed out the long lapels of his deep-red coat. "It is not your job to force that snake to leave. If you had an ounce of brains inside that vapid head of yours, you would know this." He paced around behind his desk and sat down in the chair.

"Let us think this through, as you should have done, shall we?" He crossed his legs and peered up at the girl who licked her lips and nodded once.

"Excellent." He folded his hands. "The bridge is an interesting place to plan this assault. Easy to block the exits so no one interrupts you. And you limit her escape routes."

Vaniel nodded.

"It is also very public. Have you any idea how many people use those bridges? Did you even think about *who* might be using them at the time you decided to have your fun?" His voice became harder. "And what might have happened if you *had* been seen?"

It took Vaniel a moment to realize she was expected to answer. "They would have seen what I did?"

Dalan glanced to the ceiling, praying for patience. "Yes, of course. And how would that look, the daughter of Lord Palatan Sablehawk assaulting a fellow Eyas? How do you think it would reflect upon him, upon your house, if his daughter were to be barred from the Hawks, an Eyas forever?"

Vaniel shook her head, "I did not—"

"Did not think? That much is obvious, child." He leapt to his feet again. "Your father and I have worked too hard to maneuver your family into the position it is in for your childish antics to blow our plans to the Shadows."

"But I was trying to help! And I did. I found out just what a freak she is. She tried to attack me. The others will swear it."

"And she will swear she did not! You have no proof!" He strode around the desk. "There is not even a mark on you. You claim she assaulted you, and you will be laughed out of the throne room."

"But the bridge! It was damaged. Surely that—"

His hand struck her before he could even think. Her whole body jerked to the side with the impact. "SHE IS A SECOND TIER EYAS!" he yelled into her ear. "No one will believe she so much as touched magic! Let alone damaged a bridge that has stood since the palace was raised. And did you ever think about the sympathy for her your attack might engender? No. Because apparently *thinking* is not something you are capable of."

He closed his eyes and took several deep breaths before reaching into his coat to retrieve a handkerchief. "Fortunately for you, the dog's claims of your assault on her have little more proof." He handed her the cloth then walked to his window, giving her the dignity of wiping away her tears in private.

Whispers at the Altar

"But know this, Vaniel Sablehawk. I do have plans for that abomination. And if you get in the way of them again with some unasked for childish prank you will wish you had never come to the Roost. Do you understand?"

There was a soft, "Yes, sir."

He turned around and walked to retrieve his damp handkerchief. He paused, tilting her chin up so he could look her in the eyes. "I love you, Vaniel. As though you were my own daughter. But this is bigger than you or me. I hope you understand that. This is about the safety and security of the entire elven people. I cannot afford to let anything jeopardize that. Not even you. If you do so again . . . I will end you. And trust me, your father will not say a word."

YEAR 2

Resurrection

Christa crept through the chapel doors. It was her first time back since she ran out during Chorus and, as she passed the threshold, she could swear she heard that awful voice softly laughing at her. She shuddered and shuffled forward. The sooner she got this over with, the sooner she could get out of here.

The chamber looked different without the crowd of worshipers. Less religious but even more grand. The statues in the alcoves loomed over her, hands clasped in prayer or held aloft in adulation. Their sad eyes followed her, examining. As much as she hoped to see it, there was no compassion in them. No encouragement. Only disappointment.

She couldn't help but run her hands self-consciously over her scant inches of hair. Sinna had done her best with what was left, but evening everything out had cost even more length. Even a month later she had yet to get used to it, and the looks everyone gave her were wearing thin. Westrel had even cut hers in the same style, so

Christa would feel better. But for some reason it looked better on her. At least the white had faded. No one could give Christa an explanation for that.

She focused on the floor five paces ahead as much as possible and tried to move faster. Just get it done. Director Namarian—Uncle Namarian, though she couldn't get used to the idea of having one—stood in the center of the amphitheater, speaking with a woman Christa didn't recognize. The woman's hair was pitch black threaded through a net of silver stars that continued down the simple but elegant midnight-blue gown she wore.

Christa paused, remembering what Sinna told her. With hair like that, this woman must be very important. No. That was just custom. She couldn't let herself think that way. And Christa had to reach Namarian before he left. Cornering him had taken weeks. Whenever she caught a glance of him he was always walking away. She tried his office, but he was always out. And she wasn't about to wait for him there; she had too much to do.

Ten shuffles away, Christa saw him glance her way. She smiled as brightly as she could with those statues menacing over her, but his face remained impassive. A half second later he looked back to the woman. Christa's stomach sank, and she quickened her steps. She wanted to yell, to get his attention, but she knew it would be rude, especially here.

She arrived within an "elven" polite speaking distance as his conversation ended and he turned—away from her.

"Director Namarian. Would you spare a moment to speak with me, please?" She tried to say it just as Mama taught her all those years ago. She even remembered to add a curtsy.

Director Namarian stopped, and Christa watched his gaze flit from her to the woman he had been speaking to. The pause stretched uncomfortably before he faced Christa.

"Of course, Christabel. What can I do for a future Hawk?"

•Whispers at the Altar•

His tone was flat and formal, and it beat Christa's stomach even lower. She waited, unsure now how to proceed. She didn't want to talk in front of this stranger, but would it be unseemly to ask her to leave? "I . . . um. I wanted to ask you a question," she hazarded. "About the Creator. Um . . . something personal." She glanced to the woman and put on her most innocent face.

"I see." Director Namarian gestured toward one of the alcoves. "If you will excuse us, Your Highness."

Christa took a full step toward the alcove before the address registered. She nearly stumbled. Your Highness? As in . . . Queen Elisidel? Should she turn around and curtsey again? Would that just make her look worse?

"Of course, Director." The voice was clear, tinged around the corners with mirth.

But Director Namarian was already walking past and there was no time for another curtsy if Christa wanted to catch up.

"Now what questions can I answer for you?" he asked as they reached the alcove.

Christa cleared her throat and glanced once in the direction of the Queen. She was already exiting through another set of doors. "I had a question about . . ." Christa tried to remember the script she memorized, but the lines wouldn't come. She cleared her throat again. "I just . . . I heard that it was possible to—" She let go the folds of her skirt she had gripped in her hands and forced them still behind her back.

Director Namarian waited silently.

"That some Divinists could bring back the dead. I was wondering how that worked."

His eyes narrowed. "Why?"

Christa was suddenly painfully aware of the carved figure stooping over her in contrite humility. She took a deep breath and a small step forward. Better to get this over with. After all, if there was anyone here who would feel as she did, it was her uncle. "I want to bring Mama back. I was hoping you could do it."

The director took a step back. "What?"

"Bring her back," Christa pleaded, advancing another step. "You can, can't you?"

"No." He said, horror showing on his face for a brief instant. "I will not."

Christa stared at him, taken aback by the vehemence in the words. "Why not? She was your sister. Don't you want her back?"

His voice rose slightly. "I realize you are new here, Christabel, but even you should know that to ask such a thing is not done. Yes, some Divinists can resurrect those who have passed. But it is not a power we have at our whim. None of our power is. Our magic is not just skill. It is a relationship. We are only able to do what we are allowed to do by the Creator."

Christa frowned. "That's stupid. Why have the ability to do something and then forbid yourselves from doing it? Why even know how? And what does he have against me getting my mama back?" Christa glared up at him.

Namarian frowned. "Do you think I do not wish her back? Do you think your grief is greater than my own?" His voice rose, heedless of the heads that turned. "She was my sister! My companion. We walked through all our lives together until she met *your* filthy father!"

The words echoed through the hushed chamber, and only then did Namarian remember where he was. His voice dropped to a hissed whisper. "She is gone, Christabel. Leave her in peace. Or do you think you know better than the Creator when his gift of life should be taken? He has a plan, and life goes according to it."

She threw her hands up. "So that's what you'll hide behind? His 'plan'? His *plan* is for you to lose your sister? His *plan* was for me to—" She barely kept herself from telling him.

"Well, I can't sit back and be so accommodating. My mama was *not* meant to go! She was not meant to leave me alone. She loved me. She still loves me. And she wants to be with me."

"Enough! I will not stand here and listen to your blasphemies in this holy place. You will not speak of this again. That is final. Do you understand?"

Christa shook her head in disbelief. "I understand. I understand that if you loved Mama even half as much as I do, you'd get on your knees and you'd *make* your Creator give her back." She stalked off. She had to. The urge to hit him was growing too great. She couldn't even think of names to call him as she paced back across the floor.

He called to her, but she ignored him. He wasn't going to help her. And neither were the rest of the Divinists. She'd have to find something else. Some other way. There had to be one. With all the knowledge stored here, all the books, there had to be something that would help her. And she would find it.

Christa slammed another book closed and pushed it across the table. It nearly fell off the other side, but she didn't care. The thump as it closed made the few other library patrons glare, but she didn't care about them, either. It was the tenth book she'd skimmed through today, and the tenth book that hadn't helped. Worse, all ten, while they claimed to tell the story of the early elven church, had taken every opportunity to describe how utterly backward and barbaric the humans were.

She stood, stretched, and gathered the ten useless tomes from the table. She still had a couple hours before dinner so there was time for one more round of pointless searching. She ignored the signs telling her not to shelve books and walked through the stacks replacing them where she found them. It felt wrong to leave the work for someone else.

She was so focused on trying to find where *A Brief History of the Church and the Barbarians* went, she almost collided with Silvana coming around a corner. Christa let out a strangled cry, dropping the last six books she held.

"You scared me to death, Silvana!" She tried to keep her voice to a hoarse whisper but still got shushed by two other students.

Silvana put a hand over her heart. "Likewise. What are you doing sneaking about in this part of the library? I didn't think you had much interest in religion." She didn't mention Chorus. She didn't need to.

Christa knelt to recover her books. "Trust me, I don't. I was just trying to find something."

"So you don't. But you do?" Silvana smiled. "What are you looking for? Maybe I can help."

Christa paused for a second, one hand hovering over *Tillieman's Guide to the Creator's Faith.* "I don't think you can," she said, picking up the tome and stashing it in her arms with the others. In truth she could use the help, but would Silvana help? Or would she just tell her how wrong she was for trying? Or worse, tell Director Namarian.

"Oh, come on. You obviously need help, and I know this library far better than you. Give me a chance."

Christa placed *Church and the Barbarians* on the shelf and searched for the next spot. "It's personal. I need to know something."

"What could be personal to you about the history of the elven church when you don't even go to Chorus?" Silvana followed her, keeping a pace behind.

"I don't care about the history. I need to know how something is done."

•*Whispers at the Altar*•

"Why don't you ask your uncle? I am sure Director Namarian would be happy to explain anything you are wondering about. And it would be easier than poking around these dusty things."

Christa let out an exasperated sigh. "I can't. It's personal." She got another shushing and lowered her voice. "He wouldn't understand."

Silvana gave her a look. The same one Mama gave her when she knew Christa was lying. "Then tell me. I am your friend. You can trust me."

Christa paused with a book half-shelved. "Fine." She shoved the last book into place and faced Silvana. "But you have to promise not to tell anyone else."

Silvana nodded. "I promise. Now what is so secret?"

"I'm trying to figure out how the Divinists bring people back from the dead."

"Why?" Silvana tilted her head to one side.

Christa took a step forward. "Because. If I know how they do it maybe I can figure out a way to do it, too."

"Christa, that is not possible." There was only a hint of condescension, but it was there. "You—"

"I know, I know. I'm not a Divinist, so I can't use their magic, so the ritual won't work. Besides that, it 'isn't done.'" She sighed and leaned back against the bookshelves, folding her arms in front of her. "But I have to try."

Silvana said nothing for several seconds. "You can't bring her back."

"I have to."

"Why, Christa? Why can't you let her go? People die every day. Don't you think everyone would bring them back if they could?"

"I just have to. The . . . the nightmares aren't getting better."

It was true. At least once a week now she woke covered in sweat with images of dense forests filled with clawing hands or crumbling rock monsters chasing her into wakefulness. The younger her was always there, always giggling, and always pointing her to..."

Silvana gave Christa a level look. "That isn't the reason. Why?"

109

"Because . . . because it's my fault!" she hissed, earning another glare from a passing librarian. "There. Now you know. Happy?"

Silvana shook her head, reaching out to pat the air between them. "You are no killer, Christa. I am sure whatever happened was an accident."

Christa wiped at her damp eyes with one hand. "You don't know me. You have no idea what I've done."

Silvana reached her hand further as though to console her, but lowered it with a sigh. "I do know you. I know you wouldn't purposely hurt anyone or anything. And I don't blame you for wanting to bring her back. But you have to let this guilt go. Let *her* go."

"Why? What's so wrong with bringing her back?" A boy turned to shush her again but Christa glared at him hard enough it stuck in his throat. "You and Namarian both tell me it's some sin to want to find a way to bring her back. A way that has even been used before! But you can't say why. Because there is no reason why. You just don't want to take the trouble to help. So, fine. Don't help me. I don't care. Just stop telling me to stop trying." She moved to push past Silvana, but the girl stepped back out of her way.

"I am not . . ." She hurried to catch up. "I will help you, Christa."

"Yeah, right."

"Christabel!"

Something in the tone made her stop before realizing she had.

Silvana sighed. "I will try to help you. But please. Please, try to consider that this isn't the best way. That maybe . . ." She struggled to find the right words. "Maybe she *was* supposed to go."

Christa scowled, but Silvana continued before she could say anything.

"Regardless. I will try to help you. But you know this ritual won't help. It is a Divinist ritual, and they can only do what the Creator lets them."

"And apparently the Creator wants my mother dead."

Silvana sighed. "Everyone has a time. But there are powerful items, created by Divinists, which may allow you to bypass the ritual."

Christa narrowed her eyes, considering this. "The force of the ritual is stored somehow in the item? Then all I would need to do is release it." She grinned. "Where are they?"

"I don't know," Silvana said with a shrug. "But if anything with that kind of power exists, it would be here in the palace."

Christa nodded, thinking. "Wait. Why would the Creator allow this jealously guarded power to be stored somewhere it could be used by anyone?" She watched Silvana. She still wasn't sure she could trust her.

"I don't know. It may not exist at all. I am not promising anything. I just thought it might be a better place to search."

It made sense. Christa was getting nowhere researching the ritual itself. "All right. We'll try it. I know some history books that might help."

They spent the rest of the hour flipping through catalogues of registered patents for magic items. Silvana was sure if anyone had developed something along the lines of what they needed, it would be listed there. They had no luck, though there were enough catalogues to last months at the slow rate Christa could research.

Still, she walked away feeling more optimistic about her search than she had in weeks. Silvana even agreed to meet her every day for an hour before morning chores to help. With both of them looking, it should be no time before they found it. Assuming it existed at all.

TOWN

The crack on the head broke through Steven's troubled dreams, shattering images of giant snakes and Mother's mad cackling. Groaning, he fumbled around until he found the offending apple. He'd throw it back at Brogan, but that would mean opening his eyes. And losing part of his breakfast.

"Get up, you sack. You don't have much time if you want to get any more of your breakfast in your belly before we go."

Steven cracked open one eye and brought the apple up to take a nearly blind bite. "Where are we going?"

"To town. Unless you want to start eating the mice out of the grass." Brogan was relaxing in one of the chairs at the table, his foot propped up on Steven's much newer chair.

Steven had made it himself, along with his bed and everything else he needed to live in Brogan's hut. The old man made it very clear shortly after they left the swamps that if Steven wanted to stay with him, he would be responsible for his own care. Steven didn't mind, though.

Brogan showed him how to find the wood he needed, taught him to shape and carve it into the proper shapes. They weren't perfect, but they were the result of his own sweat and blood, and Steven was proud of them.

"You mean I actually get to come this time?" Steven crawled out from under the skins covering his bed and stumbled to his chair.

"That was once, and I told you before it wasn't my fault." Brogan said through the apple in his own mouth, pieces falling out to color his unbrushed beard. "I wasn't used to having some pup that needed looking after every hour of the day."

Steven waited patiently for the foot to be removed from his chair before sitting. "You left me here without any food for a week."

"You didn't die, did you?" He pushed a half-eaten pan of potatoes across the small table then stood and began collecting what few things he would take with him.

Steven's smile, already wide from the scent of garlic and onion wafting off his breakfast, widened as he watched the old man. It had been a difficult year for both of them. The idea that someone would actually *want* him living with him was as foreign to Steven as having someone to look after was to Brogan. But gradually, Steven realized Brogan not only wanted him around but genuinely cared about his well-being. The lessons on carving had been the first of many. It was a door opened to a bright new world and—though it hurt his eyes at times—Steven was fascinated by each new thing he found there.

The potatoes were gone long before Brogan finished his meager packing. But Steven still had to tend to the garden, the chickens, and the pigs before they could leave. It was well past sunup before he joined Brogan on the grassy hill overlooking the tiny hermitage.

"Packed?" Brogan grumbled, using his thick walking stick to lever himself up.

Steven gestured to the small bag filled with his few belongings and hoisted an empty pack on his back. "All set."

"Good. On the way you can identify and gather the twelve treatments for cramps and stomach distress." He walked down the hill with his shuffling gait, leaning on the staff hard enough to leave a trail of divots for Steven to follow.

"All twelve?" He fell in line, already wondering if maybe it would have been better to stay and take his chances eating mice.

"Yes. And now you can also explain just how to prepare each one as you find it and any dangers associated with them."

Steven suppressed another grumble. He knew from experience it would only get worse. He could refuse to do it, but that would ruin any chance at dinner. So, he began scanning the ground around him, repeating the names of the plants he needed and trying to picture each one in his mind. It was going to be a long day.

When he finally found the twelfth plant, Steven had to name each kind of tree they passed. Then it was listing the summer constellations in order and pointing out their locations. No matter how quickly he finished one task, Brogan always had another for him. Some were even fun, and all of them sped the hours past at a rate Steven never would have expected.

It was the morning of the third day, as he was naming the most dangerous insects and how to avoid them, when they first caught sight of the town. Steven stopped, staring at the crowd of buildings. There must have been two score of them at least. One was twice as tall as his hut, towering over the antlike people walking around them. Beyond the town, a small lake glistened, reflecting the rays of the morning sun rising behind him.

Brogan walked a few more steps before turning around. "It'll be fine. Just stick close to me. They're just people."

Steven nodded mutely, then hurried to catch up as Brogan started off again. "But . . . then why don't you like them?"

"I don't like noise. People are people. Some are respectable, some are horrible. But all of them make noise. The more people, the more noise."

"Did you used to live here?" Steven couldn't help taking advantage of the opportunity to get some rare information about his mentor.

"Not here," was all Brogan answered.

Steven wasn't sure if he meant he didn't live here, or he wouldn't discuss it here. So he tried another angle.

"Do you know a lot of people here?"

"Enough to get our business done. We'll get some cooking supplies. Maybe another sow. Nails. A new hammer to replace the one you broke. Few other odds and ends. Shouldn't take more than a few hours."

Again, not a real answer. Steven decided to drop it. When Brogan didn't want to talk about something, there was no point in pestering him. Instead, he went back to examining the town.

Most of the buildings were squat and round, just like Brogan's hut, made of close fitted logs with mud filled cracks and the same reed thatched roofs. An area on the far side, near the lake and its short piers, was cleared and a score of cloth stalls surrounded a pillar or totem of some kind—Steven couldn't see it very well. But it was the large log building that drew his attention most.

He couldn't imagine living in something so huge. It stood in the center of the village, an ancient tree surrounded by its saplings. Round, like the houses, but tall and windowless with a high peaked roof.

As they got closer, the people of the town pulled away his attention. The sheer number of them was overwhelming. A horde, some dozen at least, of dirty children in coarse brown clothes chased each other through muddy alleys. Meanwhile, the adults sulked in doorways and along the edges of the only road, or hurried from place to place like beetles afraid to be caught in the open.

•Whispers at the Altar•

Steven edged closer to Brogan, barely resisting the urge to cringe against him as one grimy little girl nearly bumped into him as she bolted past.

"Are towns always like this?" he whispered.

Brogan shook his head slightly. "Stay close to me."

They passed into the shadow of the towering building Steven admired from afar, but from this range he found little to marvel at. Dark and unwelcoming as the people crouched under its wide eaves, it loomed over the road. The gloomy interior, glimpsed through the yawning doorway, was pierced only by what scant rays of sunlight managed to filter through the shield of tarred thatch above or stab through chinks in the log walls. Steven couldn't make out the far side, or even the center of the single open room with any certainty, but he shivered nonetheless. Picking up his pace, he reminded himself over and over: It was just a building.

A glance at Brogan showed the same worry Steven felt. Obviously this wasn't the reception Brogan was used to. Steven watched the people more closely, his own suspicion growing as it met with theirs. Most looked away rather than meet his gaze, mumbling some curse or complaint for some ears other than Steven's. One wizened crone stood in the lee of her door wearing what may have been a perpetual frown as she watched them pass by. Steven stared back. He couldn't help but wonder if she was a mother. What were her children like? Did they have the same distrust etched into their faces?

Brogan led him quickly along the muddy thoroughfare and into the cleared area by the harbor. Here the people were everywhere, and Steven was reminded of Brogan's words earlier. But for all the three-score people milling about the stalls, there was little noise. In fact, the only noise he could remember hearing since entering the town was the muffled sound of children running. Shouldn't they have been laughing? Didn't children laugh when they played? It seemed they should, despite his own inexperience.

"Something isn't right here," Brogan said as he pulled Steven aside. "I'm going to get what I can quick, then put as much distance between us and this town as possible before we make camp. Don't leave my side. Understand?"

The order was hardly needed. Steven wanted nothing more of town. In fact, he doubted he would ever want to leave the hut again.

Hand in hand, they walked to the nearest merchant, a thickly muscled farmer slouching before a wall of course sacks piled behind him. The man examined them with narrowed eyes, but he said nothing.

Brogan met his gaze, a deep frown on his face. Steven knew that frown. It was the one that told him Brogan wasn't going to put up with any more of his nonsense. "Well met again, Arin. Five silver for two bags of flour. Another five for a bag of sugar if you happen to have one. Same as last time."

Steven looked at Brogan in confusion. Silver? When did Brogan get money? This was definitely something to bring up later.

"You're not from town," the man stated in a thick rumbling voice.

"What difference does that make? I've bought from you before. Twice a year, in fact. My silver's always spent the same as anyone else, hasn't it?"

The man's lids narrowed further, bare slits hiding muddy brown eyes. "You're not of Ssanek. I only sell to Ssaneks now."

"Don't be a fool, Arin. You've sold to me for years. What does it matter what I am or am not?"

Steven watched the veins in the man's neck bulge.

"I'm no fool, old man. I know my place. Perhaps you need to be taught yours."

Others were starting to turn toward them, the man's voice rising easily over the bare murmur of voices filling the market. Steven tugged on Brogan's sleeve.

"I only sell to other Ssaneks," the farmer ranted. "So either take the oaths before the priest or get off."

•Whispers at the Altar•

"Light of creation. I'm gone for six months and this whole backward town gets itself a new religion?" Brogan took a step back, shaking his head. "Who is this Ssanek? He better be willing to sell me some flour."

Brogan's hand griped Steven's arm painfully tight. The others were walking toward them now, their eyes hard and faces set like stone masks.

"You had best watch your blasphemies, old man. Ssanek protects us."

Ssanek protects us. The crowd murmured in echo.

Arin stalked out from his stall, his long strides easily keeping pace with Brogan's.

"Ssanek makes us strong."

Ssanek makes us strong.

Steven glanced about frantically as Brogan continued stepping calmly backward. They were being herded, like Steven herded the pigs back home. There was only one opening now, and that was dominated by the wooden totem.

"Ssanek has chosen us as his people."

Ssanek has chosen us.

The totem. Steven looked up at it closely for the first time, and his knees nearly buckled. It was so familiar. A thing from his nightmares. A great snake with wings stretched out as if to cover the sky.

"And so, we serve Ssanek!" The giant of a man shoved one meaty fist into the air as the whole market echoed.

Brogan waited, leaning on his staff, seemingly oblivious to the storm around him as he waited for the noise to die.

"What is your choice, old man?"

Steven looked down, unable to keep his gaze on the totem. There was something odd about the ground. The scrubby grass was tinged an unusual dark red, like a giant stain around the base of the icon.

"Well. It doesn't look like I'm going to be getting any flour today," Brogan sighed and shifted slightly, his hand never loosening on Steven's arm. "Which is a shame. I was really looking forward to some fresh bread. But, if those are my only choices . . ."

119

Allan C.R. Cornelius

There was a flash accompanied by a sound like thunder cracking beside him. Steven was sure his ears were broken. Brogan pulled his arm and, unable to see or hear, Steven stumbled along.

They were nearly out of the town before the single white spot covering his vision began to dissolve into a blur of shapes, and well outside before he could hear more than a high-pitched ringing. He saw no one from the town pursuing them, but still it was two hours before Brogan let him sit down to rest for a moment.

"Was that magic?" He tried not to yell, but it was so hard to really hear anything.

Brogan gave a small smile and shook his head, sitting close beside him to speak into his ear. "No such thing. At least not for you and me."

Steven wasn't so sure he believed that, given what he had seen in the swamp. But then that certainly wasn't anything he could do. So maybe Brogan was right after all.

"Just some powders I mixed together. They can't actually hurt anything. Not seriously anyway. But they do have their uses."

Just some powders, Steven thought with a chuckle. He would have to learn that one. "What about the supplies?"

Brogan's smile faded. "We'll have to go to the city. The king will want to know about this cult anyway."

Steven's stomach sank. A town had been bad enough. He didn't even want to think about a city.

Patriots

The city—his city—was beautiful at sunset. It was Dalan's favorite time of day. The way the sun glimmered off the rooftops of the estates and caught the far-flung towers of the palace. It was an ever-shifting rainbow punctuated by the diamond sparkle of the Observatory far above. She was his true love. His only love. Always constant and always welcoming. He would do anything to protect her, to help her. And anyone who wouldn't . . .

"Come, Dalan," Secretary Iyian called from his chair across the sitting room. "Come join us. You are being a terrible guest."

"Yes, Director. Come. Sit." Lady Corannel pulled gently on his arm, offering one of those breathtaking smiles that won her a union with House Sablehawk some three centuries ago.

"My apologies," Dalan said with a bow, acquiescing. "I find I am not very pleasant company today." He crossed the large room to take a seat at one of the three couches facing each other in the center. The chamber was beautifully decorated in the latest Imilierian fashion.

Subtle gilding along the paneled walls, rich oak furniture carved into designs no hand could accomplish without the aid of magic. He was especially fond of the chandelier, hung with twenty miniature lamps that changed their hue almost imperceptibly based on the mood of the owner.

In this case that owner was his host, Lord Palatan of House Sable-hawk, one of the most powerful elves outside the walls of the palace itself, and his oldest friend. The lord sat in one of the two throne-like chairs that completed the circle of seating, twirling a long-stemmed goblet of honey wine in one hand. Even his deep red tunic threaded with gold seemed designed to complement the room's decor.

"Nonsense. No doubt you are merely troubled by the rumors of conflict with the Anathonians." He looked to Elirel, the fifth of their company, for agreement.

The Mentalist shrugged from where she sat opposite the lord. "I do not pretend to guess the depths of his mind, Milord."

"And she knows better than to invade it, I wager," Corannel said, taking the seat beside her husband with barely a rustle of purple skirts.

"Most certainly. That would be illegal," Elirel answered. "Is my lord referring to the reports from Agent Talaran regarding the dispute between the Dwarves and the Anathonians?"

Dalan shook his head. "Dwarf attacks on those near-humans do not concern me. If they cannot deal with such petty incursions, they deserve their fate." In truth, the idea of both parties wasting their strength on each other was appealing. The Anathonians, while possessing a deep culture nearly as old as the elves, were a little too near to human for his taste. Darker, more noble of bearing perhaps, but the similarities were just too close. Dalan was sure there must be some common ancestry.

"But surely you see the possibility of such activities spreading further north?" Palatan said. "Are our own borders to be next? What then? Too much trade flows through both nations, and not only mine."

Whispers at the Altar

"I assure you the danger is not as great as you may have been led to believe," Iyian cut in, leaning further back in his seat. He gently swirled the wine in his own glass, but his eyes never left Palatan's. "I have read Agent Talaran's report. Any danger to our borders you may have heard of is grossly exaggerated."

"Perhaps," Adasian interjected, drawing all eyes to where he sat with his sister, both forgotten. "But fighting will disrupt trade nonetheless. And a disruption in trade, even if we are neutral, will mean a loss of income."

Palatan shifted toward his son with a smile. "Just so. And what would you do, young Adasian, were you in my shoes?"

The boy—no, nearly a man now Dalan reminded himself—sat up straighter. "I would send envoys to both parties. Unofficially. Make it clear to both that it is in their best interests to ensure that certain caravans pass unmolested."

"Why unofficially?" Palatan prompted.

Adasian shrugged. "Why should we care if our competitors' caravans go missing? In fact, I might even let slip just how happy that would make me. War is a dangerous business after all."

Palatan laughed and set down his glass to clap. "Excellent. You will make a fine Hawk."

Dalan had to agree. The boy had a keen eye for finding just the right way to manipulate events. Much like his father. He would make an excellent ally. Unlike his sister.

"So, you see," the secretary said. "Play your cards right, and you could even profit from this. However, I was speaking of our boarders rather than economics."

"Well, that is certainly good news." Lady Corannel ran one hand through her raven hair. "From what I have heard among the courtesans, we have enough trouble brewing in our own palace. With that . . . half-human you let into the Roost."

Dalan turned to Elirel, as did everyone else in the room. It galled him that the woman could sit there and grin in their faces after what she did.

"Yes. Well, as Director Elirel explained to me," Dalan said, "she believed it best to keep our enemies in plain sight rather than risk them hiding like snakes in the grass at our feet." He sighed and refocused his gaze back to the lady. "Not a completely unwise strategy."

Elirel nodded. "Had we refused her, what would have prevented her from traveling elsewhere? From infiltrating another city where she could lay in wait, perhaps even trained in secret by Marellel or one of her friends? Trust me. It is better to have her here where we can see what she is doing and what she is learning."

"Perhaps," Palatan muttered, taking a delicate sip of his wine. "But I still would rather she were elsewhere than the heart of our power. I believe we will regret this decision in time."

Dalan shook his head, "Besides. *Can* we see what she is doing? Vaniel's actions have made it nearly impossible for me." He glanced briefly at the silent Vaniel, sitting with her hands folded in her lap beside her brother. "The Queen, Marellel, and Aerel, all know I support you, and that I am against the girl remaining. Vaniel's actions were immediately taken as mine. They are watching us both more closely than ever."

"I agree that she should be watched," Secretary Iyian said. "But she is only one issue in a sea of problems. Surely there are more important—"

"Yes, you are right," Palatan interrupted. "She is below any of us. A headache, yes. Even a headache that may grow into a full sickness of not tracked. But not an object of immediate concern. We need someone closer to her level. Someone to keep tabs on her, to know what she is doing, even what she is thinking."

His eyes focused on Vaniel.

Dalan watched her look up with wide eyes into the ring of faces.

"Me? How . . . how can I do that?"

Whispers at the Altar

Dalan shrugged. "You wanted to help. Isn't that what you said? You just wanted to help? Now is your chance."

"But . . . she would have to trust me. She hates me. And I would have to spend *time* with her." Her voice broke as she leaned toward Palatan. "Father, please. Mother . . . don't make me do this. I am sorry for what I did. I will do anything to make it up—"

"You will do this." Palatan's eyes narrowed. "You will prove you are worthy to be a Hawk and deserving of the title you will one day have. Because if you fail, you will not be given another chance."

Dalan watched her gaze flick from the cool impassive stare of her mother to the stern glare of her father. He watched as the implications sunk in, and a measure of pride straightened her spine and steeled her gaze.

"I won't fail you, Father."

Palatan rose, mirrored by Corannel. "See that you don't, daughter." He paused, then turned back to his guests, all smiles once more. "Now is everyone ready for dinner?"

Dalan rose, took Elirel's arm, and followed the others into the hall. They were right, of course. The half-human was currently only a minor annoyance. But he hadn't gotten this far by ignoring minor annoyances. He looked forward to hearing what information Vaniel was able to recover. He knew, in his gut, that the half-human was the keystone. She was the piece that once removed, would start the slide ending not just with her expulsion, but with Palatan Sablehawk on the throne.

CITY

It took Steven and Brogan over two weeks to reach the city, starting with the three-day trek back home. They hadn't planned on being gone longer than a week, and the animals needed to be let into the field, else they would break out on their own. Plus, Brogan wanted to leave some precautions in case any people from the village came snooping. It was no secret to them that he lived nearby.

By the time they finished at the house and the real journey to the city began, Steven was through with the excitement of travel. The ground was hard, the food was dry, and his legs ached in ways he never could have fathomed. He couldn't understand how Brogan did it. The old man just kept going, wispy white hair streaming behind him as his legs churned over the rocks and scrub grass. The only talking now was Brogan's muttering to himself. It was a habit Steven had long ago become accustomed to, but it had increased dramatically since the village.

The incident at the village was worrying him, that much was obvious. But trying to get anything more out of the old man was like squeezing water from a stone. So, Steven was left to his own miserable thoughts and nightmares. They had come back since the village. The same dreams he had after Brogan first found him. The same dark scaled shapes. Only this time the altar was in the middle of the village, with all the people there cheering mother on as she stabbed him in the chest. Her eyes were always the last thing he remembered when he woke. Burning pits of green fire.

Steven shivered despite the summer heat and quickened his pace to come up alongside Brogan. He cleared his throat once. Then waited for a pause in the muttering.

"Brogan? I have a question."

The old man started. "Don't sneak up on an old man like that. I'm frail."

Steven chuckled. Right . . . frail." He schooled his expression, however, at the sight of Brogan's scowl. "Sorry. I had a question."

"Humph. And what is that? If it's 'how much farther' again I suggest you keep it in your skull."

"No. I just. I was wondering about the creatures. You know, the ones from the swamp?" This had gone much better in his head.

"Yes, what about them?" Brogan hitched his pack, as stuffed as Steven's own, up on his shoulders.

"You've told me that everything was made, and that it was made for a purpose. Even if we don't know by what or for what."

"Yes?" He vaulted over a log then waited while Steven sat down and swung his legs over.

Steven dropped onto the ground again and looked at Brogan as though he were crazy. "What purpose could there be in making them? They're evil."

"Who says?" Brogan shook his head and marched off across the shallow valley they had entered. Steven hurried to catch up.

Whispers at the Altar

"They tried to sacrifice me to . . . to something. Ssanek, I guess. I would say that makes them evil."

Brogan raised his hands over his head in mocking assent. "Oh, well if the great Steven says so then it must be true."

"Well . . ." Steven blustered, "what do you think?"

Brogan stopped and turned to face him, his expression serious. "I think they are no more evil than the people in that village. Or in the city. Or you, or me. Remember it was your mother who held the knife. Evil isn't a race or a people, Steven. Oh, it's real enough. But we would only be so lucky for it to be so easily spotted."

Steven furrowed his brow. "So, you think they're being used? Controlled?"

Brogan sighed, and Steven could see his frustration. It was a common enough emotion. "I'm saying that we all have choice. You, me, those villagers, and even the lizard people in the swamp. We all have evil in us." He turned to keep walking. "What do you think would drive those people in the swamp to turn to Ssanek? Do you think they woke up one day and decided to commit human sacrifice?"

Steven mulled that over. It wasn't an angle he'd ever approached it from. "I don't know. Maybe they were afraid of something?"

Brogan gave him one of his rare smiles. "He *can* be taught. Fear is a powerful motivator. It makes us do all kinds of things. Some good, some bad. I'm sure the villagers are afraid of a lot of things. A bad harvest, the fishing going dry, not being able to protect their loved ones . . ."

"Are you saying—"

"I'm saying that they have a reason. It isn't a good one, and it certainly doesn't make it right, but it's a reason. And the first step to helping anyone is understanding them."

Steven thought in silence as he walked. It made sense. But who could be trying to push them? No one even knew they existed. But if Brogan was right, perhaps there were others like them. Ones who didn't follow Ssanek. The idea brought a whole new light to his thoughts.

Steven knew what the word *city* meant in an abstract sense. The same way he knew what *mountain* or *ocean* meant, even if he'd never seen them. But nothing in the definition, or the warnings Brogan gave him the day before, could have prepared him. He knew now why Brogan chose to live in the middle of nowhere. He couldn't understand how anyone could live in such a crowded, noisy, filthy, miserable place.

There was a castle, a giant structure of stone walls and blocky towers that stood up on a hill. But any sense of grandeur was lost on Steven. It felt too . . . superior. As though whoever lived there was determined to put as much space and as much stone as possible between himself and the crowds below.

Steven huddled close to Brogan, nearly hugging him in his effort to keep from being jostled, trod on, or lost. Dozens of people tramped through the narrow, clay street—all in a hurry to get somewhere. Shopkeepers yelled out of their shops, peddlers called out from street corners, and beggars pleaded with every passerby for whatever they could spare. Here and there a pair or trio of men and women dressed in dirty armor with dirtier tabards walked, one hand on their spear, the other on their belt pouches. It was terrifying chaos wearing the trappings of civilization, and Steven wished with every step they could turn around and go home.

" . . . to stay close," Brogan was saying, barely audible through the noise. "And once we get inside, let me do the talking. He won't care about anything you have to say, trust me."

Steven nodded, and though Brogan couldn't see it, he didn't ask for any other confirmation. His attention was taken by the packed earth causeway leading up to the looming gate of the castle.

As they started up the causeway they left the bulk of the crowds behind. Steven was able to relax slightly, but the sight of the guards watching their approach from atop the gate and its companion towers did little to ease his mind. Half looked bored, others amused, but none friendly.

"What business do you have here, old man?" one of them above the gate shouted down.

Brogan waited until he was ten paces away before he even glanced up. When he did, Steven noticed there wasn't a hint of a crook in his back or a squat to his legs.

"Tell His Majesty King Steven that Brogan is here with news and council that concern him greatly."

"Brogan?" a second guard called down with a laugh. This one's armor was only slightly less dirty than the rest. "Is that really you? My, but you've gotten old."

"And you've gotten fat and lazy. There was a time when you would have had the gate open for me by now, Malerik."

"Guilty on one count at least, old friend," the guard shouted down, clasping a hand to his belly. "But I cannot claim credit for the gate."

Brogan's eyes narrowed. "What do you mean?"

"That your last visit left a poor taste in the king's mouth. He left standing orders against your admittance."

Steven could hear Brogan growling under his breath, though he couldn't make out the words.

"Tell me your message, old man," the guard continued. "I will take it to the king. If he deems it necessary to speak with you, you might still gain your audience."

"Doorman and messenger boy now, Malerik? There was a time when your ambitions were greater."

"Aye. And there was a time when we were both younger and ambition far more tempting. Tell me your message, and let us see if fond memories and bad news win out over hurt feelings."

131

Brogan sighed. "I have news of a danger to the king's lands. A religious cult rising to the southwest."

The guard waited, but when Brogan said no more he shook his head. "Is that all? Some religious zealots out in the country?"

"I won't yell my counsel up from Steven's doorstep through a mediator," Brogan fumed. "If he wishes it, he may let me in so we can discuss it. If not, I'll leave."

"Fine, fine. I'll tell him. Just don't be surprised by the answer."

The guard walked out of sight, and Brogan threw his hands in the air. "Imbeciles. Give an imbecile money and this is what you get."

Steven followed as he stomped over to a short abutment of wall and sat down. "The king's name is Steven?"

Brogan glanced up from under lowered brows. "Caught that, did you?" He shrugged. "I wouldn't make too much of it. Steven's a common name."

"I see." He didn't pursue it, but decided to file it away for another discussion. "So, what did you tell him last time that made him so mad?"

Brogan coughed. "That his wife had once been less than faithful to him. Before they were married, of course."

Steven smiled. "And you knew this how?"

"I wasn't always old, now was I?"

"I don't imagine she took your admission any better than the king did," Steven said through a laugh.

"No." Brogan stood, walking back to the gate. "She was already dead."

Steven followed. "So why tell him?"

Brogan shook his head. "It was wearing on my conscience. And I was too much of a fool to see what harm it would do."

The rest of the wait passed in silence, Steven trying to imagine what his friend had been like as a young man, and Brogan . . . lost in whatever thoughts of the past or present most concerned him. Steven couldn't guess which those might be. It never occurred to Steven that Brogan might have real feelings, ones beyond frustra-

◆Whispers at the Altar◆

tion, annoyance, or the occasional flash of anger. The thought that he might have loved someone once sounded somehow . . . wrong. Not like the idea of Mother loving someone, but similar.

"What do you want, Brogan?"

Steven looked up to find another, older man standing above the gate. Presumably King Steven. After all, he wore no armor. Instead he wore a red tunic edged in black over a tan shirt; an iron crown sat on his head. And he was clean.

Brogan sighed. "I would have thought you would treat your friends better. But I see I was wrong."

"I treat my friends with respect, old man. Perhaps you should have done the same. Now speak your piece and leave my doorstep, or we'll see just how many pins that withered body of yours can hold."

Brogan mumbled to himself, arguing by the sound of it, shook his head a few times, then sighed.

"Very well. I am here to warn you. The village of Ceerport has fallen under the sway of a cult spawned from the worst parts of the Wilderness. I have reason to suspect dark and potentially danger-ous practices there."

The king laughed, tossing his blond head back. "How very myste-rious. But do you have any proof? Have they refused my rule? Have they withheld their taxes? Or would you have me put one of my own villages to the sword, people who trust me for their protection, on your word?"

"Of course not . . ." Brogan grumbled.

Only Steven heard the "fool" at the end. He couldn't understand how this king could be so casual about this.

Brogan took a second to compose himself. "I would counsel you to investigate. If they are truly benign, they should not fear a few questions from their liege."

"Fine. I will send a patrol out to see what these fishermen are up to. Is that all?"

"There were monsters!" Steven said it before he could even think about it. Every gaze that up to now had ignored him, now focused on him now.

"Monsters?" the king asked incredulously.

Brogan groaned next to him, but it was already said. No matter how much he wished he could take it back.

"Yes. In the swamp. They . . ." He debated how much he could tell this king. Brogan didn't seem to trust him. "They have a symbol. I saw the same symbol in the town. It could be an inva- . . ." His voice died under the weight of all those eyes.

"Thank you very much for your astute assessment, boy." The king mercifully moved his gaze back to Brogan. "You should teach your servants better manners, old man. Now get off my porch."

"An invasion?" Brogan scoffed. "Didn't I tell you to let me do the talking?"

Steven dodged an old woman carrying a basket of beans and talking animatedly to her equally old friend. "Technically, you told me to let you do the talking once we got inside. We never got inside."

Brogan's hand snapped out to cuff him across the ear but paused mid-flight. He sighed. "You're right. And maybe the fool will take your warning for more than the ramblings of a peasant boy. At the least I don't see how it could have hurt." He turned down an alley that smelled of excrement and rot.

"Where are we going?" Steven asked, stopping at the alley entrance.

"To see a friend." Brogan didn't even pause. "Someone who can carry a message."

"To who?" Steven hurried to catch up, stepped in something soft he didn't want to identify, and nearly fell into a mound of trash.

"Friends."

Steven rolled his eyes, righted himself, then moved cautiously forward. He caught up as the alley exited onto another narrow street running away from the main traffic. Two more turns and an angry cat later, they came to the ruins of an old watchtower closed with a weather-beaten but still very sturdy looking door. Steven stopped, expecting Brogan to knock. Instead, the man fished around in a pocket for a minute before producing a worn brass key, which he slid into the lock. The tumblers rotated with an audible click, and a second later the key was gone and Brogan was climbing up a crumbling stone stairway.

"So, your friend lives here?" Steven whispered, closing the door behind him, but there was no answer. "And how do you have a key to the city's old watchtower? This thing must be a hundred years old."

"More like thirty," came the echoed answer from around the corner of the spiraling stairs. "It was my first try at architecture."

Steven couldn't help but chuckle. At this point, nothing about Brogan amazed him anymore. Taking the steps carefully, he soon lost track of how far ahead Brogan was until he came around a final turn and up into what must have been a middle landing but was now the top. Half the roof was gone, letting the bright summer sun in to shine on dozens of pigeon coops.

"These are your friends?" he asked.

Brogan was already crouched over one cage, gently handling the gray bird within.

"And who feeds them? I mean, it can't be you."

"Ashes, boy," Brogan grumbled as he worked on the bird. "Do you think you get to my age without knowing some people? Now are you going to stand there gawking or are you going to do something productive?"

Steven looked around at the cages of cooing birds. "What do you need?"

"Well, come over and watch so you can see."

135

Steven walked closer to watch over the man's shoulder. He was tying a small rolled scrap of parchment to the bird's leg.

"The bird is trained to carry the message to a friend. As are several others, to other friends. The king won't take our warning seriously, but there are plenty of other people who will."

"Couldn't we go back to the village and . . ."

"And what? Root out the evil? Convince them to change their ways?"

"We have to do something." Steven retrieved another bird as the first flew out the hole in the roof. "We can't just sit around and wait for more people to join that cult."

Brogan shook his head, eyes watching Steven. "Listen to me. We are not going back to that town. It isn't safe. And besides, there isn't anything we could do there. What we need is information. Are there other towns affected? Other cities? I have friends that can give us that. If we go back to that village, we're alone. With these birds, we have friends."

Steven nodded sagely. "Pigeon friends."

Brogan laughed. "Yes. Pigeon friends."

Friends

Sinna let Christa walk ahead a bit while she reached down to grab a handful of snow out of a drift. Christa was right. There were advantages to taking their walks through the park outside the palace, and this was one. The snowball hit Christa square in the back of the head with a thump.

"Hey!" Christa turned, but the grin on her face belied the anger in her voice. "That was cold."

"Of course," Westrel said. "I think that was the point."

Sinna giggled and walked up to help brush snow out of Christa's short mop of hair.

"Ooo, no. You can stay right there," Christa said, one hand held out. "I don't trust you."

"I p-promise. I just want to help."

"Exactly," Westrel said, walking up as well. "It isn't as though she would think of sneaking a snowball down your dress."

Icy cold flooded down Sinna's back, and she spun to face Westrel with words that wouldn't come out through the chill.

The fight lasted a good half hour. It was a beautiful day with clear, blue sky and a nice crispness to the air. The snow lay gathered in piles like yesterday's afterthought. By the time the conflict was over, they were all wet, cold, and laughing hysterically. None of them had come out, dressed for playing in the snow—it was too nice out—but somehow that made it all the more fun.

They were wandering back for new clothes—Christa's white dress especially needed replacing as Sinna might have used a little magic to dump an entire drift on her—still suppressing spurts of laughter when Sinna saw someone sitting alone in the snow under a tree, well off the path.

"Isn't that Vaniel?" She pointed to the figure briefly, not wanting to be rude.

Christa sniffed. "Who cares?"

"She looks upset." Sinna slowed, indecisive. It was true Vaniel was a spoiled brat who picked on anyone she thought below her. She had done horrible things to Christa. But it didn't feel right to pass by anyone in pain.

"We should go s-see what's wrong," she decided, turning off the path. She half-expected Christa to protest, but she said nothing. Instead, she followed a few steps behind, a small frown on her face and Westrel protectively at her shoulder.

Vaniel refused to look up as they approached, there was no way she couldn't hear them. Sinna made sure to make the right amount of noise. She didn't want to scare the girl, after all. She just sat there, head buried in her knees, arms wrapped around her legs. Her entire body would shake occasionally—with sobs?—and as they got nearer, Sinna could see a sheet of expensive, carefully creased, parchment clutched in one hand. Sinna stopped three paces out, the furthest polite distance, and cleared her throat.

"Um . . . V-V-Vaniel? Is s-s-something wrong?"

"Go away," came the muffled reply.

Sinna took a step closer instead. She couldn't help it. She heard Christa and Westrel come up beside her. "We w-want to help. Do . . . do you want to t-t-talk about it?"

"Yeah," the word dripped with sarcasm. "I am sure you would love that. We can all make fun of the bully. Finally get your chance to give her what she deserves."

"No. It isn't like that."

"True. If we wanted to make fun of you we would be doing it," Westrel said.

Sinna glared back at her. Honestly! Didn't she know when to have some tact? Sometimes she was worse than Christa.

"We won't make fun of you, Vaniel. I promise. What's wrong?"

"I am ruined," she snarled as she looked up. "Here, go ahead and read it." She brandished the letter at them. "It will be all over the Roost by tonight anyway. You might as well get your laughs out now, like they did."

"Who?" Christa asked as Sinna took the paper. The letter was short, written in crisp, firm lines with a seal at the bottom.

"My so-called friends," Vaniel spat. "The ones who didn't laugh ran as fast as their socially minded feet could take them."

"Is this . . ." Sinna asked, pointing to the seal.

Vaniel only nodded, dragging one arm across her damp eyes.

Christa and Westrel crowded around her, reading over her shoulder.

Vaniel,

I have informed you on numerous occasions that your evaluations and your progress at the Roost are unaccept-able. You should be well into your third tier by now, as your brother was. I cannot fathom what is holding you back—whether it is an unwillingness to commit yourself or some mental flaw. Regardless, my patience has reached its end. I cannot allow you to be a constant stone around the neck of this house. My house. As you seem determined to walk your own path, I see no choice but to allow you. Henceforth, all support and privileges associated with House Sablehawk are removed from you. Attested by my seal on this document and those submitted to the Office of Nobility this 75th day of Autumn, in the 316th year of Queen Elisidel.

Lord Palatan Sablehawk

"What does he mean, 'all support and privileges are removed'?" Christa asked, scrunching up her face.

"It means he has disowned her," Westrel answered for her. "She has no family. No status."

Sinna handed the letter back, but Vaniel just looked away. "But w-why? Because your progress at the Roost is slow? I mean, I didn't think you were m-m-moving any slower than a lot of others."

"Not as fast as he did," Vaniel muttered. "Or Adasian. 'Why can you not be more like Adasian?'" she mimicked. "Adasian understood that without even having to be told . . . Adasian is the perfect son, he will make a fine Hawk someday. While you would be better off as an Attendant.'"

"That's stupid," Christa said. "And . . . just . . . wrong. You can't control how easy things are for you." She walked over and sat down next to Vaniel.

Sinna couldn't help but smile. Christa was always ready to rally to a cause. She sat down opposite Christa, though not as impolitely close. "Of course it's stupid. And horrible. I . . . I'm sorry, Vaniel."

She scoffed. "For what? You have never done anything to me." She turned to Christa. "I am the one who should be apologizing. I have been . . . awful to you. The things I said . . ." One hand reached halfway to Christa's erratic hair. "And the things I did to you." She shook her head. "You really shouldn't be sitting next to me now."

Christa just looked at Vaniel for several seconds. "No. Everyone makes mistakes. I know I've made plenty. And everyone deserves a second chance."

Vaniel shook her head. "I have done more than make bad choices. I was . . ." She glanced at all of them. "I guess I was jealous." She faced Christa once again. "You had friends. *Real* friends. People who actually cared about you. My own family didn't care about me. Not really. And the other Eyas . . . I knew they only stayed around me because of who my family was. And sure enough, as soon as I didn't have that anymore . . ." She sighed. "And then there were the classes." She thumped the side of her head against the tree. "They all came so easily for you. Like how my father expected them to come for me. It was like . . ." She shrugged sheepishly. "It was like you were the daughter he really wanted, not me."

"Aside from being a half-human freak you mean?" Westrel said. She was still standing, her face an impassive mask as she watched Vaniel.

"Westrel!" Sinna could understand being suspicious, but that was just rude.

"No! No, she is right. I did all kinds of horrible things. As I said, the bully is finally getting what she deserves. It is a kind of justice, I guess."

"There's nothing *just* about abandoning your child," Christa said. "It's hurtful and horrible and . . . *wrong.*" She pounded a fist into the cold ground. "You should show him. You should show him exactly what he threw away. What classes are you having a hard time with? I'll help you. We can start tonight."

Vaniel's eyes widened. "You would do that? But—"

"We'll all help," Sinna added. "As much as we can. I mean, you're an I-Illusionist, right? We can't help much with that. But we can all help with the regular classes. Right Westrel?"

Westrel smirked. "Of course. I am more than happy to give whatever help I can to any of my friends."

Vaniel was practically beaming. "You are all too kind. And I know I don't deserve it. But I will . . . I will do something . . ." She snapped her fingers and a wide grin spread over her face. "I know." She leapt to her feet.

"Really, you don't have to d-do anything," Sinna said, climbing to her feet as well.

"No. No, this I do have to do." She faced Christa. "For you. I have hurt you more than anyone. Just . . . just meet me back here in half an hour." Her eyes took in Christa's still wet clothes. "Make it an hour."

"But," Christa tried to interject, but Vaniel was already hurrying off toward the Palace, almost running.

"And wear something nice!" she yelled back over her shoulder.

Sinna opened the door to Christa's room and made for the wardrobe. She probably didn't trust Christa's idea of "dressing nicely," and Christa was more than happy to let her do the work.

"Start undressing while I find something suitable." Sinna tossed new undergarments over her shoulder to Christa then pulled out two dresses to examine. "Goodness, are the clothes I gave you the only ones you have that aren't w-white?"

Christa grabbed a towel to dry off with and started changing. She gave Sinna a good-natured scowl. "I like white. I'm used to it, and they make it easy to get dressed in the morning."

"Tsk tsk, Christa. You are a strange mix of p-practicality and eccentricity." She pondered for a moment, then placed the blue dress with white lace cuffs and hemming back. She handed Christa the other, a green satin gown cut with dark red pleats and a wide, scooped neck. "No white. It's a special occasion after all."

"What do you think Vaniel wants to show me? I mean, what could I need to get dressed up to see?" Christa asked as she dressed.

"I haven't the faintest, but Vaniel having a change of heart is cause enough for celebration." Sinna busied herself picking up the wet clothes and tossing them down the chute. "I can't believe someone's own f-father would cut them off like that."

Christa frowned. She knew all too well what that felt like. As soon as she read that letter she understood exactly the pain that was lodged in Vaniel's heart. The betrayal.

Sinna paused at the chute. "You don't suppose she's lying, do you? I mean, as some sort of trick? It's exactly the sort of thing she would do."

Christa thought about that. Vaniel had always been mean, even vicious, but she had never been subtle. "I don't think so. I mean, why go to all this effort? She's never had a problem making my life impossible before."

Sinna shrugged. "I don't know. I just don't want you to get hurt again."

Even after Christa got the dress on and arranged properly Sinna still wasn't satisfied. "Something else . . ." she muttered to herself. "I know. I h-have just the thing in my room. Oh! And you'll need some proper shoes as well. Westrel has the perfect pair, and I think they should fit. Stay here. I'll be right b-back." She was out the door before Christa could say a word.

Christa laughed to herself. It still sometimes felt a little weird having friends. And now even Vaniel was a friend. The world was a strange place.

She stood there waiting for a while, but as Sinna didn't immediately return she picked up a brush and ran it through the tangled mess of not even shoulder length hair. She was just starting to get used to it. She could see why Westrel found it appealing. It was definitely easier to manage. Maybe she would keep it like this.

Whispers at the Altar

Sinna hurried in a few minutes later holding a pair of green slippers in one hand and a small red bag in the other. "S-Sorry," she offered as she handed Christa the shoes. "Westrel couldn't find the shoes. And she had to lecture me about trusting Vaniel. She's certain the entire thing is one giant trick. I had to convince her that we weren't blindly following."

She blew out a long breath, tucked some hair back behind her ear and reached into the bag to pull out a short silver chain. It bore a single silver pendant, a dragon coiled into a circle with a small ruby for his eye. She reached forward and fastened it around Christa's neck then motioned for her to look in the mirror.

"P-Perfect," she declared.

Christa didn't know what to say. She fingered it where it lay, inches below her neck. She never seen anything so . . . delicate. And to be wearing it! She glanced over to Sinna with a worried expression. "Oh, thank you Sinna, but I can't. I mean, what if I lose it?" Christa lost things often. She had lost Mama's tiny porcelain doll playing princess in the garden. It had never been found, and Christa had cried for hours imagining how sad her mother must be.

Sinna pished. "Then I guess that'd be too bad for you. It's yours now. But it's actually impossible to lose. It's enchanted to return to you if you ever do lose it or it gets stolen. Now . . ." She rubbed her hands together and motioned for the door. "Vaniel *did* say an hour."

They arrived back at the tree along with Westrel, who Christa noticed did look more gruff than usual, to find Vaniel already waiting for them, practically bouncing from foot to foot.

"Much better," she said, looking over Christa's new apparel. "You look beautiful. And I have just the thing to complete it. She produced a long impossibly thin chain of white metal from her pocket, at the end of which hung . . .

"Mama's ring!" Christa rushed forward to cup it in her hands like a fragile butterfly. "You found it?"

145

Vaniel blushed as she let the chain drop into Christa's palms. "I may have 'borrowed' a Discerner from my father to find it. And not with the best of intentions I have to admit."

"You were going to keep it?" Westrel said, taking a step closer.

"Was. Yes," Vaniel faced her unabashed. "But it belongs to Christabel, and I am returning it." She turned back to Christa. "I never should have taken it. It was a horrible thing to do. I can't tell you how sorry I am."

Westrel muttered something Christa couldn't hear, but she didn't care. She had Mama's ring back. She kissed it, then held it up by the chain.

"It is adamantine," Vaniel said as she took the ends, fastening the clasp around Christa's neck. "Unbreakable."

Christa tucked the ring under the neck of her dress where it hung out of sight. She glanced over to Sinna and they shared a smile. "Thank you, Vaniel. Thank you for doing the right thing." She paused, considering. "But surely you didn't ask me to get all dressed up just to give me this?"

"Of course not. The rest is a bit away. Follow me." And she headed off across the field toward the back of the palace.

Christa followed, bouncing along beside Vaniel, with Sinna and Westrel behind. She couldn't remember the last time she was so happy. With few exceptions, everything was going very well. There was nothing better, she decided, than an enemy turned friend.

They rounded the side of the palace and started down the other side. Down the slope of the hill, on a large flattened portion, a great many people were scattered over the large fenced off training field. Each group of two to four were locked in combat with each other and the ring of metal and clack of wood echoed across the open space between. Christa turned to Vaniel, certain that she would finally explain what this was all about.

Whispers at the Altar

"My father knows pretty much everything that happens in and around the palace," she said as she ambled down the hill. "I heard him talking the other night about someone who had come to stay here."

"Who?"

But she just gave a sly smile and quickened her pace.

When they reached the fence line she paused, walked left a few dozen paces, then pointed out across the field to a group of three men.

Two were locked in combat with long wooden swords. The third, some kind of instructor, watched with arms crossed over his chest. Of the two fighting, one was a tall, slender, elven youth Christa guessed to be about Sinna's age. The other was not elven at all.

He almost looked human except Christa had never seen skin that dark auburn before. He was also both taller and broader than any human she had ever seen, with dark curly hair matted down to his head from the sweat that also covered his bare chest and back.

She watched as the two darted around each other, clashed together, then separated to pace about once again. Christa noticed the non-elf's sword was also different, wider, curved and single-edged as opposed to the straight, thin, double-edged blades the elves preferred.

"His name is Kadin," Vaniel explained. As Sinna and Westrel caught up. They all leaned against the fence.

"I don't understand," Christa said, looking at Vaniel. "You brought me over here to see one of the Queen's Guard trainees?"

"He is an Anathonian," she hurried to explain. "From the south. He showed up about a month ago asking to join the Queen's Guard. It really made my father angry, but after he bested a few of their most promising students they agreed."

Christa watched the dance of combat as she leaned on the fence with Sinna and Westrel. She'd seen plenty of fights. It was pretty common among the children back home. She'd even been in a few, something she wasn't proud of. But this was something else. It appeared to be a very lethal dance, even with the wooden swords they were using. Something about that lethality made her stomach queasy.

147

"The other one is Seanan," Westrel piped in, drawing all eyes to her. "We practice with the Queen's Guard as part of Corporalist training. Seanan is good, but I would put my money on Kadin. Seanan tends to rely on his quickness too much. Likely he does not expect Kadin to be as agile as he is."

The duel concluded in a flurry of movement and flash of weapons Christa couldn't begin to follow. The result was the elf collapsed to the ground with the Anathonian's sword at his back. The instructor seemed satisfied, said a few words as they stood back from each other, then departed. The duelists bowed to each other and were about to follow when Vaniel called out.

"Kadin!" She waved a hand in the air attracting the attention of both. They looked at the girls for a moment, then Seanan said something, clapped Kadin on the shoulder, and laughed as he followed the instructor.

Christa glowered at her. "What are you doing?"

"Calling him over, of course. Sinna didn't get you all dressed up so you could ogle him. I wanted you to meet him. He is the closest thing to a human you are going to find here."

"What?" Christa couldn't believe what she'd heard but she didn't have time to say anything more as the young man stopped a pace away and watched them expectantly. Instead, she faced him, a slight frown on her face.

The silence stretched as Vaniel looked back and forth between Christa and Kadin. Christa had no idea what the girl expected.

"Hello, Kadin," Westrel filled the void, a small smile on her face. Was she enjoying this?

Kadin gave a short bow then removed a slip of paper from his pocket and handed it to Vaniel. Christa leaned over to read it.

Hello. My name is Kadin. It is a pleasure to meet you.

Christa looked from the paper to the young man then over to Westrel.

"He is mute," she answered, her eyes more on Vaniel than Christa. "He hasn't said a word since he got here. Next time you might want to get to know the person you are trying to arrange with your new friend."

•*Whispers at the Altar*•

"Arrange?" Christa repeated.

Vaniel's eyes went wide. "I . . . well, I only thought that you would both appreciate being with each other." She took a step back, looking between Christa and Kadin whose brow had furrowed. "Because you are both . . . you know . . ."

"Freaks?" Christa said softly. "Because who else could either of us possibly find attractive? So you bring me down here thinking I'll fall head over heels for some sweaty . . ." She gestured vaguely toward Kadin. "You don't even know him! Or was it that we were the only ones deserving of each other?"

"No!" Vaniel looked to Sinna for support. "No, I swear it wasn't like that. I just thought . . ."

"I should have known," Christa turned to storm off. "I should have known you hadn't really changed."

"I swear I was trying to help," Vaniel called after.

But Christa was having none of it. Of course Vaniel would want to introduce her to that sword-swinging brute. In her mind, they were perfect for each other. Both non-elf freaks. She couldn't believe she'd been so blind.

"I hate to say, 'I told you so,'" Westrel said as she and Sinna caught up to her.

"But you could have *t-tried* to talk to him, Christa," Sinna said. "I'm sure he's very nice."

"That isn't the point," Westrel said. "Vaniel had nothing to base that arrangement on other than him not being an elf. She is just as racist as she ever was."

"You're not being fair, Westrel. It's how she was raised. You can't expect her to ch-change the way she thinks in one day. She *was* trying."

"Enough," Christa shouted. "I don't care right now if she meant well or not. It hurt. I thought I could trust her."

"Give her some time," Sinna said softly. "No one changes in a day."

Westrel shook her head. "And some people never do."

149

Christa considered that, and wondered which category Vaniel fell under. She wanted so much to believe Vaniel had changed. But was she deluding herself?

The knock at Christa's door that night was not unexpected.

"Come in."

The door edged open, and Vaniel slid through. Christa put down her Advanced Mathematics book.

"I wanted to say I am sorry. Again," Vaniel clutched several books to her chest. "And to ask if you would please help me study."

Christa considered her for a long moment, but in her heart she already knew the answer. Everyone made mistakes. And everyone deserved another chance. Just like she deserved another chance with Mama.

She scooted over on the bed. "Of course I will. Just don't try to 'arrange' me with anyone else. Deal?"

Vaniel sighed. "Deal. Now maybe you can explain these equations to me," she said as she sat down primly on the side of the bed. "Because I can't make heads or tails of them."

Essence

Sheets of paper flew as Christa threw open the classroom door. Breath caught in her throat as her gaze flicked around the empty room. She was late, but the class should still be here. Then she saw the message, written in sparkling silver, still hanging in front of the room.

"Class in the yard today."

Dark of the Pit! She might still have time, though. Clutching her books to her chest she fled down the hall to the nearest bank of tubes.

She was frustrated with herself for being late. Again. Partly because of the trouble she would be in, but mostly because she'd been looking forward to this lesson since her first day here. Instructor Laisel was teaching the new Third Tier Eyas to touch the Essence for the first time today. It was her first step in trying to find something useful to do with this magic. And she was missing it!

•Allan C.R. Cornelius•

It figured she would be assigned mopping duty this morning. And of course Adasian would casually kick over her bucket and flood her fresh clean floor with filthy water. She could still hear his laughter as he gave the most insincere apology ever made. The sound echoed within Christa's head, and she clenched her fists as she ran. Vaniel was right. Her brother was a pig.

Meriel, the other girl assigned to the chore, hadn't even offered to help clean up. She'd just kept her head down, pretending the whole thing wasn't happening. All morning spent re-mopping and now she was rushing about like a madwoman trying to get to class before it was too late.

She reached the tubes and slid to a stop at the nearest. She hated them. They still made her feel as though her stomach were somewhere other than where it ought to be, and she couldn't get the hang of stopping at the right floor. Still, ground floor was easy. An auto-stop kept you from pulverizing yourself.

With a deep breath she stepped in, thought *down*, and fell. She squeezed her eyes shut, unwilling to brave a peek at the floors rushing past without so much as stirring her hair. It was all she could do to keep down the sweet rolls she had for breakfast. Fortunately, the trip lasted only a few moments. Opening her eyes, she ran as fast as she dared for the front doors.

She burst out into the bright artificial spring sunlight of the palace yard, passed inches from bowling into a courtier, and scanned for her class. It didn't take long. They were sitting under a tree, arrayed in a semi-circle around Trainer Laisel. She could tell, as she hurried over, that Laisel had already begun the lesson so there was no hope of sneaking in. Instead, she hustled over and prayed she would at least not be called out.

"Ah, Christabel," the instructor greeted, watching her approach. "I hoped you would be able to join us."

Christa stopped short, blushing as the other students broke into a chorus of giggling. The only friendly face was Vaniel's, who sat at one end by herself. None of the other Eyas' wanted anything to do with her. The other noble children knew she was below them, and the rest had either been too bullied by her to trust her or were afraid of what her brother might do if he caught them socializing with her.

"Enough!" Laisel cut through the laughter with a single word, stopping it as suddenly as it had started.

"Ma'am," Christa dropped a curtsy, trying to keep her attention focused on Trainer Laisel as she fought back the embarrassment, "I'm sorry I–"

"We can discuss the why and the consequences later. For now please take your seat."

Christa dropped to the ground in the nearest convenient space only to feel something damp start to crawl up through her skirt. Glancing down, she saw the mud the other students had been avoiding.

"It suits you, sad-ears," Darnel, one of Vaniel's former hench-girls, whispered sweetly from two spots down. Which only inspired more giggling.

Groaning, Christa got up and moved again, next to Vaniel, who offered a sympathetic smile and motioned to her own muddied dress. Christa smiled back.

Unfortunately, moving didn't help. The water had already seeped into her white skirt and would take hours to dry out. Not to mention it was the second dress she'd dirtied today. She was so distracted that she missed most of what Trainer Laisel said.

" . . . while all of these other classes and subjects are important, as you are now all Third Tier Eyas, it has fallen to me to carry you through the first steps in your main course of study. Now, to review what you should all already know, who can list for me the three forms of magic?"

Everyone looked around, waiting for someone else to raise a hand until a boy at the other end nudged his up.

"Yes, Haranan?"

153

"There is Divine magic, those whose power comes from the Creator himself. Essence magic, which is manipulation of the creation itself. And Corporeal magic, which is the rarest and involves using your own mind and body."

"Excellent. And what are the six disciplines?"

Christa was surprised to see Vaniel's hand go up. She never answered questions.

"Vaniel?"

Vaniel cleared her throat. "Practitioners of Divine magic fall into either the Divinists, the religious leaders who protect and heal, and the Naturalists who primarily work with crops and weather. Essence magic is either focused on the control of the individual elements that make up the Essence, Elementalism, or the restructuring of the essence itself to form temporary images and objects, Illusion. Lastly, Corporeal magic includes Mentalists, those who use the power of their minds to influence others or develop great insight and understanding, and Corporalists, who can exercise incredible control over their own bodies even changing how they look."

Laisel clapped softly. "Very good, Vaniel. A near textbook explanation. Now all of you have been told your talents lie in Essence magic. And we have already touched on what that means. Can anyone expound on that specifically?"

"It means we can touch the Essence in some way," answered Darnel, glaring at Vaniel as she did so.

"And the Essence is?" Laisel prompted.

Darnel shrugged. "It is everything,"

"That is, perhaps, a too simplistic answer. Anyone else?" Her gaze focused on Christa. "Christabel. How would you describe the Essence?"

Christa swallowed and glanced around, clearing her throat. "It's pretty much how it sounds, I guess. I mean, it's what everything is made of. Like if the world were a dress," she used an example currently very close to her, "the thread would be Essence. Only . . . it isn't

•Whispers at the Altar•

just dresses. And it's everything between the threads, too . . ." She trailed off as soft laughter rose from the circle.

"Quiet please," Laisel cut in, silencing the class again. "That isn't a bad analogy, Christabel. The Essence is everything, but it is more than just everything we see, it is everything in between. The wind ripples along it. The air is filled with it. It is the very building blocks with which the Creator fashioned our world. Each of you has the ability to interact with this Essence in some way and to some extent. As a side note, as you may guess, you will not all manipulate it in the same way, nor will you be able to use it to the same extent. My advice is, during your training, try not to compare your own progress in any one area to anyone else's. While you may be slower in one area, there may be others where you will excel."

She paused before leaning forward ever so slightly. "Now who would like to be the first to try to touch the Essence?" A ring of hands shot up, Christa's among them, but in the end Laisel started at the end opposite Christa and worked her way around.

Christa tried to pay attention, desperate to absorb everything the others were doing. Unfortunately, the process looked very personal. Laisel sat in front of each, held their hands, and talked to them as they closed their eyes. Before she knew it, Christa was deep in a conversation with Vaniel about where and when they should have their next study session and what Vaniel should bring.

Christa jumped as Laisel sat down in front of her and took her hands. The woman's large patient blue eyes looked straight into Christa's. "Alright Christabel, just like I told the others," she said.

Only Christa had no idea what she told the others.

The patient look faded ever so slightly. "Pay attention, Christabel. Focus," she admonished—an admonishment Christa had heard a lot in her fifteen years, and particularly in the past two. "Close your eyes and focus out. Use all of your other senses." She paused. "Close your eyes, Christabel."

155

Christa clamped them shut as tightly as she could, trying to make up for her delay.

"Now, focus out. Touching the Essence is like touching anything else. First you have to reach out. Some find it helps to use their hands, but it isn't necessary. You are reaching out with your self, with the Essence within you. To do that you need to feel everything. You need to feel the grass under your feet and the breeze kissing against your cheek. The smell of the flowers from the gardens and the cooking from the kitchen. The sound of my voice and the murmur of the fountains. You have to feel all of it."

Christa tried. She tried to still her mind and concentrate. To focus on each thing as Laisel listed them. It was hard. Her mind wanted to wander off to one thing or another. To her other lessons, to her friends, to her chores, to Adasian. Then it wandered to an image of her mama. One she often pictured. She was sitting with her in the forest outside the village, learning to read. They were laughing together. Christa could almost hear her loving voice urging her to try again.

And she did, she gritted her teeth and focused. And all the sensations around her sharpened, became more and more acute until she nearly couldn't bear it. The grass was tiny blades against her skin, the cool breeze a freezing wind, Mama's ring like a millstone hanging from her neck, and Laisel's soft breathing like the panting of a wolf in the night. All the while, a stinging heat suffused everything as though she were standing too close to a bonfire. Time slowed as she tried to reach further, to feel more. And just as she thought she might, a shrill voice sliced through all her concentration.

"Look at her hair!"

It all came crashing down, jerking her back into her painfully plain reality.

She opened her eyes and looked around, then tried to grab a handful of hair and examine it. There was nothing unusual about it. Then she noticed every face staring at her with an expression that sunk her heart in her stomach.

"What? What happened? What did I do?"

Laisel blinked several times. "What did you feel, Christabel?"

"Just what you told me to. I felt a bit of everything. Only . . . more."

The trainer stood up and moved back to her spot under the tree, taking the time to school her expression as whispers flitted around the circle.

"Yes, well, I think all of you have the right idea. I would like you to practice opening yourself to one sense at a time. Go through each of them ten times. Just one at a time," she repeated, focusing on Christa. "Take it slowly."

The others set to their practicing with more than one glance at Christa. All except Vaniel, who was openly staring.

"What happened?" Christa whispered.

"Your hair," Vaniel asked, trying to look as though she were practicing. "It was turning white. Just like . . . before."

She didn't need to be any more specific. They both knew what she meant. No one could tell her why it happened before; she doubted they could now. But it obviously wasn't normal. Which was just what she needed. Another way to stand out.

She was about to begin her own practice when she spotted Silvana sitting by one of the nearby fountains, watching. Christa waved, and Silvana returned it, adding a wide smile. That smile swept away the fear. So what if she was different? Being the same was boring, wasn't it?

Sinna watched Christa over the top of her Advanced Mathematics book. She'd agreed to come up to the Observatory to study together, but Christa hadn't stopped fidgeting since the moment they sat down. Sinna had become used to Christa's near constant toying with her skirts, or tie strings, or bows, or whatever else happened to be nearby. But this was excessive even for her.

"W-will you just tell me, Christa? You're obviously barely holding something back. I don't think I'll get any studying done until you sit still."

Christa took a deep breath. "So, I had my first Essence lesson today," she said in a voice that did a very poor job of sounding nonchalant.

"Oh?" Sinna answered. She knew how much Christa had been anticipating this. She'd talked of nothing else for weeks. "How did it go?"

"I'm not sure." A hint of confusion crept into her voice. She set her book down and squinted at Sinna. "But I think I must have done something wrong."

Sinna set her book down as well. Nothing with Christa was ever normal. Or boring. "What do you mean?"

"Well, I did what Instructor Laisel told me. I tried to feel everything. At first it was hard, but I kept trying. And I thought it was working. Everything *felt* so much it almost hurt. Then when I tried to do more it all went away." She frowned. "I thought I had done it right. But Instructor Laisel didn't seem happy. And everyone was staring at me."

She sighed and raised a hand to Sinna. "Kind of like you're doing right now."

Sinna closed her mouth.

"Christa . . . I-I think you did it. But I've never heard of anyone touching on their first try. You weren't supposed to be able to. As far as I knew it wasn't even possible."

Sinna cursed herself. She could see the fear creeping into her friend's eyes. "But that's g-good. It's what you wanted, isn't it?"

Christa chuckled. "I guess. I mean . . . yes. It's great! I guess it's a bit frightening is all." She leaned back against the crystal wall, staring up through the ceiling. "Oh, and then there was the thing about my hair."

Sinna shook her head. "What about it?"

"Oh, Vaniel told me it started turning white again. Everyone saw. Apparently it went away a few minutes later, but . . . I wish I knew what was going on."

•*Whispers at the Altar*•

"I know. So do I." And she meant it. Something definitely wasn't right. There was no way Christa should have been able to feel the Essence her first try, not to mention her display of magic on the bridge. It just wasn't possible. She laid the tips of her fingers on Christa's knee.

"We'll figure it out. Together."

YEAR 3

Progress

"Gah!" Sinna threw the spoon across her room.

"Still not working?" Westrel asked, not even glancing up from her book as she wiped off water drops.

"No." Sinna turned in her chair and leaned back against the desk. "I've t-t-tried all kinds of metal, in water with all kinds of s-s-saline levels. I just can't g-get the right reaction."

"There is the possibility that it is not . . . possible." She looked up. "Besides, why do you *want* something to rust?"

Sinna leaned forward on her knees. "Because. If I can understand how to make it rust, maybe I can understand how to *keep* it from rusting. Permanently. Can you imagine what that would do for farmers? For ship captains?" Her mind buzzed with the possibilities.

Westrel raised an eyebrow. "Sounds pretty important."

"It would be incredible! I can't tell you how much time we spend on my family's farm keeping all our tools from rusting."

"Hours a day?"

Sinna's excitement faltered. "N-no. But enough time to be really annoying."

Westrel laughed. "Sounds as if you are trying to magic your way out of a chore."

Sinna tried her best to imitate Director Marellel. "If j-just one young elf has a few more minutes to spend chasing her brother through haystacks, I will consider my experiments a s-success."

They both broke into laughter and it was several minutes before Sinna even thought to look at her desk again. "Thanks, Westrel. I needed that."

She smiled. "I am sure you will get it. At least you found something to work on that you are passionate about."

"Oh, I'm s-sure you'll find something. You still have plenty of time."

"I will find something. But the odds of it being anything I can get that excited about are low."

"Why?" Sinna stood and gathered up the bowls and silverware that comprised her experiment. "I think everything about your m-magic is fascinating. The things you can do . . ." She gestured with a fork, trying to think of the right words. "Th-they're incredible. Much more interesting than just moving elements around."

"Perhaps. But Director Aerel wants all our proposals submitted to her before the end of the season. And I still have little idea of where to focus, let alone a specific proposal. You are trying to help your family. My family is in the Vanguard. Patrolling the forests, ready for an attack from the humans that I doubt will ever come." She sighed and closed her book. "Not something I want to get involved in, let alone develop some technique to improve."

"You don't want to be assigned to the V-Vanguard? I thought they were practically begging for you."

"They are. General Quiran has even spoken to Director Aerel. But I don't want it. At least the director is holding off making any decision. I think she is waiting to see if anyone else requests me."

•*Whispers at the Altar*•

Sinna tucked her experiment equipment into a box under her bed and sat down beside Westrel. "What do you w-want?"

The Corporalist shrugged. "I would be a great asset to the Vanguard. Logically Director Aerel should recommend I be assigned there."

"That isn't what I asked, though."

Westrel chuckled. "Intelligence. Like a *real* Hawk." She sighed. "But my family is counting on me. The status they would gain within the Vanguard, were I assigned there, would be significant. I do not want to let them down."

"I'm sure they'll be proud of you no matter where you end up. Besides—"

A knock on the door stopped the conversation abruptly. Sinna silently chided whoever it was. Their timing was annoying to say the least. "Yes?"

The door cracked open revealing Vaniel's black hair and dark eyes. "It's Vaniel. Can I talk to you for a minute?"

Sinna reached over to give Westrel a squeeze. "We'll finish this later," she whispered, then waved Vaniel in as she walked back to the chair at her desk. "Come on in."

Vaniel closed the door behind her then stood there looking between them. Sinna didn't blame her for being nervous around Westrel. She hadn't made a secret of the fact that she was more than skeptical of Vaniel's "conversion." Sinna just wished they would both get along.

"What is it?" Sinna asked, motioning to the spot on the bed next to Westrel.

"I wanted to talk to you about Christabel." Vaniel sat down on the very edge of the bed, focusing on Sinna.

"What about her?" Westrel asked, leaning forward.

"I am not sure how to say this, and please don't tell Christabel. I am not sure how she would . . . react."

Sinna leaned forward as well, running one hand along the braid of her hair.

"What w-would she be angry at you for telling us?" She and Christa were best friends. They told each other everything. Vaniel was probably overreacting to something.

She took a deep breath, "I noticed a few weeks ago that Christabel was acting . . . odd. Even for her. She is almost never in her room. She sets very strict times for our study sessions, and when I ask what she does with the rest of her free time she changes the subject."

"She's busy. The girl studies more than she s-sleeps. I keep telling her it isn't healthy but—"

"I know. And that is what I thought it was, too. But it nagged me. So I . . ."

"You have been watching her," Westrel stated.

She nodded. "Not all the time," she hurried to add. "Just now and then."

"I am sure. And?" Westrel didn't seem surprised in the least.

"She has been spending a lot of time alone in the library. Searching through Divinist magical artifact registries." She sighed. "It could be nothing. But I can't think of what she might be looking for. It isn't as if any of her classes should have her anywhere near those kinds of books."

Sinna leaned back. Christa hadn't mentioned anything about this to her. "Divinist Artifacts?" She looked to Westrel for any ideas but she only shrugged.

Sinna tried to remember anything Christa might have said about Divinists or even Divinist magic. "The only time I've even heard her mention D-Divinist magic is when she first got here. I was telling her about the different kinds of magic and what they could do. I mentioned Divinist magic, and she got so excited." Sinna smiled as she remembered. "She really w-wanted to be able to do it. I was a little sorry for her when she found out she couldn't."

Westrel cocked her head to one side. "Maybe there was something specific about it she wanted to do. Something that she is looking for another way to do."

"I suppose." Sinna shook her head. "But I didn't t-tell her much specific. It was all generalities."

"Do you remember what you *did* say?" Vaniel asked.

Sinna thought hard. "Something about some Divinists being able to raise the dead, I think. But you don't think . . ." She looked from one face to the other. "I mean to t-try to do that without the Divinists . . . That would be blasphemy."

"This is an awful lot of guessing," Westrel said. "We don't *know* anything. She could just be curious. You know how Christa is. She wants to know everything, and she is never willing to wait until she is supposed to learn it."

"I am sure you are right," Vaniel said. "But I at least would feel better if you both talked to her about it. I am sure we are jumping to conclusions, and I know she will tell you exactly what she is doing if you ask."

Sinna nodded. "I don't see h-how it could hurt. Do you want to come, too?"

"No, thank you," Vaniel stood. "I don't want the fact that I was watching her to cloud the issue. If there even is an issue," she added hastily.

"Come in," Christa called, her eyes never leaving the book she was hunched over. She heard the door open and felt Silvana step in before the latch clicked again. She wasn't sure how she knew it was Silvana. She just did. Something about the way the hairs on the back of her neck pricked when she was around.

"Are you ready to study?"

Christa frowned at the cheerfulness in Silvana's voice. "Not really." She leaned back in her chair and stared out the window of the empty classroom.

"What is wrong?" Silvana moved into her view, beside the window. The slight breeze lifted her hair into the sunlight like an ethereal halo.

"What's wrong," Christa shoved the book back a bit, "is I've spent the last year searching through catalogues for a resurrection artifact that doesn't exist."

Silvana bit her lip. "I never said there would be . . ."

"No. You never said there would be. But you did say you knew the library. You said it was possible. That it would be my best bet."

"It still is." She fidgeted with the front of her skirt.

"No, Silvana. It isn't. And you knew that, didn't you?"

"I don't . . ."

Silvana was fidgeting fiercely now. And Christa knew why. Because she did the same.

"Don't lie to me."

Christa's anger rose, the Fire rising with it. It was the same Fire that had burned inside her repeatedly over the years. It had only grown more distinct since she began touching the Essence. More . . . present.

"I looked it up. It's against the laws of the church to make such an item. And for the very reasons I brought up!"

Silvana took a step forward. "Christa, I just wanted to—"

"Wanted to what?" Christa snarled, leaping to her feet. "Because you didn't want to *help* me."

"Christabel Sellers." Silvana stiffened, her eyes hardening. "I have only ever tried to help you. Since the first day you came here."

"Then you—"

"No!" The shout forced Christa back a step. "You have had your say. Now listen. Yes, I lied to you, but I tried to tell you the truth, and you wouldn't listen. I hoped, given enough time, I could convince you of the folly of what you were trying to do. I hoped you would outgrow the need. That time would help you forgive yourself. But you refuse. You are obsessed, Christa. It isn't healthy. Why haven't you told your friends about this? Or Marellel? Because you know they would stop you. Because you know it isn't right." She leaned

•Whispers at the Altar•

forward, eyes glistening. "Please, Christa. You *must* let her go. *Please.*
It wasn't your fault."

"NO!" Christa swept her hand in front of her, a wave or force blowing
the book off the desk. "You're wrong! This is the only way. The only
way Papa will ever love me again and the only way we can be a family
again. I *will* bring her back."

"It was her time, Christa," Silvana pleaded. "She's happy now."

Christa's hand clenched and the desks around her shuddered and
vibrated away. "Happy without *me*, you mean."

Silvana blanched. "No. I didn't mean—"

"Happy now that she isn't raising a monster."

"What?" Silvana took a step toward her. "Christa, that isn't what I—"

"Get out," Christa whispered.

"Christa, please . . . Let me help you."

"Get out!"

Ten desks, all of those around Christa, flew through the air, crashing against the wall where Silvana stood. But Silvana was gone, the
door swinging open.

Christa's chest heaved, reveling in the sensations of the Essence
flowing around her. Like a warm cloak pulled tight around her. A
cloak that promised more power than she could ever need. And the
Fire flicking below the surface.

Then the truth of what she'd just done struck her and she collapsed
back into the chair, sweat pouring down her face. She was glad Silvana
was gone—there was no denying she had been holding Christa back—
but the way Christa had done it. She shivered in the breeze. What if
she'd hurt Silvana? Or worse yet, what if she hurt Sinna or Westrel?
What if Director Dalan was right? What if she was dangerous? What
if the voice in her dreams was right? She was still chewing on this
thought when Sinna and Westrel walked in.

"Christa?" Sinna peered in around the corner. "Are you all right?
W-we heard a . . ." She stopped as her eyes caught the tumble of
desks near the window.

169

Christa saw a flash of fear in Sinna's eyes, and the look was enough to break her heart. No. She would never do anything to hurt Sinna or Westrel. Or any of her friends. She would rather die.

"I'm all right," Christa muttered, walking over to pick up one of the desks. "Just . . . trying something new."

Sinna's face brightened as she accepted the lie. "Oh. Well remind me to stand far away the next t-time you do that." She walked over to help right the desks.

"Or behind you," Westrel said, standing near the door.

Christa could see in her eyes that she knew something else was going on. It made Sinna's blind trust even more painful. She set the desk down and turned to find Sinna staring at her as well.

"What?"

"You know you can t-tell us anything, right Christa?" Sinna asked as she sat on the edge of the desk she just placed.

"Of course." Christa glanced back and forth between them. "What's this about?"

"Just . . ." Sinna gestured lamely with one hand, "if there was a-anything bothering you. If you need to—"

"Have you been researching Divinist Artifacts in an effort to bring your mother back?" Westrel interrupted, earning a glare from Sinna.

Christa sighed, buying herself a second to think by picking up the book she'd thrown from the desk. In a way it was a relief to have the secret out.

"I-I understand why you would, Christa," Sinna added, obviously taking her silence as an admission. "Not that I really know what you are feeling . . . But I know you miss her fiercely."

Christa nodded, eyes never leaving the book. "But it isn't possible. They won't let me."

They said nothing.

"You know, I can't even remember what she looked like. Not really. I used to be able to picture her when I closed my eyes. But now it's all blurry."

Whispers at the Altar

Still they said nothing. Just two hands on her shoulders.

She set the book, *Magical Artifacts of the Ancient Church*, on the desk. "I suppose if the Creator is so determined to keep her, all I can do is hold onto that blurry image as long as I can." But the pit if she was going to stop trying. There had to be a way. The very fact that they didn't want her to find it only made her more determined to do so.

RETURN

Steven nearly jumped out of his skin as the bird flew through the window. "Brogan, you have another one!" he shouted, taking a moment to calm his racing heart. The past few months had seen their usually peaceful retreat turned into a hostel for pigeons. Steven didn't know if bird messaging was a common practice—Brogan said most people hired someone to carry their messages—but he couldn't imagine the mess if it was. Cleaning pigeon poop had become a regular chore for him.

Brogan came in from the garden, brushing his hands off on his breeches. "That would be Aaron, the last of them."

"Thank the Maker of All. I've already had more of pigeons than I ever wanted to." Steven set the book down carefully on the table, covered it with its cloth, and walked over to get the bucket. They always felt the need to let go whenever Brogan removed the message. As if they had been holding it in the entire flight just for him.

Allan C.R. Cornelius

This one was no different, and as Steven cleaned the mess it made all over their kitchen table, Brogan worked the scrap of paper off its leg. Steven tried to get a glimpse as Brogan read it, but he didn't need to. The old man's face was more than enough confirmation. Another positive. That made six other towns with cult activity.

Brogan walked to the window to set the bird free then studied the faded map he had pinned to a square of wood. "Six towns," he muttered. "That we know of."

Steven tossed the water from the bucket out the same window and threw the rag on the pile to wash later that day. "But why aren't they in any of the cities? And why isn't there any activity south of here?"

Brogan sighed. It was a weary sound that Steven wasn't used to hearing. Even as old as Brogan looked, Steven had never known him to show it.

"We don't know for sure there isn't some influence in the cities. It's far easier to hide when you have so many more people to hide among. All we really know for certain is that it isn't isolated to our little Ceerport." Brogan reached out to place a little pin in the far north, the home of their latest pigeon.

Steven shook his head. "No. But we do know it's related to something going on in the Wilderness. Something that began a little over two years ago. I know that . . . thing, is the same thing they're worshiping. I think we should go back where it all started, see if we can find anything to tell us what they're after."

"No. We can't risk that. I don't know if you were just lucky the last time or if they let you go on purpose, but it isn't safe." He set the map down and walked over to his chair, easing himself into it.

"So, what? We just sit here? Wait for something to happen? We already waited to see how big the problem was. Now we know. It's big. When are we going to do something about it?"

Brogan smiled. It was barely a hint of one, but it lit up his eyes all the same. "Ah, to have the fire of youth again. But no. Going back into the Wilderness right now could only result in us being killed.

174

Whispers at the Altar

But!" he held up a finger, forestalling Steven's argument. "But . . . it may be time to return to the village. I would like to see for myself what has happened over the past year. It may be we can get an idea of what they want without entering the Wilderness at all."

"I'll get the animals ready for us to leave." Steven was halfway out the door before he even finished the sentence.

"Not this time."

Steven turned around. "What do you mean?" They had to take care of the animals.

Brogan walked over to his trunk and removed his pack. "I mean you aren't coming. It will still be dangerous. This way the house can be tended, and you can stay safe."

"Safe?" Steven scoffed. "As if I could survive here on my own if anything happened to you."

Brogan chuckled. "Oh, I'm sure you could. You're very resourceful." He stuffed some clothes into the sack.

"Exactly. I can help you. I know you just want what's best for me, but I'm fifteen. I'm not a child anymore. And what if something does happen to you? What if *they* do something to you? They know I live with you. What's to keep them from finding me? And how safe will I be then?"

Brogan closed the chest and faced Steven.

Steven stood up as straight as he could. He expected to see disapproval in those eyes. But he saw only love. And he realized that was the real reason he wanted to go so badly. Because he loved this crazy old man, too, and couldn't bear to think of him facing danger alone. Steven had never known his father, didn't know what it was like to have one. But he thought it must be something like this.

"Fine. You can come. But only because I'd hate to see the state of this place when I got back. You'd probably spend all your time picking dandelions in the fields." Brogan shoved food into the pack. "But you better hurry. I'm not waiting around for you to be ready."

Allan C.R. Cornelius

Chores done in record time, Steven was packed, ready, and waiting for Brogan at the top of the hill. There were no lessons on this trip. The possibilities of what they might find in the town weighed too heavily on both their minds. The hours of walking were wiled away in silence broken only by the crunch of their boots on the dry summer grass and the buzz of grasshoppers leaping to escape the feet of these intruders. At night, the sawing of crickets droned loud enough to keep Steven awake, and the fire drew hundreds of moths eager to sacrifice themselves in the flames. Steven was reminded once again how much he hated traveling, and vowed for perhaps the hundredth time to never do it again. What had he been thinking?

It was a long and miserable three days, and the nearer they came to the end, the lower Steven's stomach sank. His mind filled with all kinds of horrible predictions of what they would find. What if everyone in the town was dead? What if they were all transformed into those lizard things he had seen in the swamp? What if they were waiting in ambush, ready to capture him and Brogan, tear out their hearts, and devour them while they still beat?

Each scenario played itself out in Steven's imagination over those three days, until he couldn't bear to think about it but couldn't manage to think of anything else.

On the third day, Brogan turned south. He wanted to circle around the town and approach it from a new direction. Steven couldn't argue. His thoughts of ambush had been steadily growing.

When they crested the large hill on the south side of the town, Steven was surprised to see little difference from the last time they were there. His imagination had invented a hundred different horror stories, each more destructive than the last, and a part of him fully

‣Whispers at the Altar‣

expected the town to be gone completely. Or at least a smoking ruin. But there it sat, huddled up against the shore of the sad little lake. If anything, it had grown. A wall now surrounded it, though he couldn't fathom where they would get that much stone, and some of the squat buildings were definitely new.

"Well, that's going to make things more difficult," Brogan muttered as he pointed to the wall.

"It looks like that gate house is the only entrance," Steven said. "Unless we want to go for a swim." Though the wall wasn't very tall, it wrapped in a firm near circle, anchored on both ends by the lake.

"It might be our only way in, but it's an obvious weakness." He looked at Steven sternly. "Never trust an obvious weakness." He hustled forward. "Better get off this hill. If they have any sentries they may have already spotted us."

The walk into town worked Steven's nerves raw. He couldn't stop thinking of all the time they were giving the townsfolk to prepare something. Brogan angled them further east, toward the lake, until they were walking along its coast. The rushes and weeds that choked the bank provided a modicum of cover from observers, but as they grew closer Steven could see there were no guards along the wall to see them anyway. He also saw that it wasn't built out of stone but thousands of clay bricks. The corner of the wall extended into the lake, but not far. It should be a simple matter to wade out enough to work their way around.

When they were within a stone's throw from the base, Brogan crouched down, trying to take advantage of the reeds. Steven tried to imitate his quiet movements, but the ground was uneven and his feet slid away in the mud.

Splashes echoed off the wall, loud enough the whole town should have heard. But after a pause during which nothing but a general low murmur could be heard from the other side, they continued forward.

They made the base of the wall with no further trouble and waded down into the water. Steven wasn't fond of water, or at least pools of it large enough to swim in. It reminded him too much of the swamp. Anything could be waiting just feet away and you would never know until it was too late. It was an unknown and a deadly one. But he had no choice. He couldn't fight to come and then run away at the end. So, he hugged the wall as he stepped carefully after Brogan, eyes peeled for any movement in the water.

By the time they reached the edge of the wall the dirty water was up to Steven's chin. He had to walk on tiptoe with his head tilted back just to keep his mouth out of it. Brogan had resorted to swimming, but being able to feel the ground was a comfort Steven wasn't willing to relinquish.

The low murmur of voices Steven had heard earlier grew louder, and as they rounded the corner he could see why. The entire town must have been by the water's edge. Slipping around and back up the bank on the other side, they could see a crowd of people gathered in the market. In the middle rose the same totem Steven and Brogan had found themselves cornered under the last time.

They took a moment to flex limbs and stretch muscles while everyone was turned away to the totem, then crept as silently as they could along the edge of a fishing boat toward the commotion. The crowd was silent save the occasional wave of agreement, yet what they were responding to was difficult to see.

Steven spotted a window below the low eave of a house across the street and pointed it out to Brogan. They weren't going to learn anything down here, not without walking right into the crowd. Brogan nodded once then hustled over. As they crossed the center of the narrow street, a scream echoed out across the houses, cut short in a disturbingly final way.

Steven and Brogan froze, but none of the townsfolk turned. Instead, they cheered. Steven exchanged a worried glance with Brogan and they ran the rest of the way to the house. Steven gave Brogan a boost then followed up behind him, swinging up and onto the roof with a soft grunt.

Whispers at the Altar

What he saw as he peeked over the edge of the roof chilled him more than the wind through his wet clothes. The entire town, man, woman, and child, was gathered around a platform, from which the totem rose another fifteen feet. Upon the platform stood the snake from Steven's nightmares revealed completely in the glaring light of day. It was as tall as a man with arms that ended in taloned hands, but scaled from the top of its vaguely human head to the tip of its tail. The rough parody of a face looked out from its reptilian hood and regarded the assembled villagers with what Steven could only assume was a grin as it hissed and spat words he couldn't begin to understand.

Behind the snake stood nine humans dressed in rags. Their faces were downcast as they looked upon the woman who lay upon the platform with a curtain of brown hair covering her face. Even from where he crouched Steven could see the stream of blood that spilled from her and down the hole surrounding the totem.

Steven couldn't stop the shaking that took hold of his limbs. Neither could he take his eyes from the sight, even as his stomach churned and he thought he might be sick. He watched as the snake grabbed another, a young man with arms as big as Steven's thighs but who now walked forward as meekly as a sheep. The snake lifted a jagged dagger high, uttered a series of slippery sounds, then slit the man's throat to the cheers of all assembled.

Steven cried out, a strangled, feeble yelp, and ducked back behind the cover of the roof's peak. This couldn't be happening. *That* couldn't be here.

"We have to help them," Brogan whispered as he too ducked down.

Steven looked at him as if he had suddenly gone insane. "What? How? We'll be . . ." He shook his head violently, the image of that giant shadow rising from the swamp playing over in his mind.

"We have to," Brogan insisted. "Would you rather wait up here and watch them all die? Do you want that on your conscience?"

Steven just kept shaking his head, but it wasn't in answer to Brogan's question.

"We can't just run down there. Did you see the people? Armed. Every one of them. Even the children. And not just with farming or fishing tools. Swords. Shields. That isn't a town. It's an army."

"So . . . so we should go back and tell the king," Steven tried. "Wouldn't he want to know this?"

Brogan gripped Steven's arm. "Listen to me. Those people don't have time to wait for Steven to get his head out of his ass. Either of you," he added pointedly. "They have minutes at most."

A scream ripped through the air, followed by a chorus of cheers.

Steven could hear children's voices in that cheer. He *did* have to do something, didn't he? But what about Brogan? Steven had only just found someone who was kind to him. He was just learning what actual kindness looked like. He couldn't lose Brogan. The idea was more frightening then a host of snake-men.

Brogan stared at him then growled softly and gave him a small shove. "We need a distraction."

"What? What should I do?"

"This whole place is a bonfire waiting to happen. Find something to light. *Away* from me."

He gave another small shove, and Steven scrambled away as quiet as he could.

"And don't get caught. I'm too old to be rescuing people twice in one day."

Of course he would. Steven knew that. And it gave him a small spark of courage. He dropped the last few feet to the ground and took off running.

He knew exactly what the distraction needed to be. There was probably only one thing that would get everyone out of the market. As he ran, he fumbled in his pack for the powders he would need.

Escape

Steven prayed he remembered the basic layout of the town enough to get where he was going. The hardest part would be arriving there without using the main road. That would put him in view of anyone who happened to turn around. Luckily, his vague memories didn't let him down.

He ducked down a side street, left down another, and there it was. The big creepy building he saw last year. It deserved to be burned down. With how dry the summer had been so far, the thatching on the roof should be perfect for a fire. Unfortunately, Steven couldn't see any easy way up there. He needed a torch, and he had nothing on him that would work.

He ducked in the door and was immediately smothered in darkness. No windows, no chimney, just the odd brave beam of sunlight that managed to struggle through the roof. Steven sighed. He'd need a torch—just to find something to make a torch. He was just about to leave when he spotted the shadow of something large and bulky at the far end. There wasn't time to keep looking. If it was big enough, maybe he could reach the roof by standing on it.

He ran toward the object but stopped three paces away. It was a simple altar, made of a table stacked with what meager offerings a fishing community could provide. Fish bones, small rotted bundles of reeds, moth-eaten spun cloth . . . Over all of this lay the body of what Steven could only assume was the local priest. There was little left now but bones wrapped in brown vestments stained darker by blood dried years ago.

Steven paused, unwilling to touch or move the body, until another gurgled scream reminded him of the urgency of the situation. He swept his arm across the altar, but the items were dried and stuck to the wood. All he managed was to shift some of the bones through the layers of desiccated offering.

It would have to do. Leaping atop the table he brought a combination of powders from his pack. It would be harder, working upside down, but it would have to work. Rather than throw the elements onto the ceiling, he combined them, twisted the ends of the wrapping, and shoved it into the brittle thatch.

It took three swipes of his flint, but at last he got a spark out that caught the edge of the wrapping.

Brogan waited a few seconds, then slipped down off the roof as well. He would need a better position to take advantage of any distraction Steven managed. Someplace closer where he could get to the captives quickly.

Back on the ground, he made a bolt back to the shoreline. When he reached the first pier he slid to a stop and gasped for breath. The swim around the wall had been bad enough. Then lying on a roof in cold wet clothes while his muscles cramped up. Now sprinting across coarse sand. Curse this Ssanek. Brogan had been perfectly happy growing old in peace and quiet in his little house.

Brogan took a deep breath and scrambled out from under the pier, heading for the next one. He didn't have time to feel sorry for himself. The Maker had given him work to do, and he meant to see it done. Another scream emphasized just what was at stake. This was about more than just his old bones and muscles.

As he reached the third pier he took another moment to rest while he waited for the distraction. There were only six captives now. Four women, two barely old enough to warrant the name, and two men. The snake-thing—Brogan wished he knew what else to call it—was talking again. Brogan couldn't make out a word, but the villagers didn't seem to have any problems.

If they had been paying attention, they would have seen the smoke rising from behind them. Brogan tried to will them to turn around. The snake-man reached for the next sacrifice, a girl of perhaps eighteen years, dragging her forward to the totem with one clawed hand.

Turn around, you fools! Brogan pulled a knife and clamped it between his teeth. He wished he could yell it. He briefly thought of shouting an alarm from his hiding place, but he couldn't afford drawing their attention toward him.

The snake raised the knife in the air then stopped.

Someone in the crowd yelled.

The yell was picked up by others and within moments the cry of "Fire!" was driving the crowd to action. It was instinct, as built in as breathing. Fire was the oldest enemy of all.

Brogan rushed to action as the chaos fell. Running from his hiding place, he pulled from his pack what to anyone else would look like an ordinary ball of dried mud. He slid under the raised stage, aiming for the front. Slants of light through the boards guided him to the stairs. He jammed the ball against the stairs, then crawled toward the back of the platform.

A swift kick exploded the ball in a cloud of black smoke. More cries of alarm followed, but Brogan was too busy crawling out and finding the captives to pay much attention. He found them, caught between panicking along with everyone else and taking the chance to run despite the ropes binding their hands and feet.

He grabbed the knife from his mouth, reached up, and snapped through the rope binding the closest captive's feet. Then moved to the next as he yelled at her to run for the water. Two more followed in quick succession. Then a slender shape slid out of the smoke and yellow eyes locked on him.

Within seconds a quarter of the roof was alight. By the time Steven made it out of the building and down the road the smoke was rising in swirling clouds. Steven couldn't help a terrified laugh. It wouldn't take them long to see that. He ducked down between two dilapidated shops and stopped for a second to think. He hadn't thought about how to get out. He was near the middle of town, which meant now the crowd of villagers would be between him and the lake. The only other way out was the gatehouse.

Between the shaking in his hands and pounding of his heart he was sure he was about to explode. But he took a deep breath and ducked back out onto the street anyway.

He decided to sacrifice stealth for speed and turned out onto the main road. It was the fastest way to the gatehouse. As he sped down the crusted clay, he tried to dig through his pack for what he would need. There wasn't much left, and bits of clothes and food spilled out as he searched.

He was so absorbed with the search he nearly didn't see the two guards walk into the road from the gatehouse. He skidded to a stop, as surprised as they were, then ran down a narrow side street.

"He must have set the fire!"

Steven cursed as he heard them chase after him, but there was still a chance. If he could find another side street, he might be able to loop back around and catch the gate unguarded.

Only there weren't any side streets. Or any outlets of any kind from this alley. Steven cursed again. Why couldn't these villagers put roads where he needed them?

"Stop!"

"It's no use, boy!"

The wall got closer and closer, and the guard's yells louder and louder. He was running out of time.

He could try climbing up one of the ramshackle buildings, but none of them looked sturdy enough to support him. It was a wonder the wind hadn't blown them down. He briefly contemplated just taking one down, but before he could pick a suitable target he was at the wall.

He turned, the guards were seconds away.

It was the wall or nothing.

Brogan didn't wait for the snake-thing to make a move. He just reached over and cut through another rope. Then he saw the girl. The snake still had her by the hair and, with its eyes locked on Brogan's, it calmly slid the knife across her throat.

• Whispers at the Altar •

A compulsive swallow threatened to choke Brogan as he watched the girl's blood sluice down over her convulsing body.

The snake made a hoarse sound, half scream half hiss, and threw the knife into the chest of the last living prisoner still on the stage. The man, older even than Brogan, tumbled back over the edge, dead before his body touched the ground.

Brogan ran. All his age and exhaustion vanished in the flood of burning adrenaline. He could see the four former prisoners in front of him. He couldn't help calculating their odds of survival and which might be useful. Old habits died hard, and fear brought them rushing back.

He was halfway to the beach when he heard a slithering chant that ended in a hacking invective. He looked just in time to see the smoke from his globe coalesce into five vipers, each as long as he was tall, which raced toward him. Five steps later they struck him from behind.

Teeth, no less solid for being made of smoke, knifed into his legs and back. Brogan fell, barely keeping the presence of mind to collapse off the side of the pier, out of sight of the snake who was no doubt still following him. He clawed frantically at the vipers, but his hands just passed through trailing wisps of black smoke behind them.

Acidic venom pumped into his blood, burning his flesh from the inside.

A pile of ruined chairs lay against the wall. Some carpenter's rejects waiting to be recycled into something new. Steven took a deep breath and lunged for them. The furniture shifted and slid under him. He couldn't get a firm footing.

"Ha! Come on down, boy." His predicament was obvious, and the guards closed the remaining distance with grim smiles.

"There's no way to run. Just come on down, and we'll go easy on you. Mayhap the priest will only slice off your hands."

Steven's left foot slipped, dropping him down across the leg of another chair. The air burst from his lungs with a hollow gasp, and his vision darkened for a moment.

"Better climb down."

"You'll break something."

The guards were on him now, and their hands grasped at his feet. Something Brogan said echoed in Steven's mind, and he stopped fighting.

The guards pulled him to the ground in a crash of wooden furniture. Steven screamed and wrapped one hand around his ankle as he writhed on the ground.

"You broke it! You broke my ankle. You thugs. You sons of dung beetles." Steven tried to think of all the horrible insults he could.

"Now look here, boy. We warned you not to climb that."

One guard came close to grab his shoulder. Steven waited a half-beat more, then swung with the broken table leg he'd brought down with him.

The blow connected with the guard's face, throwing him back a step. Steven didn't wait around to see if it drew blood. He was up on his feet and pumping them as fast as he could.

Never trust an obvious weakness.

"Hey! Come back."

The second guard was chasing again, but he was a few steps too slow.

If Steven could summon even a shred of luck, the gate would be open, and he could make it out into the open plain. He doubted the lone guard would follow him much farther after that.

As he turned back onto the main street Steven could hear shouting coming from behind. The distraction had worked. He only hoped Brogan was having an easier time escaping than he was.

The guardhouse was ahead, and the gate was open. Finally, some good luck. Then two more guards walked out to block the gate. Of course.

Roaches! There was no turning back now, no other way to run. No wonder the lone guard had lagged behind. He knew Steven was running into a trap. Steven searched frantically for some escape. Anything. What he found wasn't ideal, but it was all he had.

With a deft spin he cut to his right, inches from the swing of a guard's sword. Steven took the stairs two at a time, climbing to the top of the wall. The high ring of a sword rang off the step his foot just left. Steven didn't pause even as he reached the top.

Step. Step. And jump.

It wasn't until Steven was at the peak of his leap that he realized just how far down he had to go. Up to now fear had been overcome by the need of the moment. Now it seemed he had an eternity to think about it as his stomach rose into his throat.

Steven tried to roll, or some approximation of it. It wasn't like he had any experience with death defying leaps. His feet hit the ground first with a snap he both heard and felt reverberate up his right leg. Then his back, followed by an ear-shattering crack like the ground itself opening under him. The rest was a jumble of dirt, gravel, and grass before he finally came to a stop some fifteen feet from the wall.

He knew the guards would be running after him. But he was terrified to move. His back felt like it was on fire, and his leg was screaming. Still, he couldn't just lie there and wait for them to skewer him.

He coughed and tried his leg first. His knee bent. But his ankle felt as though a knife had been jabbed through the joint.

He coughed again and waved at the smoke. Then realization hit him and he rolled over, tearing the burning pack off his back. One of Brogan's blinding stones must have ignited the last of the powder, and the rest of his clothes. Which in turn made the cloud of smoke obscuring him from the guards.

But not for long. An arrow sliced into the ground three inches from his hand as if to accentuate this point. Steven saw a small gully a few feet to his right and half crawled half dragged himself to it. He rolled in, biting his lip to suppress a scream as his ankle jostled off rocks and tufts of weed.

Great. At least he was out of the town. Hopefully they would be too absorbed with the fire to worry about chasing him over the countryside. Now all he had to do was find Brogan.

Brogan clenched his teeth against the pain. He tried rolling on the ground, but as quickly as they disappeared, the smoke-snakes reformed. An idea pierced the fog of agony, and he aimed his roll for the lake. He felt the cool splash of water just as he glimpsed the snake standing on the pier.

He first felt, then saw, the vipers dissipate into the lake, the magic unable to maintain their essence against the diluting pull of the water. As they faded, the pain subsided enough to let him swim. He was just about to struggle to the surface when he saw the snake through the ripple of the dark water.

A column of swirling shadow shot from the thing's hands, skimming off the waves. Where it touched, cold followed, and the surface froze in a sheet of black ice. Another bolt followed, and another, slowly turning the lake into a reflection of midnight.

Brogan swam toward where he hoped the wall ended, praying he could find some cover before his breath ran out. Darkness inched in around the edges of his vision. His blood pounded in his head.

Finally, he saw the vague outline of a ship's hull. If he could make it to the other side . . . He could barely remember why he needed to. Every thought strained to just keep swimming.

He broke the surface with a gasp followed closely by another as his lungs tried to make up for lost time in their love affair with sweet wonderful air. It was a full minute before he even thought to look for the snake. And another before it occurred to him to find the captives he'd freed.

He found no sign of the first, though the pier was blocked by the fishing boat he hid behind. But he did see a body, encased in black ice like a cruel coffin. It bobbed in the water, crunching occasionally against the streaks of frozen water left behind by the snake's barrage. That made three escapees.

There was a burst of water beside him, and Brogan threw himself back against the hull of the boat. Two heads splashed up, gasping for air much as he must have done only moments ago. A young man, perhaps in his middle thirties and a teenage girl stared at him with hollow eyes. They said nothing, but Brogan understood. That made two.

He nodded, then pointed to the same corner of wall he had rounded with Steven. He could only hope the fire held the villagers' attention long enough. And that Steven had made it out. *Please, Maker, let him have made it out.*

Steven didn't know if it was luck finally showing him some favor, the grace of the Maker, or stupidity on the part of the guards, but he managed to hobble and crawl a quarter mile down the length of the hollow with no pursuit. When he was finally certain none was forthcoming, he took the time to gather a branch large enough to fashion a splint and another to lean on. It was with these that he finally limped into Brogan's camp after nightfall.

"It's about time you showed up," the old man grumbled. "What'd you do? Get lost?"

He was crouched on a log while a young girl dabbed something green onto his back. A large man sat nearby using Brogan's knife to sharpen the end of a long branch.

"Nah. Just stopped to do a little sightseeing." He eased himself down on a rock.

The camp hadn't been as hard to find as Steven first thought. There was only one direction that was safe now. South. And though Brogan had lit no fire, he had left signs should Steven pass by. Small groupings of twigs or rocks, easy to miss unless you knew what to look for.

"What happened to you?" Steven indicated the angry looking punctures on Brogan's back.

"Porcu . . . pine." Brogan winced as the girl covered another hole with the goo.

"Your father risked his life to save us," the man said. "Earned the wrath of the Seer-spawn."

"He's not . . ." Steven started to protest but thought better. If Brogan wasn't his father, then who? He couldn't think of anyone he'd rather have.

"He told us of your part as well," the man went on. "You have our thanks. My name is Hareb. This is my daughter, Honovi."

Steven's stomach sank. His part? His fear would have seen them both dead on that platform.

Honovi nodded in his direction, and Steven thought he caught a glimpse of a smile, one that he returned through the guilt. Even covered in dirt and grime from her imprisonment and escape she was the prettiest girl he'd ever seen. Though the tattered state of her dress made him look away quickly, trying to keep the blood from his face. Of course, now that he noticed, his own clothing situation wasn't much better.

"Our people are . . . were from a village to the east and south," he continued, pointing with Brogan's knife in the indicated direction.

"It seems their village was attacked," Brogan said, thanking Honovi as she finished and then turning to face Steven and Hareb. She said something too soft to hear and handed Brogan the bowl of goop.

"Apparently they refused to join the 'Chosen,' and our friends in Ceerport didn't take that well." Brogan swiped a finger through the goop and licked it clean.

Steven blanched.

"They came in the night," Hareb confirmed. "There was a fog, the magic of the Seer-spawn. They killed most of my people. I was returning for my son and daughter when the spawn took us."

Steven remembered the strong young man on the platform. A man that looked remarkably like Hareb now that Steven made the connection. Quickly, he searched for another direction in the conversation.

"You call the snake-thing a . . . Seer-spawn. Do you know of them? Have you seen them recently?" Honovi bent down to hand him a bowl of green paste. Steven started to say thank you, then completely lost the words in her deep brown eyes. She smiled, and before he knew it the moment passed. She turned away. He looked back to Hareb to find the man glowering at him. Steven felt the blood rush to his face and immediately looked down at his ankle.

There was a long moment before Hareb answered. "They are a part of our legends. They serve Ssanek, the Winged Serpent, the Great Deceiver. A god from the ancient times. When these people came to our village preaching their lies, we saw them for who they really were. So we refused them. We should have known what would come."

Steven furrowed his brow. "Do all the people to the south know these legends?"

Hareb shrugged. "All that I have met. But I cannot speak for everyone."

Steven gave Brogan a knowing look. "So where are we going?"

Brogan ate another fingerful of goo and sighed. "We can't go home, as you well know. The townsfolk will have seen us, and they know near enough where we live. Hareb has told me he knows of a place where the survivors of his people would have gone. He has invited us."

Steven glanced at Hareb then at Honovi. She had her back to him as she scooped more of the paste into a bowl for herself. Her black

Allan C.R. Cornelius

hair hung in a curtain down her back, reflecting the starlight like bits of glass.

He suddenly felt the weight of Brogan and Hareb's eyes on him and cleared his throat. "Yes. I think that would be an excellent idea." He swiped a finger through the goo and without thinking popped it into his mouth. It tasted like pond scum.

SSANEK

Christa jumped as a pile of books dropped onto the table next to her. She looked up, ready with a scathing glare that died as she saw Sinna's smiling face.

"You nearly scared me to death," Christa whispered. "Didn't anyone ever tell you to be quiet in a library?"

"Or that you should only bring the books you actually need?" Vaniel added from across the table as she eyed the pile.

Sinna grinned. "Well as it turned out, I *do* need all of these," she answered as she sat in the nearest chair and began arranging the books around her. "What were you so absorbed in, Christa?"

Christa usually loved watching Sinna set up for their study sessions. Each book and sheaf of parchment had to have its own place, and that place couldn't change between sessions. Ordinarily Christa would move things when Sinna wasn't paying attention, just to tease her, but she wasn't in the mood today.

"Oh, just studying for Human History." Christa pushed the book away from her on the table.

"Are you in that class already? Didn't you just test for Third Tier?"

Vaniel shook her head. "No, that was six months ago."

"Right. How silly of me. A whole six months." Sinna chuckled and flipped her last book open to the proper page. "Never mind that you have covered nearly thirteen years of training in two and a half."

Christa leaned down to see Sinna's eyes. Was she jealous? "I'm sorry. It just comes easy for me. I don't know why."

Sinna pished and gave a smile that didn't quite touch her eyes. "Don't apologize for being brilliant." She poked Christa in the ribs.

"Yes," Vaniel said with a smile. "It makes one sound arrogant."

"Well, don't make me feel guilty for it," Christa said through a giggle.

"Would you like some help?" Sinna picked up Christa's book and flipped through it.

"I guess. It's not very hard. It's just . . ."

Sinna looked up from the book. "What?"

Christa shrugged. "It's wrong. It's the history of an entire race from the perspective of someone who isn't one."

"Well, I'm sure whoever wrote it did their best to be accurate. She was a scholar after all." Sinna flipped the pages, probably searching for the author.

"It doesn't matter how accurate she tried to be. She isn't human. She doesn't really know what happened, or why. Or how they think."

Sinna nodded, but Christa didn't think she really understood. How could she? It wasn't like there were humans trying to write histories of the elven people.

"Well here's a question . . ." She gave Christa a level look. "Now don't think just because I've already taken the test that I'm only going to ask you those questions."

Christa laughed. She couldn't fathom Sinna trying to cheat at anything.

"What was the cause and result of the human eastward migrations?"

"According to the apparent expert, the humans periodically migrated east due to increasing tribal conflict and overcrowding to the west. The result being increased contact and conflict with the elves. In effect they were just bouncing back and forth from one threat to the next."

"That's close enough. Now let's see . . ."

"Although how she could know what was happening in the far west is unclear. She never cites any sources. They could just have easily been enacting a religious rite. Or following food sources. Or even fleeing some threat we don't know of."

Vaniel set her book down. "That is true. But some of those could be refuted by how regular the migrations were. I mean, every six hundred years?"

Sinna nodded. "Do the humans even track things over that length of time? Do they have books?"

Christa took a deep breath and exhaled slowly. It wasn't Sinna's fault. She just honestly didn't know humans. "Yes. We do track things over that length of time. We've had writing. And books. Not as long as the elves, obviously, but definitely for centuries."

Sinna glanced at Vaniel, impressed. "I had no idea."

Vaniel just shrugged and went back to her studying.

"Exactly," Christa continued, "And how could you, with drivel like this being taught."

"But you can't say it's *all* wrong. I mean, we know they killed a lot of the first elves who tried to deal with them."

"But we don't know why, do we?"

Sinna flipped through the books then pointed to one page and read. "'They were aggressive, unwilling to listen to reason. We tried to share our knowledge and our faith but they would have neither.' That's right from someone who was there."

Christa scoffed. "But why were they so aggressive? Maybe they just wanted to be left alone. Maybe they just didn't like some strange people coming in and telling them what to believe or how to behave."

"So they killed them?" Sinna shook her head. "I don't care how you try to justify it. That isn't right."

Sinna might be right. But Christa wasn't willing to accept it out of hand. She wished she could see what had really happened. She just didn't feel she could trust anything an Elven historian told her about her own people. Besides. She could think of some reasons that might perfectly justify killing those elves. To her at least. She wasn't sure things were always so black and white as Sinna thought.

Sinna flipped to one of the first sections of the book. One Christa barely remembered. "Here's another question. Name the five most prominent human deities."

Christa rolled her eyes. "No one worships those any more. I'd never even heard of them."

"Humor me." Sinna gave another wide smile and Christa couldn't help but comply.

"Ancient humans worshiped a series of deities who each took on one of five mostly opposed aspects. Day, Night, Creation, Destruction, and Balance. None were considered evil per se. Life needs all five to continue. But there was a cult of Ssanek, the god of night, which grew particularly powerful. They believed they had summoned Ssanek and that he spoke to them in their dreams. He was said to make deals. To provide some service in exchange for payment. Anything from money or jewelry to living sacrifices."

Christa paused. He made *deals*.

"Keep going," Sinna encouraged. "So, what happened to this cult?"

"Oh." Christa shrugged. "No one knows. The book says they killed each other in a series of power grabs. But again there's no reference given."

Sinna continued to ask questions, but Christa's mind wasn't on them. She kept coming back to the same thought. What if—and she realized it was a large *if*—Ssanek was real? What if she could make a deal with him? He was a god, right? And she was half human, she must have some kind of tie to him if he did exist. And if he did . . .

Sure, there was a price, but she could always say no if it was too high, right? It wasn't like she wanted to kill anyone.

This way, no one had to know. She didn't need anyone else's help, and no one would get hurt. By slow increments Christa allowed herself to begin to hope.

Maybe, just maybe, the Creator wasn't the only one capable of bringing Mama back.

Christa kicked her door open, shuffled inside, and dumped the armful of books and parchments on the bed. She'd spent the rest of the evening after Sinna left scouring the stacks of the library for anything on Ssanek. There wasn't much. But she did find an account written by an elf who had allegedly viewed one of their rituals.

She didn't have all the things they did, but she thought she might be able to make something that would be close enough to work. She had to try.

Shuffling through the books she pulled out one with a page marked. This she took over to her desk, laying it flat before retrieving a piece of parchment. The marked page held a drawing of the ritual. Men and women with their arms raised around a pole of some kind. The pole was covered in gold except for the top where a carving of a winged serpent painted black sat.

There was a man at the base, slitting the throat of another man and letting the blood run down the pole to soak the ground beneath it. Christa was certain this was just more elven propaganda. They always portrayed humans as savages. In fact she had yet to read anything about them that didn't include some reference to human sacrifice. And this picture was so overly graphic it strained credulity to the breaking point.

Christa didn't have a totem pole. She drummed her fingers on the page. Perhaps it was only the image that was important. Perhaps if she drew it, larger than what was already in the illustration, that might serve the same purpose. She retrieved a clean sheet of paper and, ignoring the pole itself as likely being immaterial, focused on the image atop it. Christa was no artist, but when she was done she had a reasonable depiction.

She smiled, closed the book, and put it far under her bed. She wasn't sure Sinna would understand after their conversation today. She was just too . . . biased by what she'd been taught. Christa put away the rest of the books on her bed, then stood there in the middle of the room staring at the picture she'd drawn. On second viewing it really did seem pretty good. She was impressed with some of the detail she'd managed to work in. Especially around the eyes.

Christa put the picture down on the floor and took a deep breath. She felt ridiculous for doing this, but she only had the one account to go on and this was in it. Taking a deep breath she began to side-step in a circle around the picture, periodically raising her hands as she did.

There was nothing in the brief account of what the humans were saying, but the elf probably wouldn't have understood it anyway. After one circuit around, she decided maybe she should just state her request. After all, if he wanted to make a deal, he probably wanted to know what she wanted.

"Oh Ssanek," she whispered, feeling even more ridiculous, "I ask that you bring my mother back. I ask that you talk to me so I might know what you want for this service." She finished her second circle then wondered if she was supposed to circle a specific number of times. Most of this was pure guesswork. She decided to make one more circle, repeating her request. Any more than that would just feel too awkward.

As she shuffled around the third time she kept her eyes on the picture. She really was a better artist than she thought. She could swear the serpent's eyes were watching her as she circled.

The third circuit ended rather anti-climatically. No puff of smoke or voice from beyond. Just an uncomfortable silence. Christa sighed, then picked up the paper. She wasn't sure what she'd expected. She crumpled the paper, dropped it into the basket, and got ready for bed. She was grasping at straws. Ancient deities? Really?

Maybe Silvana was right. Maybe she should just let it all go. Only, she didn't see how she could. What would that say about her? If she just accepted what she had done. Wouldn't that make her the monster part of her was certain she was?

When she finally fell asleep, it was with the most vivid memories of Mama she'd had in years.

Christa didn't know this place. It was dark. Not just because of the blackened and blasted rocky landscape. Not only because of the low threatening storm clouds. It was as if the very air were made of shadow. As if someone had taken the umbra of twilight and given it substance and form.

She was standing on a hill, that much she knew, but fog shrouded its base and anything else that might serve as a landmark to give her direction. So she stood there, turning in circles as she peered out into the black.

"Hello?" The sound was consumed by the dark. "Hello?"

She thought she heard a reply. A low rumble like rocks breaking.

"Where are you?" It was impossible to tell. The sound echoed all around her. "Who are you?"

"You called to me," the distant voice growled. "Yet you claim not to know me?" It sounded amused, like the lion talking to mouse under its paw.

Christa swallowed. "S-Ssanek?"

"I cannot see you well. The ritual was incomplete." There was a noise of movement from the fog, as though a large mass were drawing closer, crushing and tumbling boulders as it went.

"I . . . I did my best." She tried to clasp her hands to stop their fidgeting, but it was like they had a mind of their own, always returning to her skirt to clench, finger, and tease the fabric.

There was no response.

"I want to make a deal. That is what you do isn't it? Grant wishes?"

"I am no wishing well!" The voice was much closer now, as if it were right beside her ear. But she still couldn't tell where it came from. "What is your desire, child?" It was faint now. She had to strain to make it out.

"I want my mama back. She died. I want you to bring her back." Christa's courage increased as she remembered she did indeed have a purpose here. She would not let Mama down. "Can you do that?"

"Certainly," the voice purred from everywhere. "But all things have a cost. Surely you know this, young one."

"What do you want?"

Again the rumbling chuckle rolled across her, echoing in her chest. "Your ritual is too weak. First, you must conduct a proper ritual."

"Tell me what to do. What do I need?"

"Blood, child," the voice rumbled, but it was no longer amused. "Dear, sweet, blood."

Whispers at the Altar

She woke with a start, the words still echoing in her mind as her heart pounded in her chest.

She closed her eyes, but the swirls of mist and shadow hovered behind them. Jerking away the covers she crossed the room to the basket. The paper was gone, replaced by a pile of still smoking ashes.

Pits, she cursed, then immediately thought better of it. What had she done? Had it actually worked? She knelt to touch the ashes, needing to know for certain they were real.

He hadn't said no, this Ssanek. In fact he had said he could do it. She jumped up, spinning around with joy. He could do it! And all it would take was blood.

She scrambled under her bed for the book and flipped it back open to the illustration. Obviously not human blood like in the picture, that was preposterous. Plenty of religions used animal blood in their rituals. There was nothing evil about that. In fact the harvest festival back home had involved the killing of a goat. And even Mama had gone to that.

She would need to do it properly, though. She would need a real totem. And that would take time. But it didn't matter.

He would make all her dreams come true.

Honovi

Even with his ankle splinted and wrapped in every scrap of spare cloth they could spare, the pain was still the worst thing Steven could imagine. Of course walking on it for miles at a time wasn't helping. At least the pain kept his mind off everything else. Most of the time.

Not in the morning when the camp was quiet and the dreams of hissing snake men and desiccated corpses were still fresh in his mind. And certainly not in the evening when they all sat around a silent campfire remembering homes that would never be again. But during the day, as they trudged through hills covered with brown grass, the pain was enough to keep any other thoughts at bay.

Which was a good thing. Because it was at those times when the thought most pressing on his mind was Honovi. He was acutely aware of where she was at all times, though he tried not to look. He'd made that mistake already. She'd caught him staring their first day, and he'd spent the rest of it walking next to Hareb.

Now, on their second day, he was trying to keep his eyes focused straight ahead and push any thoughts of Honovi's tanned shoulders, or long shining black hair, or swaying . . . He let the pain of his leg flash the image from his mind.

He couldn't understand why she kept intruding in his thoughts like this. It didn't even matter if she was behind him. The urge to turn and look at her would itch at the back of his mind like a heavenly mosquito bite, persistent and full of sweet promises. It made no sense. He didn't even know her. What if she was one of them?

It was maddening. But there was something about her. Something quiet and mysterious. He rarely heard her speak, and catching her gaze was like snatching motes out of a beam of sunshine. And when he did, he hadn't the slightest idea what to do with it.

"How's the ankle?" Brogan asked from beside him. He'd barely left Steven's side since they'd started. He even fashioned the crutch Steven was using and found the bark he was chewing to relieve the pain.

"It's fine." The wince as a jolt of pain shot up his leg betrayed his answer. He didn't want Brogan to worry. He had enough worrying him already.

"So I can see." Brogan was quiet a moment. "Have you tried talking to her?"

Steven stumbled, eliciting a sharp high-pitched gasp. "What?"

"Talking. You know, that thing people do when they want to get to know each other? It might be more productive than staring at her or ignoring her." He shrugged. "Just a thought."

Steven waited a few steps, playing it off as recovering from his stumble when really he was trying to fit the thoughts shooting around his head into actual words. "I . . . I wouldn't know what to say. I mean, she's lost everything. Her home . . . her mother. Besides. I doubt she wants to talk to me."

Brogan grunted. "You're probably right. I mean, it isn't like you would have anything in common to talk about."

"But I . . ." Steven fumbled with words.

•Whispers at the Altar•

"I understand, of course," Brogan patted him on the shoulder. "She is intimidating. I mean, she's got to be over a hundred pounds at least. And look at those eyes . . ."

Steven turned around before he could catch himself.

Honovi was walking about ten paces behind with her father. Steven's gaze locked with hers. She smiled and reached up to brush a lock of hair over her shoulder.

Steven raised his non-crutch hand in an awkward wave, as if they hadn't been traveling together for the better part of two days already. Her face brightened, and she gave a little wave back.

Then Steven saw Hareb's stern face and all the blood that had been rushing to his head and pounding in his brain fled. He turned back as quick as he could and set as fast a pace as he could manage.

"I don't think her father likes the idea as much as you do," he mumbled.

Brogan chuckled. "He likes you well enough. But I think at the moment he's torn. She's all he has left. I don't think he fancies the idea of her leaving any time soon."

"Leaving? Where would she be going?"

Brogan stopped and stared up at Steven.

Steven stopped. "What?"

"Regardless . . ." Brogan shook his head as he started off again. "Having a conversation with her isn't going to bring down the fiery wrath of her father. And it might be good for both of you, no matter what urges you might be battling."

"I'm not 'battling urges.'" Steven resisted the urge to look back at her again.

"Right. Just make sure it stays that way for now. I won't have you taking advantage of her."

"Take adv—" Steven blustered. "I just want to talk to her. Not . . ." His mouth moved but no words came out. "I would never do that."

Brogan chuckled and reached up to lay a hand on Steven's shoulder. "You're a good lad. I know you wouldn't hurt her on purpose.

But youth has a way of making us see things backward. We might think we're just being nice, helping them talk about the pain they're feeling. But really we want to expose their vulnerability. Then come in as a savior and reap the rewards."

Brogan's eyes gazed past him and Steven got the impression he was no longer talking about him. "I'll be careful."

"I know you will." Brogan said as he blinked back to the present. "And that's all anyone could ask."

By the time they made camp, Steven was sure his foot was three times larger than normal. The bindings felt as though someone were constantly squeezing against the entire bottom half of his leg in an attempt to pop it, like breaking an enormous blister.

When he could sit down and Brogan unwrapped the windings, he was surprised to find nothing of the kind occurring. The ankle was one giant ugly bruised color, along with his foot and a good portion of his calf, but it didn't look in danger of bursting any time soon.

"There is a small river on the other side of this bluff," Hareb said. He crouched down in the grass and began arranging kindling. "It is exposed, but if you are quiet, and carry no light, it should be safe."

Brogan nodded. "An excellent idea. I'll fetch some. A soak would do you well, Steven."

"No." Steven sat up. "I'll go." He didn't want to think of Brogan lugging water all that way. Just so he could be more comfortable.

"You can't fetch water," Brogan said with a laugh.

"No, I mean I'll go and soak it there. I don't want to be a bother. And I could use a good wash."

"You won't get any argument from me about that," Brogan said. "All right. Just be careful. We'll come get you when there's food to eat."

•Whispers at the Altar•

Steven sighed with relief and propped himself up on his crutch. It was going to be slow going. He didn't want to take the time to re-bandage his foot just to take it all off again. "I'll be fine," he reassured Brogan. He hobbled off as Hareb got the fire going, and in a few minutes the edge of the bluff blocked the light, and he was alone.

It didn't take long to reach the river, though it barely deserved the name. At about four paces across and five span down to its rocky bed, Steven would have called it a creek at best. But it was enough.

He was immediately glad he'd come. With the hill to his back, the land spread out and down before him in a wide valley glistening in the light of the stars. Even without the moon's light to help, he could still make out a ridgeline at the far end of the valley. Dark shapes rose to blot out the horizon.

He stood at the edge of the water, debating. It was dark, but he was awfully exposed here. Finally, he eased himself down to the ground before carefully removing what remained of his trousers. If the Servants of Ssanek found him while he was taking a bath, then that was just bad luck. At least he'd be content when he died.

Stripped down to his skivvies, he slid his good foot into the water. He let out a long breath and closed his eyes as he eased down into the exquisitely cool water. He had to lie down completely along the shore. The water lapped against his chest as he let his injured leg float with the gentle but insistent current.

Settled in, he opened his eyes and stared up at the cloud of stars above him. He could see her face there in those stars. Without even trying. Why was that? Why did she constantly hover on the edge of his mind, ready to pounce to the forefront whenever there was a still moment?

She was beautiful. But logically, what did he have to compare her against? Logically, he knew she was the first girl his age he had ever been around. So of course he couldn't stop thinking about her. He certainly didn't love her. He didn't even know her. That was it, then. His body and his . . . inexperience were getting the best of him.

But knowing that didn't give him any more strength to push her image from his mind's eye. Or the willpower to stop wondering what it would feel like to touch her hand. Just the thought of it made his heart beat faster. But it wasn't going to happen. He couldn't even work up the courage to talk to her. The very idea of it made his stomach twist. So he lay there, letting his mind wander through scenarios that would never come true.

"Is the water cold?"

Steven jumped, thrashing in the water to catch his balance and striking his ankle on one of the many rocks in the bed. He cried out, a shout of pain cut short to a tight-lipped whimper as he saw Honovi standing over him not a pace away.

"I'm so sorry. I didn't mean to scare you." Eyes wide, she knelt to help.

"It's . . . fine." Steven raised a hand as he scooted back and further into the water, now very aware of just how little he was wearing.

Warded away, Honovi instead sat down on the bank. She took a deep breath and stared into the river, her eyes glinting in its reflected starlight.

Steven wanted to say something. Something clever and yet comforting. Something witty. He tried to think of what Brogan might say, then immediately disregarded the idea. The silence stretched on as he thought.

"Did you . . . come for water?" he finally sputtered, gesturing to the waterskin lying beside her.

She glanced down and nodded. "Why did you save us?" She looked directly at him and the gaze pierced through him.

He mouthed several failed responses then looked into the stars swimming in the water. He couldn't meet those eyes. And he couldn't tell her the truth. "I . . . I couldn't let them kill you."

"But you could have died. Your father could have died. Why risk everything for strangers?" She shifted, sitting cross-legged on the bank as she stared at him.

"It just seemed like the right thing to do."

She shook her head. "That is the flowers. What swims beneath?"

Steven squinted. "I don't understand."

"Your answer. It is like the flowers that float on top of the pond. Pretty, but not what the pond is."

"You think I'm lying?" Could she tell?

Honovi only shrugged. "Perhaps. Perhaps you are lying to yourself. You say what anyone would say. Maybe it is the first thing that comes to mind. But is there nothing deeper?"

Steven blinked. What other reason could he give her? That really he had wanted to run away and never look back? An image flashed before his mind. Mother, her scarlet hair spilling onto the ground, mixing with the blood until there was no telling one from the other.

"They took someone from me once. My mother." He picked a smooth stone from the riverbed and turned it over in his hands. "I guess I couldn't let them do that to someone else . . ." It had the advantage of truth, and he could almost convince himself that he would have used that reason, had he possessed the courage to act at all. "Not that I succeeded, I guess. I mean, your brother still—"

"You saved my father for me. And me for him. One life's worth is uncountable. You saved two." She reached far forward to lay a hand on his arm. "It is more than enough."

Her touch sent tingles through his body.

She straightened, and her hand rested on the waterskins as she stood.

"Honovi," Steven almost shouted. Now that she was here, he couldn't bear the thought of her leaving. He searched his mind franticly for anything to talk about. "Tell me about your people."

Her head tilted. "Here? Would you not rather listen from in front of the fire? My father can tell the stories of my people far better . . ."

"No, I . . ." He turned the stone over and over in his hand. "I need to let my ankle soak a bit more. I'd . . . I'd like the company—your company."

She settled back down, her eyes never leaving his. Her gaze was curious and amused and veiled all at once. "What would you have me tell you?"

He hadn't thought this far ahead, of course. He cleared his throat to give himself a second to think. "Tell me about your people. I mean, I'm going to be living with them, and I don't know anything about them except for a few bits Brogan taught me and what your father mentioned two nights ago."

She leaned forward, resting her elbows on her thighs and clasping her hands in front of her. "What do you know already?"

"I know that you are of the Yahad. One of three major nations that dominate the southern plains. I know that you used to be nomads, horse people, who—" He cut off as she frowned. "D-did I say something wrong? I'm sorry, I—"

"Horse-people. It is . . . an insult," she said. "It means we are animals."

"Oh. I'm sorry." He said tentatively. "You see what I mean. I would hate to make that mistake with someone who wasn't a friend."

Honovi laughed, a light happy sound that lifted Steven's heart. "Yes. You obviously have much to learn." Even after the laughter faded, the smile remained, lighting up her eyes with more than starlight.

"There are too many stories to tell, and I do not know them all, but I will try to tell you what you must know. We," she motioned to herself and vaguely in the direction of her father, "are Yahad. But the elders tell us there was a time, long ago, when we were all one people. We traveled where we wanted and did trade with the great dark men in the east and the villages to the north.

"Then the Servants of Ssanek came. The giant lizard-soldiers and the snake-like Seers with their dark magics. They clouded minds and twisted hearts. Many of the people turned to their lies."

Steven was leaning forward now, the stone in his hand forgotten. "What lies did they tell?"

"It is said they could give people what they wanted. The love of another, wealth, power . . . But always at great cost. And never in the way the person really wanted. Ssanek is the Great Deceiver, and though his lies may look beautiful they are still lies.

Whispers at the Altar

"So many were tempted and eventually turned upon those who were not. We were divided. Brother against brother. There was war."

"Of course," she shook her head as she frowned, "I would not have believed any of it before now. I did not believe *any* of the old stories. I thought they were . . . just stories.

"The war was long and hard. They say even the north-men fought on one side or the other. Many died. In the end, the followers of Ssanek were defeated, but we were no longer one people. There was too much suspicion. Too much anger. The Makau chose to live apart. On the other side of the great swamp. We, the Yahad, and our cousins, the Chota, divided what was left of our old land. The Chota chose to live closer to the fierce men of the east, while we chose to live here, closer to the Chisarans who had ever been kind to us."

Steven watched her as she spoke, enthralled by the movement of her lips and the song-like tone of her voice. He tried to memorize her face, every curve and line, and more than once he had to force himself to listen to the actual words she was saying.

"The Shona divides us. The great river that flows down from the mountains." She pointed off toward the ridge Steven spotted earlier. "It is to the source of the Shona that we are traveling. She is the life giver to both Yahad and Chota." Honovi's eyes twinkled. "She is bathing you even now."

Steven almost jumped out before he realized what Honovi meant.

She giggled. "That is why my people will go there. It is a sacred and safe place for us. And for the Chota. A meeting place in troubled times, though it has not been used for many years."

She was silent for a long moment, and Steven had time to realize just how cold he was getting. He glanced from his clothes lying on the bank, to Honovi. As much as he didn't want the moment to end, he was afraid if he stayed in the water much longer he might freeze.

"Um. Honovi. I'm going to get out of the water now. Would you mind . . ."

Allan C.R. Cornelius

She stood, brushing off her torn and muddied skirt. "Of course."
She stood, picked up his clothes, and held them out to him.

Steven could feel his face getting hotter even as the rest of him
shivered. "Um. Thank you." He reached up to take them, taking care
to keep them up out of the water. "Ahh, you can go ahead and fill the
waterskins. I'll meet you back at the camp."

She raised her eyebrows. "Do you wish me to help you back to
the camp? Or . . ."

Steven stopped listening after the first question. The thought of
Honovi's arm around him, helping him back to the camp made his
heart thump. He wanted so badly to say yes. But the very intensity
of that desire frightened him.

"No," he said, perhaps a bit louder than he should have. "I can manage."

Honovi nodded once and bent down to pick up the skins. She
paused, and half turned just as Steven was starting to stand. "It was
good to talk to you."

Steven watched her every movement. "It was nice. Thank you for
sitting with me."

She gave one more smile and walked slowly upriver.

Steven's gaze followed until the darkness swallowed her up. And
it had nothing to do with the hypnotic way she moved.

The others were nearly finished eating by the time he made it back
to camp, but Steven didn't mind. He would trade that bath for a week
of cold meals. Two weeks. He tried to catch Honovi's eye as he eased
himself down beside the fire, but she was gathering up the scraps and
leftovers to bury. Instead he caught Hareb's.

"Do all Chisarans take such long baths?" he asked gruffly.

Steven swallowed. "I don't know. I'm not even sure if I'm Chisaran."

Hareb narrowed his eyes, leaning forward to poke the fire. "It is
important to know who you are." He glanced over to Brogan who was
busy mixing up another batch of his back-goop. "But discoveries can
sometimes come suddenly. And through unexpected circumstances."

214

Whispers at the Altar

He fixed Steven once again with those dark eyes, lifting the branch to point at him with its still glowing end. "But be careful. Any discovery should be investigated slowly. And with *great* care."

Steven could only swallow his cold rabbit and nod, noting the man's arms that Steven was certain could snap him in half like a twig.

Lessons

"Forgive me, Christabel, is General Rissian's victory at the battle of Arithia boring you?"

Blinking back to reality, Christa found every eye in the class, including those of Instructor Ophidian, gazing at her. More than a few were happy to see her get into trouble again. Only Sinna, sitting beside her, showed any sign of sympathy.

Christa desperately tried to remember what he'd been talking about. "Umm, no, sir."

"Really?" Ophidian sneered. "The vacant expression on your face suggested otherwise. Or perhaps you simply cannot be bothered to learn what I have to teach you." He walked across the semicircle of desks to stand before hers. His cold eyes squinted down. "Since this is the third time today I have called your attention back to this classroom, perhaps you would care to tell us what is so much more deserving of your attention?"

Christa looked into those eyes and wished for the hundredth time Marellel had not put her in this class. *Elementary Tactics and Strategy.* She had no idea what the director was thinking. Why would she ever need to know any of this? "I . . . nothing is," she lied.

Turning on his heels, he strode to the large circular table in the middle of the room. With a wave of his hand, a rainbow of translucent flames leapt from the surface of the table. Moments later they settled into the image of a rocky landscape, peppered with illusory forests. The shadows of nonexistent clouds crept over while, beneath them, two armies sprang from the rocks like fields of wildflowers. Spears rose to the sky in thorny thickets while miniature horses stomped and pawed at the ground.

Instructor Ophidian continued his walk to the front of the classroom, turned, and motioned with one hand to the table. "Then please, Christabel. Show us how you would have improved upon General Rissian's battle plans."

Christa looked to Sinna for help, but her friend had no more idea what he expected than she did. She made her way around her desk and into the empty space surrounding the miniature battlefield. She stopped at the edge of the table and clasped her hands behind her back to keep them from fidgeting. She could feel the blood rushing to her face as twenty pairs of eyes focused on her. This was all Marellel's fault, she thought as she tried to recall anything from the lecture to help her.

She remembered something about a trade dispute and a show of force, but she couldn't recall any details. Taking in the forces arrayed on the table, she wondered what she was supposed to prove. The elves outnumbered their foe two-to-one, how hard could their victory have been? She glanced to Ophidian who watched her expectantly, a small unfriendly smile on his face.

The expression sparked something deep in her chest. She would not give him the satisfaction he wanted. She returned her attention

Whispers at the Altar

to the table and squinted at the battlefield. It didn't take long to strike upon an idea.

"I can't say what General Rissian might have done better, but it's obvious how the dwarves could have survived." She risked a peek up and found his expression aghast, just as she had hoped.

"You think you could have defeated him, girl?" he asked, his tongue dripping with sarcasm. "By all means, show us." He made another quick motion with one hand and the forces arrayed against Christa began to move. Formations of elves churned forward in a slow march toward the lines of heavily armored dwarves opposite them.

Christa waited until the elves marched at full pace, cavalry readied in neat rows with infantry arrayed behind them. Archers climbed the nearest hills, ready to catch the center of the dwarven line in a crossfire of arrows.

"Withdraw," she whispered.

The neat formations of dwarves turned and hurried toward their edge of the table, drawing the elven cavalry after as they hurried to catch up.

"South," she whispered again, and watched as the formations wheeled. The cavalry, seeing the dwarves bunching between their pincers, surged forward.

"Halt. Turtle. Fire." The formations, dense between two tall hills, folded together to present a fortress of shields. Tiny elven arrows ricocheted off the formation, while dozens of knights fell to dwarven crossbows before they could reach the wall of spears and shields before them.

Committed to the charge, most of the cavalry attempted to break through the formation. A few opted to ride around, but found no better reception. Meanwhile, the crowd of crossbowmen shielded in the middle of the formation found them easy targets. By the time the elven infantry caught up, the knights' charge had become a slaughter.

With a final "withdraw," Christa brought the mixed dwarven formation off to their own edge, disappearing beyond it before they could be caught.

"It seems you need this class after all," Instructor Ophidian sneered as the image on the table sank back into its surface.

Christa looked up, confused but defiant. "I said I could help them survive. They did."

"They ran, like cowards. Dwarves would never do this. Their pride would not allow it. Which is exactly why General Rissian defeated them. Know your enemy, girl. It was the entire point of the lesson. You would know that if you had been paying attention. Now sit down."

Christa glared as soft laughter echoed about the room but stalked back to her seat. The spark that rose in her chest at the challenge had grown to a fire at his parting words. It wasn't her fault dwarves didn't have the sense to run. Sometimes you had to know when to give something up.

She spent the rest of the class fuming. But at least she did a better job pretending to listen.

"I thought it was a good idea," Sinna tried to cheer her up as they walked out the door half an hour later.

Christa glared as another girl pushed past her.

"I mean, you should have seen I-Instructor Ophidian's face when you tore apart that cavalry charge."

"Not good enough, apparently."

"Bah. You were going to be wrong no matter what you did. You know that. He wasn't going to let you show him up." She paused at an intersection. "Don't let him get to you."

Christa smiled wanly. "Thanks. I have to get to Instructor Laisel's office for Essence practice."

Sinna shook her head. "You're trying the t-test again, aren't you?"

"Maybe." Christa had been trying to pass the Fourth Tier test every day for a week now. But she wasn't sure she was in the mood after Ophidian.

"Well, good luck," Sinna's disapproval was obvious in her voice. She'd already lectured Christa twice on trying to take things slower. "See you at lunch later?"

Christa nodded and waved as she turned down the hall. She reached Laisel's door as the palace bells marked mid-afternoon. She took a quick moment to catch her breath, tucked some hair back, then knocked twice before entering.

She liked Laisel's office. It was smaller than Marellel's. More cozy. She was particularly fond of the wall of shelves filled with numerous odds and ends. From small statues and portraits to tiny bells and ancient lockets. She kept meaning to come early for a lesson just once so she might get a better look. But being early was not something Christa managed often.

Laisel was sitting at her desk as usual, reading. She put down the book, gave a warm smile, and motioned to the usual spot on the couch. "Good afternoon, Christabel. You are looking well."

Christa sat on the edge of the couch, trying her best to keep her hands still, even as her stomach fluttered inside. Who had she been kidding? Of course she would be taking the test again. What if today was the day?

"What shall we work on today?" Laisel asked. "Breathing? Visualization? Control?"

"I would like to take the Fourth Tier Eyas test, please," Christa stated, just as she had every other day that week.

Laisel sighed and stood to retrieve the tray. "This is *your* practice time, Christabel. I won't tell you how to use it. But insisting on beating your head against a wall that is . . ." She turned with the tray, already arranged with the required items.

Christa grinned. Laisel had known, for all her lecturing.

"I've told you before, Christabel, no one has controlled all four elements within their thirteenth year. Let alone their third. You have a brilliant mind, and it has served you well so far. But this is something else completely. Ability to see and control of the elements is something that takes practice and patience."

She set the tray down on the low table between them. "You don't have to prove yourself to anyone."

But that was just it, and Christa knew it. She might try to tell herself she was just eager to learn more, or that she enjoyed the challenge— and those might be true—but deep down she knew. She *did* have to prove herself. From her first day everyone here looked at her with false pity in their eyes. How could she, a half-human, ever learn what they knew? How could she ever succeed? She'd spent the past three years proving all of them wrong, and she wasn't about to stop now.

"I'm not trying to prove myself. I just want to be the best that I can."

"Perhaps." Laisel didn't appear convinced. "But remember. The people who matter already except you for who you are. Everyone else . . . their minds will never be changed, no matter what you do."

Christa nodded, but only half-listened. She was already looking down at the tray, preparing herself.

"Very well." Laisel cleared her throat and started into the formalities.

"Christabel Sellers you have chosen to complete the final assessment, proving that you are prepared to begin training as a Forth Tier Eyas. You are reminded that the use of magic at this level is a great responsibility not without its dangers. Misuse of magic can result in the harm of yourself and those around you. Any such harm will be counted as your own indiscretion and you will suffer the repercussions of it. Do you fully understand the new responsibilities you are requesting?"

Whispers at the Altar

"I do," Christa said absently. She would try air first this time. Get the hardest one out of the way.

"Very well. You must show me that you can exercise control over a small amount of each element. You may begin when you are ready."

Christa stared at the four bowls. From left to right they held a bright yellow feather the size of her forearm, a pitcher's worth of cold water, a small pile of stones from the pond, and a candle flickering in the breeze from the window. She let out a long breath, brushed a wisp of hair from her face, and focused.

She pushed her nerves aside and opened herself to the Essence. That was the easy part. She concentrated harder, squinting past the sunlight coming through the window. The trick was picking out the air within the greater cloud of Essence. A cloud she could now see stretched between and among everything in the room. All the elements drifted through the cloud. The slow stately grains of earth, the meandering beads of water, the minute, rushing specks of air, even the agitated sparks of fire, all of them moved and swirled around her. She could see them in the air around her, the table before her, even swirling within the form of Laisel before her. But it was the nimble specks of air around the feather she was trying to focus on now.

She had done this before, and she knew all it took was patience. The flecks of air were so small, and so fast, there was no way she could simply reach out and grab them. She had to wait and reach out with her will to form a trap around the feather. Slowly she let the trap fill with air, letting the other elements leave but keeping the air that entered. Slowly the pressure built against the walls of her will until it was like holding a soft pillow, a pillow that wanted to disintegrate through your fingers if you gripped it just a bit too tight. Then it was only a matter of lifting the pillow, and the feather lifted with it.

"Very good," Laisel whispered. "That was definitely faster than last time. But remember to pace yourself. There is no time limit and if you—"

223

Christa dropped the feather back into the bowl as she glared briefly up at Laisel.

"I apologize. I know you like to be left alone when you are concentrating."

Christa pushed back the sweat threatening to drip into her eyes. "It's fine. I'm sorry."

Laisel walked to a table to pour a cup of water. "Every student is different," she said as she handed it to Christa. "Some thrive under gentle encouragement. Some don't." She smiled, "I once had a student who couldn't seem to do anything unless I was yelling at him."

"I can't imagine how those training sessions went." Christa drank the entire cup, wiped her sleeve across her forehead, and looked back down at the tray. She should do the water next. Earth was always easy, she could do that even if she was tired. And the fire . . . She knew all too well how easily that came to her.

She turned her cup around in her hands as she stared at the bowl of water in front of her. Within moment she was back into the Essence, watching as the slippery beads of water slid over and around each other. It was like watching a bowl of greased maggots. The thought turned her stomach, and she wondered how on earth Sinna could work with this element every day.

Christa steeled herself, then reached into the bowl with her will. It didn't feel like water. There was nothing cool and refreshing about it, like when she washed her hands in the basin. It was slick and oily, the beads squishy and slimy. They were almost as impossible to hold as the air had been. Still, she forced down the bile rising in her throat and pushed around the bowl. As slick as they were, they couldn't resist her will as long as she kept the motion simple and the force solid. Slowly the water began to turn, stirring around the edges of the bowl until a small whirlpool had formed.

No sooner had it done so than Christa jerked out of the water, unconsciously wiping her hand on her skirt despite the fact that the greasy sensation was not coming from it.

Whispers at the Altar

"Excellent, Christabel. I can see you still don't like the way it feels, but you are getting better at hiding it. And, as I said before, you will find that different liquids *feel* different. Though they all react the same."

Christa only nodded as she caught her breath though she smiled inside. It was funny how Laisel could apologize for talking to her during the test, then keep doing it. She couldn't help herself. It was like asking Sinna to stop thinking the best of everyone.

The bowl of stones was next, and though it took several minutes to catch her breath, Christa didn't bother to release her hold on the Essence. Nor did she take her eyes off those flat, smooth stones. These would be easy, but still tiring. Not because they would be hard to grasp, the grains of earth barely moved at all as they ground over each other. Neither was she hesitant to touch them, there was something comforting about their solidity. But that same solidity made them stubborn. Unwilling to be moved in any way they did not wish to be.

Luckily, she was even more so.

With a grim scowl she slid her will into the bowl, the density of the stones pressing hard against it. They with eyes narrowed in concentration, she pushed. The cup she held dug painfully into her hands as she focused all her determination onto those stones. Blood pounded in her ears, but still she shoved her will against them. She was better than them, their master, and she would not be denied.

With a small jerk, one stone moved. Then another. Then they all began to turn and roll as though stirred with an invisible spoon. She stopped with a gasp for air, and the stones came to a clattering halt. Christa dropped the cup and leaned forward to steady herself on the table. Her mind was like mush. Like the time Westrel had challenged her to do more pushups and her arms had turned weak and wobbly after only ten. Except it wasn't her arms that were wobbly this time.

She vaguely heard Laisel ask if she wanted another cup of water and nodded a response. Maybe it was a bad idea to start with air.

Maybe she should have started with earth again. Maybe she should stop. She could always try again tomorrow. There was no hurry. She was tired. And after all, no one had ever passed this test this soon. No one would blame her if she gave up. It wasn't like she would be giving up forever.

The voice in her head went around and around, repeating the same excuses. But she knew what the real excuse was. It was the fire. She wasn't too tired. She didn't need to rest. She was afraid. She let herself look up at the candle and into its flame. It was so small. Surely it would be safe. But every time she came to it, every time for the past week that she had taken this test, all she could think of was Mama. Or Vaniel. Of the way she could feel the burning deep down inside her whenever she was angry.

Of the voice in her dreams reminding her what she was. A monster.

"You need to rest," Laisel's voice broke through her thoughts, forcing her gaze away from the flame. "You are exhausted. You did very well today."

Christa shook her head, leaning back in the chair as she drank the water. "I'm fine." She was so close to proving them all wrong. So close to showing them what a "half-human" could do. What she could do. She just had to show the Fire that it wasn't in control. That she wasn't a monster. "I'll be fine."

"You can always try again tomorrow."

"I'm fine!" Christa said, louder than she meant to. She took a deep breath and set the cup down. "I'm sorry, Instructor Laisel. I didn't mean to yell."

She didn't seem convinced. "You are not fine, Christabel. You are exhausted. To continue the test at this point would be irresponsible."

"No, please. I promise I'm all right. I just need to rest."

"This is exactly what I was talking about before the test." She sat down across from Christa once more. "Magic at this level is a responsibility. You have to know your limits."

Whispers at the Altar

Christa leaned forward, her hands gripping the tabletop. "But I can do this, Instructor. Please. At least let me try."

Laisel shook her head. "Why? Explain to me why I should let you push yourself this hard."

"Because I'm ready!"

"You will be just as ready tomorrow."

"No. You don't understand." Christa threw her hands up, exasperated. "Haven't you ever needed to do something, but you just couldn't make yourself do it? So you kept putting it off."

Laisel's eyes narrowed. "What can't you make yourself do?" she asked slowly.

"This," Christa gestured to the candle, nearly knocking it over. "It . . . it scares me."

"Why?" Laisel was leaning forward now, her expression intent.

"I . . ." She couldn't tell her about Mama. Or Vaniel. No one had believed Vaniel at the time, and Christa had denied it when asked. Even Sinna had gone along with the deception. "What if something happens? I just . . . don't want to hurt anyone." That much, at least, was true.

"Christabel. I am right here. Part of my role in this test is to ensure you do not do anything unintentional."

"I know. But that's the way I feel. But I'm ready to try now. And I'm afraid if I don't do it now, I might never have the courage to do it at all." She looked up at Laisel sheepishly. "Haven't you ever felt that way?"

Laisel considered for a moment as a smile spread across her face. "I have. At my first ball." She took a deep breath then nodded once. "I will let you try. But you must promise me that if you feel it is too much of a strain, you will stop. Try. But do not push yourself beyond your limits."

Christa wanted to jump over the table and hug her. "I promise. I won't push. Thank you. Thank you, Instructor Laisel."

"Fine, fine," she said with a grin. "I will be watching you very closely. You may begin whenever you are ready."

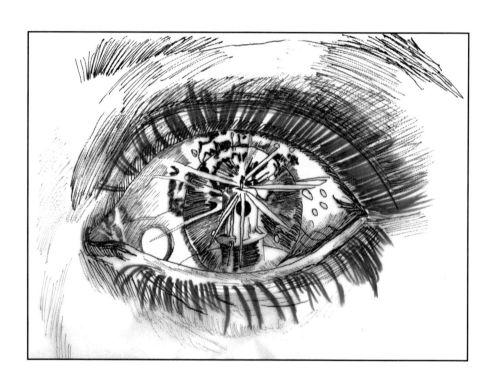

Whispers at the Altar

Christa took a few minutes to calm herself, to steady her breathing and her racing heart, and focus on the Essence. She watched it flow and dance around her, lost herself in its random chaos. Then, as her mind cleared, she looked into the flame.

For a moment everything was still. She could see the motes and sparks of fire as they dashed about within the body of the flame, only to hurtle away as rays of heat. It was mesmerizing. Beautiful.

She reached out with her will as if it were her own finger, the fear battling with determination. She could do this. She would master it. She was *not* a monster.

The finger of will grazed the edges of the flame.

It leapt, blinding. The burning from within filled her as it surged in response. There was a moment of resistance, like tearing through paper, and the room flooded with red-orange light.

A scream of pain shot through her concentration, and it shattered like glass.

FIRE

Christa didn't know if the flame or the scream made her jerk away from the Essence. It all happened so fast. But as she blinked the fire's afterimage from her eyes the situation became horribly clear.

The smell of smoke.

The scorched table and blackened stones in their charred bowl.

The flames still eating away at the sofa Laisel lay back upon, burnt hands pressed to her face.

Even with Christa's limited experience she knew this was far beyond her. Still, she rushed over and tentatively reached out to the sobbing woman.

"What do I do?"

Laisel gathered herself enough to rasp. "My desk. Middle drawer." She worked to a sitting position, hands never leaving her face.

Christa leapt to her feet, rushed to the desk, and yanked the drawer open to reveal a hodgepodge of items and papers whose purpose Christa could only guess at.

"A small box. Green."

Mad shuffling ensued as Christa ransacked the drawer. Papers flew in a cloud. She was about to up-end the entire drawer when she pulled out a coffer, slightly larger than her hand, and made of green wood. She rushed back to Laisel, skidding to her knees beside her.

Laisel barely noticed except to reach out with trembling hands, revealing a blistered and raw face. Christa jumped back, and the box clattered to the floor. She snatched it back up and handed it to her teacher. Laisel's burned hands grasped it, but her fumbling attempt to open it only dropped it a second time.

"Christabel. You need to open it. There is . . . a cloth. Place it . . . over my face."

Her breathing was getting worse, and for the first time Christa noticed her eyes were staring past without seeing her.

"I can do it, Laisel. Just hold on." She fumbled the box for a second, then flipped open the lid revealing what appeared to be an ordinary silk handkerchief. She plucked it out—it was surprisingly cold—and shook it once to unfold it, then leaned forward to lay it gently over Laisel's face.

The Elementalist sighed with relief, then brought her hands up to press the cloth against her skin. "Help me to the infirmary please, Christabel," she said in a muffled voice.

Christa helped Laisel to her feet and guided her to the door.

The walk to the infirmary was the longest she could remember. Each inquiring face was a cutting accusation. It didn't take long before a veritable train of curious students followed. She was relieved when a passing instructor stopped to help, even if he gave her a scathing look. The tears the panic of the moment had held back, were streaming long before she passed through the infirmary doors and handed Laisel off to the Healers.

•Whispers at the Altar•

Forced to watch through a window as they rushed about, Christa could only think how this was all her fault. She should have been more careful. She shouldn't have reached out to the fire so eagerly. She had known what would happen, and all her fears had been justified. Now Laisel, who had only ever been kind to her, was paying the price. Just like Mama had.

The instructor who'd helped her in the hall walked out, his lips set in a frown, and his eyes fixed on Christa. It occurred to her then what kind of trouble she must be in. What if Laisel died?

She ran. She didn't know what they did to murderers here, and she didn't want to find out. Even if Laisel didn't die, surely Christa would be expelled for this, or imprisoned. She didn't stop running until her bedroom door slammed shut behind her.

"What are you doing, Christa?"

She spun around as her heart jumped into her throat. Christa's eyes went from the closed door to Silvana, and she backed a step away.

"I let myself in. It wasn't locked," Silvana explained. "I heard about what happened. I wanted to make sure you were all right."

"I'm fine," Christa mumbled as her hands wrung her skirt like a washcloth.

"I know you, Christa." She took a step forward. "You are anything but. You need to go to Marellel. She can help you. She will want to. If you stay here . . ." She shrugged.

"Why would she want to help me?"

Silvana gave a wry smile. "You are the daughter of her best friend, Christa. If she wouldn't, who would?" She glanced at the door. "Please, Christa. Go to her. Before things get worse."

Christa sighed. "Will you come with me? I could use the company."

"I can't." She wrung her hands. "But I will wait here for you as long as I can."

"Why can't you?" Christa frowned. "She's your director, too. I'm sure she'd let you."

233

Silvana shook her head. "It isn't a good time, Christa. Please, you need to hurry."

Christa's frown deepened, but she hurried back out. She started straight for the nearest set of tubes then thought better of it and headed for the stairs instead. She really didn't want to run into anyone.

In fact, Christa was barely out of the dorm halls when she nearly collided with Director Marellel coming around a corner. The director pulled up sharp, her face an unreadable mask.

"Goodness, child. You are a disaster. Go to my office right now. Close the door and wait for me there. Don't go anywhere else, and don't speak to anyone if you can help it."

She was gone again before Christa could ask a single question, and without settling any of her fears.

Christa closed the office door and leaned back against it. She debated locking it, but decided it might seem suspicious if anyone came looking for the director. She collapsed into a chair, trying to catch her breath. She'd run all the way here.

The sun was sinking behind the opposite side of the Roost and it threw the office into shadows that lulled her toward sleep. But Christa found she couldn't close her eyes without seeing the damaged and sightless face of Laisel staring accusingly back at her.

Look at what you did, the Fire inside her whispered.

Christa's eyes snapped open. "No. It wasn't my fault. It was an accident."

An accident. Like when you attacked Vaniel? Like your precious Mama?

Christa's hands curled into fists. "I didn't mean to do it. *You* did it. You made me."

◆Whispers at the Altar◆

The Fire only laughed as it curled around her gut. *I can't make you do anything, remember? You are the master. The monster.*

Christa squinted her eyes closed, pressing the lids together until it hurt. Laisel's charred face met her, but she forced herself to look at it. "I am not a monster," she hissed.

The Fire only laughed, a cracking hissing sound that shivered every nerve.

The door opened and Christa looked up.

A weary Marellel stood in the doorway. The sun had set and the room grown very dark, but Christa hadn't bothered to light any of the globes. The dark fit her mood. It was painful when the director walked in and spoke a word that brought all the lamps to full illumination as she let the door close behind her.

"What are you doing here in the dark, Christabel? Sulking?" Her tone, as weary as she looked, made it obvious she would tolerate nothing of the kind.

Christa took a moment to shield her eyes with one arm and blink at the light. The Fire was gone, retreated to whatever part of her it slept in until it felt her weakness. "I guess I didn't notice it got so dark."

Marellel gave a suspicious humph as she walked by on the way to her desk. She collapsed into the chair and stared out the window for a silent moment before fixing Christa with kind eyes. "You will be happy to know Laisel will recover," she said. "Her sight will never fully return, and there will be scars. The Healers can only do so much."

Christa shivered. "She . . . she's blind?"

Marellel nodded, her expression sympathetic, then let out a long breath as she leaned back in her chair. "There was talk of expelling you, particularly from Director Dalan, but I made it clear how ridiculous that was. This isn't the first accident to occur during training. And Director Namarian pointed out it was your own quick actions that prevented worse damage. Still, the secretary was prepared to follow Director Dalan's advice.

"It is Laisel you have to thank for your continued education. She accepted all the blame. She told the secretary she had been pushing you too hard and had not taken the proper precautions."

"But she hadn't been pushing me at all!" Christa blurted. "It was my fault."

Marellel's eyebrows arched. "Are you calling Instructor Laisel a liar, Christabel Sellers?"

Christa swallowed, shaking her head.

"Then don't say such things. Especially not in public. Laisel has taken the blame for this mistake. In return, she has been removed from her instructor position and a new instructor has been assigned to you. One chosen by the secretary."

"But I don't want a new instructor." Christa tried to sound matter-of-fact, but the break in her voice betrayed her. "And I don't want to learn anything to do with fire."

Marellel's eyes narrowed and she stood, taking a single step toward Christa. "You will, Christabel. If you care at all for Laisel and your-self, you will." Her voice was cold, firm. "The Creator has given you power, whether you like it or not. Laisel knows this as well as I. She gave up teaching, the thing she loved most, so you could learn to use that power. She did not stand in front of the directors and shame herself so you could run and hide like a child. If you give up now, if you refuse to even attempt to achieve your potential, you burn that sacrifice to ash. Is that what you want? Because, if it is, I promise you will not leave these walls without telling Laisel personally."

Christa blinked, her mouth working but no words making it out. She settled for another shake of her head.

"What you will do," Marellel continued, her tone softening, "is work as hard as you ever have. I guarantee your new teacher will not be interested in your feelings. She will do everything to hold you back. You will have to prove you deserve to learn something new."

Christa contemplated those words. She already knew running wasn't an option. What else was there? But still, the thought of touching fire again . . .

"I'll do my best."

"I know you will, Christabel," she answered with a knowing smile. "You are your mother's daughter. Giving up isn't in your blood."

Christa bit her lip for a moment then decided to take a chance. "Director Marellel? Do you . . . think I'm a monster?"

Marellel blinked, obviously taken aback. "What? Of course not. Why would you think that?" She walked over to take the chair next to Christa.

"I don't know." Now that she had brought the matter up, she had no idea how to proceed. But the fact that Marellel so vehemently disagreed with the Fire was comforting. "I mean . . . look at what I did."

Marellel reached out to turn Christa's chin so she could look into her eyes. "That doesn't make you a monster, Christabel. Did you mean to hurt Instructor Laisel?"

"No."

"Will you learn from the mistake you made?"

"Yes, but—"

"Fire is a part of you. But no more so than your hands or your feet or any of the other elements. It is a part of who you *are*. And you cannot be afraid of who you are, Christabel. But what you are *not* is a monster."

YEAR 4

Warning

Christa tried to appear as nonchalant as possible while her stomach turned somersaults. She was nearly to the doors of the palace and the last thing she needed was someone stopping her. Granted there weren't many people about past midnight, but still far more than she expected.

She hefted her bag farther up onto her shoulder, praying no one noticed the soft fluttering coming from inside. She wasn't sure who she was praying to. Maybe Ssanek. Maybe no one. She only knew that if someone stopped her now, she would have a lot of explaining to do. Of course she had a story. She'd practiced it in front of the mirror at least ten or twelve times.

Oh, I'm just going out to the palace ground to practice.

I couldn't sleep. And I thought this would be the perfect time to practice without distractions.

That's just some sample elements to practice on.

But if someone decided to look in the bag, her explanations would have to get a lot more creative. She was being paranoid, there was no reason anyone would search her, but that did nothing to calm her roiling gut.

Two Hawks passed by, their red and brown dappled cloaks shifting in pattern as they moved. The nearer watched her intently.

Christa gave a nod of greeting, as well as a smile she hoped was neither too anxious nor suspicious. *Please don't say anything . . .*

The Hawk slowed.

Christa didn't.

"What is it, Rissan?" the other asked, turning to look at Christa as well.

Rissan cocked his head slightly. "I thought I heard something. Like . . . fluttering."

She passed them, but continued listening, her lips moving soundlessly. *Please, please, don't let them ask me anything. Please, Ssanek, don't let them ask.*

The other Hawk laughed. "Probably your stomach. Come, you aren't going to get out of asking her that easily."

More laughing. "She is not going to say yes." The voice waned as it turned away. "Have you seen the way she looks at Elinaran?"

The voices faded, and Christa mouthed a *thank you* before wiping her sweat-slicked hands on her skirt.

She passed through the doors of the palace without meeting anyone else. Once out in the palace grounds she veered off the path to a stand of firs. She walked faster now, the bag jostling against the back of her thighs with each hurried stride. The hard part was over. There were no guards until the first wall and even those were sparse. The primary worry now was from above. But the new moon and dark clouds would help hide her from any eyes that might happen to look out from the towers or bridges.

When she reached the trees, she dropped the sack with a sigh of relief and sank down in the snow to rest against one of their coarse trunks. She held up a hand, watching it tremble. Whether from the strain of carrying the bag or the stress of what she planned to do, she couldn't tell. She pressed it into the snow, forcing it to be still.

Doubts crept into the back of her mind. Creeping things that gnawed at her and had been gnawing at her ever since the first time she spoke to him. He wanted blood. How could that be right? What would he want next? Hadn't she decided not to keep secrets? Why was she doing it again? What would Sinna say?

She curled her fingers in the snow, concentrating on the cold. Letting it focus her thoughts. No. She wasn't doing anything wrong. It was just a few animals. And this was the only way. Sinna wouldn't understand. She'd been lied to all these years. It wasn't her fault; she didn't know any better. If Christa told Sinna, Sinna would tell Marellel, and all that elven bigotry would keep Christa from doing what she had to. This was the only way.

Beating back the doubts, she shoved herself to her feet. She was already getting cold and sitting in the snow wasn't helping. Picking up the sack once again, she turned even farther from the path. As she walked she sent small bursts of air to blow the snow behind her, leaving only small undulations where her boot prints had been. It wasn't perfect but it was the best she could manage and would have to do.

Christa had chosen the site carefully. As unnerving as being caught leaving the palace would have been, being seen in the middle of the ritual would be infinitely worse. So she chose a spot as out of sight as possible within the palace grounds. It was well away from any of the numerous globes that lit the grounds at night. And, as an added benefit, the edge of a tall hedge maze shielded view from the wall, while a large gazebo provided cover from the bulk of the palace.

Snow was falling in swirling gusts by the time she arrived at the spot, a bare patch of grass covered in a blanket of white. She dropped the bag then winced. She hoped the crunch was only from the snow.

She took a minute to stretch her back and arms, then knelt in the snow to open the bag.

Christa withdrew the cage first. She peered inside it, unable to see much in the near complete darkness. They were still alive. She could see the doves moving and hear them fluttering nervously. She set the cage aside, then reached in to fish out the walking sticks she'd purchased in town. After a minute of fumbling she found the ends she'd carved, one with a hole into the shaft, the other whittled down into a peg. These she slid together.

Next, came the top. Besides the doves, this had taken the longest. She had never carved anything before and had gone through countless small practice blocks before she even dared a full size attempt. Even then, this was her third try, and it barely resembled a winged snake in any but the crudest fashion. Still, she had to hope it would work. She wasn't likely to do much better.

She fit the snake to the top of the pole, then used it to lever herself back up. The snow had seeped through her dress despite the fur she wore over it, and her knees were chilled to the bone. She paced the steps to the center of the open space, then plunged the totem into the snow with both hands.

The sharpened point at the bottom barely sank into the cold-hardened ground. She gingerly let go, and the top-heavy pole started to fall to her right. With a sigh, she held it up, then reached down into the Essence of the earth, loosening it around the point of the staff as she pressed down. It sank a span more before she hardened the ground around it and stepped back to appraise it. The serpent gazed down at her with cold lifeless eyes, its tail seeming to curl around the peak of the observatory.

Christa let out a long breath, even after a month of practice moving the elements was still tiring, then walked back to the cage and looked down at it with a frown. This was the part she looked forward to the least. They were such pretty little doves. But it had to be done. Opening the little door, she reached in, wrapped her hand gently around one of the doves, and pulled it out. There were four, two mated pairs she had caught on the bridges of the palace. The bird shifted and cooed in her hand as she stroked it. She could feel its heart beating wildly beneath her fingers.

It wasn't until she stepped up to the pole that she realized she'd forgotten a knife.

"Christa, don't!"

She almost dropped the bird in surprise. Then she recognized the voice, and her stomach eased back down her throat. "What do you want?" she asked as she looked up.

Silvana stood not five paces away, barely visible in the dark and the snow, but Christa knew it was her. Christa cursed herself for not keeping a better watch, and the snow for muffling the sound of Silvana's approach.

"You can't do this. You can't go down this road," Silvana pleaded. She took two steps closer. "She wouldn't want this."

"Do what?" Christa tried first for the wild lie. Explaining what she was doing would be far more difficult.

But Silvana only gave her a level look. "You know very well what. He can't help you. He can't give you what you need."

"How do you know? All you know is what you've been taught by people who hate humans. He *can* bring her back. He said so."

Silvana stopped a handful of steps away. "He is lying. And even if he could, at what price, Christa? Look at what you are doing. And who you are becoming. Is this who you think she wanted you to be? Sneaking around at night, keeping secrets from your friends, performing sacrifices to foreign gods?"

Christa looked down at the dove cooing softly in her hand. Those doubts surging back in the recesses of her mind. "It doesn't matter. I have to bring her back. And if he can do it . . ." She looked up, wiping her eyes. "Besides, I'm not doing anything wrong. The elves practice their religion. Why can't I practice mine? I wouldn't have to be so secretive if you weren't so bigoted."

245

But Silvana would not be baited. "You don't have to bring her back. Whatever guilt you feel . . . it wasn't your fault." Silvana took another step closer. Christa could make out her eyes now, dark pools of concern. "It has been over three years. She has already forgiven you. Forgive *yourself*, and let her go."

The words stabbed through Christa, chilling her heart with doubt. Why couldn't she let Mama go?

Because you killed her, the Fire whispered. *You sent her away. You stole her from Papa.*

But it wasn't really her fault, was it?

Who else's could it be? There was only one monster there.

"Christa, she has left this world and all of its pains, heartaches, and troubles. Don't you think she is happy where she is?"

Happy to be rid of her freak of a daughter.

"No." She raised a hand to point at Silvana. "No. She isn't. She couldn't be. What mother could be happy without her daughter? Without her family? What mother wouldn't fight to get them back? My mama *loved* me. My papa loved me. And I took all of that away. I did. And I must make it right. For *all* of us." The memory of Papa's face as he turned away from her, of the way he could barely look at her even as he abandoned her among strangers, haunted her.

Silvana backed away a step. "Everyone dies—"

"No!" The fire raced down her arm, surging around her hand. "I *will* bring her back. I don't care what it takes. She loves me. She wants to be with me!"

The fire surged out of her in a deluge of flame that licked around Silvana, rolling over and around a shimmering barrier.

"I am warning you, Christa," she said, breath coming in gasps as she held one hand out before her. "If you go down this road—if you follow this thing that fancies itself a god . . ." She raised herself up to her full height. "You will never find your mother. You will only destroy yourself."

Whispers at the Altar

"I will get her," Christa growled. "No one will stop me. Not you, not him, not them." She pointed vaguely at the palace. "I will bring her back where she belongs. Here. With me. I will prove I am not a monster." She raised both hands, and the flames howled out in a tidal wave, melting through snow, charring grass, and blasting though Silvana's defense.

By the time she was able to bring herself back under control, Silvana was gone. Not ash, as Christa had briefly wished her to be. Just gone.

Christa had no idea where Silvana went, but the ritual would have to be completed quickly now. Someone might have seen her stupid outburst.

Why had she done that? She didn't want to kill Silvana.

Did she?

She shook her head to clear it. It didn't matter. Silvana was gone. And Christa had work to do. Even if no one had seen anything, Silvana would undoubtedly tell someone.

Christa sighed and turned back to the totem—a pile of ash clenched in her fist where the dove had been.

She threw the cinders into the snow and retrieved another bird. Three would have to be enough. She debated briefly, then wrenched the bird's head to the side. There was a snap and it went limp, but no blood. She needed the blood. That was the entire point. With a jerk she ripped the head off. Blood was already flowing over her hand as she held the carcass up to the pole and what life the dove had possessed trickled down the wood and melted little holes into the snow beneath.

The second and third doves followed, each as stupidly compliant as the first. When the lower half of the pole was striated with dark lines, Christa stepped back. She didn't have time to circle around. So she stood, hands raised to the figure of the snake that seemed to smile at her from above.

247

"Great Ssanek, god of darkness, giver of desires, hear my prayer," she whispered. "Bring my mama back. Bring her back alive and well. Tell me what price you require, and I will pay it. Just bring her back. Great Ssanek—"

"You have done well," a soft voice hissed.

Christa blinked and stepped back. Had the snake just . . .

"You have completed the ritual. I see you now. Body and soul. Mind and will." The voice grew louder, raspier.

"So you can bring her back? You can help me now?" She recovered her step, trying to make her voice sound firm even if part of her wanted to hide.

"Mmm. I can. And gladly. No one should be without those they love. No one should be denied the opportunity to make right their wrongs."

Christa blinked, gripping her skirt tight. "How . . . how did you know?"

There was a soft, scratching laugh. "I told you. I see you, Christabel Sellers. Would you expect your secrets to be kept from a god? But unlike some, I do not lay blame. You are no sinner. No *monster*. You are only what you are. A strong, beautiful young woman who is hurting terribly. And I want to help you."

The blood rushed to Christa's face. "What do you need me to do?"

"I can bring her back, but you must provide the gate for her to walk through. There is a way, but it will require much time. Time and study. Can you do this?"

Christa nearly fainted with relief. Was that all? "Study? Yes! I can study. Whatever it is. I can learn anything."

"Yes. So I can see. Then study this. There once were two Hawks, long ago. They died in an experiment. You must . . . recreate it."

"An experiment? I don't understand."

"Wiliran and Welsebel," it hissed. "You will understand. Complete their experiment, and you will have your mother back. Your father will have his wife back. You will all be a family once more." The voice faded. "Speak to me again when you have need. And remember . . .

I have seen you. I will always be with you." The voice faded to a whisper then was gone.

Christa stared up at the winged snake totem, and a smile spread across her face.

Perform an experiment? That was all? She felt like shouting, cheering. She leaned forward and kissed the staff again and again, heedless of the blood that covered it. Then collapsed back into the snow in exhaustion. Fat flakes drifted down from the cloud-laden sky to land on her face. She should pack up the totem. Someone might even now walk up. The idea made her inexplicably giddy. What would they think? Her laying here in the snow. Dress and hands all bloody. Dead birds scattered about a gore-streaked totem to an ancient human god.

They might think she was crazy. But she knew better. She had a goal now. A finish line. She had purpose. She looked fondly at the winged snake high above her. He would bring Mama back. And for that, she loved him.

Vaniel watched Christa kiss the pole and collapse into the snow, then ducked down further behind the underbrush to think. To tell the truth she had no idea what it was she just saw. Was Christa performing some kind of human rite in front of that totem? And who had she been arguing with? Whoever it was had been on the opposite side of Christa. Vaniel hadn't been able to get a clear view. Neither had she heard another voice, but then she hadn't dared to get too close.

So all she had right now was that Christa was sneaking out in the middle of the night, killing birds, talking to some totem, and losing her temper with some mysterious other person to the point that she threw fire at them. Vaniel bit her lip and sat down in the snow. That

Whispers at the Altar

might be enough to go to Dalan, he had always warned that Christa was mentally unstable, but he would want proof.

Rising to a crouch, she began to circle out and around to the other side. If she could catch whoever had been arguing with Christa, she might be able to convince them it was necessary to come forward with whatever information they might have. For Christa's sake. Truth be told, she hated all of this sneaking around. At least when she had bullied Christa, it had been out in the open. Not only did this subterfuge mean getting her dress soaked in snow and snagged in rose bushes, it felt . . . wrong. As disgusting as Christa was on principle, she and her friends at least treated Vaniel with respect. That was more than could be said for her own flesh and blood.

It took far longer than she thought to work her way around to where the mystery person would have had to approach. By the time she reached a point she was sure the person would have to pass, Christa had already started back to the palace. Yet, try as she might, Vaniel couldn't find a single sign of anyone passing through the area. She doubled back to the spot Christa performed the rite, now abandoned, but didn't see a single footprint.

Christa had done a thorough job cleaning up. There was no sign of blood or doves. Vaniel saw the furrow of melted snow from Christa's attack, but there were no footprints leading to or away from it. Whoever it was, they had gone to great lengths to make sure no one could follow them. Or Christa had. A breeze blew through Vaniel's wet skirt, reminding her of how cold she was, and how much colder the night was likely to get.

She kicked a clump of snow in frustration. This was all Dalan's fault. If it weren't for his cursed obsession and his stupid suggestion, she would be curled in her bed under a warm blanket. She turned and started the long slog back to the palace. She wasn't going to find anything else here. She doubted she would find anything useful tonight at all. She considered going to Christa's room to catch her trying to hide the evidence, but halfway back discarded the idea. It was already too late. Vaniel was going back to her room to dry off and try to get whatever sleep she could before the sun rose and classes started. She would sneak into Christa's room later. Maybe the totem would be enough evidence for Dalan.

Plots

The clock struck the sixth hour as Vaniel rounded the corner into Christa's hall. Which meant she had exactly ten minutes to search Christa's room if she wanted to be on time for the dinner her father was holding. She would have had more, except she would need to sneak out of the palace, take a roundabout route to her father's estate, and sneak in the servants' door there as well.

Vaniel slowed her pace to a purposeful walk as she neared Christa's door. Christa should be at dinner. She better be. This was the sixth time Vaniel had tried to get into Christa's room when she wasn't there, and Vaniel didn't have time to wait around. If she didn't have some kind of results to give her father at this dinner...

She took a deep breath and knocked softly as she prayed that Christa wouldn't be in. There was a long pause during which Vaniel dared to let herself hope, then Christa's soft voice.

"Come in."

Vaniel cursed to herself, but smiled as she opened the door and walked in. "Good evening. I wasn't sure if you would be in."

Christa sat bent over her desk, too intent on whatever she was doing to look up. "Oh hello, Vaniel. Come on in. What did you need?"

Never mind that she was already in. Vaniel just shook her head at Christa's unintended rudeness and closed the door behind her. "Nothing really. I was passing by and thought I would stop." She searched the room as she walked over to the bed. There was no sign of the totem, but there were only so many places Christa could hide it. The wardrobe? Under the bed?

"Well, you are always welcome," Christa said after a long pause, then sat up and turned to face Vaniel. There were ink stains on her fingers, as usual, and a smudge of graphite on her cheek.

"What are you working on?" Vaniel tried to think of anything to keep the conversation going as she sat down on the edge of the bed.

Christa shrugged. "Nothing really. Just drawing."

She turned to put her drawing sticks and paper back into her desk, and Vaniel seized the opportunity to steal a quick look under the bed. If the totem was under there, it was buried in a pile of books, paper, and clothes too dense for her to see it.

"Can I see?" Vaniel asked as she stood.

"If you want," Christa said with another noncommittal shrug. She leaned back from the desk.

Vaniel walked over. It was a drawing of a woman with hair down to her legs and a little girl, that much was obvious, but Vaniel couldn't tell what exactly they were doing. Hugging maybe?

"I know it isn't very good," Christa said as she fingered one corner.

"Is this your mother?" Vaniel took a stab before glancing over at the wardrobe again. It wasn't locked.

Christa nodded. "Mama loved dancing."

Vaniel looked closer at the drawing, and it became a bit clearer. The figures might be dancing.

Whispers at the Altar

"We used to dance all the time in our little garden. Sometimes Papa would dance, too."

Vaniel smiled. "My mother loves to dance as well. I still remember her carrying me around the floor at the first ball I was allowed to attend. She was the most beautiful woman there. And her smile . . ." Vaniel wiped one eye.

"What else did she like to do?" Christa asked, unaware how rudely personal the question was. "Did she sew? My mama used to sew all the time. She made all my dresses. She tried to teach me to sew, but I was never very good at it. The dresses I made for my dolls always ended up too long or too small."

Vaniel laughed as she trailed one finger down the length of Christa's picture. "No. My mother would consider that beneath her. But she played games."

"Like hide and seek?" Christa sounded skeptical.

Vaniel laughed again, louder. The very idea of her mother playing a peasant game was hilarious. "No. Not like that. She played Savik. It is an old game played with pieces on a board. She would play it by herself for hours as she listened to me take my lessons. She could even beat my father at it."

"Did she teach you?" Christa leaned forward in her chair, her expression intent.

Vaniel sat back down on the bed, her heart warming with the memories. "She tried to. But unfortunately I was no better suited to it than you were to sewing. Still, I used to love trying. And sometimes she would even let me win."

Christa smiled that infectious smile. "My papa used to do that. When we were racing. He would pretend he had a cramp."

Some of the warmth seeped out. "Yes, well my father would never *let* anyone beat him at anything. But Mother was different. She was always kind." Vaniel sighed as the last glimmers of memory were torn by the reality of the present like fog through the trees. "I should be going."

Christa stood, "Are you going to dinner? I'll come with you. I haven't had any, and I'm starving."

Vaniel waved a hand as she walked to the door. "No. I think I will go for a walk."

Christa stopped short. "Oh. All right. Do you want some company?"

"No. Thank you. I will see you at breakfast tomorrow." She closed the door as quickly as she dared behind her and started toward the nearest tube.

It wasn't until she was outside the palace that she remembered the totem, and even then she couldn't bring herself to care.

"Would you simply tell my father that I am here?" Vaniel tried to keep her voice under control, but it was getting harder and harder. It never occurred to her that Father would let the servants believe her disowning was genuine. Now Geridan, the stupid doorman, wouldn't even introduce her.

"Miss, his lordship is a busy man. He does not have time for every commoner. Perhaps if you made an appointment and came back—"

That did it. She slapped the man across the face so hard it almost made *her* cry out in pain. "How *dare* you speak to me like that? I am Vaniel Sablehawk, of House Sablehawk, and you *will* show me respect or I will see you and your family thrown into the street as paupers. Do you understand? Now let me in, and announce my arrival to my father. Now!"

Geridan fumbled for words as he backed up a step. It was all Vaniel needed. She ducked inside and stalked toward the dining room.

•*Whispers at the Altar*•

She was already late; the early socializing would be long over. The doorman hurried past her to the door, apparently having decided to let the nobles fight their own battles.

"The Lady Vaniel Sablehawk," he called into the room, just before Vaniel could break the threshold.

"Who?" called Father, louder than was necessary.

Soft laughter trickled around the table including, Vaniel saw, from Mother.

"Ah . . . very well then, Geridan. You may go."

The doorman gave a single nod and closed the door.

Vaniel found that the only empty chair sat at the far end of the table from her parents. She took it, trying to hide any sign of complaint. As far as they knew, this was where she wanted to sit anyway.

"You know, the whole point of this ruse is for others to believe it," Father was saying. "And how are they supposed to believe it if you go around saying you are still a Sablehawk."

Vaniel smirked. "Then perhaps you shouldn't invite me to dinners and then forbid the doorman from letting me enter."

"How you accomplish the tasks set before you is not my concern. What *is* my concern are the results. And if the result is to ruin my entire plan, then you will find that disownment is the least punishment I can inflict."

There was a hush broken only by the ring and clink of Vaniel serving herself. She wouldn't give him the satisfaction of an answer. She had precious little results to give, and she wasn't about to ruin her dinner with them. After a few seconds the murmur of conversation rose again, and Vaniel allowed herself to relax slightly.

Dinner passed without any other comments being thrown her way, and she was happy for it. She did find herself stealing a glance up now and then to look at Mother. But their gaze never met. She was too busy talking to Dalan or Father. Elirel met her gaze once. She sat next to Dalan but seemed barely concerned with the conversation.

•*Allan C.R. Cornelius*•

Instead, her gaze roamed up and down the table, examining each person as they ate. Vaniel met that gaze, but only for a moment. She couldn't help feeling the Mentalist was reading her mind, and she wasn't sure she wanted anyone else seeing the things she was thinking.

When dinner was over and everyone rose to adjourn to the sitting room, Vaniel hurried to catch her mother. She nearly reached out to touch her arm before she remembered herself.

"Mother, can I speak to you for a moment?"

Corannel looked to her husband, but he only walked away. "Of course. What is it, dear?"

Vaniel folded her hands properly in front of her as she led the way out onto the veranda and into the cool evening air. She didn't speak until she was sure they were alone. "Mother, this . . . this disowning is temporary, right?"

"Of course, dear. Why would you think otherwise?"

Vaniel shrugged. "No reason." She walked to the low railing that encircled the veranda and looked out over the pristine beds of roses, fireblossoms, and starflowers and the empty marble Savik board to one side. "Except that Dalan insinuated it could become permanent if I failed to produce any useful information for him." She turned as her mother walked up beside her. "You wouldn't let that happen would you?"

"Darling," her mother placed a hand on the rail beside Vaniel's, "know I love you. You are my only daughter. Losing you would be . . ." She shook her head, then smiled. "But some things are bigger than you or me. Or even your father. Some things are too important."

A stone of hurt settled in Vaniel's stomach.

"But enough of such depressing talk," her mother said, waving a hand. "I have no doubt that you will do us both proud. Now we should join the others. They will start to think we are a couple of gossips." She motioned to the arch leading into the sitting room, and Vaniel reluctantly tore herself away from the rail.

Whispers at the Altar

"Why don't we play a game of Savik, Mother? It has been ages since we played." She tried to sound more cheerful than she felt.

Corannel laughed. "Savik? I think we are both too old for such games, don't you?" She led the way into the sitting room, and Vaniel followed silently.

She tried to think of when exactly it happened. When did her mother become someone she barely knew? When did she become someone who would claim to love her then talk about disowning her in the same breath? Vaniel looked up from the carpet in front of her feet and saw her father talking with Dalan by the fireplace. It was his fault. He had turned her own mother against her. He had twisted her into something Vaniel couldn't recognize.

"Now, Vaniel," Palatan said, setting his glass of brandy on the mantle. "I have taken the risk of ruining our entire little endeavor by inviting you here and letting you dine with decent folk for the first time in over a year. I think it is time you returned some of my goodwill with some information."

"Yes," Iyian said, walking up behind her, "what does the dog do when the owner isn't looking?"

Vaniel glanced around as every other conversation stopped, and all eyes turned to her. She thought of reaching out to Corannel, but she had already walked away to stand properly beside Palatan. Vaniel was alone. Oddly, she found herself wishing Christabel were there, or Sinna, or even Westrel. But she pushed that ludicrous thought out of her head. They were the enemy. But enemy or no, they truly supported her. Unlike these vultures. But one of these vultures held her life in his hand, and if she wanted it back, she had to give him something he could use.

"I do have something to report." She gave Palatan a proper curtsy. "Father, I know that Christabel is obsessed with bringing her mother back from the dead." She glanced at Dalan, but his face was a mask. "I have also witnessed Christabel sneaking into the palace grounds

259

to enact a heathen ritual. There she raised a totem, sacrificed animals before it, and prayed to it." This was all she had, and though the gasps were encouraging, Palatan's blank face was not.

"And you have proof of this ritual?"

Vaniel's mind raced. "No."

His frown deepened.

"But there is someone who does," she added.

Palatan raised an eyebrow. "Indeed? Who is this?"

"I am not sure. But while I was watching, Christabel argued with someone. She yelled at the person. Eventually she became so angry, she seemed to lose control. As she did with me on the bridge. Only this time she threw fire at the person. There is no way they could have escaped unscathed."

"And you have found this mystery person?" Palatan asked, his voice tinged with impatience.

"No. I tried, but whoever it was did not want to be found." She took a step forward, "However, as a commoner, my abilities to persuade information out of people are limited. While your own resources are far greater. Surely this person had to have been Healed. I cannot get to those records. But I am sure you could."

Platen considered this. "Possible. What do you think, Dalan?"

Dalan, his gaze distant, blinked and turned to Palatan. "Possible, certainly. But Namarian is very particular about his records. And even should we find this person, if they have not come forward yet, the odds of us convincing them are low. However," he turned back to Vaniel with a twisted smile, "I do believe our spy has given me another idea that might work even better."

Palatan gestured for him to continue.

"This is not the first time the half-human's anger has been triggered. Whoever this mystery person was seems to have done it. Even Vaniel has accomplished it. It seems to me, all we need to do is trigger it in the right setting. A setting where there will be no lack of witnesses."

"Of course," Palatan agreed. "Why that would be proven attempted murder."

"The queen would have little choice in punishment."

"Yes. And though I do dislike the idea of executing anyone. She is, after all, half human."

Dalan nodded. "All we need is someone to make sure she is in the right place at the right time." He turned back to Vaniel. "Say, the opening dance of this year's Commencement Ball."

Sun-Pass

The alcove was hard to get to. Steven had to cling to the cliff face like some giant spider as he stepped from foothold to foothold, his new, soft, leather breeches almost tearing with the effort. But that very fact was what made it worthwhile. No one came up here.

Honovi had shown him the prime piece of solitude as soon as his ankle was strong enough to make the climb. The intervening months were now a terrifying blur.

Every waking moment had been spent huddled in the back of one of the caves, trying to forget how many people were living their lives no more than a stone's throw away. The tiny cave had helped, comforting in its closeness, but there was no escaping the fact that nearly a hundred Yahad now called the place home, with more arriving every week.

He pulled himself into the small cave and sat down with his feet dangling over the edge to wait for Honovi. The cliff dropped away below him, over a hundred span of sheer rock to the fast, ice-choked creek at the bottom. The other side of the ravine stared back at him, pocked with tiny crevices where the cliff swallows were already building their nests.

Below him, on either side of the creek, were the caves of the Yahad, while to his left the headwaters of the Shona tumbled down between two crags that formed the source of the river. The constant rush of water had been distracting at first, contributing to everything else that kept him from sleeping. But now the sound was just another part of life. He looked the other way, to the southeast, and a smile crept across his face.

Aside from the solitude, this was the reason he came up here. The ravine cut southwest, straight through the southern remnants of the Ashkeh Mountains. From here he could see clear down its length. The layers of red, gold, and orange ran like veins of precious metal, pursuing freedom as they stretched toward the window of clear blue sky and the open grasslands beyond.

Honovi slid in close beside him, and his heart sped up a little, but he didn't turn. He just waited. Slowly, the line of the sun glided east across the Shona and lit the river like flowing silver. Then the light struck the opposite wall and Steven had to squint, but he didn't dare look away. He didn't want to. The canyon caught fire in the sunlight, the walls awash in striated rivers of flame reflecting off the silver water below.

It only lasted an hour, one he spent sitting silently with Honovi. The best hour of the day. When the sun passed and the eastern wall glowed like dying embers, he turned to Honovi and found her staring at him. Her dark brown eyes caught the cliff-light, throwing it back to him in warm waves. She was smiling, but there was something else there. Something in the set of her eyes, or the turn of her lips.

"What is it?"

She leaned back against the wall of their retreat. "I would ask you the same. The way you watch the sun-pass. You are looking for something. Is it escape?"

• Whispers at the Altar •

Steven stared at her for a moment, surprised. "Why would I want to escape?" It was true he yearned to be anywhere other than a cramped cave filled with people, but up here he was just enjoying the beauty of the view. Wasn't he?

Honovi's gaze never left his. "You left everything behind. Your home." She shrugged one shoulder. "I would think you would want to go back. This place," she gestured to the ravine below, "it is not a place to stay for good. It is a place to reflect, to seek counsel, even protection, but always you must return to face what brought you here."

"I guess I never thought about it." He looked down into the ravine, watching the water rush over and around the rocks and stones in its way.

"You are scared," she said softly.

"Aren't you?" Steven looked back at her. "I mean, you've seen what's out there. We both lost our families. I even—" He shook his head. He just couldn't bring himself to tell her what he had seen in the swamp. What he had done. "Any sane person would be scared to death."

Honovi leaned forward, her hand resting on his knee.

He flinched.

She frowned and brought her hand back, folding both in her lap.

Steven cursed himself. She was only trying to help. What was wrong with him?

"To be afraid is natural. I am as well. My father, your father, all of my people." She spoke stiffly. "But none of us can remain there forever."

Steven chuckled. "Brogan's not afraid of anything."

Honovi's eyes narrowed. "Can you not see your own father?"

"He's—" Steven wanted to tell her Brogan wasn't his father. But it was all so complicated. He would probably have to explain about Mother. And what if she turned on him when she found out what he'd done? He'd never had someone his own age he could talk to. Someone who might understand. He didn't want to lose her. He needed her. But what use was it if he never opened to her?

Honovi waited patiently.

Steven sighed. "You're probably right. He's lost everything he had." The stone of guilt weighed heavily in his stomach. If only he had been able to reach Mother. To make her see what she was doing. "I wish I could do something for him. He's as lost here as I am. I mean, your people have been very kind, but it isn't the same."

"Your father misses his home as well." She leaned forward, bringing her face close to Steven's own.

The discomfort of having anyone so near battled with the urge to move even closer. He closed his eyes for a moment, enjoying the smell of her. When he opened them again, the nervousness had subsided. "I guess. I mean, I see him muttering to himself a lot. More so than usual. He's constantly complaining about how he could do more to help your people if only he had something. His books, his plants, even his pigeons."

He waited for Honovi to say something, but she sat there, staring, a hint of a smile tugging at her mouth.

"Do you think I could go back to the hut and find some of his things to bring back to him?"

"He would never allow it."

"He wouldn't have to know. I could make up a story."

Honovi laughed. "You are a terrible liar. He would never believe you. Better if you let me."

"So what would you tell him?"

She tilted her head a bit as she thought. "A hunting trip. If you are to live among us, you must learn our ways. I will take you east to hunt in the Ashkeh."

"But that's the wrong . . . oh. Right." It was better than anything he would have come up with. "Wait. You're coming, too?"

She laughed again, the sound echoing back from the opposite cliff face. "How else can I teach you?"

Steven could feel his pulse beating in his face. "But won't your father . . ."

"He may not think it wise, but let me worry about that."

"No, I mean . . ." Steven was sure his face was as red as the rocks outside. "I mean, about you and me . . . being alone . . ."

Honovi's own cheeks grew flushed, and she leaned back. "He may object. But I am of age to make my own choices."

Steven wasn't so sure. He still remembered the way Hareb had looked at him that night on the road. True, that was nearly four months ago, but Steven doubted the man's opinions had changed since. Even these stolen moments typically earned him a stern look from the man on their return.

"So then we just travel to the hut, pick up some things, and come back?"

"And hunt," she said with a nod. "The people do need food after all."

"Definitely not." Brogan poked a bony finger into Steven's chest for emphasis. "The last group to come in was from no more than a hard day's ride away. It's too dangerous for you two to be wandering off alone."

"We will be hunting to the east," Honovi said. "There will be little danger of meeting any of Ssanek's followers there."

Brogan narrowed his eyes at her. "If this is about the two of you—"

"Brogan," Steven cut in. Brogan's voice was echoing through the cave and he could only imagine what the others were thinking of their *discussion*. "We'll be fine." He kept his own voice soft and even. "I've learned from the best. And Honovi has been hunting since she was old enough to draw a bow. We'll be fine."

"If you wish to hunt," Hareb's deep voice echoed through the small chamber, "you may accompany the next hunting party." He walked in to stand in what passed for a doorway in the living-caves, effectively cornering Steven and Honovi between them. "There is no need for you to go alone."

"Father," Honovi bowed her head slightly in deference, "there is no need to slow down the hunters with . . . foal watching. We will be going neither far nor in the direction of danger."

"And besides," Steven said, still focusing his argument on Brogan—better if he didn't try to meet Hareb's eyes, "all reports are that the servants of Ssanek are raiding villages. It isn't like they're scouring the countryside looking for two people."

Brogan's frown only deepened. "Reports can be incomplete. There is no way for us to know right now what their plans are."

"Brogan is correct. It is not a risk worth taking. There is no benefit." Hareb crossed his arms, daring one of them to dispute it.

"Teaching him to use a weapon is its own benefit. We need all the hunters we can get," Honovi stated, refusing to back down. "Eventually we will fight back." She stepped toward her father, voice rising. "When that time comes, every bow, every spear will be needed." She pointed at Steven. "His may be the one that saves my life. Or yours. Or yours." She swiveled her finger to Brogan, her gaze boring into him before returning to Hareb. "I count that a benefit." She crossed her arms, her pose a perfect mirror to her father's.

Hareb frowned as the echoes of Honovi's last words chased the sound from not only their room, but also from the halls and chambers outside.

Steven looked from face to face, his gaze lingering on Honovi as if seeing her for the first time. There was certainty in her stance and defiance in her eyes. He loved seeing it. And part of him wished he could have it, even a part of it, in himself.

The silence was cut by Brogan's soft laughter. "Well, we can't argue with that, Hareb. As much as we would like to."

"The hunters could train him," Hareb muttered.

"True." Brogan sat down in one of the two chairs in the room, a comfort he had conceded to himself despite the Yahad's custom of sitting on the floor. "But I've taught him before. Trust me, he would slow them down. They'd be lucky to bring back a squirrel."

"Hey, I—" Steven turned to see Brogan already waving a hand to silence his inevitable outburst.

"And *if* they stay nearby . . ." his gaze focused on Steven with glittering intensity, "they should be safe enough."

Steven's heart skipped a beat and he looked away. He could only hope Brogan hadn't read the truth on his face. Honovi was right. He was a horrible liar. He couldn't understand how she could face her father down even now, knowing she was deceiving him. Could she do the same to himself? Had she?

Hareb gave the barest hint of a nod. "You may go. But you must stay within a day to the east." He stepped from the doorway, his gaze shifting to Steven.

Steven swallowed past the lump in his throat, nodded, and hurried out before he could give anything away, or crack under that stare.

Duel

"Are you feeling well?"

Christa glanced away from the entrance to the dining hall long enough to meet Vaniel's gaze and smile. "Fine? Why?"

"You have hardly touched your food and you seem . . . distracted." Westrel, too, was looking at her, eyes narrowed in the same piercing look she got when presented with a puzzle that needed working.

"Oh. I'm just not very hungry." She tried to sound nonchalant, but Westrel's gaze didn't falter. Christa forked a bite of pale, pink fish and chewed quickly.

"Oh, leave her alone," Sinna interrupted. "She's p-probably thinking about some young man that's caught her eye." She leaned forward conspiratorially. "You know I-I've heard she sneaks out in the middle of the night to have secret r-rendezvous. Though why she wouldn't tell her best friends who he is—"

The fish stuck in Christa's throat, sending her into a coughing fit as tears came to her eyes.

"Gracious, Christa," Sinna said as she patted Christa's back. "Must have been pretty close to the mark." She winked at Westrel who laughed while Vaniel just stared at them.

"I would say so. Next thing we know she will be asking us for a dress to wear to the Commencement Ball."

"I do *not* have rendezvous," Christa sputtered, gaining control of her breathing. "And I do not go to balls."

"Why ever not?" Sinna brushed a few tiny bits of errant fish off her skirt.

Vaniel cleared her throat. "You told me you loved to dance back home."

Sinna nodded. "And they're so much fun. Especially with friends. You get to see all the Nobles in their best d-dresses, and—"

"I told you. I don't know any elven dances." That wasn't strictly true. Mama had taught her several. But she hadn't practiced them with anyone. In fact, the entire truth was that she'd never danced with anyone other than Mama or Papa. And as much as she loved it, she wasn't too keen on the idea of trying to do it in the middle of a huge room full of strangers.

"We could always teach you," Vaniel said.

"I know. And thank you, really. But I—" Christa spotted Marellel entering the hall, "I really don't have the time. I have so much work to do."

"Right." Sinna poked Christa in the ribs. "So much work out in the gardens with . . ." She waited expectantly.

Christa tried to keep the blood from rushing to her face. Did Sinna really know? She'd only redone the ritual twice since the winter. To ask a few clarifying questions. Ssanek's first instructions had been a bit vague after all. But no. Looking into Sinna's happy, if a bit sleep-deprived, trusting eyes was enough to see she didn't really know.

"I can assure you I'm not sneaking out to see anyone. I can't imagine when I would have the time." Marellel was sitting down. Now was her chance. She stood. "I'm sorry. But I need to talk to Marellel about something. Classes. I'll see you tonight." Grabbing her tray,

Whispers at the Altar

she hurried through the chairs, winding her way to Marellel's table without looking back.

By the time she reached it, all thoughts of Sinna's teasing had fled from her mind.

"Excuse me, Marellel? Do you mind if I join you?"

Marellel looked up, her thoughtful expression turning up at the corners as she saw Christa. "Certainly." She motioned to a chair then turned to look at the table where Sinna and Westrel still sat. "But wouldn't you rather sit with your friends?"

"Hmm?" Christa sat across from the director. "Oh, no, I think they were about to leave anyway."

"I see."

Christa let a moment of silence pass as she ate three bites. She didn't want to appear overly eager, after all. "You know, maybe you could help me with something."

"I would love to if I can. What do you need?"

Christa took a long slow breath, covered by chewing a bite of leafy green vegetables with little red berries. "I was doing some research. For a paper in History. I was trying to find some information on a pair of Hawks who died in an accident. Wiliran and Welsebel. All I could find was that they died trying to perform an experiment. But finding anything on the actual experiment has been rather difficult."

"I am not surprised," Marellel leaned back in her chair. "Their experiment was considered to be foolish from the beginning. No one has ever tried to duplicate it."

Christa laid her fork down. Here was what she needed. What weeks in the library hadn't gotten her. She should have tried this ages ago. "Why? I mean, why was it foolish and never duplicated?"

"Well," she laid her own fork down and leaned forward, her face lighting up a bit.

This was what Christa had hoped for. She knew Marellel's duties kept her from teaching and that she missed it. All Christa had to do was give her the opportunity.

273

"They had a theory that you could join two points in space."

Christa squinted. How was that supposed to bring Mama back? "I don't understand."

"Suppose you could bring two places, say where we are now at this table, and . . . your room. Suppose we could make both places exist in the same place."

"Why?"

Marellel laughed. "Most people would ask *how*. The why is easy. The only thing that would separate those two places at that point would be the Essence of each place. Which at that point would essentially be the same Essence. Tear a hole in that . . ."

"And you could walk from one place to the other," Christa said with a grin. Perhaps that was it. Ssanek could bring Mama back, but he needed this to get her to Christa. Or perhaps he didn't. Perhaps it was just a test of her resolve.

"Exactly. Of course the notion is patently ridiculous. There is no way to join two places in such a way."

"Is that how they died? Trying to join two places?"

"No. I don't think they even got that far. My understanding is that they did manage to tear the Essence, and the resulting backlash of magic is what killed them."

"They tore the Essence?" Christa couldn't even begin to imagine how to accomplish such a thing.

Marellel nodded. "And died because of it. It is an excellent lesson on the repercussions of reaching too far and ignoring the advice and caution of your peers."

Her tone was serious, and Christa knew she was trying to make a point specifically to her. "I remember." She lowered her eyes. But it was possible. At least the hole was. All she needed was a way to control it and a way to connect the two places. Maybe Ssanek would have an idea of how to do that.

"So how are your friends?"

Christa blinked and looked up. "What?"

Marellel turned to look pointedly at Sinna and Westrel who were still sitting at their usual table. "How are Sinnasarel and Westrel? Sinnasarel is nearing her advancement to Hawk. It can be a very stressful time."

Christa shrugged. "Oh. Yeah. She's doing fine. I think her project is almost done."

Marellel nodded slowly. "And Westrel? Are things any better with her family?"

A sinking feeling was starting in Christa's gut. Why was Marellel asking all these questions? How was Christa supposed to know what was going on with Westrel's family? "She's fine." Christa stood, figuring it might be best to just leave. "I . . . uhh . . . I need to get to class. Instructor Ophidian hates it when I'm late."

"I understand."

Christa turned to go.

"But Christabel . . ."

She paused, half turning.

"Don't forget your friends in all your rushing around. They need you as much as you need them."

She nodded and walked away. Whatever that meant. After all, how could she forget about her friends? They ate nearly every meal together. They talked constantly. She was always there for them.

The class hurried to keep up with Instructor Ophidian and, as usual, Christa lagged behind them all. It was easier to avoid anyone sneaking up behind you that way. She had no idea where they were going. All

Ophidian had said was to follow him. So they were following him. Out of the Essence tower and across the bridge to the central tower.

It was just like him not to tell them anything. He loved theatrics. Christa wasn't sure if it was because he thought he was that clever, or if he was that desperate for attention. Either way it was annoying. Laisel had never been like that. She was always fair and straight to the point. Oh, Christa got in trouble plenty of times, but at least when she did, Laisel didn't go out of her way to embarrass her.

They stopped in the central tower before a large wooden door, somewhere between the throne room below and the library above. It was plain, no different from many of the others in the Roost, save for the iron scrollwork that formed bands across it.

Ophidian turned to face the class, waiting for everyone to gather around before speaking. "This is the Practice Room. Only a Fourth Tier Eyas or above may cross the threshold of this door. The reason for this will become obvious shortly. It is here that you will practice those techniques that are impractical to perform elsewhere. Including, but by no means limited to, combat techniques."

A boy in the front raised his hand.

"Yes, Astran."

"Is this where the old Hawks used to fight when they were challenged to a duel?"

Ophidian looked exasperated. "Yes. There was a time when challenges between Hawks would be settled by combat. But that was in the time of the Founding. I am happy to say such practices are beneath us now."

Christa thought Astran looked disappointed.

A girl, Fassiel, raised her hand. "Why are only Fourth Tier and above allowed in?"

Ophidian smiled. "An excellent question. Thank you, Fassiel. Let us go in, and I will show you." He turned, opened the door, and walked in while the rest of the students crowded in after.

·*Whispers at the Altar*·

Christa eased through last, moving just past the frame and scooting to one side as if the room itself was toxic and staying as close to the door as possible would save her the inevitable sickness. As much as the idea of dueling intrigued her, she knew better than to call any attention to herself in one of Ophidian's classes.

The room wasn't large, at least not by the standards Christa had adopted since living in the cavernous spaces of the palace. It was also empty. Not only empty, but devoid of any adornment or decoration save for a single pedestal in the center. This by itself was unusual enough to be shocking, and a bewildered murmur filtered through the small crowd.

Christa watched as Instructor Ophidian paced to the center of the room, turning to address the class with one hand resting on the pedestal and a small, amused smile on his face. She knew that smile. She hated it and the certain unpleasantness that it would bring. She ducked farther from the safety of the door, behind a taller boy.

"This room will replicate any place or environment you can think of. While it is doing so, your magic will also react differently than you are used to. You will learn the exact methods used to accomplish this in latter classes. For now, all you need to know is that any spell you cast will be altered by the room into something not altogether harmless, but not injuring, either."

Christa couldn't see his expression but she knew what it would look like. That smug smile as he took in the confused expressions of his students.

"It is easiest to understand with a demonstration." There was a pause during which Christa closed her eyes and hoped he wouldn't call her name.

"Christabel, come forward."

Christa let out a long sigh as she opened her eyes to find a nice clear path through her fellow students directly to Instructor Ophidian.

She walked forward to stand in front of him, her hands clasped firmly behind her back.

"Yes, Instructor?"

"Stand over there, please." He pointed to a spot on the opposite side of the pedestal but still in plain sight of the class. "Close the door, please," he asked the class as he walked to a spot a mirror distance from Christabel.

As Christa paced to her spot she noticed for the first time a small red stone, about the size of her fist, sitting atop the pedestal. Its surface was cut into octagonal facets that glimmered in the dim light of the few globes that ringed the room.

The door thumped shut, and the light dimmed even further as the brighter light from the hall was cut off. Christa dragged her eyes up from the stone upon the pedestal to stare defiantly at Ophidian. He said nothing but raised one hand toward the red gem. It glowed brightly, bathing the room in a bloody brilliance before flashing to an intensity so bright it forced Christa to close her eyes. When she opened them the dim light and gray stone walls were gone. She, Instructor Ophidian, and the class were standing in a green field under a bright noon sun.

Christa knew it was an illusion, but she had never seen one so complete. She recovered quickly. She wasn't about to let Ophidian think he could impress her, so she turned a blank expression back to him.

He, however, regarded her as a wolf looks at its dinner. That expression settled Christa back into the here and now, and her focus narrowed. All thoughts of the Illusion, the lights, the stone, and even the other students were forgotten. There was nothing else in the world but her and this pompous instructor who took pleasure in tormenting her. If he wanted a duel, she was more than happy to oblige.

"Now, class, something simple to demonstrate what I was saying earlier," Ophidian said without ever taking his eyes off her. He flicked his wrist and a stream of fire shot out over the green grass toward her.

Whispers at the Altar

Christa barely had time to put her arms up in front of her face and push out with a gust of wind before it struck her. It wasn't enough. A high-pitched scream escaped before she could even register the fact that she wasn't feeling any pain. And then it was over. The scream's last echoes danced in time with the flames that flickered in the grass.

Christa opened her eyes—she couldn't remember closing them—to the laughter of several of her classmates and the self-satisfied smile of the instructor. It had happened so fast. She had used fire before, but she never imagined an attack with it could be so sudden.

"As you can see," Ophidian continued, not bothering to quell the laughter, "the room does not allow you to directly injure each other. However, that does not mean you cannot injure someone indirectly."

He flicked his hand out again, but this time Christa was ready. She'd already guessed the kind of things that might hurt someone here. She wasn't about to get caught off guard again.

She anticipated the simple pull of earth under her, designed to trip her, and stepped quickly to one side. Throwing her hands out in front of her, she pushed as hard as she could at the earth between them. There was nothing subtle about her assault, but Instructor Ophidian was obviously not expecting any kind of retaliation.

The furrow of churning earth plowed through the green grass before jutting up into him just as his smug smile was turning to confusion. The attack threw him back to land on his butt with a gasp that Christa heard from ten paces away. She barely noticed, only registered it on an instinctive, analytical level that told her she held the advantage, and it needed to be pressed.

Taking a step forward, she shoved out again. She knew in her head that the motion wasn't necessary. The Essence needed no such physical prodding to be moved. But while Instructor Ophidian's gestures had been for dramatics, hers simply felt right. A focus for her will.

The grains of earth leapt out in a large bulge, rippling toward him like a building wave.

Allan C.R. Cornelius

"Enough!" he shouted as he leapt to his feet. The wave shuddered, buckled, then died abruptly as the grains lost cohesion until the pieces were too small to do anything with.

Instructor Ophidian blew the resultant sand back at her like stinging mist. He may have been caught off guard by her first attack, but he was still far more skilled and experienced.

The green field faded away, replaced once more by the ordinary, unadorned room. "I did not give you permission to use magic," Ophidian spat as he stalked up to her. "Let alone to attack an instructor." He paused long enough to cast a quick glance at the other students.

They stood silently by the door, though more than a few were smiling. Christa couldn't tell if it was at Ophidian's embarrassment or her own foolishness. It didn't matter. Of course Ophidian would assume it was all about him.

He took another step toward her, close enough that she could smell his breath. "I should kill you now, here in this room," he whispered so only she could hear. "It wouldn't be hard. A single effort would save all of us the ruin you will inevitably bring."

He waited as if for a response, but Christa had no idea what to say to that. No one had ever threatened to kill her before. She looked up at his face and for a moment thought he might do it. She had never seen an elf so angry. And she wondered, for a moment, why the thought didn't frighten her at all.

A long silent moment passed before he turned away. "Report to Director Marellel's office. You can wait there until I have time to explain the situation to her."

Christa walked slowly from the room, the other Eyas parting to make room for her. When she was through the doors, she smiled. A whole room where she could practice. Where she could experiment. And look at what she had done! The image of Ophidian falling played itself over and over in her head. She laughed to herself. It didn't matter what punishment she got for that, it was more than

280

worth it. Besides, the only thing she had really hurt was his pride. She doubted Marellel would punish her much for that.

But that room. It was fantastic. And a stone that could prevent magic from hurting you? Why hadn't she ever heard of that before? Why wasn't that used more? If that could be duplicated . . . it could make someone nearly invincible. You'd have to make the area smaller. And you would still have to watch out for regular stuff like swords. But still.

She grinned. She would need a project for graduation. It might as well be invincibility.

Home

Steven froze. His hands were sweating, making the bow slippery in his grip, and his legs burned from the effort of stalking after the beast. Still, he raised the weapon, sighting down the shaft. He wasn't a very good shot, but the range was good. Barely.

He took a breath . . . let it out . . .

And the rabbit bounded three paces further along to another patch of grass.

Steven cursed it silently but vehemently as he lowered the bow again. They had been playing this game for the past thirty minutes. Steven would close to just within range, then the demon bunny would merrily hop five to ten paces farther. It was toying with him. And Steven cursed all rabbit-kind for it.

He took another slow, careful step forward, his gaze flitting from the grass in front of him to the beast and back again. He tried to recall everything Honovi taught him. But there was too much to remember, and he was sure he was forgetting something.

Step by slow step he closed the distance again.

The rabbit turned its head, one eye peering at him as it munched on the new shoots of spring grass.

Steven raised the bow slowly, watching that evil little eye the whole time. He sighted down the shaft and let out a breath.

The string thrummed, the rabbit jumped, then flew five paces to land on its side, the arrow protruding from its neck.

"Yes!" Steven nearly jumped in the air, but his thighs were too sore from crouching for so long. Then he saw his arrow lodged in the ground a foot from where the beast had been sitting.

"Honovi." He turned to find her already striding up, bow in hand.

"I wanted to eat meat tonight," she said with a smile.

"I would have got him," he grumbled, walking up to retrieve his arrow.

"I'm sure you would have." She gave him a pat on the shoulder as she passed by. "You are getting better. But you forgot to watch the wind. It shifted just after you started. The rabbit could smell you the whole time."

"Of course I forgot something." Steven shook his head. "I think I'll stick with traps. Something that works better with me far away."

Honovi picked up the rabbit by the arrow impaling it and examined it. "I think tomorrow we will work on your strength and aim. It would help if you did not have to get five paces away before you shot."

"It was more than five paces." But Steven saw her smile and his anger fizzled. "More like fifteen," he said with a grin.

"Fifteen then." She winked and turned to walk back to the horses.

Steven watched her walk for a second, then followed. She had traded the simple knee length deerskin skirt traditional among the women of the Yahad for men's breeches of the same material. They were far more practical for hunting and traveling, but the way they accentuated the curves of her legs, punctuated by the gentle sway of her black hair over her . . . He jerked his eyes up to the back of her head. It wasn't right to stare. And the way it made him feel was . . . distracting.

Dinner was quiet. Most of their time since leaving the Shona had been spent in a comfortable silence. It was a blessing after the constant noise and crowd of the caves, and Steven wrapped the silence around himself like an old familiar blanket.

At first he had been worried Honovi might expect him to talk as they traveled. He wondered constantly about what he should say, if he should say anything, and if the fact that he did not was making her angry with him. After the first few hours those worries eased away. She seemed to enjoy the silence as much as he did, and he found that the simple act of riding next to her was enough to make her happy. He wasn't sure how he knew she was happy, it wasn't as if her mouth was fixed in a rictus smile, but he knew all the same. It was as if he could feel it radiating from her. He simply . . . knew.

Which was why he was worried now, lying under his blanket, staring up at the brilliance of a cloudless night sky. That feeling, that *knowing* was gone, replaced by something that made his stomach twist. It had started during dinner, one she had perhaps cooked a bit longer than necessary. All he did was make a comment about how he loved eating ash. It was the same thing he told Brogan all the time. But the way she had glared at him. He could still see that look. One that frightened and worried him at the same time. And ever since . . .

"Honovi," he whispered, "are you awake?"

"Yes."

"Did . . . did I say something wrong?" He didn't even turn his head. He didn't want to see that look again, shadowed by the light of the dying fire.

"No."

He considered. Her answer didn't seem to fit with that look at all. Maybe she didn't realize it was a joke.

"I was joking about the rabbit tasting like ash. It's just something I tell Brogan when he burns the food."

"It is fine."

Good. Now she understood. Now she should be happy again. Steven waited. Ten minutes passed.

He still wasn't getting that feeling. There must be something else wrong.

"Is something else bothering you?"

There was a heavy sigh and the sound of her rolling over. "Go to sleep, Steven."

Maybe she needed a good night's sleep. Maybe she wasn't feeling well. She'd told him to go to sleep, and Steven knew that when he wasn't feeling well, the last thing he wanted was to talk to anyone. He let out a deep breath and closed his eyes.

The faded edges of sleep were just reaching him when he heard her sniff.

"She was a good cook, my mother. She could roast a rabbit perfectly."

"It was fine, really. I . . . I'm sorry I said that." He turned over to look at her, but her back was to him.

"She could make a meal out of nothing." She chuckled, or maybe it was a hiccup. It was hard to tell. "Or at least it seemed like it. She could make sweet bread that melted in your mouth. She kept telling me she would teach me how."

Steven's mind whirled as he tried to think of something to do, something Brogan might have told him that would apply. But all he

Whispers at the Altar

could bring up were the five treatments for vomiting. Silence fell as he thought, and the silence dragged as he started to become desperate.

"What happened to her?" It was the only thing he could come up with but he regretted it as soon as it was out. The last thing he wanted to talk about was mothers.

"She was taken. I left the hut to get water. Father and Hadi, my brother, were out hunting. They met me at the well. We talked. When we came back to the hut . . . it was as if she disappeared."

Steven thought of his own mother, how she would just leave sometimes. "Maybe she had to go somewhere."

Honovi shook her head. "There were others. The village searched for them. They followed tracks west, but then a rain washed them away. We never found her."

"I . . . I'm sorry," He reached out one hand to trail a finger lightly down her back, but jerked it back as she rolled over to face him, dark eyes glinting in the starlight as the embers painted her face in long shadows.

"What was your mother like?" she whispered, as if the stars might hear them trading dark secrets.

"Why?" Steven blurted before he could think. The shadows on Honovi's face shifted, and he could tell he had fractions of a second to avoid another mistake like the one at dinner.

"I mean, I didn't really know her that well, I guess. She didn't talk much." That much at least was true. He took a deep breath, trying to sort through what he could and couldn't tell her.

"Your father doesn't mention her at all. Does he miss her?"

Steven fingered a leaf of grass between them. "He didn't know her. He isn't actually my father. I just think of him that way because he's the only one I've ever known."

"Oh." Silence but for the soft sound of her shifting under her thin blanket. "Was she pretty?"

Steven smiled. "Yes. Very. With long red hair. I remember watching her brush it. Sometimes, when she was very happy, she would hum to herself."

Honovi's fingers touched his, wrapping around them gently. His heart flew into his throat, beating wildly.

"She sounds lovely. I would love to have met her."

His heart sank like a stone in a pond. "I don't think you would have."

"Why not?"

"She was . . . angry. A lot. She didn't say much to me and when she did . . . it wasn't like the way Brogan talks to me, or the way your father talks to you."

Honovi's eyes narrowed slightly. "What kind of things did she say?"

He shrugged. "It's not important. I know she loved me. She just showed it differently than you or Brogan." It took a second to realize what he'd said. "Not that I'm saying you love me. I mean how you show it to your father and Brogan shows it to me. Not that it would be bad or anything, I guess—" He faltered as she squeezed his hand.

"I know what you mean."

"Oh."

"Sometimes I imagine she's still alive," she said. "Father tells me it's foolish. But what if she is?"

"How would you know?"

She shook her head, a barely discernible motion in the dark. "I don't know. But the alternative is . . ."

He had no idea what to say or do next, so he just lay there, watching her face. It was several minutes before he realized he could feel it again, her happiness. Not as strong as before, perhaps, and still tinged with sadness, but it was there.

"Thank you," he finally came up with.

"For what?"

"For coming with me. For teaching me. For talking to me the way you do. It's nice. Brogan is great, but . . . he doesn't act the same way toward me."

She chuckled. "You're welcome. And thank you as well."

"For insulting your cooking?"

The chuckled erupted into a laugh. "Well, yes. For always being honest with me. And for letting me talk to you when I need to."

Steven couldn't help joining in the laughter, though a sharp pain ran through it. Honest? Like how he was honest about whose idea it was to save her? "I think I have the better end of that deal. But you're welcome."

He wasn't sure how long after that he fell asleep. He only knew how disappointed he was when he woke up to find her no longer beside him, her hand no longer in his.

The afternoon sun beat down on Steven's head as they stalked up and around the familiar hill overlooking the hut. He wiped his forehead with the sleeve of his shirt for what must have been the twentieth time since they started up the hill. He knew it wasn't only the heat. His heart was hammering in his chest, had been ever since they spotted the ruins of the barn half an hour ago.

He had expected as much. Still, the idea that someone might be there was wreaking havoc with his nerves. Honovi suggested they climb the hill for a better view. Of course the hill was a perfect place for anyone to keep watch. No lookout would miss their approach. There was no cover save low rocks and tufts of high grass. But no alarm had been raised thus far. A good sign.

He looked to his left, straining to spot Honovi crouched behind a patch of grass. He could barely make her out, about six paces away. She was looking up the shallow rise, bow in hand. Then she was gone again, moving toward the top. He shifted his bow from hand to hand as he stretched his cramping fingers, took a deep breath, and rose into the half-crouch she had taught him.

His legs burned. They'd started off sore from yesterday's hunting, and he could only imagine what they would feel like tomorrow. Still, he did his best to ignore them and kept inching forward, his eyes set on the lone elm tree that dominated the peak of the hill. He knew every nook and cranny of those roots. There was cover enough there for both of them if they kept low enough.

He caught sight of Honovi again about twenty paces from the tree. Actually, she seemed to materialize next to him out of nowhere and nearly startled him into crying out. Steven closed his eyes for a second then glared at her with what he hoped was a *Don't do that again* look and not something closer to *You nearly made me pee my pants.*

She only smiled, then lowered herself from her half-crouch onto her belly, cradling her bow between her arms and chest. Slowly, using her feet and elbows, she wormed her way forward a pace then turned to look back.

Steven gave a single nod and mimicked her, glad to be able to stretch his legs out fully. About halfway the pain in his elbows, knees, and legs had him wishing he could stand again. But Honovi showed no signs of slowing, so he gritted his teeth and pushed through.

Steven knew there was a particularly large hollow between two roots. There they should both be able to huddle together without being seen by anyone below them. He tapped her boot, waited for her to turn her head, then pointed in the direction of the cover. But as they came to the edge Steven realized that it must have been some time since he used the hiding spot. Either that or it had shrunk dramatically.

Still, Honovi slid in, curling in on herself to give him as much room as possible. Steven crawled in after squeezing as much of himself as he could into the tight space. There was an uncomfortable moment when he realized he was practically laying on top of Honovi, their faces a mere inch apart, but then they were looking up over the root, and any other thoughts fluttered away.

◆Whispers at the Altar◆

The hut was still there, but it was a wreck. Nothing remained of what had been the garden, the pens for the pigs, the chicken house, the fences, even the stones that made up the little walkways between the buildings had been torn up and tossed about. The roof was burned and collapsed while the windows were empty. The front door stood blackened and ajar, leaving a yawning opening into the shadowed interior. His home was vacant and hollow. Bones left to rot in the sun while the scavengers picked them clean.

Even steeled for the worst, Steven couldn't help the pain that pierced his heart, nor the regret and anger that followed close after.

"I'm sorry," Honovi whispered.

Steven pressed his lips together, holding on to the anger to beat back any tears that might threaten. Instead, he focused on searching the rubble for any signs of life. There were none. No smoke, no horses, no remains of a camp, and definitely no one walking about.

He stood as smoothly as he could manage with protesting muscles, despite Honovi's whispered protest. He was halfway down the other side of the hill before he realized it could be a trap. But by that time he didn't care. He heard Honovi catch up, walking a step behind and to his right. He didn't turn to look at her. Didn't take his gaze from the ruined front door.

He reached out to slam the door open and stopped. Instead, he stood there, staring in. The fire had claimed much, but he could still make out enough. There, against one wall, was what used to be his bed. The scorched remnants of the table lay on its side against the opposite wall. Chests were opened, and their burnt and tattered contents scattered about the room as if they had exploded.

Steven looked back to the door, reaching out a hand to brush against it.

"So many memories," he murmured.

"That is home," Honovi whispered. "Memories."

Her hand touched his back, and he tried to draw strength from it.

"But I lived here such a short time. How can there be so many memories? The first time I walked through this door. Watching Brogan burn dinner. Listening to him teach me about . . . about everything."

"Time doesn't matter. It was home."

He walked two paces in and reached down to pick up a small knife. "He taught me to carve with this." He hefted it with a smile, then turned a slow circle, searching the room. He found his chair smashed and half-burned in one corner. He let out a deep breath. "Everything's gone. Everything."

He thought of Brogan living here for years. How many more memories must he have? How much more loss must he feel? He thought of Honovi, of all her people. All their homes. All their memories. Everything they were.

Honovi walked to him, stepping carefully over the detritus of what used to be his life. "Not everything. You and Brogan are alive. That is what matters. It is not the stone and furniture that makes home. It is—" She bent over to move a shelf dislodging a half-dozen large black lizards hiding from the heavy afternoon sun. Honovi staggered backward in surprise as they hissed and skittered across the floor to other shadowed parts of the ruin.

Steven reached out a hand to steady her. "I hate lizards."

Honovi took his hand in hers as she looked around the single room. "Should we get what we came for then?"

She didn't say that the place gave her the creeps, but she didn't have to. Something about it was wrong. This wasn't home any more. Something else had moved in, and it wasn't just the lizards.

He nodded, and together they sifted through the wreckage. The same thought kept running through his mind. That this wasn't really his house. That wasn't the chair he used to sit in. Those weren't the dishes he used to wash. It all belonged to
someone else. It helped. Or maybe it was Honovi's hand in his own, her fingers twined between his.

It took nearly half an hour of searching, and they were both covered in ash by the time they were done, but the time wasn't wasted. Three of Brogan's books had survived the fire, buried under a collapsed section of wall. And while all the pots of plants had been broken, a few had survived, digging their roots into the packed dirt of the floor. It took another fifteen minutes to transplant them, most of the time spent looking for anything to serve as a pot.

An hour after arriving, Steven was carefully placing everything into a sack, along with a few other odds and ends, when Honovi grabbed his arm, shushing him furiously and ducking down under the ledge of a window.

Steven ducked, shoved the last few things in, and then crawled over to the window. "What is it?" he whispered, but Honovi only glared at him and indicated the window with a quick motion of her eyes. He started to slide up to take a peek, but her grip on his arm tightened, and she pulled him back down.

It was only then he noticed how wide her eyes were or how fast her pulse was racing. Then he heard it, too.

The frequent but slow tread of multiple horses walking. Then the soft murmur of conversation.

" . . . sayin' I don' understand why we gotta patrol this area, know? We been through 'ere a dozen times already. Ain't no one live anywhere near 'ere no more." The voice was loud and grating. The exact opposite of the soft commanding voice that answered.

"We all 'eard you the first dozen times today, Makon. Now shut up and start drawin' the water."

There was a series of loud crunches, feet hitting the ground, then the noise of several people walking around in the yard outside where the fence had been and where the well still stood.

"Don' know what's got his knickers in a bunch," the first voice muttered. "Jus' sayin' it makes no sense is all." There was a grunt, followed by the creak of the well's wheel.

293

Steven's gaze was locked with Honovi's. His knees hurt from where they were pressed into the rubble beneath the window, but he dared not move. The well was only ten paces away at the most.

"He's afraid of *them*," a third man said. "And you would be too if you had a lick o' sense. You keep carryin' on like that . . . You know what they'll think."

"I ain't disloyal," Makon hurried to say. "I'm just as Chosen as either o' ya."

The creaking stopped, followed a moment later by the splash of the bucket falling down the well. When the wheel resumed its nerve-grating side of the conversation, Steven took the opportunity to shift his leg slightly. It didn't help.

"Don' matter what ya are. Matters what *it* thinks ya are. An' ya can bet it heard ya complainin' 'bout its orders all day."

"So? Man ain't allowed to complain? Geesh, ya sound like my wife."

They were obviously from Ceerport or some other village taken by the servants of Ssanek. But it sounded as if something else was with them? One of the Seers? Steven could barely focus through the pain in his knee.

Honovi shifted, pulling away her hand to silently draw an arrow and lay it to the string of her bow. Her mouth was set in a hard, determined line. Steven shook his head. He could see what she was thinking, but there were at least three of them. Even if they caught them by surprise . . . the risk was too great.

Honovi glared at him and nodded at the window.

The squealing of the well stopped, and there was a long silence.

Steven held his breath. Had they been heard? He reached for his bow. It wasn't there.

He looked around the ransacked room. Not there either. Then he remembered. He'd left it on the hill, forgotten under the tree in his rush to get down to the hut.

•*Whispers at the Altar*•

The splash of the well bucket made him jump, disturbing the pile of stones he crouched on and sending a few sliding down with a soft rattle.

"Fine. Get yerself taken. One more sacrifice. No skin off my nose. Jus' make sure you water the horses before ya do." There was a grumble and the sound of footsteps walking away.

Honovi started to rise, pulling back the arrow as she did.

Steven pulled her back down, shaking his head.

Her eyes were like fire as she pulled her arm out of his grasp.

It's not safe, he mouthed.

She mouthed something back, but it was too fast and too angry for Steven to make sense of. He wasn't entirely sure it was even in Chisaran.

"Hey! Look at this." The cry came from some distance away, perhaps up the hill.

Steven's heart sank. His bow.

Footsteps traveled away from them, but he knew they would be coming back. He reached out to tug on Honovi's arm. *We have to go.* He motioned to the back of the hut and a crack in the wall they could crawl through. *Now!*

She shook her head again and rose, peeking over the broken sill of the window.

Steven cursed to himself and inched up until he could see as well.

It was his bow. One man stood at the foot of the hill holding it out for the other two. Four horses stood by the well, two drinking from buckets as the others nibbled on what meager half-dead grass grew nearby. Steven's throat went dry. Where was the fourth rider?

As he watched, the three men turned to look at the hut and Steven's heart leaped into his parched throat. He dropped down to the ground. "We have to go. Now," he whispered.

Honovi glared at him and started to crawl away. But not before muttering, "We could have defeated them."

Steven didn't care. He just wished she would move faster. Let her be angry, at least she would be alive.

They were halfway across the room with the noise of the men already back at the well when he saw the lizard. A black one, longer than his forearm, sitting on a piece of burned wood, pale green eye staring at him.

Steven tried to shoo him off, but the thing refused to move. Then he saw another lying up on the ruins of his bed. And another on the sill of the window they had just left. Two more by what used to be the table. Another in the fireplace. All watching the two of them as they crawled through the dust and ashes.

Honovi saw them, too. She looked at him with worried eyes.

Then, as if being spotted was their cue, the room erupted in a high-pitched keening as each lizard's mouth opened to add to the chorus.

Steven and Honovi scrambled to their feet.

Steps and shouts echoed behind them.

They half-ran, half-stumbled to the opening in the far wall. Honovi reached it first, started to leap through, then recoiled with a cry.

Steven turned from looking back over his shoulders at the three men, armed with hatchets and bloodied hammers, to see something blocking the exit.

Some *thing*, for it wasn't human, at least not fully. Dressed only in ragged trousers, one side of its broad, muscular chest rippled with tiny flashing scales of green and yellow. Those scales traveled over its shoulder and down the twisted and multi-jointed right arm to end in a four-fingered claw twice as large as a hand. The black talons of that claw glistened wetly in the sun.

But it was the head, the face, if face it could be called, that arrested Steven's steps, even making him stumble back two steps. The scales rose over it, covered it like a hood, but from within that hood he could see the glint of orange eyes and the emptiness of slitted pupils.

Allan C.R. Cornelius

It smiled, revealing rows of teeth crowded into a too-small mouth. They jutted out at odd angles and overlapped each other in a forest of needles that dripped thick, pale, green ooze down a chin that ended in a single jagged horn.

The footsteps stuttered to a halt behind them.

"Guests," the thing spat, its voice a low, guttural growl. "How lovely."

TUTORING

"You are troubled, child," Ssanek whispered through the roiling shadows.

Christa sighed, sitting on the smooth, black onyx that stood conveniently beside her. "Oh, it's just Ophidian. He's having me copy this treatise on the first recorded Elementalists again. Says I left parts out last time."

Ssanek chuckled. "Did you?"

"Maybe." She kicked a stone, sending it clattering off into the mist that surrounded her. "But it was so boring. And I've already read it at least three times."

"You think he hates you."

"Obviously! I mean what other explanation is there?"

"Indeed. You are human. The elves have always despised my people. Jealous of their adaptable minds and their fearless spirit. You have a power they will never know or understand."

Christa smiled. "Is that why I'm learning everything so much faster?"

"Of course. You, child, are a marvel that has never existed before. The union of elven magic and human mind. They have no idea what you are capable of. And that terrifies them."

Christa's smile grew. "So I'm not a freak?"

Ssanek's laugh was like a landslide of scree and boulders. "A freak? No, child. You are a wonder. A beauty. A queen. And you should be treated as no less. By *anyone*."

Christa jerked awake, the echo of Ssanek's words still ringing in her mind. She enjoyed talking to Ssanek. He always knew what to say. She couldn't help but laugh, though, as she wiped the drool from her cheek and the pages of her book—not very queenly. Then the third evening bell rang, and she leapt to her feet with a curse, knocking over her chair. She must have fallen asleep copying pages. Now she was sure to be late.

She pulled her cloak tight as she stepped onto the bridge from the Elementalists' tower. She couldn't help running a hand through the now shoulder-length hair under her hood. She would much rather have gone through the yard than challenge the bridge and the memories it conjured, but she was in far too much of a hurry to take the long way around.

Winter was in full force. The Commencement Ball was only weeks away, but the snow was already piled knee deep in places around the palace. Even with her cloak pulled close and the hood thrown over her head, Christa couldn't avoid the biting wind that whirled across the spans of the Roost. Even the bright afternoon sun did little to offer respite.

She was halfway to the central tower when she heard a voice calling her name, the sound faint as the wind carried it away. She paused, turned back, and spotted a small group of figures hurrying toward her. It took a moment of squinting to recognize them, and even though the sight brought a smile to her face, she couldn't help feeling a bit annoyed at being delayed.

"Christa!" Sinna called out again as she hurried to a stop. "F-Fancy meeting you here." Westrel and Darian came up behind, making a little half-circle as though to keep their friend from escaping.

Christa could never understand how Sinna walked about in freezing weather with barely more than a summer cloak. It just wasn't natural. "You're lucky to find me here at all," she answered, hiking the strap of her satchel further up her shoulder. "I was on my way to the library." She started walking again. She didn't want to give the impression she was trying to avoid them, but she did need to keep going.

"We'll walk with you then," Sinna said, skipping over to walk beside her. Westrel and Darian fell in step behind, apparently content to let her harass Christa for now.

"How did you even know it was me?" Christa asked, turning to peer at Sinna.

"There really aren't many people here as short as you who go around in thick white cloaks with a permanently mud b-bedraggled hem. I took a chance."

Christa chuckled and looked down at the hem of her cloak, which was even then dragging along the worn surface of the bridge. "I take it this isn't just a visit to say hello?" She glanced at everyone.

"Of course not," Westrel said. "Though you have been very lax lately about spending time with us. If we didn't know better, we would think you were avoiding us."

Sinna's light laugh made it obvious that was a ridiculous notion. "No, we were just talking about the b-ball. We were wondering if you had picked out your dress yet."

"I hear Tamaran is fond of green," Westrel added with a sly smile.

"And I've heard he'll be there," Sinna confirmed.

301

Tamaran was the latest in a string of young men Sinna had attempted to arrange Christa with. It seemed they did not disagree with the principle of Vaniel's failed attempt. Only the method.

Christa took a deep breath to force down the frustration and raised her hands, stopping at the door to the library. "Look, I don't have time for this." She tried her best to keep her tone friendly. She knew they were only trying to help. It was the same every year.

"I have a mountain of work from Instructor Ophidian that needs to be done and, as if that wasn't enough, Director Marellel has given me a student to tutor in Essence. I barely have time to sleep, let alone go to balls or pick out dresses or worry about who is going and what colors they like."

There was a moment's silence before Sinna spoke up again, her enthusiasm refusing to be dampened. "We'll just talk to Director M-Marellel and have her lift some of the work so you can go."

"Don't you think I've tried?" Christa asked, exasperated. "She can't. Something about how Instructor Ophidian was appointed by the secretary so only the secretary can dictate any changes to the way Ophidian teaches."

"But you're the best student I've seen, Christa," Sinna tried. "I've seen you breeze through p-practices. What could he possibly be assigning you that takes so long? Is he giving you tasks above your level?"

Christa huffed. "I wish. Exactly the opposite. I've never been so bored, even in History. We haven't tried anything new in months. He just keeps hammering away at the same manipulations I mastered six months ago, while having me copy entire chapters out of Essence theory books from the library."

"He is holding you back on purpose then," Westrel noted.

Christa gave a shrug. "Whether it's on purpose or not doesn't matter. What matters is right now I have to get to the library to tutor this Alainel. Then I have to finish copying twenty pages for Ophidian for my Elemental Theory class, followed by a complete analysis of the battle of Wikker Ridge for him for Tactics class. Then somehow have time to finish my chores from this morning."

"But you must be allowed to go to the ball. Surely Director Marellel can do something about that!" Sinna insisted.

"You're more than welcome to try. But I wouldn't get your hopes up." Christa turned, her hand reaching for the handle of the door.

"We will talk to her, Christa," Westrel affirmed. "In the meantime, try to relax."

Christa gave her a smile she hoped was reassuring then walked in out of the cold, closing the door behind her.

Of course she'd left unsaid that she also had research to do for the experiment. Compared to that, a ball really was trivial.

She quickened her pace as she entered the library. The warmth was refreshing, and ordinarily she would have taken a moment to let it seep into her bones, but she was very worried about being late. She didn't know much about Alainel, but she didn't want to make a bad first impression with someone she was supposed to be teaching. She stopped long enough to throw the hood back from her head and hike up the satchel on her shoulder again.

Christa found Alainel in one of the dozens of study rooms off the library. She was sitting with a quiet air of false patience that bled annoyance. She was young. She couldn't have been at the Roost much more than ten years. Which would put her in her early thirties. Still, to Christa's eye she wasn't more than a young teenager. It was a view only reinforced by the petulant gray eyes gazing at her imperiously from a face framed by careful ringlets of pale white hair. Even her close-necked cobalt blue dress with its white lace at the cuffs and tiered hem shouted superiority. Something Christa thought odd from someone of such an obviously low social station.

Christa took a deep breath she hoped wasn't visible and offered her brightest smile. "Alainel? My name is Christabel, but you can call me Christa. Director Marellel asked me to help you with your Essence practice." She took a step forward and held out a hand.

Alainel looked at the hand, then back up to Christa's eyes, leaving her arms crossed over her chest. "You are late, Christabel. I do have other things to do, you know."

Christa cleared her throat and walked to the chair across from Alainel to sit down, setting her satchel on the table between them. "Yes, I'm sure you do," she muttered. There was a moment of silence as they stared at each other. "So," she tried to put as much cheer as she could into her voice without sounding ridiculous, "what do you find to be the hardest part of seeing the Essence?"

Alainel raised an eyebrow. "Seeing it."

"Well, yes. But there must be something your instructors asked you to try. I would think some part of that would be causing you difficulty."

"I have been able to see it," she stated. "Just not for long."

Christa considered, finding it easier to think when her eyes were focused on the wall behind the girl. "I can take you through the same way I learned. Maybe you will find it easier than what you've been trying." Alainel gave a shrug Christa took as an assent. "Go ahead and close your eyes."

Alainel rolled her eyes before closing them, adjusting her crossed arms to make herself more comfortable without giving up a bit of her disdain.

Christa suppressed an exasperated sigh and tried to focus. "Now reach out with your senses. Try to feel everything. Try to feel everything you're touching and everything you can hear. Let yourself relax, but focus at the same time. Stretch out and try to feel everything you can."

"Maybe I could focus if you would stop talking," Alainel muttered.

A deep calming breath. "I'm just trying to help you, Alainel. If you need me to stop talking, all you have to do is ask." She watched the girl as the silence closed in around. Alainel was anything but relaxed. In fact, to Christa, it looked more like she was playing along, waiting for time to pass so she could leave.

◆*Whispers at the Altar*◆

After ten minutes Christa could stand it no longer. "Alainel," she said, trying her best to be encouraging, "you need to relax. You're never going to get it if you don't let yourself relax."

"I am relaxed!" Alainel snapped back, opening her eyes just long enough to glare at Christa.

Christa's hands clenched, but she managed to keep her voice calm. "Perhaps something else," she said more to herself than Alainel. It was obvious she wasn't trying, but there had to be some way Christa could get through her arrogance. She tried to think of things that relaxed her, but all that came to mind was Mama. When she had first touched the Essence, it had been remembering Mama that helped her. Even now, all she had to do was think about the times she spent with her and she felt much better.

"Alainel," Christa whispered, in deference to the girl's supposed concentration, "why don't you try thinking about something relaxing to you? For me it's my mama. Maybe there is someone that helps you feel peaceful or a place like one of the courtyards or a garden."

"What I would find relaxing is being taught by someone who had the faintest idea what they were doing," Alainel grumbled, opening her eyes once again. "It is obvious you have no idea how to help me, and no wonder."

"What is that supposed to mean?" Christa shot back, her mask of calm beginning to fracture. She was tired of coddling this spoiled brat.

Alainel smiled condescendingly. "How could a half-human possibly know how to teach an elf to use magic? It isn't a part of you the way it is us."

"Really? Is that why I could see the Essence the first time I tried? Is that why I've done more in three years than any of you have done in fifteen?"

Alainel rolled her eyes. "Of course. Your humanness is tainting the way you should be learning. I heard about what happened with Instructor Lisilan. You might have learned to use magic, but you will never learn to control it. You will never understand it the way we do. And that is why trying to learn from you is a waste of time. All I will learn is how to do it wrong."

Christa lurched up, her fists clenched as she glared down at the girl. "Why you smug, self-righteous, arrogant, pile of . . . sheep vomit! If you're so superior, figure it out on your own." She rushed out of the room, but not fast enough to avoid hearing Alaina's parting thrust.

"Exactly what I am talking about."

Sinna jumped and spilled the water she was pouring as her bedroom door slammed open. She spun around, splashing more water on the floor. "What in . . ." She took a deep breath as she saw Christa and barely bit back an admonishment. The girl was obviously upset, but Sinna still wanted to yell at her. Sometimes Christa's lack of manners was anything but charming.

"What's wrong, Christa?"

"That . . . spoiled little brat," Christa fumbled, pointing vaguely toward the door. "Not only does she refuse to listen, or take anything I say seriously, she actually . . ." Christa growled in frustration.

"Alainel?" Sinna asked, trying to piece things together.

"Yes, Alainel!" Christa confirmed as if it should be obvious. "That little toadstool."

Sinna sighed. If she wanted to go to the ball, she desperately needed to get some work done. But that wasn't going to happen as long as Christa was in one of her moods. She walked over to sit on the bed, motioning for Christa to have the chair. "Calm down, Christa. She didn't want to listen?"

Christa ignored the offered chair and took up pacing. "That's putting it mildly. It was more like she ignored me. She actually told me she didn't have to listen because I wasn't an elf. As if the fact that my

•Whispers at the Altar•

father was human has anything to do with whether or not I know what I'm talking about."

Sinna tried to keep her voice calm. "Maybe she didn't understand what y-you were trying to tell her."

Christa stopped and looked at Sinna incredulously. "I was telling her to relax. I don't think that is so hard a concept. She wouldn't even do that. She had no respect for me at all. She arrived intending to do nothing I asked of her."

"So what did you do?"

Christa threw her hands up, "I got mad. I told her she could figure it out on her own and I left. She wasn't going to listen to me."

Sinna's eyes widened. "You yelled at her? And stormed off? Don't you think that's a little childish? I mean . . ."

"Childish?" Christa took a step forward. "She insulted me. She refused to listen."

Sinna's back stiffened. "She's a child, Christa. You're s-supposed to be the adult. How can you expect to convince anyone else you're mature enough to handle more responsibility if you don't have the backbone to stand up to a child?"

Christa's eyes narrowed. "I've stood up to more in the past four years than you could imagine, Sinna."

"Yes," Sinna said flatly. "So you're fond of reminding me." She tucked her feet under her. "So why should you care what Alainel thinks of you? She wouldn't listen, fine. Tell Marellel. I'm sure she wouldn't be happy to hear a student wasn't showing someone the proper respect. But don't r-run away."

"Sure, then Marellel will think I can't handle my own problems. Or worse, the little brat will deny everything, and Marellel will think I'm making up stories to cover my own incompetence."

Sinna had a brief vision of smacking Christa right across the face to bring her to her senses. Were all human teenagers like this?

Instead, she shook her head. "I hate to say it, but you obviously c-couldn't handle this problem. And that's not such a bad thing. Everyone fails sometimes. Marellel knows that."

"Oh, and wait until Ophidian hears about it, because you know he will," Christa rambled on. "He'll use it as even more ammunition that I'm not ready to advance and keep me doing the same. Boring. Stupid. Useless. Exercises." She accentuated each word with a stomp on the stone floor.

Sinna scooted back on her bed. She'd never seen Christa like this. She had always had a temper, but this tantrum was beyond the norm.

"Christa, it will be fine. You just need to show Alainel you're in charge. Don't give her an option. If being nice won't work, then be mean. You goal is n-not to be her friend, it's to make her learn. And as for Instructor Ophidian . . ."

She paused, uncertain how to put it. "I think you need to stop p-pushing so hard. Not everything needs to come right now. Have you ever stopped to think there might be a good reason he isn't letting you progress?"

"Pushing?" Christa blurted, spinning to face Sinna with eyes alight. "I'm telling you I've been doing the same basic lessons for months, Sinna. Months. This isn't about me showing him patience, it's about him hating me."

She took a step forward.

"He hates me because I'm human . . . because of what I can do . . . because I'm better than he is."

She took another step forward and the water in the bowls started to steam.

"That's all I've gotten from anyone here. They don't even know what humans are but they hate them. They hate them because they're afraid."

Christa took another step forward, and Sinna shrank back against the wall as water started to boil and the bowls and silverware began to bend.

"Well guess what? You *should* be!"

Whispers at the Altar

A spray of steam shot into the air out of hopelessly twisted and melted bowls. Disfigured spoons clattered to the floor.

Sinna cowered, avoiding the steam as her eyes flitted back and forth between the desk and her friend. Christa only growled as she spun and stalked from the room, the door booming closed behind her.

Sinna stared at the closed door for a second, her mouth gaping, before leaping up and running to open it. She looked both ways down the hall, but Christa was nowhere to be seen. Sinna walked back into her room, waving her hand in front of her face, and opened her window to let the steam drift out.

"Was that Christa that just stormed out of here?"

Sinna turned to see Vaniel standing in the open doorway, her face as much a mix of concern and worry as Sinna assumed her own must be. What in the world had got into Christa? It wasn't like her to explode like that. At least, not at her.

"Yes, it was. I d-don't think she is having a very good day." The attempt at levity fell flat. Sinna stood in the window enjoying the cool breeze on her back and looked back at her experiment. It was ruined. She would have to start over.

"Did she break anything?" Vaniel came into the room and began trying to clean up the mess that was Sinna's project.

Sinna smiled. Whatever Vaniel had done before, she had been nothing but kind since being disowned. And not just to them. Sinna hadn't seen her so much as raise her voice to anyone in years. Which was more than she could say for Christa.

"You don't have to do that," Sinna said as she walked up to her desk. "I'll clean it all up later."

Vaniel nodded, setting the few twisted spoons she had picked up on the desk. "Do you think we should tell someone? It isn't like her to act like this."

Sinna considered that. Vaniel knew as well as Sinna what Christa's temper was like. But whatever the reasons behind it this time, there was no excuse for it. She should tell Marellel. Not to get Christa into trouble of course. Sinna was mad, but Christa was still her friend.

"Maybe Director M-Marellel," she finally decided, "she'll want to know if one of the Eyas are acting oddly."

"Exactly. And after all, it is part of our duty to keep an eye on each other," Vaniel said. "To help each other."

Sinna chuckled. "Exactly."

"You know," Vaniel said as they walked out the door, "maybe she needs some distraction. Some fun. I know just the thing."

SHOPPING

"Come in."

"There you are. We've been searching everywhere for you." Sinna was practically skipping as she, Westrel, and Vaniel walked into the empty classroom where Christa was studying.

Christa couldn't help but grin. Just the sight of them was usually enough to push all her dark thoughts to the side. Not out of her mind, but as near as they ever were.

Sinna walked over to lean against a table. She wore a smile that appeared to hold back some world-altering secret.

"What is it?" Christa asked. She knew that look.

"Oh, I was walking through town on an errand for Liranan and saw the most p-perfect dress for you to wear to the ball."

The ridiculous grin grew as she spoke, and Christa couldn't help rolling her eyes. "Not this again." She leaned back, enjoying the warmth of the nearby fire.

"You should go this time, Christa," Vaniel pleaded.

"Why this time?" Christa had heard all kinds of reasons. She was curious what they had come up with this time.

"Because apparently Director Marellel is under the impression you are in desperate need of some . . . diversion," Westrel interjected as she sat next to Sinna. Her eyes twinkled as they always did when she was plotting. "She seems to have recently learned that you are under a great deal of stress."

"And where would she have gotten that impression, I wonder?"

"We never said so," Westrel shot back. "Not exactly. But whatever conclusion the director came to, she told us you had two choices. You could go to the ball, or you could spend the entire night doing dwarven conjugations in her office."

Christa frowned. "She's going to punish me for not going to a ball? That's hardly fair. Not to mention it makes no sense to give me more work to do when I'm already—" She caught herself before she could say it.

"Exactly," Westrel said, not needing magic to read Christa's mind. "She seems to also believe it will have the added benefit of furthering your education, being a part of such an important elven cultural event."

"Oh, come *on* Christa," Sinna pleaded. "It will be fun. You're turning something that would be a great time into a chore. You said before you couldn't go because of all the work you had to do. Now Marellel has made sure you can go. So y-you have no excuse."

"And it isn't as though you will be alone," Vaniel added "Everyone is going. Sinna, Westrel, Darian. Even me. You will have plenty of company."

Christa sighed. "That doesn't mean I have any less work to do." But still, she knew what it meant to Vaniel to be around all those people who would be looking down on her. The fact that she was going, too . . . "It doesn't sound as though you've left me much of a choice," she said with a smile.

"Sure we have. You could do conjugations." Westrel grinned. "There are *always* choices."

Christa couldn't help but laugh. "At least if I'm late with any of my work for Ophidian, I can tell him its Marellel's fault. All right, you connivers. I'll go. And I suppose I'll even try to enjoy myself, though I don't make any promises."

"Excellent!" Sinna clapped her hands as she stood up. "Now that's settled, we should go take a look at that d-dress."

Christa sighed, "I have dresses."

"Oh please, Christa, this is the C-C-Commencement Ball. It marks the graduation of the newest group of Hawks, the founding of Ellsabae, and the raising of this very palace—according to legend. You can't wear just any dress." She raised a finger as Christa opened her mouth again, "And don't bother arguing you don't have any money. You know very well Westrel and I will be more than happy to cover the c-cost as we've said before."

"Though even if they didn't, I am sure Director Marellel would be happy to," Vaniel interjected.

"Indeed." Sinna looked out the window. "So . . . since you're not doing anything right now, I think today is perfect for an outing into the city."

Christa thought of protesting. She had a test to study for, and it was freezing outside, but the break would be nice. And she did enjoy going into Ellsabareth. She rarely had the chance. "Fine, I'm tired of arguing. Let me get some proper shoes, and I'll meet you in the yard."

Within half an hour she was walking out the palace doors, half-listening to her friends prattle on about dresses, sashes, cloaks, and jewelry. They were topics Christa had very little experience or interest in, but she tried to listen to be polite. She loved walking through the park surrounding the palace. The heavy snows of winter were starting to melt away under the youngest rays of spring sun, and there was a freshness in the cold air that gave subtle hints of the riot of color that would soon be washing over the hill. By the time they reached the silver gates leading out into King's Square, she had lost the conversation completely. But since no one was addressing her, it didn't seem to matter.

As they passed through the square, she couldn't help letting her eyes linger, as they always did, on the spot where Papa stood as she walked away nearly four years ago. Neither could she help the twist of heartache and anger it put deep in her stomach. She missed him. She missed his laugh, his smile, his reassuring hugs. But she'd lost him before they ever got to Ellsabareth. And only bringing Mama back would convince him to love her again.

Christa shivered and looked away, ahead past her friends, dreaming of what it would be like.

Before long they were ducking into shop after shop and Christa was thrown completely out of her element. She never imagined there were so many variations in color, style, and embellishment for something as simple as a dress. She doubted she could ever be on time to a class if she had even a fraction of these options in the morning.

Still, it was fun to watch the others going about like bees in a spring garden, ogling this dress, feeling this material, calling each other over to share their discoveries. They were all beautiful, and after a few hours she began pausing longer by certain gowns, trying to imagine herself wearing them. She never could. They were far more extravagant than anything she had considered wearing in her wildest dreams. But it was fun to try.

"Don't think we've f-forgotten about you, Christa," Sinna interrupted, catching her standing in front of a delicate white gown. There were white roses embroidered down the skirt that moved on their own in an unfelt breeze. She stood behind Christa, peering from the dress to her. "You should try it on," she declared at last, motioning to a clerk.

Whispers at the Altar

Christa started to object, but then Westrel was beside her. "I wonder what the male past perfect tense for *dance* is in dwarven."

Christa could only laugh and accept the inevitable. "Dwarves don't have a word for dance, Westrel."

"Ahhh. Perhaps you should live with them sometime. But in the meantime . . ."

They spent the next hour and a half finding the perfect dress. It was a process the others enjoyed far more than Christa. No matter what she liked it was too simple, or not flattering, or the wrong colors. But then Christa found several of Sinna's choices to be far too extravagant and some of Vaniel's downright embarrassing.

After much debate, they settled on a deep green dress, overlaid with a red floral cutout, with short off-the-shoulder sleeves. Christa had to admit she loved the way it looked on her. She was even a bit excited about wearing it, though that took a plunge when they walked out, and Sinna immediately started talking about finding the proper shoes. And jewelry. And underthings.

It was dinnertime before they finished. They found an outside table at a small restaurant near the shops, and Christa relished in the simple pleasure of sitting. Her hands kept drifting up to finger the new earrings Sinna insisted on buying. They matched her necklace, with small silver dragons, wings folded as though diving, and a small ruby set for each eye. They reminded her how lucky she was to have such friends.

The cool evening air made her shiver, bringing her thoughts back to her surroundings and what Sinna was saying.

"What, you don't like him, Christa?"

"Hmm? Who?"

They all laughed. "Don't mind her, Sinna. She is probably just thinking about who *she* might see at the ball. You notice the dress she picked was green."

Christa couldn't help the blood rushing to her face no matter how she tried to play it off.

"Indeed I did." Sinna patted Christa's knee. "So you know for sure D-Darian is coming?" she asked Westrel, reverting to the previous conversation.

"Yes, he told me both he and Levilian would be going. He asked if you had an escort yet," she added with a small smile.

Sinna couldn't keep the color from her cheeks. "And what did you tell him?"

"That you did not, but would not be opposed to the idea."

Sinna sniffed and tried to adopt a more dignified pose. "Not at all, if he were the r-right sort."

"And by 'the right sort' you of course mean Darian," Westrel added with a smirk.

"He would qualify, yes." Sinna barely suppressed an ear-to-ear grin, but it dissipated as she squinted over Vaniel's shoulder. "Wait, isn't that Director Dalan?"

Vaniel's expression fell as she twisted around. "Yes, it is."

Christa peered across the street, spotting the overweight elf in meticulously maintained robes browsing through a display of men's clothing set out in front of a shop. She too frowned. "What is he doing here?"

"Seems to be doing a fair bit of shopping himself," Sinna mused, indicating the stack of parcels hovering behind him. "Wonder if he's getting ready for the ball as well."

Vaniel shrugged as she turned back around. "I doubt he misses one. He is very close to several of the more powerful nobles."

"I do not see why he would need any new clothes," Westrel commented. "He could always Illusion his own to whatever he wants, correct?"

Sinna chuckled. "Ah, but then he wouldn't be k-keeping up with the latest fashions. Didn't you know four button coats are all the rage with the royals this season?"

They both laughed, but Vaniel's face was a mask.

Christa groaned. "Oh, good Creator, he's coming over."

◆Whispers at the Altar◆

They fell silent as they all watched him cross the street, angling directly toward them—all but Vaniel, who seemed to shrink in her seat.

"Good evening, ladies. An excellent evening for a dinner under the early stars. Doing a little shopping for the ball I take it?"

Westrel took an obvious look around at the bags and parcels arrayed around them before answering, "Why yes. However did you guess?"

"Were you s-shopping for the ball as well?" Sinna asked, interrupting before Westrel could say anything truly disrespectful.

"Me? No no, I was just out taking a stroll . . . window shopping as it were." He glanced around and appeared to see Christa for the first time. "Ahh . . . good evening, Christabel. I hardly recognized you out of the palace corridors. Director Marellel let you out of your cage, did she?"

Christa glowered, but pushed down the urge to say something she might regret. "Director Marellel has asked that I attend the Red Ball."

"Has she?" he asked, his false joviality shredding away. He forced a smile. "Yes, well I guess she would consider that her duty. I suppose she feels it an excellent opportunity for you to . . . observe more of our traditions."

"Isn't that . . ." Sinna began, but Christa cut in, her voice as flat as the director's.

"Actually I think that was exactly what she thought. She seems to place a high priority on my learning about and understanding elven culture. Probably because it is, in fact, my own culture. Wouldn't you agree?"

Director Dalan stared at her for several seconds before shaking his head minutely. His expression shifted to that of an adult explaining something to a child. "You left your culture, if culture you could call it, behind years ago. I am quite sorry, my dear, but as much as you try to play at being an elf, as hard as you try to twist your way into our society, you will never be one of us. This will never be your culture. I believe Director Marellel does you a great disservice by deluding you into thinking otherwise."

"She b-belongs here as much as any of us!" Sinna said. "She's more t-t-talented than anyone I know. And she's s-smarter than most!" Her voice carried clearly over the conversation of the other tables.

He turned that same condescending look to Sinna. "I don't expect you to understand. For some reason, you have forged a friendship with her." His face made the words appear sour in his mouth. "But magical talent does not make an elf. It does, however, make one dangerous. Especially when combined with just enough brains and far too little wisdom."

Sinna's eyes fell, and Christa was instantly reminded of her tantrum in Sinna's room. She never had apologized for that. She just assumed Sinna forgave her.

"Sir," Westrel spat the title, her green eyes flashing, "only a fool would call Christa 'dangerous.' Anyone who took the time to know her would know she wouldn't intentionally hurt a fly. Besides, it is ridiculous to assume someone is dangerous purely because they have magic. By that estimation, all of us are dangerous."

The director's expression grew serious, the false sugar gone as a shadow grew over the table. "We are. All of us."

He stared hard at Christa but she only glared back. She was dangerous. And he was smart to fear her.

"And youth often cannot fathom the wisdom of its elders, Westrel Tala," he continued as he turned back to regard her. "You would do well to remember that when speaking to a director of the Roost. I assure you I did not attain my position by being foolish or ridiculous. Your friend should not be here any more than a dwarf. If you doubt me, ask her. I am sure she could give a long list of ways she does not belong among us, let alone at one of our most important cultural events."

He focused back on Christa. "Don't go, child. Instead, run. As fast as you can. Run back to your people. Where you belong. If you do not . . ." he paused, "you will wish you had." Then, with a flourish of robes, he spun and stalked back toward the King's Yard.

Sinna let out a long breath and shook her head. "I'm sure Director Aerel will hear about that."

Westrel gave a snort and shrugged. "It won't matter. I am sure she would have said the same." She sighed and tore her eyes from the director's retreating back. "What a bigoted, pompous, self-indulgent sycophant."

Sinna shook her head, "You shouldn't talk about him that way. He's a director." She paused, biting her lip. "But he really was out of line about you, Christa. It sounded like he was th-threatening you."

"He was." Westrel said. "The only question is what he thinks he can do about you going. After all, you were ordered to go."

Christa was still watching him go. "It doesn't matter. But he just made me happy I am."

Shadow

The sun was burning low behind a haze of clouds when Steven first spotted the shadows of the cliff face to the south and what appeared to be a sickly fog huddled against it. Then he saw the trails of campfire smoke lifting from the fog, and his throat went dry. The putrid mist clung to the base of the low, cave-riddled cliff, and spread out over the plain before it like a noxious vapor issuing from a score of hungry mouths.

Steven glanced back to check on Honovi. Her head was up for the first time since the Ssaneks—as Steven had taken to calling them over the past two days of trudging—had tied the ropes around her wrists. He tried desperately to catch her gaze, but her eyes were hard and distant as they looked through him to the cliff beyond.

"Turn 'round," one of the regular Ssaneks growled as he shoved Steven in the back with the haft of his smith's hammer.

Steven complied. There was no reason not to. Honovi hadn't said a word to him since their capture, despite his attempts to get any kind of reaction from her. She wasn't likely to start now. Instead he focused on the back of the *thing* that led them. The monster had spoken barely more than Honovi. It would croak out single word orders, along with significant amounts of spittle, when it was time to make or break camp, but otherwise it seemed content to leave them be. In fact, Steven got the impression that it regarded the act of speaking to even the other Ssaneks as beneath it.

Another hour brought them within the first tendrils of the green-black mist. Sentries stood watch just within, their forms darker shadows within the already deepening dusk. Steven had a last glimpse of the sunset, a burst of angry red that burned through the clouds. Its defiance brought a smile to his face. Then another painful shove into his lower back drove him into the mist, and the sun disappeared.

The fog enfolded him, wrapping around him like an oily cloying embrace. He shivered, though he was covered in sweat, and immediately wished he could take a bath to wash off the feeling. It reminded him too closely of the swamp. Of Mother. But there would be no escape this time. No deaths other than his own and Honovi's that would slake the horrible presence he could feel pressing in through the mist.

They passed the first sentry, a tall, gangly woman wearing only a creatively applied smearing of gray mud caked to her darkly tanned body. She crouched on an outcropping of rock, a long spear tipped with sharpened bone cradled in her arms, and as they passed she turned to watch with large black eyes in mud shadowed sockets.

Steven jerked his head back forward. He could hear her low throaty chuckle following him. The mist was suddenly colder, its touch like incorporeal claws scraping against his clammy skin, drawing their talons across his neck and face. He tried to draw his dirty shirt closer around him, but it didn't help. He tried to think of home. Of Brogan. Of lying under the stars with Honovi. Of her laugh. But all that would come were images of Brogan weeping with worry and grief, of Honovi's blood spilling over an altar of snakes, and his own

Whispers at the Altar

screams as his body was subsumed into the altar to be slowly ripped and broken by fang and coil.

Before long, the dull glow of fires illuminated the gloom around him. Tents, crude lean-tos, and threadbare blankets littered the ground around the fires. And, within the struggling light of each fire, groups of haggard men and women ate, drank, and tended to their meager gear. Some wore the rough homespun and tooled leather of Chisarans. These looked at him appraisingly as he passed, wide wicked smiles blooming on their faces. But most were obviously kin to the sentry he saw earlier, dressed in nothing more than dried mud, their heads uniformly shaved. He could feel their stares, filled with excited yearning, long after he passed. He didn't want to know what they were yearning for.

What surprised him most was the number of Yahad at those fires. Dozens huddled in the gloomy dark, their deer and ganox skin clothes stained red and their looks cold and empty. Their eyes reminded him of Honovi's.

He risked a quick look back and caught the glimmer of a tear on her cheek. She was staring at her people, her mouth partly open, the question obvious even if it never left her lips. It was a question Steven asked himself even as his captor shoved him forward again. Why would the Yahad join them? Didn't they know what the Ssaneks had done? Or were they captives, doing what they had to in order to survive?

He wasn't so sure. The looks on their faces were not of a people oppressed or downtrodden. They were hardened, determined, and angry, not at the Ssaneks, but at him. At Honovi. It was all happening again. The same lies that tore her people into three tribes ages ago was tearing at them again. It was gnawing them into even more pieces, wearing them down until they were fractured, fragmented. Then Ssanek would consume them all.

He remembered the map in Brogan's hut with all its pins stuck in towns, each successively farther north. If it was this bad down here, what was going on up there? Were there armies like this one razing the cities of the Badum even now? Had the king of Chisara heeded Brogan's warnings at all? Steven could only hope, but the mist told him that was foolish. There was no hope. Not against a god.

The chaos of tents and fires grew more crowded as they neared the cliff face. Steven could feel the press of bodies around him, even if the mist prevented him from seeing all of them. Still, no one tried to approach them. In fact, though Steven and Honovi earned their fair share of stares and gawkers, no one wanted to meet the eye of, let alone approach, the beast that led their group through the camp.

Then, as abruptly as if there had been a physical barrier, the tents stopped. There was a stretch of grass more black than green and farther ahead, crouched under eighty-five span of dark granite, a precise half-circle of tents larger than any they had seen so far.

Their leader stopped and turned to the three Ssaneks bringing up the rear. "Leave. I will inform the Seer that you performed adequately."

The three men needed no further prompting. With barely muttered thanks they turned and fled into the shrouded jumble of the main camp.

The beast turned to its prisoners, grabbed each of the ropes binding their wrists and dragged them forward behind it.

Steven stumbled into Honovi as they were forced to half jog side by side to keep pace with its long strides. They kept stepping on each other's feet, and more than once one or the other nearly fell as they were inadvertently tripped.

The inner camp was lit by several large bonfires that cast flickering shadows through the fog, illuminating nothing fully. Larger shadows, dozens of them, moved among the fires. They were only vaguely human and, as Steven passed through the ring of tents, their vague shapes materialized into forms he immediately wished he could forget.

What may have once been a woman sat on a rock and chewed a leg of some raw meat he did not want to identify. Though its bare head and torso retained all the remnants of humanity, its naked torso ended in the long, inverted legs of a frog tipped with talons the size of Steven's fingers. A *thing* the size of an enormous dog, its body covered in spines as long as Steven's forearm scuttled right up to him. Its red eyes glinted as it grinned up at him and licked its wide pale lips with a long, anemic, forked tongue.

Steven jerked back, but the monster leading them whirled a back-handed fist that sent the squat beast tumbling back. Steven had a quick glimpse of waving chitinous legs before it flipped back to its feet, hissing and spitting. Their guide didn't even pause.

Three large tents, their charcoal cloth barely visible in the putrid fog, rose in front of them. The light of the bonfires barely filtered through to this inner cloister. The only light came from the coals of two enormous braziers, which stood on a low wooden platform twice the size of Brogan's hut. In the center of the dais rose a post wider than Steven and likely three times as tall. On the capital of the post was carved an enormous winged serpent, the light of the coals illuminating its pitch scales and gold tracery in harsh reds and jagged shadows.

The bottom thirteen span of the pole were stained black.

Steven remembered all too well what took place at those poles. Honovi's shoulder leaned into him, and he turned his head. Her eyes were wide, the dirt on her face tracked with the few spent tears she had allowed herself. He tried to smile, tried to think of something he could say. Anything. But he knew it was useless. There wasn't anything to say.

Thankfully, they didn't stop at the platform. But the idol's gaze bore into him as they passed.

Instead they were led ten paces past to a black pit in the ground nearly three paces across. The rancid smell of decay oozed from the hole, and Steven remembered a dark clearing in a swamp. Worms wriggling in his toes. And frogs, hundreds of frogs. This smell was worse, like every time he'd ever been sick had been condensed and drained into this one stygian abyss.

He tried to pull away, the bile rising in his throat, his stomach churning. But the thing was too strong. With one sweeping motion it flung them forward. Steven's feet slid on the slimy grass, Honovi knocked into him, and then they both tumbled over the edge.

The fall was mercifully quick. Steven hit the bottom with a splash on his hands and knees, sunk to his chest in water and mud. The smell assaulted him, overwhelming his senses before the water had even calmed. He barely had time to sit up and lean his arms against the wall before he was sick. It was several minutes, when even the smell of his own vomit mixed with the muck couldn't urge any more out of his stomach, before he could focus on anything else.

"Honovi?" He coughed. He hadn't tried to speak above a whisper in days. Even the coarse rattling he managed sounded far too loud in his ears as it echoed up the shaft.

"Where are you?" The pit was a void in front of his eyes. He couldn't even see his hands. The fog obscured any stars or moon and what little light had existed in the inner camp must be far above them. He stood, and tried reaching out his arms, feeling ahead as he took timid steps along the wall.

His hands touched something softer than rock, but were immediately pushed away.

"Is that you? Are you hurt?" He took another step forward, then immediately back again. What if they weren't the only ones here? "Is that you?" he whispered.

"Yes," came the gruff reply. "Leave me alone."

Steven ignored her. She obviously wasn't thinking straight. "Are you hurt?" He tried reaching slowly toward her again and again his hands were knocked away, followed by the sound of her splashing further away.

"Leave me alone. This is all your fault."

Steven paused. Swallowed. "I was trying to help."

"If you had let me shoot them at the hut none of this would have happened," she hissed in the dark. "We could have escaped. Now they are going to kill us. If we a are lucky."

"I didn't want you to get hurt. There were a lot of them."

"We could have made it."

"What if we didn't? I just didn't want you to get hurt." He took another step forward. Surely she could understand that. She knew what it was like to lose someone.

"Better there, fighting, then slaughtered here like cattle. I can't believe I ever told my father your spear might make a difference."

Steven blinked back tears. "I'm sorry. I just—"

"Did not want me to get hurt. Yes. Good job with that. Now leave me alone."

He heard her splash even farther away, and he leaned back against the wall. She didn't understand. What if she had attacked them and been hurt? What if she had been killed? He was protecting her. He *had* to protect her.

But she was right. Look where protecting her had landed them.

He closed his eyes, though it made no difference in what he saw. Lying down was impossible, and there was no way he was going to sit in this sludge. Even standing, it came up to his knees. So he settled back against the jagged rock wall and tried his best to gather what sleep he could. But try as he might to ignore them all the possible horrors of tomorrow replayed themselves in his mind over and over.

Honovi would die horribly. Brogan would be wracked with worry, not knowing what happened to him. He could hear Mother sneering it at him. *Your fault. It's all your fault.* Like everything always had been. And when exhaustion finally did claim him, it was her face he dreamed of, her blood spilling over the altar, his hand on the knife. But it was Honovi's voice hissing from her mouth. *All your fault.*

TEMPTED

Sleep was occasional at best, interrupted by nightmares and cramps in his freezing legs. The only mercy was that by the time a tinge of light brightened the sky and offered vague illumination to their pit, he couldn't smell its stench any longer. Whether that was because he had lost the sense forever or it had simply been overloaded enough to shut down, Steven didn't care. At least his stomach had ceased bubbling like a pot.

As the light brightened, sifting through the fog layer in a diffuse haze, Steven saw that the pit was not actually as deep as he had feared. On the contrary it was only a bit more than twice his own height, though the knee-deep water chock full of refuse and debris made it seem even shallower. In fact he would have considered climbing the craggy wall had it not been for the sheen of moisture that covered it and the fact that his hands were still bound. Not to mention the army just over the lip.

But it was Honovi's stirring that brought him fully back to reality. She leaned on her side against the wall opposite him, her head lolled to one side. As she woke fully, she gave a deep groan and turned away from him to prop herself up with her bound hands.

"How . . . how are you feeling?" Steven tried. He had to say something, didn't he?

She glared over her shoulder but said nothing.

"I was thinking," he continued. "And I guess this is my fault. But I want you to know, I'm going to fix it."

She scoffed. "You cannot fix this. You know it."

Steven shook his head. "I know that I'll try. I know that I won't stop trying. I won't let them hurt you."

Honovi sighed deeply and shook her head. "You still do not understand."

"What? What don't I understand? I told you it was my fault. Isn't that what you wanted?"

She said nothing, just leaned against the wall stretching her back.

Steven looked back up at the sky. Fine. She didn't want to talk. It wasn't doing any good anyway.

His gaze fell to the prison walls. What if he *could* get out? As hard as it was to believe, as much as the *presence* in the fog wanted him to think it was impossible, he had to believe it was. For Honovi's sake. In the end, he would need some plan for how to get past the hundreds, perhaps thousands of cultists surrounding them. The caves? But there was no telling where they went. He shook his head.

One thing at a time.

He might be able to climb out, with Honovi's help. But he would need something to work with once he was up there. He patted down his pockets. The Ssaneks had been very thorough in their search of them both. He turned up a bit of string, now soaking wet, and a small metal pick he used for separating powders for Brogan.

•*Whispers at the Altar*•

"You had that all the time?" Honovi muttered. "We could have used it. To cut the ropes or . . . to stab one of them."

Steven stared at her. "It would take us forever to cut through a rope with this," he said, trying not to sound condescending. He looked again at the walls. The dull light gave the moisture a metallic sheen. One webbed through with silver.

No. Not silver. White.

He squinted then smiled. "We can use this," he whispered.

She looked at him as though he were crazy.

"No, really. See this?" He pointed to a vein of white about as wide as his finger running through the granite. "This is whitefire. I might be able to use it."

"To do what?"

He paused. He really wasn't sure. It was highly combustible. But they had no way to light it. Not to mention that it was so damp he wasn't even sure it would catch at all. It didn't matter. For once he could see the faintest glimmer of hope in her eyes, and he wasn't about to let that fade.

"Look. I may not know anything about hunting a rabbit, but Brogan taught me a lot about plants and minerals. I know this. If we can remove it, then I might be able to use it after we get out of this hole to cause a distraction. Then we slip out."

She narrowed her eyes, doubtful.

"I'm not going to let them take us without a fight again."

She stared at him for a long moment then nodded slowly. "What do you need me to do?"

"Listen. If you hear them coming, tell me. I doubt they know what this stuff is, or they never would have put prisoners here. But I'd rather they didn't know we were up to anything."

She nodded and Steven turned to face the rock. He looked at the long thin piece of metal dubiously. This had better work. Please he prayed. Please let this work.

It was slow going, made even more so by Steven's urge to stop every time he heard something moving past their hole. Several times he had to stop for a few minutes as one of the grotesque mutations from the camp would pause at the edge of the hole. They would peer down with clacking mandibles or dripping tongue, a hungry gleam in their eyes. A few would laugh or cackle as they eventually walked away, but even more disturbing were those who left as silently as they came. The hardest part was finding somewhere to store what powder he was able to remove. At first he was catching it in his hand, but even as damp as it was, he wasn't comfortable handling it.

Honovi solved that problem. She managed to find a small pouch among the debris floating in their prison. It wasn't big, Steven could barely fit three fingers into it, and it was soaked. But after a firm wringing, Steven decided it would do as well as anything else. It certainly wasn't going to make the whitefire any damper than it already was.

After an hour and a half, Honovi insisted he show her what he was doing so he could take a break. He couldn't bring himself to object even if he'd dared contradict her. It wasn't easy work. You had to lean close to the wall, scraping with one hand while holding the other underneath to catch the grains as they fell. After an hour and a half, his back was killing him, and he was pretty sure if he could feel his calves at all tomorrow, they would be burning.

By the time the light failed to the point they couldn't see the veins, the pouch was so full they could barely close it.

"Will this be enough?" Honovi asked as she tried to bend her back in a way that wouldn't put her face into the water.

Whispers at the Altar

"I'm not sure. It really depends what we try to do with it." Steven longed to sit down. He had never realized how much of a blessing it was. By now even sitting in the foul water didn't sound so awful.

He was staring at the water, trying to decide if relieving the pain in his legs was worth it when Honovi broke the silence.

"What do you think is in this water?"

Looking up, he saw her face was even now dissolving into the growing dark. "I don't think I want to know. Why?" She paused and frowned as if trying to decide whether to say something.

"I have to pee."

Steven blinked. "Oh. Um. No problem. I can just turn around." He did so, glad the dark made it impossible for her to see the blood rushing to his cheeks.

"But I don't want us to be standing in it," she whispered.

A soft laugh escaped before Steven could catch it. "I don't think that's our biggest worry right now. Besides, we probably already are." He thought he heard her trying to climb up the wall.

"Why do you think that?"

"Think about it. This is probably where they store all their prisoners. I doubt any of them had a better place to go then we do."

Silence.

"Cover your ears."

Steven shook his head but tucked his bound wrists under his chin and did his best to cover his ears.

"Get out!" someone above them bellowed.

Steven spun around just as he heard Honovi let out a sharp cry and fall into the water. A roughly humanoid figure stood silhouetted against the harsh crimson of the fires diffusing into the mist.

How did he get so close without them hearing? Steven reached down to help Honovi out of the mire. There was a moment of frantic movement as she presumably righted whatever she had been in the middle of doing when she was interrupted.

"How?" Steven shouted back, moving to stand in front of Honovi in case this *thing* had better vision than he.

The figure kicked something, and Steven heard a swishing sound against the rock wall. A rope? He felt along the wall until his hands closed on it, a length as thick as his wrist, knotted for climbing. He also remembered the pouch of whitefire clenched in one hand.

He tucked it in his pants as smoothly as he could. He hadn't expected the Ssaneks to come for them so soon. He didn't have any kind of plan, and plan or no, he would need a lot more whitefire than one pouch.

"Very nice. Except for this," he held up his bound hands.

"Besides," Honovi added, now fully recovered, "why should we? If you want to kill us, come down here and get us."

The figure's hands clenched and unclenched as if the conversation were taxing its patience, and for the first time Steven noticed long claws on those fingers. Its head turned slightly as if it were considering or listening to something they couldn't hear, revealing an elongated snout where a nose and mouth should have been.

After a moment it nodded. "Very well. I will bring you."

With a splash of water, it leaped into the hole. Steven barely had time to register it was there before it crouched and leaped again, powerful legs carrying it up and over the lip, Honovi gripped in both hands.

"Honovi!" Steven cried as she disappeared from sight.

But a moment later it was back. Steven was better prepared this time, managed to beat his fist futilely against its chest once. He might as well have been beating the wall. One clawed hand grabbed each shoulder, and there was a moment of sheer terror as his stomach was left in the pit and the rest of him traveled up and out in an effortless bound.

He was thrown like a sack on top of Honovi, who was still recovering from her own trip. He rolled off, still trying to catch his breath, only to find the lizard-thing looming over him, a long, broad, double-edged sword in its hand. The light of the braziers was now more

Whispers at the Altar

than enough for Steven to recognize one of the beasts that had haunted his nightmares for three years. Legs like small trunks, broad scaled chest, and thick arms that ended in fists the size of melons. But it was the eyes, those yellow slits above the white-toothed maw that held him.

"Now get up," it spat. "If it was up to me your blood would already be mixing in the vat, but I don't imagine he'll care too much if a bit of it spills between here and there. Now move!" It gestured toward the large gray tents some thirty paces away.

Steven scurried back then stood and helped Honovi up as well. His muscles protested, but he overruled them. After all, this was what he and Honovi wanted, to be out of the pit. Whether he was ready or not, this was likely the only chance they were going to get. He ran his hands over the pouch—it was still there—and started walking in the indicated direction. Honovi walked beside him, as weary as he had ever seen, but her eyes were as bright and defiant as ever.

The three tents they approached were all lit from within. The middle one was more like a pavilion, at least as big as a house, and the dull red that glowed through the cracks in the cloth gave few recognizable shadows. The other two sat off to either side and were bright with lamps and candles. Steven couldn't make out the shadows of people in either one. But there was one figure between them that made his blood run cold.

A snake, large as a man, with arms folded neatly across its body, regarded them with eyes lit with an inner poisonous, green light.

Steven wanted to hold Honovi's hand. Wanted to cry into her shoulder. Drag her away. Or just run screaming into the army. Let them kill him. Better that than to face this thing again. He stopped three paces away, unable to make himself go any farther no matter the sword at his back.

"Welcome, Steven. Son of Arica. Son of Ssanek." The Seer swayed as it spoke, its bright eyes hypnotizing in the dark. "I must apologize for your treatment. Those who found you were not aware of who you are. Of your importance." He gestured with one hand to the

335

giant lizard behind them. "Remove their bindings. They are guests. *Honored* guests."

"We are no friends of yours!" Honovi shouted as the guard sliced through their ropes. "Give me a blade, and I will show you Yahad hospitality for Ssanek."

The Seer raised both hands, placating. "Peace, young warrior. You will understand everything in time. For now, I ask only that you refresh yourselves." He gestured to the two brightly lit tents. "Inside you will find food, water, clothes . . . even a hot bath. And if there is anything further you wish you have only to request it. There will be attendants outside to supply any desire."

"What if we don't go?" Steven croaked, finding his voice.

The Seer frowned. "If that is your wish, Lord Ssanek is amenable to you returning to the vat until you are prepared to accept his hand of friendship."

"Fine." He took Honovi's hand and began leading her to the tent on the right. He couldn't bear the thought of her going back into that hole. He reached the entrance, Honovi trailing reluctantly, but the two reptilian attendants, who looked a lot more like guards, blocked his way.

"There is a tent for each of you," the Seer said, his silky voice slipping over the distance.

Steven turned on him. "We only need one. Now tell them to let us in."

It shook its head. "I'm afraid I cannot. Lord Ssanek wishes to speak with you, and what he says is for your ears alone. On this I cannot compromise."

Steven looked at Honovi. He saw her mouth the word *no*. But they couldn't tell when they would have a chance to eat again. If they did escape they would need all the energy they could get. And they wouldn't get far in the ruined rags they wore now.

"It'll be all right," he whispered. "Just don't listen to anything they say. And be careful. I imagine if they wanted us dead we would be already, but you never know."

She nodded and squeezed his hand tight before letting go. "Don't listen to him. He lies."

"I know. I'll see you soon. Remember . . ." he patted his hip where the pouch was still wedged. She took a step back, and the guards withdrew. Then with a deep breath he slipped through the tent flaps.

Honovi watched the flap settle back into place, stared at it for a moment, then turned. She strode to the other tent, as dignified as possible with her soft boots squelching every step and rank water dripping from her pants, threw open the flap, and slapped it shut behind her. She stood there, eyes closed as she tried to tamp down the fear speeding through her body with every frantic beat of her heart. She wanted to believe in Steven. She wanted to have faith that he had a plan and that his plan would work. But she couldn't see how they could survive this.

By slow silent degrees, the fear subsided to a dull ache in the pit of her stomach. Only then did she open her eyes. The tent was opulent. Almost ridiculously so. Paper lanterns in bright blues and deep violets hung from the polished pine poles and thick animal skin rugs lined the floor. To one side, an enormous metal tub full of steaming water sat next to an equally large brazier of warm coals. On the other side, a table as big as a wagon wheel lay covered with plates of grilled venison, steamed carrots, and dark bread. There was even a wheel of cheese and actual butter. Her stomach growled loudly. There hadn't been real butter since . . . since she met Steven.

Between the bath and the food sat a bed. It was larger than any she'd ever seen, and covered in quilted blankets and large pillows. On its foot lay a change of clothes, clean and neatly folded.

Honovi shook her head. They thought of everything, didn't they? What was the price of all this? The stories said that Ssanek offered nothing for free. There was always a price. A horrible price. Like those monsters out there. What had they received for their deformity? Or had they taken those forms willingly? That thought was far worse.

She began walking around the tent. If they wanted her here, so be it. But she wouldn't accept any of their *hospitality*. She stopped at the bath, running a hand over the edge of the tub and feeling its warmth soak into her. She dipped one finger into the water and watched as the dirt floated away, dissipating to nothing. There was a metal ball sunk into the water, and the scent of bath salts and minerals permeated her mind and soothed her fear. A bath would be so relaxing. And she was so filthy.

She shook her head and moved on. It wasn't worth it. There was no telling what was in that water.

She passed by the bed, trailing her clean finger over the warm thick blankets before she stopped to look at the clothes. There was a silky black dress with shimmers of silver that danced in the lantern light. Even better, there were new underclothes. Made of the same unrecognizable cloth. Oh, and new leather shoes. None of it was a color she would have picked and certainly not a style she had ever worn. But they looked so comfortable, and her clothes were so torn and filthy. By now they clung to her like a second skin, and the stink was horrid.

She turned away reluctantly. As nice as they would be, she was going to be escaping soon, and even if her clothes were disgusting, they were still better suited for running. The shoes though . . .

As she arrived back at the table, her stomach growled again. It all looked so good. And she was so hungry. Steven had said it would be all right. He said they would already have hurt them if they meant to. It wouldn't be poisoned or anything. What would the point of that be?

She fingered a slice of carrot. It was warm, still steaming in the bowl.

She picked it up. It was just a carrot.

Maybe if she just had those. Then she could curl up on the floor for a nap while she waited.

She looked at her hands, filthy save for the tip of one finger, then turned to look at the bath. It would be disgusting to eat like this.

Well . . . maybe she could just wash her hands.

COMMENCEMENT

The scrap of paper under her door would have gone completely unnoticed in all Vaniel's bustling about her room if she hadn't been expecting it. She sighed, then determined to let it sit until she was done with her hair. Going to the ball was going to be nerve wracking enough. She definitely wasn't going to do it with less than perfect hair. Then there was jewelry. And Glamour. Oh, and she had to pick out just the right pair of shoes.

But eventually she ran out of ways to put it off and was standing over the note wishing it would just go away. Part of her had wanted Christa to take Dalan's advice. But she was too stubborn. The threat had only made her want to go to the ball even more. But Vaniel should be happy about that, shouldn't she? It meant Christa would finally get what she deserved, and Vaniel would have her title back. Her family back. So why did she feel like she was going to be sick?

With a deep sigh she snatched up the letter and flipped it open.

Make sure she is on the dance floor for the queen's dance. I will take care of the rest. We will be rid of her, and you will have your title. Do not fail.

As much as Christa hated to admit it, she was looking forward to the ball. The excitement that consumed Sinna and smoldered in Westrel had spread until Christa couldn't help feeling it as well.

She had never been to a proper ball. Sure, she had attended the various town festivals back home, and she always loved dancing at them, but this was different. There had never been anyone she was looking forward to seeing then.

She wasn't sure what she expected now, but the contagion was strong enough by the evening of the ball that, as she dressed, her hands refused to do as they were told. She stopped several times, scolding herself as she pressed her palms against her stomach to ease the fluttering inside and the trembling outside. In fact, she just finished when Sinna came waltzing in, breathtaking in her pale rose gown.

"Good gracious, Christa," she gasped in mock annoyance. "You still aren't ready? W-we'll be late." She examined the dress, making sure everything was in order. "You know we're supposed to meet . . . everyone else in the courtyard in less than half an hour."

Christa knew that by "everyone" Sinna meant Darian. "Well, I'm not used to dresses like this. It doesn't feel right." She tugged on the neckline, cut far lower than she ever wore.

"Nonsense," Sinna batted Christa's hand away. "You look fine. We just n-need to do something with that hair." She paced around, inspecting it with a frown. It had regained most of its length and now fell in layers down to the middle of her back. "Up, I think." And as Sinna moved her hands, Christa's hair lifted and curled on its own. It was disconcerting, like a small army of invisible hairdressers on the attack. The door opened again, and Christa turned her head.

Sinna growled in annoyance. "Keep still Christa, or this will come out all wrong."

She barely got a glimpse of Vaniel, and barely recognized her when she did. The gauzy white and gold dress and tightly curled hair cascading down her bare back were one reason, but something about her face made her almost a stranger. Her nearly black eyes arrested Christa's gaze as she slid between Christa's chair and the mirror then leaned back against the vanity.

"Aren't we ready yet?" she asked with a small laugh.

"Christa is dawdling," Sinna answered, pulling Christa's head back to center again. "I told you to hold still, Christa. If you keep on, I'll have to start over. V-Vaniel, do you mind?"

"Not at all." She appraised Christa, the same way Sinna had. After a moment's thought she moved her hands in small movements inches from Christa's face.

Christa tried to be grateful. She knew they were trying to help, but she was beginning to feel like a child's doll.

Five minutes later they stepped back, very pleased with themselves. "There," Sinna stated with a nod of finality. "Now put on the necklace, earrings, and of course your shoes, and we should be ready to go."

Christa took up the jewelry, donned the necklace, and snuck a glance in the dressing table mirror as she put on the earrings. She couldn't help staring. She didn't recognize the girl she saw. True, this mystery woman had the same brown hair, but it was smooth, shining, and arranged above her bare shoulders in interwoven waves Christa could never have accomplished. Her eyes were the same hazel, but too large, bold, and bright. Her face had the same features, but some inner glow beamed out that had never been there before. "What . . ." Christa stammered, raising a hand to touch her face and brush against her hair.

Vaniel laughed. "It is just a simple Glamour I have been practicing. Trust me, it is still you. I just added a few touches. I have heard the humans use powders and oils, but a bit of Illusion works far better."

"Right, now can we get g-going?" Sinna urged. "Or the ball will be over before we get there."

Christa nodded and fastened the earrings as quickly as she could. Sinna and Vaniel were already walking out the door as she slipped on her shoes and took one last peek in the mirror. She couldn't believe it. For the first time in her life, she felt . . . beautiful.

They ran into Westrel on her way into the Elementalist halls. Christa guessed she must have used one of Vaniel's Glamours as well. Her normally short scarlet hair fell around and past her shoulders in tight curls that perfectly matched the shade of her bare shouldered, red dress, and her green eyes arrested Christa's gaze whenever she glanced in their direction.

Westrel fell in beside them. "I passed Darian on the way up. I told him we would be down shortly."

Christa leaned over to Vaniel. "Did you?"

"What, Westrel?" she asked, glancing over absently. "No."

Christa frowned. "Are you all right?"

Vaniel's thoughtful expression turned back to a smile. "Of course. Why?"

"You seem . . ." Christa shrugged. "I don't know. But you're sure you're fine?"

Vaniel gave a firm nod. "Have you ever wondered if you were doing the right thing?" she blurted.

Christa blinked. "Sure. Lots of times." Memories of the first time she performed the ritual to talk to Ssanek came to mind.

Vaniel walked closer, leaning over and lowering her voice as Sinna and Westrel talked in front of them. "How do you know?"

Christa thought about that for a moment. "I guess I try to follow my heart. I try to let it tell me what it really wants, and then I do what I have to."

Vaniel seemed to consider that. "What if you don't know what it is that you want?"

She honestly couldn't think of a time when she didn't know what she wanted. Ever since she lost Mama it was all she thought about. "Then I guess I just . . . lean on the person I care about the most. And who cares about me." Christa reached down to take Vaniel's hand, squeezing it tightly as she gave an encouraging smile. "What is all this about?"

Vaniel looked down at their hands in surprise, then returned the smile as she gave a tentative squeeze back. "Nothing. I just . . . wasn't sure I did the right thing . . . suggesting that you come."

Christa laughed. "Oh, so *you* were the one who put the idea in Director Marellel's head. Don't worry. I'm kind of glad you did. It might be fun. At the least I can't wait to see the look on Dalan's face."

Vaniel gave a small laugh and was about to say something more when they arrived at the tubes. Christa gave her hand another squeeze before stepping into one.

It did no favors to her already fluttering innards. Darian waited for them by the doors in a black coat over a stiff shirt—that matched Sinna's dress perfectly—and black trousers tucked into boots that rose halfway up his calf. There was a short squall of greetings and compliments, and they made their way out into the yard.

Christa had never been down during one of the balls. She usually spent the time locked away in the library taking advantage of the peace and quiet. The yard was always lovely, but tonight . . . Looking up, Christa saw tier upon tier of branches rising into a clear night sky. Tiny lanterns she at first mistook for stars hung from the interwoven limbs, casting a golden glow on the gently falling snow. No, not snow, she realized, petals. Gentle breezes stirred and blew thousands of tiny petals of white, pink, yellow, and red into the most wonderful spring shower Christa had ever seen.

"Keeping an eye out for someone?" Westrel asked, a wide grin playing across her face.

Christa rolled her eyes. "No. I just didn't know they decorated the yard."

Westrel gave an unconvinced assent. "Tweaked the Illusion actually. The lanterns are no more real than the trees. Or the leaves. Really, I would have thought by now you would come to expect this."

"I don't think this could ever become normal for me," Christa said with a shake of her head. "Every time I think I've seen it all . . ." She looked for Vaniel and found her walking silently behind them. She still looked worried. Christa tried to smile even more, to show her how much fun she was having.

As they walked they were joined by other elves. There were Hawks from the Roost, Guardsmen from the barracks, and Nobles from their estates. Each arrayed in the most beautiful dresses and finest suits of every color imaginable. It was a kaleidoscope that made Christa's head hurt as she tried to take everything in. This was exactly why she stayed in the library.

Christa and her friends slowed as they neared the Royal Tower at the center of the palace. The crowd made it impossible to move at more than a crawl toward the large, open doors.

Westrel leaned closer. "So did you ever let Tamaran ask you?"

Christa blinked as she looked back at her. "What?"

"Christa, you have gone out of your way to avoid him. If I didn't know better, I would say you were afraid of him." She leaned a bit closer. "Or maybe you did want him to ask you."

Christa furrowed her brow. "How do you figure that? Not that I was. I barely know him."

Westrel grinned and shrugged her shoulders. "Some men like a good chase." She indicated Sinna in front of them with a nod of her head. "Sinna's been letting Darian chase her for nearly a decade."

Christa would never understand that line of thinking. "I can assure you I am not giving anyone 'a good chase.'"

"If you say so. No need to get defensive." Westrel gave a wink that made Christa shake her head in frustration, which of course made Westrel laugh harder.

"Name and title, miss?"

Christa started. She hadn't even noticed she'd arrived at the door.

"Name and title, miss?" the doorman asked again in a voice that betrayed only a hint of annoyance.

Christa stammered for a second but was saved by Vaniel. "Christabel Sellers, daughter of Chrysolbel Vitarius, Fourth Tier Eyas of the Roost."

The doorman nodded, made the announcement, and then motioned for her to enter. Christa gave Vaniel a grateful smile, then waited just inside the door for her.

"Name and title miss?"

Vaniel blushed and murmured something Christa couldn't hear before hurrying past.

"Vaniel, Third Tier Eyas of the Roost," the doorman announced, his voice echoed through the chamber, and the absence of a family name or title echoed just as loudly.

Christa took Vaniel's hand again, gave it another squeeze of encouragement, and pulled her along as she hurried to catch up to Sinna and Darian. Her steps faltered, however, as she realized just where she was.

A solid circle of trees, their trunks melded together, made up the walls of a room three times larger than the tower she'd entered. They soared up above her, their branches arching together into a high ceiling. The same star lanterns twinkled through the petal shower, and Christa found herself wondering where all those petals went. And why only a handful ever appeared to be in the women's hair. And, for that matter, why none clung to Darian's or any of the other men.

At the far end, raised upon a small hillock, grew two trees that couldn't be real. One shone like burnished gold, and the other gleamed pale silver. Their branches rose and intertwined, ringing tiny leaves together in the soft breeze like wind chimes. But their bases, shaped as naturally as the grass beneath them, were two high-backed thrones.

"Stop gawking like a c-commoner, Christa," Sinna teased, pulling her arm and bringing her back to the group. "You're holding up the line."

"Are those . . . ?"

"The thrones? Yes, of course. This is the th-throne room after all. Where else would they hold a ball?"

Christa blinked and forced herself back into the moment. "How should I know?"

Sinna tsked. "I'm sorry. S-sometimes I forget where you're from. It seems like you've always been here."

"Thank you, Sinna. Really. It's good to know at least someone thinks I fit in."

Westrel walked up to join them. "Of course you fit in. And it is time you acted like it." She peered over Christa's shoulder. "You should dance with someone."

Christa couldn't help giggling. She was unaccountably giddy. "No, thank you. I saw some food, I was thinking about trying that. But I promise I'll experience as much elven culture as I can tonight."

"Oh, we will make sure of it," Westrel said.

Darian cleared his throat. "Are you up for a dance, Sinna?"

They took each other's hands and strode out onto the floor.

"I need to find someone," Vaniel said hurriedly. "I will be back." And then she was gone, too.

Christa looked at Westrel. "Don't let me keep you. I'm sure half the young men here are anxious to dance with you."

Before long she found herself standing alone against the wall, but she didn't mind. There were so many things to see and people to watch she doubted she could ever get bored.

She watched Sinna and Westrel dance for a few minutes then, at her stomach's insistence, ambled to one of the tables laid out with a variety of food she barely recognized. There were some of her favorites, like the dark pudding that tasted of sweet almonds, and those little crackers that fizzed on your tongue. She had just decided on a chocolate covered pastry of some kind when a voice from behind startled her.

"Not very adventurous of you, Christabel."

She spun, scattering a tray of small pink fruit through the grass. "Director Marellel! What do you mean?"

The director stood behind her with Director Namarian who wore the same tightly controlled expression he always did when she saw him. Marellel smiled and with a wave of her hand rolled the fruit into a pile, lifted the pile into the air, and deposited it into a nearby bucket. "If you want something unusual, you should try the *salisshim*." She motioned to the far end of the table, but it was so crowded Christa couldn't tell which selection she meant.

"I will," she offered. She wasn't sure what else to say, so she stood there toying with her skirt and wondering if it would be rude to eat her pastry in front of them as the awkward silence lengthened. As it was becoming truly uncomfortable, Marellel cleared her throat, stepped forward to stand next to her, and gazed out over the dancers floating across the grass. "So tell me, Christabel. What do you think of the ball?"

"I don't know what to think." She faced the dancers, glad for the excuse to look away from Director Namarian, and peered through the crowd for a glimpse of her friends. "It's incredible."

"But?"

Christa bit her bottom lip as her fingers traced the embroidered patterns in the tablecloth. "I don't know. Maybe I'm just not used to it. It's a lot to take in all at once." She glanced over to Marellel.

"Perhaps. Or—"

"Marellel, how nice to see you. I wondered if you would come. And Director Namarian, I don't think I have ever seen you at a ball, what a pleasant surprise."

Christa turned along with the others to face Director Dalan and another man she had never met. The director was in his finest. His coat was so embellished with gems Christa found it ridiculous and, though she didn't dare check, she was sure more than a little Illusion enveloped him. The stranger was an exact opposite, his dark brown coat plain and buttoned high.

Marellel smirked. "I needed the time away from my office. After all, there is only so much work you can do before it all begins to run together. So many threads floating in the wind get hard to track. Before you know it, you have made a mistake." She turned to Christa. "Christabel, I don't think you have ever been introduced. This is Iyian, Secretary of Intelligence." She motioned to the stranger.

Christa gave a hurried curtsy and a murmured "How do you do?"

"Ah, Christabel. I've heard so much about you from Director Marellel," the secretary said. "She speaks very highly of your abilities. And your potential."

Christa had no idea what to say. "I . . . thank you," she managed, not wanting to stand there saying nothing.

"Oh, it isn't me you should thank." He seemed satisfied, however, and focused his attention to the two directors. Obviously, she wasn't worth his time. "Have either of you seen Director Elirel? She should be here by now."

"I believe I saw her as I came in, but she doesn't appear to be in the throne room now," Namarian answered, his head sweeping to scan the crowd.

Christa had no intention of standing around where she was obviously not wanted, and began taking slow steps back as the conversation shifted away from her. At the third step, she turned and finally took a bite of her pastry as she walked away. She had promised her friends she would enjoy herself, and there was no way that was going to happen around that group.

She raided a few more food tables, then found a spot along the wall to sit where the roots formed a nice bowl and she could look down

•Whispers at the Altar•

into the small valley of the throne room. The music was full of the high ringing of harps, like rain in the pond, counterpointed by the long slow singing of strings as the wind kissed the new flowers. She listened to it and watched the dancers as she ate, swaying in place and careless of the crumbs she left in her lap. Then she saw Vaniel hurrying toward her with . . . that mute boy from the practice field? Though he was barely recognizable fully clothed and not drenched in sweat. Her swaying stopped, and she frowned.

"There you are, Christa," Vaniel said as she came to a stop and tried to catch her breath. "Now, I know what you might be thinking, but this is not that." She looked back and forth between the two of them. "I wanted to apologize to both of you for what I did before. I didn't understand at the time, but I think I do now."

She faced Christa. "I was wrong to make assumptions. Just because you are half human, does not mean you could only have feelings for another human. You could have feelings for . . ." she shrugged, a slightly hysterical smile on her face, "anyone, really.

"And I should have gotten to know you," she turned to Kadin, "before I . . . tried to . . ." She laughed nervously. "Well. That was it. I just wanted to say I was sorry." She stood there a moment more, then just turned and walked away.

Christa stared after her. She hadn't even stood up. "That was . . . odd." She glanced over at Kadin as he turned back to her. He nodded, then walked up a few paces, retrieving a book of paper from his coat that he handed to her.

On the first page was written, *Hello. My name is Kadin. It is a pleasure to meet you.*

Christa chuckled. "Yes, I remember." She handed back the book, then noticed that her lap was covered in crumbs and remainders of the treats she had eaten. She hurried to brush them off and stand up at the same time, though why she should care, she certainly didn't know. And why did everything about her dress suddenly feel like it needed fixing? She forced her hands that were about to adjust

351

her dress to be still and an awkward silence fell, broken only by the music and the sound of shuffling feet.

It's good to see you, he wrote. *I'd heard you might be coming.*

Christa tried to find Sinna or any of her friends in the throng of dancers, but even Vaniel had vanished. Why would he care if she was coming? "Thank you." She tried to think of anything else to say. Anything at all.

She was saved by a peal of trumpets that brought all conversation to an abrupt halt. The dancers stopped and made their way to the edges of the clearing as the music died and silence settled over the crowd.

Christa finally spotted Sinna and Westrel standing with their partners off to one side and gave them a wave, which was returned enthusiastically. They must be enjoying themselves far more than she presently was.

A softer trumpet call sounded through the clearing and a procession appeared through a gap in the trees. Christa had imagined royalty often. What she saw entering the hall of trees exceeded all those wild fancies, and she stared without realizing it.

Queen Elisidel entered first. Her dress was like molten silver, and where it flowed the grass glimmered like morning dew. A circlet of twisted gold and silver vines sat on her head, and her dark eyes held kindness Christa could feel from across the room. She was reminded of their first "meeting" in the chapel years ago and couldn't help but hope the queen did not.

Next, six of the queen's guard in the blue and silver livery of the palace, entered, led by a tall, serious warrior whose uniform was unadorned, save for a silver brooch in the shape of a leaf that pinned his cape. At his side walked a woman Christa recognized from her time at the Roost as Director Aerel. She carried her beauty as effortlessly as the gown that glowed like a fading ember with each movement.

The procession stopped in the middle of the grove, and the honor guard fanned around their charges, leaving the queen alone in the center. There was a hush. The serious man who led the queen's guard stepped forward. He bowed to the queen, took her hand, the music struck up again, and the couple began to dance in wide sweeping circles around the grass. In moments, the lawn filled with couples, and Christa once more found herself alone by the wall.

There was a tap on her shoulder, and she turned to see Kadin gesture to the couples dancing then look back to her with raised eyebrows.

She giggled for reasons she couldn't comprehend and shook her head. "Oh, no. I can't dance. I don't know how. Not this dance anyway. I mean I danced all the time back home. I actually really like dancing. Sometimes I just dance around my room . . ." She forced herself to stop talking.

Thankfully, Kadin seemed relieved and pointed to himself, shaking his head before putting pencil to paper once again.

Would you care to go for a walk out in the yard? The noise makes it a bit hard to talk.

Christa couldn't help but chuckle at the irony, but she couldn't argue the point. Still, she didn't want to abandon her friends.

She looked out and saw Vaniel watching them. She could almost feel her willing Christa to go with him. At least she had been a little more subtle this time.

Christa waved to Vaniel then nodded. "Thank you, that would be nice."

She led the way out through the tree wall and into the yard. As she passed through the doorway, the music diminished but remained drifting in the background, while the voices died away almost entirely.

Christa wandered aimlessly through the enormous trees. Looking up, she could see the lamps in the branches had been dimmed to near darkness, leaving only the replica of actual stars blazing from the dome above them. She turned back to Kadin only as he tapped her shoulder again. He was so quiet, it was easy to forget he was there.

You like the palace?

"I suppose. I don't spend a lot of time down here, though. Sometimes I don't leave the Roost for weeks at a time. Don't you? Like the palace, I mean." She brushed some loose hair out of her face.

He shrugged. *I thought it was impressive when I first arrived. But over the years it's lost some of its charm.*

Christa could understand that. Even for her, most of it had lost its initial splendor.

He screwed his face in concentration as he wrote. *Perhaps because it doesn't seem natural. They want to make it how they want it, not how it is.* He shrugged again.

"So you think they should leave well enough alone and let it be the same all year?" Christa had never heard anyone speak poorly of how the elves did things, and she realized she was hearing another non-elf's perspective for the first time.

He pondered a moment. *I think if they could, the elves would try to Illusion everything. Some things are more beautiful as they are. Plain.*

Christa's cheeks flushed as she remembered the Illusion Westrel had put on her. "But not everything is beautiful."

Kadin shook his head. *I think you can find beauty in anything, if you look hard enough.*

"Even death?" Christa asked, grabbing the first awful thing that came to mind. A shadow passed across his face, and she immediately regretted saying it. "I'm sorry."

He shook his head. *It's fine. It was honest. But yes, even in death there can be beauty. Or maybe, because of it, something beautiful can come.* He shrugged again as she lifted her eyes from the paper.

Christa was surprised to find they were standing at the palace doors. She couldn't think of any reason to stay. So upon Kadin's invitation, she gave a deep curtsy and walked out into the cool night air. The contrast was striking. Despite the appearance of autumn, the palace had been warm, now the breeze made her shiver as it ran over her. The wind had chased away any clouds, leaving it naked save for the twinkling of stars. All at once, Christa thought she understood what

Whispers at the Altar

Kadin had been saying. These stars, though perhaps less bright and perfect than those in the palace, were all the more beautiful for their authenticity and honesty.

She stood, transfixed, until something heavy and warm draped over her shoulders. Clutching at it, she looked back to Kadin. Possibly due to the lack of his cape, she noticed for the first time how different he dressed from any of the elves. His coat was simpler, deep blue with a white sash traced diagonally from shoulder to hip. Rather than a sword, he wore a small dagger from a belt of polished leather. The only item that sparkled at all was a silver stag pin centered on the sash over his right breast.

She thanked him for the cape and stepped down the path leading into the rose garden. They walked in silence. It was nice to feel the cool air on her cheeks while the rest of her remained warm under the cloak, and pleasant to let the scent of the flowers beside the path wash over her.

She stopped at a fountain, a flight of birds captured in stone while trickles of water flowed from wingtip to wingtip to fall into the pool below. Kadin stood beside her, watching the water with an unreadable expression.

"When I was a girl," Christa broke the silence, "before I came here, I lived in a small town where my papa worked as a hunter. Our house had a garden. I used to think it was enormous." She scoffed. "I would play in it all the time, often much later than I was supposed to. Mama would have to come out and find me. I would even sneak out of bed sometimes. I loved to walk barefoot in the cold grass. Sometimes, when she was supposed to be putting me to bed, she would walk with me in the garden. She used to tell me stories about the stars." Christa wiped a bit of moisture from her eyes. She was suddenly so empty. Like a great hole had opened inside her. Or perhaps she had just stumbled into it.

She sighed. "It's funny. I haven't thought of that in years." She looked to Kadin with a wide smile. "Thank you."

355

You're sad.

Christa turned away to wipe her nose with a cloth as she shrugged. "I just miss her. Sometimes I feel like she was my whole world, and I never really knew it until she wasn't there anymore."

He nodded, paused for a second, then held up a finger. Sitting down on a nearby bench, he took off his short boots and stockings. He then faced the fountain and buried his bare feet in the grass that bordered it. Christa laughed, and hurrying forward to sit next to him, kicked off her own shoes and did the same. She couldn't help closing her eyes at the feel of cold damp grass on her sore feet. When she opened them again, she found Kadin holding out his paper for her.

I grew up on a farm in the country. I know how you feel.

Christa laughed and pulled the cape closer as she squeezed grass between her toes and watched the water trickle. "Do you miss it?" she asked after a long but comfortable silence.

He nodded. *Often. This place is much different from anything I've ever known.*

"I know what you mean. Most of the time I feel like a complete stranger. I don't know if I'll ever feel like I belong here." She peered down at her bare feet poking out from under the hem of her skirt. "But if you miss your home so much, why don't you go back? I mean, they have people there who can teach you to fight, right? And then you could be with your family."

She turned to find him staring at her with a sad look. She started to apologize but he bent down over his paper.

I can't go back.

Christa frowned. "Why not?"

I did something. It disgraced my family. So I came here to find a way to bring them honor again.

Christa's heart sank. "I'm sorry." She had no idea what else to do or say. "I . . . My mama died when I was a girl. It was an accident." Her voice trailed off.

Kadin faced her, one rough hand reaching out to take hers. *I'm sorry. But I think she would be proud of you. Of how brave you are.*

She couldn't help a short ironic laugh. "Brave?"

Not everyone could come to a foreign land, to a school where no one of their race has been admitted, and learn the most challenging and demanding of skills.

"I don't even have a race," Christa muttered.

No. You have two. And you belong to both.

Christa scoffed. "I don't belong anywhere. I don't even want to be here. Not really. I mean, I act like it, and I try to convince myself I do. But sometimes I daydream about going back home. Of living there in the town with Mama and Papa. But then," she sank deeper into the cloak, "I know I can't."

I know how you feel, Christa. I feel like an outsider here, too. It doesn't matter if other people think you don't belong. What matters is what you feel and if you are determined to find a place for yourself. I'll make you a promise. If you finish your training, I'll finish mine. I'll stay if you stay.

"Promise?"

He nodded.

She nodded once in return and reached out to give his hand a firm shake.

"Deal."

She turned back to the fountain, stretched out her legs, and stifled a yawn. "I should be getting back. I'm afraid I'm not used to staying up late."

Kadin stood and helped her to her feet. They ambled in silence to the gate of the palace, shoes in hand. It was nice to be with someone with whom she didn't feel pressured to talk but whose very presence was reassuring. They saw no one else as they entered the yard and headed toward the nearest Roost tower. When they reached it she slid the cape from her shoulders and handed it back. "Thank you, Kadin, for the walk. I enjoyed it." She glanced to the Royal Tower.

"I should let my friends know I'm going back up. I'm afraid they'll never forgive me for not dancing."

He took the cape on one arm and gestured to the larger tower.

"Oh, you don't need to come. I'm only poking in for a minute."

He chuckled, fastened the cape back around his shoulders, and offered his arm.

"In that case." She took his arm and started off. She tried to pretend the contact was meaningless, but she was sure she was going to sweat all over him. She tried to focus instead on putting one foot in front of the other without tripping. The throne room doors seemed an eternity away, but when she finally passed through them, Kadin's arm was the last thing on her mind.

Sinna and Westrel stood roughly ten paces away along one wall, and Sinna, red-faced, was yelling at Director Dalan.

Chosen

Honovi woke to the sound of soft but insistent tapping. She didn't want to wake up, let alone get up. Her dream had been so warm and comfortable. She couldn't remember anything about it, even here in the half space between it and waking, but she knew it was wonderful.

Still, the tapping wouldn't go away.

"Ten more minutes," she mumbled, rolling over and pulling the thick covers further over her head as she buried her face in the soft pillows.

"I'm afraid your presence is necessary," came the low thick reply, muffled by distance. "Please clothe yourself and exit the tent. I am to escort you."

Honovi growled and poked her head out of the covers, blinking in the soft light. "What are you talking about, Father? Of course I'm dressed. Escort me where?"

The interior of the tent slowly came into focus, and she couldn't help a smile as she remembered. Not at the caves then. She should have known. She never would have slept that well there. How long had she been asleep? She stood, stretched, and for the first time realized she was stark naked.

Her tattered rags lay in a pile next to the somehow still steaming tub, along with several plates with no more than scraps of food left on them. She giggled. She must have crawled right into bed from the bath. But then why weren't the blankets wet? She shrugged. It didn't matter.

"Lady Honovi. Did you hear me?"

Honovi sighed. "Yes, yes, I heard you. I'll be out in a second."

She picked up the new clothes from where they had fallen on the floor as she slept. They were even more beautiful than she remembered. The long sleeveless dress had an airy skirt that reached nearly to her ankles. True, it showed a bit more of her chest then was probably proper, but she somehow doubted Steven would mind. Besides, she thought with a frown, it wasn't as though there was that much to show.

The cloth tingled as she pulled the clothes on, like tiny sparks against her skin every time it moved against her. It woke her up instantly, setting every nerve alight in a way that made her close her eyes to enjoy the feel of it against her.

She found a brush on a tray by the bath and ran it through her hair. She was prepared for the worst—it felt like weeks since she'd been able to brush her hair—but found that it was smooth and thick. She didn't think it had ever been like that. But it was hard to remember. Then she slipped on the new shoes and strode out the door.

The reptilian soldier waiting for her did not seem surprised. He simply gestured toward the platform in the near distance and then fell in beside her.

Of course he was sent to *escort* her. Not *fetch* her like some prisoner. She was a guest. An honored guest. She could probably ask him to do whatever she wanted right now.

She glanced to one side as they neared the steps to the platform, its altar-pole towering above them, and saw a pit. There was some-

Whispers at the Altar

thing vaguely familiar about it. Like something from a dream. But it would have been a very bad dream, and she didn't have those now.

They reached the top of the platform, and Honovi walked over to stand close to one of the enormous braziers. There was a bit of a damp chill in the air and the warmth was welcome. She smiled to the two others on the platform besides herself and her escort, the Seer, and another reptilian larger than any she'd yet seen. She noticed then that there were a large number of the deformed monsters arrayed in a half-circle around them, their eyes focused, though she could see little else of them but vague outlines.

"Welcome, Lady Honovi," the Seer said, breaking the silence. "I am pleased that you could attend. I hope you found our hospitality accommodating."

Honovi drew herself up proudly. "It was fine." She couldn't help feeling there was more a person of her status should say, but what it was eluded her. "Thank you." It was odd to say but it never hurt to be polite. And she *was* thankful. She had never felt so alive. So important. She was just average, a girl of no consequence from a family of no consequence.

She frowned. She didn't like thinking about her family. Why didn't she like thinking about her family?

The Seer tilted his head in an odd writhing motion. "Is something wrong?"

"No." Honovi put it out of her mind. It wasn't important right now. "Nothing. I was just wondering why I'm here."

"Ah. You haven't long to wait to find out. Here comes the guest of honor now."

Honovi followed his long pointing finger to see Steven approaching from his tent. She had to suppress a laugh when she saw him. He looked so funny in his torn and muddy clothes. It was nearly impossible to tell where the mud stopped and his unkempt brown hair began.

"Didn't you give him a bath? New clothes? Food?" She turned to the Seer, indignant.

"Oh yes. But I'm afraid he did not trust us. Perhaps you could convince him for us?"

She nodded, still watching Steven. It was silly of him not to trust them. After all, nothing had happened to her. He must feel terrible and hungry, all for no reason.

As he mounted the steps, his gaze met hers, and he seemed to recognize her for the first time. His expression shifted. Surprise and desire battled there. Honovi's cheeks and neck burned. He'd never looked at her that way before. But in the end it was disappointment and determination that took hold. It was a mix that Honovi didn't understand. Was he disappointed with *her*?

He was escorted to the middle of the platform between Honovi and the Seer and directly before the altar pole.

"What do you want?" Steven asked the Seer.

The snake shifted its posture in something vaguely resembling a sigh. "I want what is best for you, though you may not believe it."

Steven barked a laugh. "Then let us go."

"I am prepared to do precisely that, given the right circumstances."

"What do you mean?" Steven sounded wary, but he crossed his arms, waiting.

"Someone else will explain." The Seer strode toward the pole and bent down to pick up a large urn decorated with symbols Honovi didn't recognize. It raised up the urn to the foggy sky then began hissing some strange language. The soldiers picked up the chant, echoing it out over the camp.

Honovi couldn't understand the words, but still they hurt to hear. Like coarse sand being scraped over her ears. The chant ended in a final yell, and the Seer poured a thick, dark-red liquid down the bottom length of the pole.

For a moment nothing happened, then a soft red glow spread through the fog above the pole. The blood that had poured down through the platform rose. It slid up the pole, over the idol, and into the coalescing fog, drenching it crimson. Honovi took a step back, then another, as the fog coalesced and took form and shape. She tore her gaze away to look at Steven. His eyes were wide, his face devoid of any color, but still he stood his ground.

After a minute even the shouts of praise ceased, and Honovi looked back up to find the ridged and scaled head of Ssanek peering down at them. It was fog, from the blood-drenched teeth to the crimson eyes, but that made it no less real.

"Finally," it said in a voice that carried easily over the camp and perhaps beyond. "It is good to see you again, son."

Steven shook his head. "I am not your son. Brogan is the only father I have ever had."

"Perhaps. But you are my son nonetheless. It was your mother's blood that opened the gate for me. Your mother's blood that runs now through me. And it is for this reason I have been looking for you."

"That's not true," Honovi said, but it came out as only a whisper. There was no way Steven would have summoned Ssanek. She caught Steven's eye as he glanced at her, and she could see the worry there, the fear.

"What do you want?" He focused on Ssanek, taking a step forward. "Why don't you tell your lackeys to kill us and get it over with?"

Ssanek laughed in great pealing rumbles. "Straight to the point. Like your mother. If that is what you wish . . . They have not killed you because I wanted to give you something. Whether you accept it or not, you are my blood, and I am not without kindness to those who serve me."

"Like them?" Steven pointed to the mutated figures encircling them. "If that is your *kindness,* you can keep it."

"Yes. I chose them, and they in turn chose to serve me. You, too, have a choice. I know you. I have seen into your very soul. You wish more than anything to keep this girl safe. To keep your adopted father safe. That is what I give you. A chance to live out your days with them. Alone. Unbothered by the cares of this world. No servant of mine will harm you or any of your descendants. You will be safe and free to enjoy your privacy."

Honovi's heart leapt. Of course. It all made sense now. This was why the Seer and the Soldiers were treating them so well. She took a step toward Steven, trying to will him to say yes. They could be together. He looked at her, and her heart sank. Why did he look so sad?

"I would be abandoning everyone else," he muttered.

Ssanek chuckled again. "Who else? The list of people who care about you is very short. *I* care, so I offer to keep you safe. Your adopted father cares for you, but you know he would be happy for the chance to live as he once did. And *she* cares."

All eyes were on Honovi now. She cleared her throat. "I do, Steven. I believe him. They have been so good to us." She rushed up to him, took his hands in hers, and held them to her chest as she looked up at him. He simply had to understand. "I've been afraid for so long," she pleaded. "I don't want to be afraid any more. I want to be safe. He can do that. *You* can do that."

"Listen to her. Is my offer so distasteful? A father wanting the best for his son."

Honovi watched as Steven's eyes flitted back and forth between them before finally settling on her.

He withdrew his hands from hers and paced to the brazier she had stood next to. "I'm sorry, Honovi," he said as he stared into the embers.

His back was facing the altar pole, but from her angle she thought she saw something round drop into the bowl of the brazier. It reminded her of something. Something important, but she couldn't quite remember what.

"I'm sorry I couldn't protect you," he continued, turning back to her.

She shook her head, "It doesn't matter—"

"It does. You need to hear this." He paced back to her, to stand with his forehead nearly touching hers. "I couldn't protect you in the hut. Trying to is what got us here."

Whispers at the Altar

The hut? She tried to remember. Something about being angry. Angry that he wouldn't let her do something. But it was blurred behind how happy she was now.

"And I can't protect Brogan. I wanted to at Ceerport. We were watching your family get . . . sacrificed. I was so scared. I just wanted to leave."

Honovi frowned. Ceerport. A memory flashed. "But. You saved me. Didn't you?"

Steven shook his head slowly. "Brogan did. I argued with him. I was afraid something would happen to him. I wanted to help, but . . . By trying to save him, I would have lost you."

Honovi's mind was like a fog with events and feelings blurring together. "But . . . but you can save me now. That's all that matters."

"No. I can't." He stood up straight and turned his head back to Ssanek. "I can't save her, and I can't save Brogan. Every time I've tried has only hurt them or someone else. They might die tomorrow, or they may grow old and die later. All I can do is be here for them now while the Maker allows us to be together."

He paused and bit his lip. He was scared. Worried about something. She looked up at Ssanek, and his face didn't seem so benevolent any more. The blood of the ritual dripped down from its fangs to land hissing on the platform while eyes like small flames blazed and flared in a twisted and grotesque skull.

"This is not an offer I will make again, son," came the rumbling reply edged with anger.

Steven looked back at her, gripping her shoulders gently. "I'm sorry I can't protect you, Honovi. But you don't need protection, and you don't deserve a cage. You deserve to be free, like all the Yahad. And I will fight to give that to you. I will fi—"

His final words were cut off by a deafening explosion.

Her feet left the ground, and she was thrown back as a blinding white light punctuated by streaks of burning red spread from behind Steven. He landed on top of her, driving the air out of her lungs even as she heard horrible screams come from all around.

He was still holding her shoulders as he rolled with her. Once. Twice. And then she was falling again and the light, like all the stars in the night sky condensed into one burning mote, was blocked by the platform.

She hit the ground on her side with a bone-jarring jolt. Spots danced in front of her eyes, but nothing felt broken. She wanted to lie there a moment, recover, but Steven was already pulling her to her feet.

"We have to run!" he shouted into her nearly deaf ear. "Come on!" He kept pulling on her, and after another second she stood.

He planned this, she thought. The whitefire. How could she have forgotten the whitefire? Her mind was filled with fog that she couldn't quite see through.

She followed him as she tried to clear her mind. He stopped, turned, ran back. There was yelling, fire, and a booming voice calling orders she didn't understand. What had Steven been saying? On the platform. It had been something important. She knew that now, though she hadn't thought so then.

He pulled her down behind a tent as lizard soldiers ran past.

It was something about the village. And her brother. And her. A clear image showed through the fog. Steven walking away. Leaving her to die.

"You would have left me," she muttered, her vision finally focusing clearly. "You lied to me." She yanked her hand out of his grip.

Steven turned to look at her, his eyes wide. "Can we talk about that later? We could end up dead right here if we aren't quiet."

Honovi glared but said nothing. Her savior was just a coward who lied to get her to . . . She turned away, but followed as he took off running again. She couldn't believe she let herself believe him.

The dress kept distracting her as she ran. Every touch of it on her skin, rather than making her feel more alive, was now like rubbing a rash or sunburn. She wanted to tear it off. Oh, but he'd probably like that. He probably enjoyed her pining like a simpleton after him. She

growled to herself as they rounded another corner, running straight for the cliff now.

"Where are we going?"

"The caves. We can't get through the camp. I've been trying. Our only hope is that one of those caves exits somewhere else."

"What?" She slowed, nearly stopped, then hurried to catch up. "Your plan is to run into a cave and hope we can get out?" For the first time she noticed he was carrying a burning branch. "What is that for? Are you trying to let them see us?"

"I'm sorry, were you planning an escape while you were enjoying your nice warm bath? Is there some escape route hidden in that new dress?"

A flash of guilt only fanned her fury, and she nearly hit him. The arrogant jerk. How had she ever—"Soldiers!" she warned. There were three closing fast to their right, including the enormous one from the platform.

"I know. I think we can make it." He started fumbling in his shirt with his free hand.

The cave was close, twenty paces at the most. But the Soldiers were faster by far.

"We aren't going to make it."

"Yes, we will, just run."

Honovi yanked up her skirt and ran, passing Steven easily.

The Soldiers, jagged swords in hand, roared in protest as she slipped into the utter black of the cave. She slowed, then heard a sharp sound of metal striking stone, and Steven ran into the back of her.

"Move!" He shoved her hard in the back, and she stumbled forward. Steven's branch was barely enough to see four paces in front of her.

"I can't see!"

"Just—"

The Soldiers roared as they rounded into the cave behind them, the sound amplifying into the cave until Honovi thought her ears would burst, but it was cut short into a cry of pain by another explosion.

Whispers at the Altar

A rush of wind tossed her forward as the cave was for a moment thrown into sharp relief.

She landed on hard stone, driving the air from her lungs as she heard a crack like thunder above her.

Then the pitch dark returned, and all she could hear were the rocks breaking and falling from above her.

This was his plan?

Loss

Christa covered the distance as quickly as she could without running or tripping over her dress. For Sinna to be this angry, Christa couldn't imagine what must be going on.

Sinna's words pierced the distance. "...no, you l-look at her and all you s-see is your own bitterness toward a people she's left b-behind. You're filled with hate and f-f-fear for people you don't even know! It makes me sick, and if that's what you call being 'loyal to the crown' then the c-crown could use a few more rebels!"

Christa's stomach clenched as she caught the last lines of Sinna's tirade. Of course they were arguing about her. As she approached, the director's eyes locked on her, and his smile grew across his wine-reddened cheeks.

"Ahh. Speak of the Dark One... I hadn't seen you for some time. I thought you left." He glanced pointedly to Vaniel who looked horrified to see Christa. "But like a mongrel dog you keep coming back."

Christa stopped short. Did he just call her a dog? "Yes. I wanted to say good night to my friends. I didn't realize I would be interrupting."

"Child, you have done nothing but from the day you arrived. Yet I don't expect you to care. Why would you? This is all some experiment to you, isn't it? Another way to strip away our traditions."

Christa took a deep breath, trying her best to control the anger kindling deep inside. "I'm as much an elf as you. I care about the people of this nation and their traditions."

Dalan chuckled, but brighter spots of red formed on his cheeks. "I care more about my people than a human monster like you could possibly understand," he hissed. "Enough to protect them from *you*! An elf? You, child, are an abomination. From your birth to your freakish abilities. Your traitorous, pit-cursed mother should never have been allowed to leave."

The kindling of anger flared white hot.

Let me burn him . . . Please. Let me peel back the blackened flesh from his bones.

"Even now you can barely control yourself. Let it out, pit-spawn. Show us all what you really are. Show us what that witch foisted on the world with her barbaric lechery."

"Stop!" She heard the word echoed by all her friends, their hands outstretched to her and eyes pleading. In a vague way she even sensed Kadin's hand pulling on her arm, but there was no time to discern the meaning behind it. Beautiful Fire burned everything away.

It seared through her veins and scorched her mind. Her oldest friend. The only one that knew all her secrets. And now it came to her defense as any good friend would. She gave no thought to resistance or fear. She wanted the Fire.

Needed the Fire.

And the Fire was happy to oblige.

There was the briefest resistance, like burning through paper, and it streaked toward the cockroach in front of her, enveloping him. There was giddy joy. Exultant satisfaction. Then it was gone. The

•Whispers at the Altar•

flames still surrounded the cockroach, his extravagant robes ablaze, but something blocked the Fire from touching him.

Then there were hands on her, forcing her down. People shouted what might have been her name. Did she have a name? Or did the Fire burn it away?

She tried to use it on the grasping hands, but it was like shoving against a wall. She could feel the barrier shudder, but it wouldn't break. The Fire promised it could. If she only surrendered a little more of herself, there was nothing it couldn't break.

There was a face in the flames. It was a familiar face. One she cared about. She couldn't let the Fire take him. Slowly, reluctantly, the flames receded and the face became clearer. Kadin? Yes, that was his name. And hers was Christabel.

Why was she lying face down on the ground?

Why were swords leveled at her, their points mere inches away, the soldiers grim faced and tense?

"Christabel Sellers!"

She recognized that voice and craned her neck up to look at Marellel. It was only then she realized someone was on her back, his knee digging in as he twisted her arms up between her shoulder blades. It made craning her head to see Marellel excruciating, the angle impossible to maintain.

"Get off!" the director yelled. "I have placed a shield around her, the same as every other Hawk in this room. If she can push through that . . ." She sighed. "Just let her up."

The weight released and Christa breathed deep. Kadin helped her up, but another guard kept her hands gripped tightly behind her back. Apparently he wasn't taking any chances. Never mind that she could burn him to cinders without them. Her stomach twisted, and she focused on Marellel, forcing the visual out of her mind.

"What in the Pit were you thinking?" She addressed Christa now, leaning close to hiss the words through clenched teeth.

Christa could see Dalan behind the director, his clothes still smoldering in places as he brushed off soot. But her gaze was captured by Marellel's stare. The director's blue orbs were filled with equal parts crushing anger and boundless disappointment.

"I don't know," she whispered. She honestly didn't. She remembered for a moment, she had wanted, needed, to kill Dalan. As horrifying as the thought was to her now. She remembered Silvana in the snow. But it was their fault, wasn't it? They deserved it, didn't they? Everything was all muddled in her head.

She sought out her friends. It was hard to meet Marellel's stare. She found them huddled behind the director, their faces crowded with fear and pity. Even Sinna had little comfort to give.

"You don't know? How could you . . . ?" Marellel sputtered and raised a hand.

Christa flinched, but the blow never came.

"Get her out of here. Take her to the Vault."

The guard turned her to the door and gave a little shove. She stumbled forward, turning to catch one last look at her friends. Instead she saw Dalan smiling like the cat that swallowed the mouse. He even had the nerve to wave.

The trip to the Vault was interminable. What did she do? She hadn't even realized the Fire was so close, so ready to leap to her call. No, she couldn't use that excuse. She knew. She had always known. She just ignored it. She deluded herself into thinking she had it under control, that she was the master and not the other way around. She wanted to hurt Dalan. Wanted it with every part of her after what he said about her mother.

It wasn't the Fire's fault.

It was hers. It was always hers.

"In here," the guard grunted and shoved her forward, snapping her back to her surroundings.

She barely had time to process the sterile room before the steel door closed with a clang that echoed through empty halls.

⁕ Whispers at the Altar ⁕

"You can't stay here," the guard said.

Christa turned, confused.

Then he spoke again. "I don't care. You are not in the guard yet so you will have to wait outside."

There was another pause, this one longer. Christa wished there was a window or even a slit in the door so she could tell whom he was talking to.

"I told you, I don't care. You aren't authorized to be in here while there is a prisoner here. Now get out before I throw you in a cell, too."

Christa was surprised she could hear him through the thick door. He must be yelling. She wandered over to the bed, a thin mattress on a solid but sparse metal frame, and sat down. It was the only piece of furniture in the room. The only interruption in the gray stone monotony of walls, ceiling, and floor. There wasn't even a lamp, just a faint mournful green glow emanating from the rock.

She never wondered what an elven prison looked like. But now, presented with nothing else to do, she thought it should be more comfortable. All the elves she knew were used to a measure of extravagance. Even if this cell were carpeted and the bed given a warm comforter with a feather pillow, they would probably weep.

The thought of her friends was a rock in her gut. She'd let them down. All of them. Especially Marellel. Christa had given her word she'd try her best, train as hard as she could, but in the end she played right into Dalan's plan and ruined everything. Now she didn't know what they would do with her. Did the elves execute criminals? She'd never heard of it, but then she'd never heard of anyone trying to commit murder in the throne room. Or anywhere else for that matter. They resolved their differences in a more "civilized" manner.

And what about Mama? Christa hid her face in her hands and stared into the dark behind her fingers. There was no way she would be allowed in the library now. No way to research the experiment. Mama would be gone forever. Even if they sent her home, which she supposed was a possibility, Papa still wouldn't want her.

"Ha! Did you see her face?" Dalan yelled as he tossed his coat over a chair. Vaniel heard the door click shut behind her as she trailed the procession into the director's office.

"The child's or Marellel's?" Elirel asked with a smirk.

"Both," Dalan answered with a grin. "Neither of those fools had the slightest clue what they were walking into."

"Of course we were lucky she walked into it at all," Adasian said, looking pointedly at Vaniel who still stood just inside the door. They all turned to look at her.

Vaniel was reminded of animals. Dogs, looking at a piece of meat. Their faces were vicious and ugly. She turned to Corannel, but hers was no different from theirs.

"Yes, child," Palatan sneered, "why exactly did I see you introducing the vermin to that Anathonian trash when you should have been bringing her to us?"

Vaniel frowned. They *were* animals. All of them. Each snarling for a piece of the small game they had finally run to ground.

"Because she doesn't deserve what you are trying to do to her." She stood up straighter. "She is just a child trying her best to get through a difficult time."

Dalan laughed, the red splotching his cheeks as he threw back his head, but Palatan's gaze was ice cold. "You had better watch your tongue, child. I—"

"I am not your *child*, remember," Vaniel spat. "I am not a Sablehawk. And thank the Creator. Because that house is just a cave full of selfish wolves gnawing at old grudges like bones as they fight over who has the cleanest droppings. And when they run out of bones, they gnaw on each other."

· Whispers at the Altar ·

Corannel gasped. "Vaniel!"

Vaniel fought the tears back as she looked at Corannel, at the woman who used to be her mother. "You all deserve each other." She turned to go.

"Walk out of that door and you will be without a family forever," Palatan hissed.

"I already have a family," she said over her shoulder as she opened the door. "And we don't use each other like tools for our own gain."

Christa couldn't tell how long she sat, but she must have slept at least a little. When the harsh light of the open door woke her she was lying down.

"Come, the directors are assembled for your trial." The guard stood to one side of the doorway, letting the full light of one torch blaze down on the bed.

Christa blinked and squinted. "Already?" Her voice sounded rough in her ears, as though she'd been forgotten for years instead of hours.

The guard didn't answer. He just stood there at attention, spear point and breastplate dazzling the light between them.

She never would have guessed a grand ball filled the throne room mere hours before. Though the walls and ceiling appeared the same, it was comparatively empty now. Queen Elisidel sat in her silver throne at the far end. Seven rugged wooden chairs faced away from the thrones in a semi-circle beneath them, and two rows of benches faced them. Before the chairs stood the directors, and at the benches stood her peers, each a stiff figure with hard eyes watching her slow approach.

A quick glance up at Marellel revealed little sympathy. A scan of the secretary and other five directors showed even less. Then she saw Kadin standing with her friends to one side in the benches, and her heart bounded. His eyes held no sadness, horror, or disappointment, only understanding.

Christa was led, flanked by a half-dozen guards and just as many Hawks, to a solitary stool set in the vertex of the chairs. She sat and, unable to see Kadin without turning around, found a safe spot in the grass a pace ahead to stare at.

"Christabel Sellers," the secretary's thin voice broke the silence, "you have been charged with treason. Specifically, you used magic in the throne room of Queen Elisidel. In doing so, you attacked, with the intent of murdering, a director of the Queen's Hawks. Do you understand these charges?"

"Yes." She didn't bother to look up, didn't want to meet all those eyes.

"And do you have anything to say in defense against these charges?"

Christa thought for a minute. She hadn't expected to be given a chance to say anything. But what was there to say? It was all true. She *had* wanted to kill him. And the thought of him staring at her now with the same self-satisfied grin he'd worn when she was escorted out, made her want to do it again.

"No."

"So you admit you attempted to kill Director Dalan?"

"Yes. But I didn't mean to," she hurried to add. "It just . . . happened."

"Lack of control is not an excuse." Dalan blurted. "This is exactly what I warned you all about when she was admitted. I warned you her human blood could not be trusted. That she was incapable of the discipline required to—"

"Yes, Director Dalan," a high clear voice interrupted. Christa didn't recognize the speaker. She guessed it must be Director Aerel. "We are well aware of your warnings. But that vote is past. She is here, and she has been taught."

"Exactly," Marellel said. "And I would remind the council that Director Dalan is far from innocent in this. His actions during the ball were completely inappropriate. Not only did he insult Christabel and her mother, a Hawk in her own right, but he threatened—"

•Whispers at the Altar•

"Director Dalan's actions will be dealt with at a later time and in a more private forum," the secretary said.

"Indeed." Aerel said. "The issue before us tonight is what to do with Eyas Christabel now."

"There are only two real choices."

The deep baritone was too familiar and carried a flood of memories. The square, her father hugging her goodbye, his refusal to help bring Mama back—it all came tumbling through the walls of self-defense weakened by her stay in the vault.

Director Namarian continued. "We send her back or we keep her here. If we send her back, we can only trust her word she will not use what she knows for some nefarious end. If we keep her here—"

"She *must* be punished," Dalan interrupted again. "And her word cannot be trusted. She has already broken one oath."

"Unfortunately, I must agree with Director Dalan."

Christa didn't recognize that voice, either. It was warm. Earthy. It made her think of a warm summer rain in the woods. The kind that made everything fresh.

"She cannot go back to the humans. They will not understand her, and I doubt they would welcome her. If she cannot control her abilities here, I fear the slightest slip there would mean her death."

Christa swallowed.

"Then keep her here," Namarian said. "I propose she be confined to the palace. She has taken an oath to serve the queen. Let her keep it."

"Even as a servant she could not be trusted within the palace." Christa could feel the venom dripping from Dalan's words. "She should be confined to the Vault."

"Until when?" Marellel's voice was tense. Christa knew that tone. She had experienced it often. "You might as well kill her now."

"She is a traitor!" Dalan's words echoed through the room. "And *you* brought her here. You begged for her to learn our secrets, and you fought for her to stay. Even when it was obvious to everyone else how dangerous she is. How many more of our people does she need to hurt before you admit your folly? Or . . . or is it more than folly, Director Marellel?" His voice dropped. "Perhaps she is not the only traitor in our midst."

"Enough!" A voice like a clear bell rang through the room.

Christa looked up. Her gaze met the queen's as she stood above the others, and Christa couldn't look away. Those dark eyes, like clear night skies, held hers and laid bare everything she knew and felt.

"We have heard your arguments, but it is not your place to pass judgment on a servant of the Crown. That responsibility is mine alone." She turned to look at Dalan with narrowed eyes as if daring him to say otherwise.

Dalan bowed in acquiescence. "Of course, Your Majesty."

Queen Elisidel watched him for a long moment before turning back to Christa. "Christabel Sellers, daughter of Chrysolbel, Fourth Tier Eyas of the Roost, you are guilty of attacking, with the intent of killing, a servant of the Crown. You have betrayed the trust we placed in you and shown yourself to be a danger to anyone around you. As such, you are immediately removed from training. We cannot trust you with the knowledge you have and will not trust you with any more."

Christa's heart sank, and her eyes watered. She would never be able to complete the experiment for Ssanek. She would never see Mama again. Never hear her voice or dance with her in the garden. And Papa would never forgive her.

"However, you are sworn to me and to my service, and I do not release you from that oath. You will serve in whatever capacity the Seneschal finds for you within the palace." The queen stepped down, weaving her way through the director's chairs, leaving a trail of bright, glistening grass behind her. It occurred to Christa that Queen Elisidel still wore her dress from the ball. She stopped a pace away, and Christa knelt in the soft grass without remembering when she left the chair. A vague scent of mint and new spring flowers drifted up to meet her.

•Whispers at the Altar•

"Look at me, child."

Christa lifted her head, meeting those fathomless eyes again.

"When I say we cannot trust you with the knowledge we have given you," she spoke so only Christa could hear, "it is in full seriousness." She withdrew a vial from some unseen pocket of her dress. It glowed dully as she raised it up for everyone to see.

"This is a philter made from the Arkius stone," she said, more for those assembled than Christa's benefit. She lowered the vial in front of Christa's eyes.

"This is the same stone that veins the walls of the Vault, with which you are already familiar. It is not of our Essence, and so inhibits the manipulation of Essence around it. Ingested, it will bond to you, to your Self." She paused and the barest hint of sadness crept across her face. "You will still be able to feel the Essence, but you will never again be able to touch it or shape it."

Christa stared at the vial, its glow sickly in the warm spring light of the throne room. "Will it hurt?"

The queen nodded once. "It will. But not for long."

Christa swallowed. "I don't have a choice, do I?"

Another glimpse of sadness echoed in her eyes, "I am afraid not, child. It is this or life in the Vault. You chose your path earlier tonight."

Christa reached out to take the vial, the glass like a chill cup of milk at breakfast, only with poison inside. "How did you know you would need it?"

"There was only one outcome."

She couldn't argue.

Pulling off the stopper, she took one last glance back at Kadin before swallowing it down as fast as she could. It tasted exactly as it looked: cold and diseased with a gritty texture. She thought it must be what swallowing an earthworm whole from the garden would feel like. The potion crawled down her throat, settling in her stomach with a nauseating lurch that almost caused her to throw it back up on the queen's silver slippers.

Allan C.R. Cornelius

She took a step back, grasping the chair for support as her vision swam and tiny pinpricks ran up the inside of her gut. The nausea turned to pain, and she doubled over, grasping her stomach. A murmur ran through those assembled, a concern like that of an audience at a play, but Christa didn't hear or care.

Then, as quickly as it came, the pain left, and her vision cleared. Still, she was acutely aware of something *else*. Something there. Like a fog before her eyes, a numbness in her fingers, or a cold clogging her head. Instinctually, she reached out for the Essence, but it was like striking a prison wall. She could hear beyond it, could smell the wider world, but the wall would never again let her experience it.

"It is done," the queen declared to the room at large and walked back to her throne, sparing one last pitying look at Christabel. "This court is finished."

Another murmur swept through the crowd, accompanied by much head shaking. Those assembled stood, waited for the queen to leave, then began to disperse. Christa peered up at the director's chairs searching for Marellel, and found her just in time to watch her turn away. Of course. Why would she stay? Christa was no longer her student.

Slowly Christa was left alone in the throne room. She stared after Marellel, still trying to break through the wall within herself, slamming against it with fists of will only to feel its cold, gritty, indestructible face.

"Christa?"

The voice was soft, timid, and in her frustration Christa almost wanted to hit it, too. Instead, she turned. Sinna was reaching out a hand to her, unsure what to do. Kadin stood beside her, a rock in the storm, while Westrel, Vaniel, and Darian stood behind.

"Christa, I . . ." Sinna stopped, then tried again. "I'll help you move. They won't let you stay in the R-Roost now."

"Of course, that doesn't mean we won't be seeing each other," Westrel said. "They can't keep you from eating in the Roost dining hall. It is open to anyone in the palace."

Darian gave an encouraging smile. "We are just trying to say you are not alone here, Christa."

"Never." Sinna nodded.

Vaniel nodded agreement, tears streaming down her face, but said nothing.

Christa tried to be grateful, tried to show it, but could only manage a weak nod of her own. "Thank you, everyone. But I think right now I just want to be alone."

There was more murmured encouragement and a few hugs before she was able to extricate herself. She didn't know where she was going. She just needed to get out of that room. She thought about stopping in the library, it usually made her feel better. She got so far as to place her hand on the door before letting it drop. What was the point? She couldn't go into any of the sections that mattered. Not anymore.

She walked on, letting her feet take her wherever they wanted as she stared out the occasional window. At first she looked at the city, spreading out below her as she climbed above it. She wondered what it was like to live in it. She imagined herself opening a small shop, perhaps a flower shop, there in the courtyard with all the trees. She could grow the flowers in her own little garden, then arrange them in vases for all the women walking by. She could be happy there alone. Without the pressure and demands of the palace.

But of course she couldn't open a shop. She belonged to Queen Elisidel. She had sworn an oath. Or at least her child-self had. How dare they trick her? How dare they manipulate a child, promising everything she ever wanted and only demanding her life in return? What was life to a child? She would grow old here, older than she could even imagine now. All those years in service to royalty who would only reward her with more life to serve them with.

She struck a doorpost as she walked through it, and the warmth of the Fire spread in her chest. She grinned. It was still there. They hadn't banished it away with everything else.

Her closest and oldest friend. She held it, and it warmed her, comforted her. It whispered to her of revenge, of the palace in flames. They would scream for help. But she would just walk away, like they walked away from her.

But none of that was possible. The Fire was there, but it was as alone as she. Trapped in the same prison.

She walked out onto the floor of the Observatory and gazed out across Ellsabareth. From here she was sure she could see the very edges of Ellsabae. She paced to the center, eyes fixed to the northwest, to home. She wasn't afraid of falling any more. How could it be worse than living like this? The walls vanished as she reached the center, and she was suspended, floating over the palace with the city far below.

Home had to be there. Right *there*. She strained, piercing through the haze of the horizon. Of course she couldn't see it. But the desire, the *need* didn't care about such minor inconveniences. She thought of Papa, of his kind, bearded face and strong arms always so eager with a hug. She remembered the town with its little garden, so much more real than any here, and the skins stretching in the woods behind their house. She remembered it so much it hurt, twisting in the back of her head like a knife.

She didn't care. She had to see it just as she did in her mind's eye. She *had* to see it.

The knife of pain twisted with a jerk and she screamed, dropping to her knees. When she opened her eyes, stars swam before them, but she barely noticed.

It was there!

Whispers at the Altar

The town, the garden, the little houses . . . all of it. She was hovering over it, as she had been hovering over the palace seconds ago. She turned a slow circle, then gasped as she saw him.

"Papa!"

But he didn't turn. Couldn't hear her. Whatever magic had brought her here would not give her that. It was a tease. A vision and nothing more.

He walked out of the little one room cottage they lived in, leaning against the fence that ran around it. It was night and the lone lantern in front of their house made a golden halo for him to stand in as he searched the sky, directly at her.

She wished she were closer, able see his face.

And she was.

She was on the ground in front of him, as if she were standing right there. She wanted to run up to him and give him the biggest hug. But she knew the magic wouldn't let her.

He was older. Gray ran through his hair in solid streaks, and lines crossed his face. Had she been at the Roost *that* long? But he was still Papa, and the sight of him filled her up. She forgot about the trial and the potion and magic and friends. She could do without all of them if only she could stay here with him. She'd find another way to bring Mama back. There must be something else Ssanek could do. Then they would all be together again. And Papa would love her again. She knew it.

Then *she* came. A woman Christa didn't recognize walked out of their house. What was she doing in *their* house? She walked up to Papa and put her arms around him, holding him like Mama had.

"No!" Christa screamed. "Stop it!" She tried to force herself forward, to pull the woman's arms from Papa, but the magic wouldn't let her. She reached for the Fire, but the prison walls laughed at her. Christa screamed at her again.

Then her father turned and kissed the woman, and the screams caught in Christa's throat.

He . . . he loved her?

Her eyes caught the ring on the chain around the woman's neck.

She reached up to feel the ring she wore on her own chain. Mama's ring. She gripped it tight as her eyes filled. There was no going back. He loved someone else. He didn't care about Mama or her. He had forgotten them.

There was a tingling in the back of her head, and her surroundings blurred through her tears. There was someone holding her. Arms wrapped around her, squeezing slightly. Papa? No, she was back in the palace now. She leaned back, blinking past the tears to see Kadin's face.

"Kadin? What are you doing here?"

I followed you. I thought you could use a friend.

Christa managed to smile. "Thank you."

What happened? You were yelling?

He didn't mention she'd been yelling at no one, but Christa could imagine what it must have looked like. "I . . . I saw something. A vision maybe." She sighed and shook her head, trying to wipe the tears off her cheeks. "I'm not sure what it was."

Kadin only nodded and continued to stare at her with concern.

"I'm alone, Kadin." She leaned against him, trying to pull his arm around her like a blanket.

No Christa. Never alone. Never.

Depths

The air was heavy with dirt and debris. Steven tried to take a deep breath but winced as an edge of pain sliced through his lungs. He coughed on the dirt he breathed in, and the pain cut even deeper. The plan definitely could have gone better.

The mutants Ssanek had chosen reacted faster than Steven expected, cutting off all the most direct routes out. Leaving only this.

"Honovi?" His voice cracked, and he launched into another agonizing coughing fit. When it finally subsided he was able to take a few shallow breaths and check for broken bones.

"Honovi?" His voice came out in a ragged whisper this time.

"I'm right here," she answered from somewhere a pace or two ahead.

All his limbs checked out, a miracle in itself considering how close he'd been to the blast, so he crawled up to a sitting position. Pain flared through his chest. Great, a broken rib.

"Are you all right? Did you get hurt?" He fished around in the void for the torch, trying not to move any more than he had to, but couldn't find it.

"I'm fine. Nice escape." If her sarcasm could have shed light, he wouldn't need the torch.

Steven paused in his groping to stare in her general direction. All that work and she was mad at him? What had she expected? He tried to shove the thoughts away—there were bigger problems right now—but they only shifted to the side.

"I lost the torch," he said as he groped further forward. "Can you feel it anywhere around you?"

"Here," she said after a moment of brushing noises along the floor. "How are you going to light it?"

He flailed about until he found her outstretched hand and the torch within, took it, and placed it between his knees. "I kept some of the whitefire. If I do it right, I should be able to use a rock and the powder to light the torch again."

"Right. Assuming you don't bring the whole cave down on us."

Steven took a calming breath. "The Soldiers were right behind us. Another couple seconds and we both would have been dead. I didn't have a choice."

He ignored her vague grunt and focused on the torch. They were both under a lot of stress. The image of Honovi in that revealing dress paraded before his mind's eye in the dark. He growled softly as he forced the picture away and concentrated on the small fingertip of whitefire.

"Problems?"

He ignored her. A few seconds later the powder caught and the blackness was consumed in blinding light. He turned away, blinking as his eyes adjusted, and looked past Honovi's crouched form.

The jagged dark granite walls and ceiling of the cave pressed in around them as if still intent on crushing them beneath its weight. It didn't have far to go. There was barely enough room to stand where they were, and it only narrowed as the cave burrowed deeper into the cliff. He wondered how far that would be. Had he chosen well? Or had he only ensured they would die of thirst, buried alive while their enemies waited outside?

A soft rumble from the entrance made him turn back that way, listening. It was completely collapsed, some of the boulders bigger than two or three of him. There was no way the Soldiers had lived through it. He would love to take credit for it, but the whitefire should not have done what it did. The only explanation was that there had been more in the rock of the cave mouth.

"What are you doing?" Honovi was on her feet now, brushing at that ridiculous dress. She probably didn't want it to get dirty.

"Shush."

"What?" The single word echoed through the cave.

Steven held up a hand as he inched closer to the rocks. He wasn't sure whether to be grateful for the slide or not. Once again he thought of the narrowing passage leading deeper into the cliff. *Please let there be a way out.*

Tap tap tap.

There it was again. He shook his head and struggled to stand.

"Come on," he whispered, turning to take Honovi's hand. "We have to get out of here."

"Out?" She pulled her hand back. "Out where?"

There was a hysterical edge to her voice that grated on Steven's already frayed nerves. He moved past her, pulling his arm tight to his chest to keep the pain at bay. "Anywhere that isn't here. They're digging through."

He held the torch forward with his free hand and walked as quickly as he could manage deeper into the darkness. After a few seconds he heard her steps behind him.

"What did he mean?" she asked after a minute of blessed silence.

Steven squinted into the dark. The tunnel had already narrowed to the point that it would be uncomfortable to pass one another. He didn't answer. He didn't feel like asking what she meant, even though, deep down, he knew exactly what she meant. If he pretended he didn't, maybe they wouldn't have to talk about it.

"What did he mean?" she asked again, more insistently. "He said you were his son. He said your mother's blood summoned him. What was he talking about? What *else* have you not told me?"

Steven sighed, turning right at a fork purely because it was wider. He had to crouch now, and his chest was throbbing in pain.

"I don't want to talk about it."

"You don't want to talk about it?" She gave a mirthless laugh. "How about how you wanted to leave me and my father to die? Should we talk about that? Or maybe how you lied about the rescue being your idea—"

"I never said that. Brogan did."

"And you went along with it!" A mist of pebbles fell over them, but Honovi didn't seem to notice. "You could not bear to see someone taken like your mother was, remember? Who took your mother? Who poured her blood over that altar?"

"Fine. I lied. I already told you that. I already said I was sorry." The tunnel had shrunk to a fissure now. He had to turn sideways just to move forward. "I was wrong. What do you want from me? It isn't like you're innocent, either."

"What?"

"You know what. I told you not to listen to him. I told you not to trust him. And there you were, dressed for a party and spouting his nonsense."

"You said it would be all right. I did exactly what you told me to."

"What?" He stopped and turned his head to look back at her despite the pain in his chest. Her face was a collection of shadows barely illuminated by the torch he held on the other side of him. But the anger etched into it was all too obvious.

"I told you to be careful," he said. "Anyone could see that was a trap. And you fell right into it. I was depending on you, and you joined *him*. A regular servant of Ssanek. He used you, and you let him. You even liked it didn't—"

The blow to his jaw staggered him forward and into an outcrop of rock that drove itself into his injured ribs.

He cried out, and the torch dropped from his fingers.

"I am *not* his." She glared at him, face shadowed in the slanted light. "I am not the one he called *son*. And you weren't there. You do not know. You do not know anything about me. You are a traitor. A spy. A coward hiding from his own fear."

She pushed past, carelessly flattening him against the wall as she did, snatched up the torch, and continued on.

Steven glared at her back. He couldn't believe he ever could have been tempted to spend the rest of his life with her. The light dimmed as she struggled ahead. *He* was the traitor? Couldn't she see what she had done? Shadows, she was still wearing the proof of it! He rubbed his jaw with his free hand. The dark was almost complete now, her form a bare shadow in the distance, then it vanished altogether. Struggling to his feet, he hurried after. There was no way he was going to let her leave him behind. Even if they were just going to die of thirst in here.

He wouldn't give her the satisfaction.

An hour later he was still walking behind her, the silence between them as palpable as the rock walls that pressed in on either side. The pain in his chest was unbearable now, and he was about to ask her to stop for a short rest when she halted so suddenly he almost ran into her.

"What is it?" he asked as he fought down the cry of pain.

She whispered something he couldn't hear.

"What?" He tried to look around her, but the walls were too narrow, and he couldn't make anything out that would explain her behavior.

"I said I cannot see anything," she hissed back at him. "The walls, the ceiling . . . they disappear after this point."

"Well it's about time this cave gave us some breathing room. What are you waiting for?"

"What if there's something there?"

"Like what?" Steven was losing what little patience he had left. "You'll see any hole in the floor before you step in it, and if there was some beast out here . . . well, I imagine it would have eaten us already. Or it will soon leap out of the darkness and kill us. Either way, standing here isn't going to do us any good."

"Thank you for the comforting words." Honovi waited a moment more, then stepped out into the black. She turned left, keeping at least one wall comfortably close, and lifted the torch as high as she could to spread the light. Even so, it was like a small candle in an ocean of black.

Steven crept along behind, using the wall for support now while his eyes strained to see anything past the disturbingly small circle the torch lit. The light wavered in time to Honovi's shaking arm, setting the shadows of stalagmites dancing as the two intruders shuffled passed. He wanted to say something to her, to comfort her, but he knew any comfort he had to give would sound like a lie. Not to mention she probably didn't want to hear anything from him regardless.

So they walked in silence, and the wall stretched on forever. He didn't know how long they followed it before his hand began to feel the irregularities in its surface. Not the jagged edges and rough planes, those had long ago become normal. These were smooth spaces surrounded and pierced by deep grooves. The closer he looked at them the more the patterns took shape, forming into enormous pictures carved into the cave wall.

"Stop for a second," he whispered. Something about the chamber made him not dare to raise his voice any louder.

Whispers at the Altar

Honovi turned. "Why?" The torch threw shadows across her face that made her look even more frightened and worried than he knew her to be.

"Just for a second. I want to look at this." He backed away from the wall, trying to take in the entire scene carved upon it, but their torch was too dim to illuminate the whole of it. He snatched the torch from Honovi's hand and paced back and forth in an attempt to see it all.

"It looks like a mural carved into the rock. See, these look like people gathered together. A whole crowd of them."

Honovi walked up beside him, one hand tracing along the collection of figures. "Warriors? Look, they carry weapons. Spears and clubs. And . . ." her finger stopped under a figure carrying a long pole topped with what could only be a winged serpent.

Steven swallowed and stepped further down the wall. "There are more here." He pointed to where the stream of people became a crowd jostling together. "But what are these?" He bent closer, trying to make them out, and Honovi slid toward him, obviously unwilling to be left at the edge of the torchlight. There were other poles, with other icons: a fly with a human skull, a rodent of some kind with two heads, a bird with four wings, and many more. The people holding them crowded forward beside monsters whose forms were too confused to make out in the eroding wall. All of them pushed together until it was impossible to tell one from another or human from beast.

Honovi backed away from the wall, tugging at Steven's shirt. "We should go. We should not be here."

Steven backed away a step, but didn't turn. "Look, they're all going up. It looks like they're attacking something. And see, up there?" He pointed to the very edge of the torchlight's illumination upon the wall. "There's some kind of altar with a reptile eye or something over it. And those other creatures around it, what are those?"

Honovi pulled harder. "I don't care. I want to leave. Please . . ."

Steven shook his head. "This could be important. Boost me up, so I can get a better look at it."

Honovi blinked at him and her eyes hardened. "No. We need to go. This place is evil. I can feel it."

"Probably just feeling that bath again," Steven mumbled as he turned to look for a stone big enough to serve his need. He didn't know if she heard him or not, but he didn't really care. If she couldn't understand that this was important, then she really was a fool.

He found a stone and managed to push it over without Honovi's help; she was sulking while still trying to stay within the bounds of the light. After maneuvering the stone into place and taking a short break to allow the piercing pain in his chest to subside, he stepped up on the rock and raised the torch high.

"I think it's an altar," he whispered, as much to himself as to Honovi. "This eye, it looks odd. Not so much like an eye as a rip or a hole. The edges are all fuzzy. And these things around it, they don't look like the people down there. The heads are different, and they have big ears."

"Fine, can we go now?"

"Some of them look like they are protecting the altar, but others seem to be running toward it. Maybe even *through* it." Steven squinted. These carvings had to be incredibly old, older than Honovi's stories about her people being swayed by Ssanek, yet here his symbol was. And who were these other people? Elves? He'd never seen one, but he knew they were supposed to look inhuman. And what was the eye? He looked around the wall for any other clue, but there was none to be found.

He crawled down, and Honovi snatched the torch back out of his hand.

"Now if you are finished wasting our light . . ." She stalked off without a look back.

Steven saw other carvings, larger depictions of the icons from the mural, but they offered no further explanation, not without stopping to examine them further, and he knew Honovi wouldn't do any such thing.

The image was still haunting his thoughts when they finally stumbled, torchless, into a rocky valley and a cold pale morning. But even as they set a roundabout course back to the east and the Yahad camp, all he could be sure of was that Ssanek had been haunting this place far longer than any of them guessed. And he was not alone.

YEAR 5

Breakthrough

The sun beaming through the windows shone off the gold inlay of the book Sinna carried. It danced and jerked in bright stripes across the walls, shifting with every step. She smiled and adjusted the book as she passed the next window to watch the light catch on the small jewel imbedded into the cover. She sent it scattering over the walls in a rainbow of color that weaved up and down with each step, finally landing on Vaniel's face.

"Ow!" she called and staggered back in mock pain.

"You are in a good mood," Westrel said, shielding her eyes from the light.

Sinna laughed as she helped a grinning Vaniel to her feet. "Yes, I am. Because *I* rusted a spoon last night. All the way through." She sighed contentedly. "And I was able to watch it happen. Do you know how d-destructive it is? I mean, you see things rusting all the time, but it's like a disease." She shuddered, but even remembering the solid metal crumbling away to fine powder couldn't dampen her smile.

"That is wonderful!" Westrel said. "Do you think you will be able to repeat it?"

They came to an intersection, and Sinna paused to think before taking the right-hand passage, which, unfortunately, angled away from the windows. She hoped she was going the right way. She had only been in the Attendant's Tower a handful of times, and never this low.

"I think so," she returned to the conversation without missing a beat. "The trick was the right level of a-air, and then having the right catalyst. Now that I know all that I should be able to do it whenever I want. Which means I can start really looking at ways to prevent it." She almost skipped down the hall. "I've gotten so much done since—" Her step faltered. "You know. The trial."

Westrel nodded.

They walked in silence, slipping past attendants going about their assigned duties or coming back to their rooms after a day's work. Sinna tried to think what it would be like to be one of them, serving the queen without magic, but it was hard. Not because she was a stranger to work—growing up on a farm saw to that—but it was getting harder to remember what it was like to not have magic. It seemed she'd always had it, that her life had always revolved around it. It was a part of her. She thought of Christa and sweat dripped down her spine. For the hundredth time she wondered what Christa must be feeling.

"What about your project?" Vaniel asked.

Westrel sniffed. "I have had to abandon my first idea. It turns out manipulating body shape is difficult enough without trying to form it around something else. I could never maintain it for more than a few seconds."

Sinna stopped to let some Attendants carrying a tub of water pass. "I see." She didn't really—Corporalist magic was entirely beyond her—but it seemed the right thing to say.

•*Whispers at the Altar*•

"It is unfortunate. Can you imagine the benefit of being able to hide a message inside yourself? Or a weapon?"

She shook her head. "So did Director A-Aerel approve another project?"

"She did. I am going to try my hand at Empathic Healing."

Vaniel scrunched her nose. "I have heard of that. Transferring an injury to yourself then healing it. Isn't that impossible, too?"

Westrel shrugged. "That is exactly what Director Aerel said. But I have an idea that hasn't been tried yet. And at least it interests me more than the last project."

Sinna pulled up short, counting the doors since their last turn. "I think this is it." She knocked, then pulled the latch. "Christa? It's us." There was a vague sound of assent, and Sinna opened the door further.

The room was small—even to Sinna who was used to the close confines of the Eyas quarters—and rectangular, with a bed on one side and a small writing desk on the other. A window at the far end was open and let in the same cheerful sunlight Sinna had been playing with earlier along with a breeze of fresh spring air. The breeze rustled the pages of dozens of books. They sat everywhere. Laid open on the desk, stacked on the floor, leaning against the lamp globe's stand in the corner, and scattered across the bed. Save for one corner of the mattress where Christa sat, hunched over a volume thicker than Sinna's arm.

Sinna pushed the door open further as they all piled inside, then clicked it closed behind. "I didn't know they gave A-attendants tests to study for," she said. She meant it to be funny but immediately regretted it.

Christa looked up with a blank expression, but her eyes lit up as she saw the book Sinna carried.

"You brought it!" She practically leapt off the bed, sending two books tumbling off.

"Yes, it is good to see you, too," Westrel said with a wink.

401

"Oh, I'm sorry," Christa tiptoed her way across the floor to give each of them a tight hug. "Of course, it's great to see you, too. Please, sit down." She looked about for a place then began shifting books around to make room on the desk chair and bed. "I've been so busy I haven't had a chance to clean up at all. I've been too busy cleaning up everywhere else. You wouldn't believe the mess a hundred horses can make. And that isn't even counting the dishes in the kitchens and . . ." She dropped back down on the bed, motioning eagerly for them to sit. "Well, I've been trying to keep busy, as you can see."

Sinna sat on the edge of the desk chair. "That's great. I'm glad you're still taking advantage of the library. Speaking of which . . ." She handed the tome she was carrying to Christa. "I hope it's the one you were looking for. It took me quite a while to find."

Christa took the book and immediately began flipping through it. "Yes, yes, this is it." Her fingers drummed on the cover, a sure sign she was concentrating. Sinna knew all Christa's quirks.

The silence grew, punctuated by the rasp of paper as Christa turned pages.

"S-so . . . how are you doing? I mean, besides being busy." Sinna glanced to Westrel and Vaniel for help, but Westrel just sat on the bed with a curious expression, watching Christa read, and Vaniel was looking out the window.

"Fine." A rustle as she flipped through a large section of pages before stopping to scan another.

Sinna finally caught Vaniel's eye, and they shared a look of frustration.

"Kadin said he has been to see you a few times," Vaniel tried. "That is good."

"He sends his best as well," Sinna added. "He couldn't come. He was b-busy."

"Yes!" Christa jumped up again, her finger glued to a spot on the page.

Sinna flinched back in surprise.

"I knew I read it somewhere. See?" She held out the book, looking back and forth at all of them. "Oh." Her expression fell. "I was looking for something I read about while doing a paper for Laisel. See here," she sat back down, holding the book out so they could see. "Vitarian is writing about his theories of the nature of the Essence. It was pretty dry stuff, and I forgot most of it, but then I thought I remembered this part here." She scanned down a paragraph. "Here . . . he says, *It is quite possible that the Essence, for all the abuse it easily takes from our daily manipulations, is far more fragile than we think. True, it binds and builds everything we know. But I believe it is in a way less like the stone and mortar of a building and more like our own flesh and bone. Just as our bodies are surprisingly resilient when young and properly cared for, so is the Essence. But this implies that the reverse is also true, and that the Essence can, in fact, become injured if not cared for properly. Further, and perhaps even more troubling, it implies that the Essence may indeed grow old, and with that age, become more brittle and fragile.*

Christa looked up expectantly, but Sinna could only blink at her. "I'm sorry, Christa. I'm not f-following what you're trying to say. I mean, it's awful to think that the Essence could grow old and brittle but . . ."

"Does this have to do with your . . ." Westrel searched for the right word, "punishment?"

"No, nothing like that. But it was the last piece I needed for something else." Christa sat the book aside and leaned forward conspiratorially. "But I'm going to need your help."

Sinna didn't like this. Christa had that look on her face. Like when she conned her into skipping class to drop water balls on people in the yard. Nothing good ever came when Christa had that gleam in her eye.

"W-what do you mean?" Sinna asked. "What do you want to d-do?"

Christa's fingers picked at her dress. She was nervous.

"I want you to help me say goodbye to my mama."

"What?" Vaniel leaned in closer. "I thought she was dead."

"H-how do you mean, 'say goodbye'?" Sinna couldn't help whispering. "And what does this have to do with what you read?"

Christa took a deep breath and clutched her hands in her lap. "I want to recreate the portal experiment of Hawks Wiliran and Welsebel. They had a theory that you could join two points in space. I think I found a way to make it work. If I'm right, I could connect where I was, to where Mama is, and talk to her."

Sinna shook her head. "D-didn't they die trying this?"

Christa nodded. "Yes. They were torn apart in a backlash of raw Essence. But I know things they didn't."

Westrel's eyes narrowed suspiciously. "Like what?"

Christa took up a piece of paper and quill and began drawing on a book. "On the night of the trial, I went to the Observatory. I was able to make it . . . look somewhere else. Not just at the city."

"But you didn't have magic," Vaniel said. "How could you make it do anything?"

Christa shrugged. "I don't know. I just know that I did. Wiliran and Welsebel couldn't focus their portal. That was their problem. They tore a hole in the Essence but without any point to connect it to. They only had half of the portal. But if I use the Observatory to connect that place to another place . . ." She gestured to the picture in her lap, but Sinna couldn't make heads or tails of it. Christa definitely should not be an Instructor.

"So you're saying that y-you can make this portal work," Sinna said. "But, Christa, your mother isn't anywhere that portal can see. She's . . . g-gone."

Christa looked back and forth between them with wet eyes. "Maybe. But I have to try. Please. When she left . . . We weren't . . . We were arguing." She sighed. "If there is a sliver of a chance that I could talk to her one last time. Tell her I was sorry. Wouldn't you want that if it was your mama? And . . . and think of what it could mean if I was right. For everyone."

"Christa," Westrel said softly, "you can't go where she went. You can't bring her back."

"No, I know that. I'm not trying to bring her back. Just talk to her. I just want to make things right between us."

Sinna gestured to the book. "By tearing up the Essence? They d-died trying to do this." She stood and crossed to the window. It was crazy.

Vaniel took Sinna's seat. "But how can you make it work? Even if you can use the Observatory without magic, you can't make the portal."

Sinna scoffed. "No, that's what she n-needs one of us for."

Christa wiped a hand across her eyes. "That's right. But I have something else they didn't. I know how to keep the magic from hurting me. Us."

"How?" Westrel asked.

"The Dueling Stone. It prevents any magic from directly harming another person within its area."

"But what if you're wrong?" Sinna asked. "What if you m-make a mistake. A small miscalculation. What if the S-Stone can't handle the power you're dealing with? We could all die, like they did."

Westrel nodded. "And more than that. Have you thought about what it could do to the Essence itself? What if it were permanently damaged?"

"I know." Christa looked up at Sinna pleadingly. "It's dangerous. And I know I'm asking a lot. But you're the only people I have to turn to. No one else will help me." She turned to Westrel. "I promise I've thought of everything. I can do this. *We* can do this." She looked to Vaniel. "She's the only family I have left who still loves me. I just want to make things right with her."

Vaniel swallowed, her gaze locked with Christa's, then nodded slowly. "I will help you, Christa. I trust you."

Sinna sighed heavily. She didn't like this. It would certainly involve breaking rules and sneaking around.

"I will help as well," Westrel said. "But you need to explain every detail of what you mean to do. And you have to promise to call the whole thing off if any of us feel the risk is too great."

Christa nodded eagerly, and all eyes turned to Sinna. She hated to be the one to say no. She knew how important Christa's mother was to her. But . . .

"I c-c-can't, Christa." She walked up to kneel in front of her. "This is d-dangerous. To you, to us, to the Essence. And it . . . it isn't healthy. I thought you had given this up a long time ago. We talked about it. I know how much s-s-she means to you, but this isn't the way."

She could see the disappointment fill Christa's eyes, and it broke her heart. "I'm s-sorry."

"Fine," Christa said flatly. "Just promise you won't tell anyone else."

Sinna sighed. She should. She knew she should. But with all her friends looking at her, she couldn't bring herself to. She looked down at the floor. "I won't say anything."

The sounds of packing were such sweet music to Dalan's ears, he couldn't resist stopping in the doorway to watch.

"Taking your leave of us, Direc—pardon me—*Hawk* Marellel?"

"I am sure Ophidian will be wanting the use of his office as soon as possible," Marellel answered without turning around.

"Yes, I am sure." Dalan wanted to gloat, to tell her what a fool she had been. He wanted to laugh in her face as she levitated the boxes of her belongings out of his life. But that would be beneath him.

"What will you do now? Has Director Ophidian granted you an assignment?" He took a step back to allow Elirel to walk in, three crates floating in front of her.

"Thank you, Elirel," Marellel said, giving her a smile. "Those stacks over there are ready to go if you don't mind."

Elirel laughed, "Not at all."

"I hadn't really given it much thought, Director Dalan. But as the decision is in Director Ophidian's hands, I don't imagine I need to."

"Of course. But surely there is a preference you would like me to relay on your behalf. Instructing, perhaps?"

She froze, eyes glaring up at him. He hadn't been able to resist. Of course she would never teach again, not after the fiasco that was currently scrubbing pots in the kitchen.

"Perhaps," she muttered, before levitating the stack of crates she had filled with books. "If you will excuse me? Elirel, I will be down in my office. If you could take those stacks to my quarters I would be very grateful."

"I will meet you down in your office when I finish," Elirel called out as Marellel squeezed past Dalan.

Elirel spared a glance for Dalan. *After all, we must be gracious in victory, mustn't we?*

Dalan scowled. *Just play your part. And stay out of my head.*

Elirel smiled back that too-wide smile.

He would have to replace Ellirel next. But not now. Now was the time to celebrate, to consolidate, and to firm his footing.

There was still Queen Elisidel to worry about.

Christa stood at the foot of the Ssanek pole, its length already stained nearly black with the blood she had poured over it again and again. Each time before had been to report failure, to plead for more information, to beg for a clue. But not this time.

She looked up at the stars spilling across the cloudless sky and smiled.

"Great Ssanek, giver of gifts, merciful and loving, hear my prayer. I have fulfilled your request. I have the knowledge you seek."

She looked at the graven image on the peak of the staff and fell to her knees, arms raised toward it. "Hear me, Ssanek. Speak to your servant."

"I hear you, most beloved servant." The carved snake twisted, its head peering down at her from on high. "Speak. I am listening."

Christa fought back the giddy joy she always experienced when speaking to Ssanek. An excitement like when she was a little girl the night before her birthday. "I know how to complete the experiment. But I can only open the portal to a place I can visualize. Someplace I have seen."

The snake bobbed its head. "You will open the portal to me. I will have your mother. Open the portal, and I will send her through."

"But . . ." Christa muttered, her heart hammering in her chest. She did not want to ask what she knew she must. Yet at the same time she yearned for it.

"But I have not seen you, Ssanek. I cannot power the—"

Her mind split open with a painful crack, like a jolt of lighting tearing her thoughts in two. She saw an altar, a writhing, shifting shrine of living snakes stained black with blood.

And she saw Him.

His enormous serpentine form wrapped around the altar in glittering black coils. His leathery wings lay tucked against his sides and dozens of lobster-clawed creatures scuttled here and there across him, ministering to him. The scaled head turned and its eyes, like pits filled with the dying embers of worlds, consumed her.

It seemed an eternity before a jolt of soft earth striking her head broke through.

•Whispers at the Altar•

She blinked, back in the palace grounds once more. Tears streaked her face as she pushed herself up.

He was . . . power. She could never have understood. Never fathomed. The urge to do whatever he would ask surged within her. To be so cared for by something so powerful, that he would give her anything she asked for . . . .

She looked back up to the idol atop the pole, but it was only a poorly carved block of wood again. The connection was broken. But a part of her could barely contain the need to see him again.

And she would. Soon.

Council

The laughter echoed behind her, never growing nearer, but still Honovi ran. The wretched black dress was a constant reminder. One moment sliding across her skin with jolts of shivering pleasure, the next scraping her flesh like gravel.

She tried tearing it off, heedless of who might see, desperate to be rid of it, but it was always there. Like the taunting laughter that followed her through the pitch black caves. She couldn't remember how long she had been running. She couldn't even remember starting.

"You can't outrun me, little slave," the voice rumbled. "I will always be there. I have *seen* you. Seen your desires, your fears, your very soul. And you will always be mine."

She tried to run harder, but the dress was suddenly longer, tangling her feet. She fell, and he laughed. It was louder, right behind her. She struggled to get up, but the dress wrapped around her, bliss and torture folding over her.

Then *his* face. Its lines burning in the dark, etching into her mind.

"You will always be mine."

Honovi jerked awake with a cry, tears stinging her eyes. Her heart beat so hard she thought it might burst as she heaved air into her lungs. She threw off the covers then squeezed her eyes tight in relief.

There was no dress. It was burned. The first thing she did after arriving back at the Cliff-Home.

She jumped out of bed and ran to the fire pit. Yes, it was there, half in ashes though the fire had burned out around it. Frantically, she gathered more kindling and logs.

She pulled her nightshirt closer as the new fire caught, its smoke tracing up and out the small hole in the ceiling of the cave. She watched the dress burn. Ssanek's words seemed to echo in the pop and crackle of the fire. Had he seen her so completely?

What *did* she desire?

A home? Safety?

Steven?

She shivered despite the fire's heat, remembering waking up naked in that cursed bed, unable to remember anything she'd done. The feeling of joy, of peace, as she walked out. Ready to do whatever the demon asked.

No.

She stood up and tossed one last log into the pit. She was Yahad. She would not be claimed like some timid cow by him or anyone else. Throwing open the chest, she tossed clothes onto the bed. The Council was today. Likely it had already started while she overslept and wasted time here whimpering over a stupid dress.

Father had forbidden her from going to the Council as part of his punishment. He was "keeping her safe." She scoffed. How young did he think she was? And besides, how safe was anyone now? Even here. She had seen the Lord of Lies' army. No one was safe anymore.

"They came in the night. They stole our horses, our cattle, burned our crops. How will we live? We have nothing." The man stood in the center of the Hall of Council, pleading with the elders before him.

It had been going on like this for two hours. Every story the same. Steven sympathized with them, but even with his limited command of the tribesmen's language, he had quickly realized the extent of the Ssanek incursion. How many times did the tribe elders need to listen to the same account from a different person?

Brogan had said in one of the rare moments he wasn't glowering at Steven, that tribal law gave every family the right to air their grievances before the Council. But the futility of it all was wearing on Steven. These people weren't calling for action. They were asking for handouts. And while he was certainly in favor of aiding those hurt by the Ssaneks, every hour wasted made their enemy that much stronger.

The man finally sat down, his grievance acknowledged by the Council, only to be replaced by another. Steven groaned, earning a stern look from Brogan, and tried to get more comfortable on the stone seat.

The Hall of Council wasn't really a hall at all, but a large, natural, amphitheater. The canyon widened here where some feature, long since eroded to dust, had caused the waters of the Shona to gather before draining out. Whether by some wild chance or, more likely, hard work, the walls of the canyon had been carved into rows of tiered seats leading down to the floor of the canyon. There the waters of the Shona still flowed, cutting the theatre directly through the middle.

On the west side of the river sat as many Yahad as could squeeze into the seats. To the East, the Chota barely filled the benches. Steven

•Allan C.R. Cornelius•

had heard that only those settlements nearest had come to the meeting. The others, neighbors to distant Anathonia, would wait and see. An attitude which sounded suspiciously like "wait it out" to Steven.

Yet another Yahad stood up to speak and Steven perked up. It was Hareb. Surely he would bring the meeting around to the real topic of discussion. Steven watched as the enormous man stood to the center of the hall and waited for the elder's full attention.

"I am Hareb, of the Atsin, of the Yahad. I speak for my village. Six seasons ago we were attacked by the servants of the Lord of Lies. They came in the—"

Steven groaned and stopped listening. This was ridiculous. He briefly wondered where Honovi was. Obviously Hareb hadn't adopted Brogan's punishment of constant observation. Steven hadn't been allowed out of Brogan's sight since they returned a week ago. Which only meant even more nights cooped up inside the caves. He'd thought of asking Brogan to come with him so he could watch the Sun-pass, but the thought of doing it without Honovi was too painful.

He pushed her out of his mind before it could latch onto her, and forced himself to focus on Hareb's voice. Anything was better than reliving the ache and solitude of the trek back.

" . . . nothing left. From the Moseya plains to the swamps, our lands have been pillaged and our people slain. The time for action is now. The elders must call for an assembly of all the families. We must ride against the Ssaneks before any more have cause to bring grievance to the council."

Steven blinked, leaning forward on the edge of his bench as the Yahad side of the theatre erupted in cheers, hoots, growls, and chants. Now we were getting somewhere. Never mind that the side where the Chota sat was silent save for a scattering of low murmurs.

The youngest elder, his hair only half turned to white, stood. He raised his arms and the crowd slowly fell quiet. But it was the oldest, a man gnarled and bent like a tree in the wilderness with skin so wrinkled Steven wasn't sure what his face even looked like, who spoke. Even as old as he was, his voice echoed clearly through the amphitheater.

"It is not your place to tell the Council what it must and mustn't do, Hareb, of the Atsin, of the Yahad. Your eyes see but a piece of the whole. Ever has the purpose of this council been to gather the entirety of the image. Only then may wisdom guide our choice."

Steven jumped up, unable to believe what the old man said. "You have been told everything," he shouted down. "We've all listened to it all morning."

Grumbles were echoing him all down the half circle of Yahad. Steven looked around and saw more than a few nods.

And Honovi. She stood at the base near the river, probably just arrived. Then sun glinted off her dark hair as she looked up at him.

Steven swallowed and faced the elder.

"You have not been given permission to speak," the old man said.

"Indeed," Hareb agreed, his brow low as he glared up at Steven. "This is a matter for Yahad. And however you may have been near to becoming one, you never will be now."

Steven blinked and glanced at Honovi who was staring at her father's back with probably the same expression Steven now wore.

"You are Chisaran," Hareb continued. "Chisarans began this. They are no longer to be trusted."

Brogan tried to drag him back down to his seat, but Steven pulled away.

"You're wrong. You may have been attacked by Chisarans deceived by Ssanek's lies, but they aren't the only ones fallen to him. I know. I walked in their camp as their prisoner. So did she," he pointed briefly to Honovi, unwilling to meet her eyes. "Many have been lured by his promises. Yes, Chisarans. But Yahad also. And Makau. Some follow out of fear, others out of lust for blood. Some follow so completely they have given their own bodies to him, chosen by him as vessels for terrible gifts. And there is more." He stood up on the bench as more and more turned to face him.

"The Soldiers of Ssanek from your own stories are walking in your lands. This is not an army of one people, and it is not the only army. Do you think the Lord of Lies strikes only against you? Do you think he leaves the people of the North in peace?"

He pointed down to Brogan. "This man knows the true extent of Ssanek's reach. The demon comes against all of us. And he is doing it now. While we wait and 'gather the entire image,' he grows."

Steven looked at Hareb. "We must fight him now. Before more are drawn to his lies. Before more of our people betray us."

Hareb gave the barest hint of a smile, but the elder was not impressed.

"And how, *child*, in your great wisdom, do you propose we go about this crusade?"

Steven paused, the sound of his own pulse crashing in his ears. Every head was now turned toward him, and any ideas he might have had were chased out of his mind by those expectant stares.

"Well . . ." he cleared his throat, trying to buy some time as the elder watched with a look disturbingly similar to the one Brogan wore when Steven was about to make a fool of himself.

"Well. I would think the solution is obvious." He waited a beat, but the elder didn't take the bait. Of course not. "You take every warrior you can muster and attack their army before it grows any bigger."

Brogan groaned below him, and the elder opened his mouth, probably to say how simple and ridiculous Steven was.

"No," Steven interrupted. He remembered something Honovi said and the spark of an idea started to form. "Not all of them. Some of them need to come with me. To the swamp."

The elder blinked, in surprise. "With you? The swamp? Why?"

Steven shifted his feet, but it would do no good to back down now, and the more he thought about it, the more sure he became that this was the only way.

"Yes. Your tales say that the last time Ssanek came, he was only defeated when the one who summoned him was dead. I know the

Seer who summoned him." He glanced at Honovi, but she was the only Yahad in the theatre *not* looking at him. "I was there."

There was a rush of noise as everyone began talking at once, and more than a few Yahad drew weapons. Brogan took a step closer, his eyes narrowed threateningly, and Steven was glad for the support, but no one made a move toward him.

It took several minutes for the young elder to quiet the crowd.

"Can you explain how you came to be involved in such a dark ritual?" a wizened but spry Chota elder asked.

"My mother brought me there. To be sacrificed. I didn't know it then, but I think Ssanek offered her something. Something she truly wanted. In addition to the chance to be rid of me."

There was no response, only expectant gazes.

"I . . . we struggled. She died. Her blood is what completed the ritual." More murmurs. "But that isn't the point," Steven shouted over them. "The point is that I saw the Seer who performed the ritual. I will never forget him. And if he is the key to defeating Ssanek, then the demon will keep him close. Possibly near the altar where the summoning took place. Let me take a group of warriors. I know the way. While you distract Ssanek with an attack on his army, we will pass through the swamp and kill this Seer. Then we can send this demon back where he belongs."

The crowd erupted into another fountain of noise, and this time Steven complied when Brogan tugged him back down to his seat. He couldn't think of anything else to say anyway. It was all pretty straight forward as far as he was concerned. He watched as Yahad yelled at each other all across the theater. Those who agreed with Hareb were obviously eager to seize on any plan that made a modicum of sense. Steven doubted they believed the expedition into the swamp would succeed, but it was an excuse to march.

At least he had gotten them to really talk.

•Allan C.R. Cornelius•

All except the Chota, who sat impassively on the other side, watching and listening.

It took nearly a quarter hour for the elders to bring the crowd under control once again and as quiet fell, Hareb stood up once more.

"You are wise, elders, and the families trust your judgment. But it seems there are many who believe it is time to strike back against those who would steal not just our homes or our livestock, but our very people."

There was a murmur of protest, but he cut it off with the raising of one large hand. "I believe the Chisaran in this, that the lies of Ssanek have always placed brother against brother. Is that not what the old stories say?" He turned to the elders for confirmation and the ancient one nodded slowly.

"If this is so, then by not acting we may one day find more Yahad outside this council than within." He turned to the Chota. "And the Chota will find all lands west of the river closed to them. And then their own battle against temptation will begin." He paused, eyes searching the tiered seats. "Or perhaps it has already. Who can say?"

He spun to stare right at Steven. "Chisaran. Your plan has promise, though you speak without knowing the difficulties within it. Who will go with you? Who will you find to risk everything on . . . a chance? What if the Seer you seek is not there? What if the Lord of Lies sees this gambit and lays a trap?"

"Then I will face it with him," Brogan yelled as he stood. "I have lost everything else already. He is all I have left."

Hareb smiled.

"I will go with him," came a cry from the foot of the stands.

Everyone turned to see Honovi standing forward, back straight, and Steven watched Hareb's smile disappear.

"No," Hareb said, "you are my daughter and I forbid it."

"You cannot!" Honovi took another step forward. "I am past the years of instruction. I make my own choices."

Whispers at the Altar

"What is this man to you, that you would leave your father and follow him to death? Your place is here."

"He is nothing to me. My reasons are my own, and I need not reveal them to anyone." She turned to face Steven, and he could feel the cold fire in her eyes even as they glared at him from the floor. "I will go."

Hareb fumed. "Then I must go, for all I love goes with you, Chisaran."

"Go then," called the ancient Yahad from the stage. "There are times when wisdom can be found in the will of the people. Go. The families will march behind you."

OBSESSION

Vaniel tried to stand as nonchalantly as possible against the wall as other Eyas passed back and forth through the hall. She also tried to calm the frantic beating of her heart, but she was having roughly equal success with both. It wasn't as if she was a stranger to breaking the rules. But she had always had the reassurance of her family name before. Now there was nothing. It was a terrifying feeling. And exhilarating.

"Calm down," Westrel said, standing next to her. "We aren't doing anything wrong, really. We are just borrowing it for a bit. It isn't even going to leave the palace."

"Then why aren't we asking permission?" Vaniel looked down the hall at the doors to the dueling room. A class was filing out, but that didn't mean much. They were fourth-tier, so any number could have remained behind to continue practicing.

"First, because it would be a huge hassle. Second, because they would probably say no." Westrel grinned wickedly. "And third, because this is more fun."

Vaniel couldn't help smiling back. "Maybe. But my stomach is tied up in knots."

"Just follow my lead. I know what I am doing."

Vaniel nodded and watched the last of the students trickle out, followed finally by the instructor.

"It is time." Westrel pushed off from the wall and walked, calmly and purposefully to the doors.

Vaniel hurried to follow, trying very hard to keep herself from glancing around to see if anyone was watching. *Just walk like you would any other day. You're just here to watch your friend practice. Nothing unusual about that.* She flinched as Westrel reached the doors and, with a casual motion, flicked one open and strode inside. But there was no one else in the room.

Vaniel breathed a sigh of relief and started to close the door behind Westrel, but she shook her head.

"I can't believe you left it in here," Westrel called back as she paced to the pedestal. "I swear, if your head wasn't attached . . ." She paused and waved for Vaniel to continue the conversation.

"Oh. I know. I have been so absentminded lately," she said as she took up her position outside the doors. As only a third-tier, she couldn't enter. Her job was simply to keep a look out while Westrel did her thing.

There was silence except for the shuffling of feet inside the dueling chamber and the passing of unconcerned people in the hallway.

Then silence.

Would something happen if she picked it up? Vaniel had never heard of anyone even touching it before. You didn't have to. Could it even *be* picked up? Was it fastened somehow? Was there some kind of alarm?

Whispers at the Altar

"Here it is," Westrel exclaimed, the signal that she had the stone and was coming out.

"Thank goodness you found it," Vaniel said over her shoulder. Her heart was pounding like she'd sprinted a mile, and she had the sweat to go with it. "I don't know what I would have done. You are a life saver."

"I know," Westrel answered. "Now let's go get some dinner."

Vaniel could only nod. Dinner sounded great right now. Anything else sounded great right now. She turned to see Westrel walk up to the door, then stop.

No, she didn't stop. She rebounded. As if she had just hit a wall.

She tried again, walking slower this time, and her body pressed against the threshold as if it were sealed by an invisible door.

"What is it?" Vaniel whispered.

Westrel frowned and stepped out of the doorway. "I don't think they want it to leave the room."

Vaniel rolled her eyes, "Of course they don't." She thought for a second. "Can *you* get out?"

Westrel's hand emerged through the doorway. "Seems I can. Just not if I am holding the stone."

"Vaniel, are you feeling all right?"

Vaniel spun to see Marellel not two paces away and walking toward her.

"Um, yes. I am fine. Why?"

Marellel stopped, squinting at her. "You don't look well. Do you have a fever?" She reached out a hand to feel Vaniel's forehead as Vaniel took a step back.

"No, really, I am fine. I just. I just had a hard practice." She took a step to her right, away from the dueling room in case Marellel got the wrong idea.

But Marellel didn't seem to notice. "I see. Be sure to drink plenty of water at dinner." She started to move on then paused and turned back. "I should have said something before, but I am very proud of you. For the decisions you have made."

423

Vaniel tried to swallow and coughed instead. Did she know about the spying?

"Oh, and can you tell Christabel I would like to see her when she has a moment. Nothing urgent. Just . . ."

Vaniel had never seen the director—former director—look so . . . unsure.

"I wanted to talk."

"Of course." Vaniel nodded, anything to get her to leave.

"Thank you." Then she turned and walked away.

Vaniel waited until Marellel was around the corner before turning back to the dueling room. That was too close.

"I think I have an idea," Westrel whispered. "If I can leave, and it is only the stone that can't, then maybe . . ."

"What?"

"Maybe I can meld the stone into my body, and the room won't be able to tell the two apart."

"You mean like your project? I thought you said it was impossible."

"It was. At least for any length of time. But I would only need to maintain it long enough to step through the door. Less than a second. I should be able to do that."

Vaniel bit her cheek. "Is there any danger to you? I mean, you have done this before, right?"

Westrel nodded. "Sure. Plenty of times. Just . . . not with stone. Or anything magical in nature. I suppose there is the possibility that it wouldn't come back out with the magical properties intact."

"What?" Vaniel barely kept herself from shouting. "We can't break it. It is a relic, as old as the Palace."

"I am sure it will be fine. I just need to keep track of it *very* carefully." There was a pause. "You may need to help me through the door. I don't think I am going to be able to concentrate on anything else."

Vaniel shuffled from foot to foot. "All right. It sounds like our best chance. And you will give up if it starts to go bad."

"Of course," Westrel gave that wicked smile again.

Vaniel couldn't help smiling.

She watched as Westrel focused on the stone in her hand, while the other raised the bottom of her blouse, exposing toned lines of rigid muscle. Slowly, she pressed the stone against the skin of her stomach. Vaniel had never seen Westrel's magic so closely before. It was both sickening and fascinating at the same time, and she couldn't look away.

The more Westrel pressed the stone against her, the more her body reacted, stretching skin over it, opening, pulling the stone in. It was like watching someone stabbed in slow motion. The farther it went in, the more Westrel bent over, her face contorting with pain and concentration.

"Westrel? Westrel, are you all right?" Vaniel tried to reach in to pull her out but the doorway wouldn't let her through. "You have to come forward. I can't get to you."

With a final shove and a groan, the last of the stone sunk in, the skin melded back over it, and Westrel doubled over. "Now," she rasped as she staggered forward.

Vaniel grabbed her hand as it passed the threshold and hauled her friend as fast as she could through the door.

There wasn't even a hint of resistance.

Christa looked up as she heard someone coming up the steps.

"I hope you appreciate what we had to do to get this." Vaniel climbed the last steps into the Observatory and leaned back against the wall, Dueling Stone in hand.

Westrel followed, slumping down to sit only a pace further along.

Christa jumped up at the sight of them. "I do. Truly I do." She ran over to give Vaniel a quick hug, then motioned to the center of the floor. "Put it right there."

Everything was coming together. Christa could barely think for the butterflies churning in her stomach. She couldn't believe this day had finally come. She would succeed where full Hawks had failed, do as Ssanek had asked, and tonight, she would be with Mama again.

Her hands trembled with nervous excitement. She'd been up all night thinking of the things she would say when she saw her mother.

She took one more look at the books she'd been setting out when they walked in, then waved Vaniel over. "Now you'll stand right here. I've laid them out in case you need to reference anything, but it should be fairly simple. The Essence will become thicker at the center of the room, near where I am. When I tell you, all you need to do is tear it at that point. That will open the portal. Meanwhile . . ." she paced back to the center of the room, "the Dueling Stone protects us from any of the magic backlash."

"And what do *we* do?"

Christa turned to see Westrel standing again along with . . . Kadin?

"Wait . . ." She walked over, shaking her head. "You don't need to be here, Kadin. Neither of you do."

Westrel told me what you're trying to do. It's important to you. I want to help.

They didn't need to be here. *He* didn't need to be here. She didn't want to put any more of her friends at risk than she had to. Besides, something about him seeing what she was doing was . . . embarrassing?

"Fine. But there isn't anything for you to do up here." Christa smiled. "But come to think of it . . . I could really use both of you downstairs. This is a lot of magic up here. Someone might see. I don't need anyone interrupting."

"You want us to be guards?" Westrel asked, quirking one eyebrow.

The blood rushed to Christa's head. "Please?" She tried her best to communicate just how much she didn't want Kadin to see this in

•Whispers at the Altar•

that one word. And perhaps it worked. Either way, Westrel shrugged and clapped Kadin on the back.

"Looks like we are on guard duty."

Christa sighed and gave Westrel a grateful squeeze on the shoulder before turning back to Vaniel. It was time.

"I don't really like this, Christa," Vaniel said from where she sat next to the open books. "Tearing apart the Essence . . . It feels wrong."

Christa forced her best smile. "I know. But is it any more wrong than manipulating it on an elemental level or using it to create whatever we can imagine?" Christa sat down and took her friend's hands. "I need you to try. Please. I promise, if it starts to go wrong I'll stop." Of course it would have to be going pretty wrong . . . and it was moot anyway because it *would* work.

"And exactly how do we do that?"

"Oh, that's the easy part." Christa straightened her back, squeezing Vaniel's hands in hers one last time. "The Essence is like our own bodies. Even when you cut it, it wants to grow back together. You'll just knit the Essence back, like stitching a wound."

Vaniel gave a hollow laugh. "Yeah, easy. Except I have never done anything like this before."

Christa grinned. "I know you can do it. Thank you for all of this, Vaniel. I can't tell you how much it means to me."

Vaniel gave a wan smile.

"Ready?" Christa asked. Vaniel nodded, and Christa closed her eyes.

She took a shaky breath and concentrated. She filled her mind with the image Ssanek gave her. The god floated there in her mind, wings flapping slowly.

She focused on his sinuous body, on the way it writhed and twisted, thicker than any tree but supple as a willow branch.

She pictured his face, the rows of stark white teeth, the brilliant red of his knowing eyes, the altar of writhing snakes, and the crab-like servants scuttling over his body.

She brought it all into focus. She bore down on it until she could swear it would imprint itself forever onto the backs of her eyelids. The great god there forever for her to see.

The familiar twisting began in the back of her brain. The room was trying to find him. She pressed harder, her nails digging into her palms, her eyes squeezed so tight it hurt. *For you, Mama. For you.*

She collapsed to her hands and knees as the pinpoint of pain wrenched itself in the back of her brain. The pain shattered her carefully formed image, but it didn't matter. She didn't need it anymore.

"Now, Vaniel!"

"Right ... I ..." Vaniel's disembodied voice drifted across Christa's concentration like a spring breeze. "I am trying to get a hold ..."

Christa blinked back against the splotches of light hovering across her vision and the headache she could feel coming on.

"There. I think I have a grip."

Christa looked down between her hands and bit back a scream.

Snakes writhed under her, their scales soaked in blood, their frilled spines razor sharp. The altar. And fetid swamp all around her. She jumped to her feet.

He was there, towering above her. A monument of strength in living, breathing form. His wings blotted out the stars as they flapped, and his eyes ... She couldn't look away from his eyes. She shivered, her blood turned to ice in her veins. She could hear Silvana faintly, warning her. Telling her what going down this path would do. But Silvana was wrong. She needed power. The power to bring her mother back. Power the elves' Creator denied her.

And this, this was power.

"Open the portal, Vaniel."

"Christa, are you sure?" The voice sounded as if it was right next to her ear.

Christa reached out, searching for Vaniel's hand. She found it and clung to it. She poured all her uncertainty and doubt into the grip until there was nothing left but determination.

"Do it."

Silence.

And then a scream. A shriek of excruciating pain.

Christa hunched forward, releasing Vaniel's hand and covering her ears. The scream was more than pain. It was despair. It was anger. It was anguish.

Christa wrenched her eyes open, fighting against the wailing screech. The altar was gone, as was the swamp. Vaniel stood next to her. Westrel and Kadin stared from the far wall, weapons drawn, facing . . .

A crack hung in the air just out of arm's reach. It was an open wound in space roughly the height and width of a full-grown man. Its jagged edges were red and raw as an infection and crimson blood wept from them to fall and sizzle like acid on the crystal floor. The scream of pain kept time with the tears, reverberating from the crack in a wail of despair.

Christa's heart beat against that despair. She had done it. She had opened the portal!

But where was her mother? Shouldn't Ssanek be sending her through? All she saw between the lips of the gash was a void. Not the usual darkness of night, or of a room without a lamp. An emptiness so complete it hurt to look into.

"Close it!"

Christa turned to see Sinna standing beside Westrel and Kadin at the top of the stairs. "No! Wait. She'll come."

Westrel ran to her, her feet slipping on the rift-blood that sluiced across the floor. "It isn't working, Christa." She had to yell to be heard. "You promised." She turned to Vaniel. "Close it."

"I can't." Vaniel yelled back. "I can't knit it back together!"

"I don't care," Christa pushed Westrel away and stood in front of the gash. She looked again at the blackness and caught the barest hint of movement. It wasn't a void at all.

A rumble echoed out of the abyss.

Everyone stopped. Even the wailing seemed to fade.

Whispers at the Altar

Christa took a step forward. She knew the sound, had heard it waking and sleeping for years now.

It rolled out of the crack again, like a peal of thunder, or a rolling boulder. Or a long, deep chuckle.

A reptilian head, its scales devoid of light or reflection, appeared in the hole. "You have done well, little servant." The voice rumbled like low thunder. "You will be rewarded."

"Where is my mama?" Christa demanded.

The mouth parted and a long, forked, red tongue slipped out to lick across the edges of the portal, drinking the rift-blood. "All in good time, little morsel."

"We made a deal! I kept my end. Now keep yours." She could feel her friends shifting uncomfortably behind her, could hear their murmurs of confusion. This wasn't how it was supposed to happen. They weren't supposed to find out.

"My brilliant, angry child . . ." the rumbling voice cracked. "All you did was arrange the meeting. A deal requires each side to *give* something. And you have given nothing. Yet."

Long talons at the apex of each bat-like wing gripped the gateway on either side. There was a deafening scream, and the crack widened with a sound like cracking bones and tearing sheets until it stretched from floor to ceiling fifty span above. Rift-blood flowed from the wound in streams driving Christa and her friends back as it hissed and spat against the floor.

Ssanek's head, ridged and scaled, with stark white horns jutting back, thrust through the opening on a long sinuous neck, its mouth wide as it drank from the fountain of rift-blood. It laughed again, reveling in the waterfall washing down over it, then its eyes, the pupils like pits encased in streams of lava, peered down at them.

"Mmm, I smell your magic. Delicious, delectable, delightful magic. Especially . . ." the horrible orbs focused on Christa, "you. The little servant all too willing to follow her master's bidding. You have been loyal, and love like yours should not go unrecognized. Your reward will come first, though I doubt you will cherish it."

There was a ringing of steel, and Kadin stepped in front of her, curved sword held before him in both hands.

"Ha! A brave defender. But futile. Yes . . . little servant, you will be a feast! A delicacy!" The words sent waves through the air, staggering Christa back. "And then I will splay your remains across my altar, as the last drop of your soul is squeezed from your broken body." The forked tongue slithered across its mouth in anticipation.

"Go back to where you belong, pit-spawn!" Westrel yelled as she moved beside Kadin, daggers flashing in her hands.

"You'll not have any of us." Sinna stood beside Christa, one hand steadying her.

Christa fumbled for words. He had lied to her. He never meant to give her anything. The elves had been right. *Sinna* had been right.

The beast's laughter rumbled through the tower's crystal walls as its serpentine body rose, the clawed wings stretching through the portal. "Children. Children who believe they can stop a god. *Children!*"

The anger in the final word left Christa's ears ringing. They were all going to die. The Fire hammered at its prison walls within her, powerless. She glanced to the exit. She could run. She wasn't any use in a fight now anyway. She saw Vaniel, huddled against the wall, her eyes wide in fear as her hands waved in front of her in a vain effort to close the rift.

Kadin was the first to rush forward. He beat his sword down against the demon's body and the blade slid against scales as empty of color as the void between stars. Westrel ran to flank the opposite side, her daggers flashes of red light against the dark as they reflected the light of the rift boundary.

Christa should run. Maybe she could get help. Christa thought of all the people below them. Would they all die, too? Surely there were enough Hawks to defeat this. She should run and get them.

Whispers at the Altar

Sinna opened her hands to a roaring current of fire that stabbed upward, licking against Ssanek's neck and face but throwing no shadow into the abyss of the rift beyond.

Christa shielded her face as the finger of flame burning its image into her vision. But she knew it was useless.

"No. Sinna, the stone," she yelled. "The stone protects him."

And, as she feared, when the fire died she found no reason to celebrate. The rift was wider, its blood now an inch deep across the floor of the Observatory—Why wasn't it falling down the stairwell?—but none of that blood belonged to Ssanek.

"Where is it?" Sinna's voice cracked with hysteria.

Christa could only shake her head. "I don't know."

Sinna growled and ran off, presumably to find the stone, but Christa knew it was hopeless. She had seen Ssanek's power. What could any of them do against it?

With a growl, Ssanek swept his clawed wings fully through the portal. One sweep caught Kadin across the side and sent him flying like a doll through the air to crunch against the wall. His body fell to the floor in a splash of rift-blood and didn't move.

Westrel leapt back and twisted impossibly far to avoid another claw. Her daggers flashed in a blur as she struck the wing, slicing through its membrane like paper.

Ssanek roared and brought both wings across in a scissor before him. Weasel leaped one, dipped under the other, but slipped as she came up. She righted herself, but not quickly enough as Ssanek's open maw crashed down on her. She thrust out, piercing the roof of the demon's mouth, but it was as if he never felt it. The jaws snapped shut over her arm, and she collapsed to the floor, screaming.

Christa cried out, and Ssanek's enormous head swiveled to regard her. "Now, little morsel. Are you ready for your reward?"

Christa took a step forward. All of this was her fault. She had to find a way to fix it. She could do this. Fire or not. She could beat him.

433

She saw the books at her feet, floating in the rift-blood.

She saw Ssanek's claws scratching against the flawless crystal floor.

And the portal . . . Ssanek must have been in the way when Vaniel tried to close it. He couldn't make one of his own or he wouldn't have needed her.

And she smiled.

"I think I'll let you keep it," she spat. "Sinna! Use the rift-blood. Don't try to hurt him, just push him back as hard as you can. If we can get him back, the Essence should close on its own."

Sinna stared back at her in confusion, then brightened and gave a wicked grin. "You want b-blood?" she called to the beast. Pulling her arms in, Sinna streamed the oozing blood through the air to her. It met in front of her chest, pooling into a ball before blasting out at Ssanek's body. Even as it left she gathered more, pouring it toward her and shooting it at him in a constant, battering stream.

Ssanek slipped on the blood-soaked floor, his claws scrambling for purchase even as he writhed under the pressure. Back a pace, then three more. His mouth opened, trying to swallow the stream, but Sinna kept it moving, sliding to whatever part seemed most ready to give.

Three more.

"The claws! Keep his claws from getting a hold," Christa yelled as she ran forward.

Ssanek lunged, a claw sweeping down for Sinna's head only to be met by Kadin's sword as he threw himself in front of the attack. The claw drove him to one knee as his own blood flowed from his soaked shirt to join the flood below.

But the gamble cost Ssanek, and he slipped back farther, scrabbling at the smooth crystal floor. His bulk slid back through the rift, but his claws caught the edges, and he laughed again.

"I have already won, little servant. Remember . . . all sacrifices require blood. And tonight you have given me all the blood I could drink."

Christa looked at the rift and the blood that flowed from it, then screamed in frustration.

"I am *not* your *servant!*" she yelled, hurling a book at his head even as Sinna split the stream in two, hitting both of his claws.

Christa ran forward. "You *lied!*" She nearly slipped on Westrel's second dagger. "And you will *not* win!" She bent, picked up the dagger, and threw it.

The claws slipped, one after the other as the head faded back into the black, laughing.

As the last claw lost its grip, the rift snapped itself shut with a deafening crack.

Alone

"Sinnasarel Tamaran, you are charged with theft of a national relic, using said relic, namely the Dueling Stone of Amoran, to practice magic in an unauthorized location, and endangering the lives of other Eyas during said practice." Secretary Iyian read the scroll in a droning emotionless voice. "Do you understand these charges and their potential punishments?"

Sinna swallowed once but refused to fidget behind the chair as she stared across the council table at the secretary. She was also trying very hard to ignore the hostile stares of nearly all the directors.

"Y-y-yes. I do."

"And do you have any further testimony to add before judgment is named?"

"I would remind the Eyas," Director Dalan's voice was slick, oily; Sinna couldn't stand it, "that her silence on the events in the Observatory have made our decision very difficult. If she were to elaborate on them, we may find extenuating circumstances to consider."

Or put another way, she could expose her friends and get them in trouble, too. True, Westrel had insisted on taking the blame for the theft of the stone. But Sinna wasn't about to let her. She had enough problems without this. Damn Christa. To the abyss with her lies and obsessions. But Sinna couldn't make herself lay all the blame there. She should have seen it. She should never have promised not to tell anyone what they were doing.

Silence.

"Nothing?" the secretary said. "Very well. As you have elected to remain silent, and the queen, in her own wisdom, has denied our request for a Sifting. We can find no evidence to support your story of a practice session gone awry. However, even if this story is true, you have displayed a gross lack of honesty in not being forthright with us. Not to mention the serious lack of judgment in performing this 'practice session.' Therefore, Sinnasarel, you are formally reprimanded. You are stripped of any assignment you may have been given and confined to the Roost under the direct supervision of Director Ophidian until such time as he deems you credible enough to be trusted with more . . . sensitive duties."

So much for going home. So much for helping her family, her village. She could only trust now that the secretary would send someone else. And somehow she doubted it.

Curse Christabel.

Christa paused at Westrel's door, her hand raised to knock. She hadn't seen her since the Observatory five days ago since the Hawks stormed in moments after the portal closed and carried her away to the hospital. Truth be told, she hadn't seen any of her friends. Of course there had been plenty of chores to keep Christa busy, but she knew the truth. She was avoiding them.

She lowered her hand. Odds were Westrel wouldn't want to talk to her. But they were friends, and Christa couldn't go on avoiding. She had to at least say she was sorry.

She knocked before she could think any more about it.

"Come in."

Christa opened the door and peered into the room. "Westrel?" She stopped short in the doorway. She hadn't expected Sinna to be there as well. They sat on the edge of the bed, Sinna's arm wrapped around Westrel whose eyes were red with tears. Her injured arm was cradled in front of her, thin and anemic. Obviously still in the process of regrowth.

Sinna's stare was almost enough to make Christa flee back out the door. She swallowed and closed the door behind her. There was no going back now.

"Um. Hi. I just . . . I wanted to say I'm sorry. For what happened."

A weak nod from Westrel but Sinna's face was a mask.

"I just—"

"You just a-almost got her k-killed, is all," Sinna spat. "You almost g-g-got us all killed. 'Little s-s-servant,'" she scoffed, "was it worth it? Betraying your friends' trust?"

Christa could feel the blood rushing to her face. "No, of course not."

"What if he *had* k-kept his word? All of us dead at your feet, but at least you could talk to your precious m-m-mother. Would that make it worth it? How f-far were you willing to g-go?"

The Fire in her gut burned higher, matching the heat in her face. "That wasn't the deal. And I didn't make any of you do—"

"Didn't make us?" Sinna half laughed and started to stand but leaned forward instead, unwilling to leave Westrel's side. "You b-begged us. You p-promised us it was safe. You lied to us! You lied to all of us, and she p-p-paid for it!"

"That is enough," Westrel said, standing. Her gaze roved about the room before finally locking on Christa. "Sinna's right. You lied to us. You said all you wanted to do was talk to your mother. You said we were opening a portal to *her*. Whatever that was, it lied to you, and you lied to us."

Christa flinched. Somehow she would rather face Sinna's hot rage than Westrel's cold logic.

"The only reason more harm wasn't done is because the Hawks were so close. Another few minutes and—"

Christa took a step forward, "I swear, I didn't know!"

Sinna stood. "D-didn't know?" She barked a laugh. "Exactly what p-part didn't you know, Christa? The part where you were m-making deals with the devil? The part where you tricked us all into helping you?" She snapped her fingers, "Oh, of course. It's the p-part where you were being played for a fool so that vile, power hungry d-demon could destroy everything we hold dear."

"I didn't know he would—"

"I warned you! In the library. But oh no. You d-didn't believe me. I was just a stupid, b-b-bigoted elf like the rest of them. Obviously you knew better. You didn't think it through or take your t-t-time or even ask anyone else for advice! Everything with you has always been 'now.' You have no p-patience. You never have." She paced up to Christa, one finger raised until it hovered inches from her nose. "First Laisel, then M-Marellel, and now Westrel have paid for your impulsiveness. And guess who got to pick up the pieces this time? Who was r-r-reprimanded? Now you've made *m-me* a liar."

"I didn't ask you to lie for me!"

"No. No of course you d-d-didn't. But I look after *my* friends. You only care about y-you. You don't even care what you've cost me, you arrogant, narcissistic, obsessed, h-h-h-"

"Go ahead." Christa snarled. "Say it. Say it! Can't you spit it out?"

There was a loud *crack* and Christa reeled back, her face afire from where Sinna—no, Westrel—slapped it.

Whispers at the Altar

"Get out of my room, Christabel." Her words were ice.

Christa reeled back, looking between them. "Fine. I know I messed up. But I thought we were friends. And I thought *friends* forgave each other. Nice to finally know how you really feel."

Sinna scoffed through damp eyes. "You don't even know what that w-word means. When was the last t-time you really cared about anyone but yourself?"

"I guess I picked the one person I could really count on, didn't I?" She glared at Sinna one last time then stalked out the door, slamming it behind her.

She wanted to hit something, to burn something, to break something. Anything. She wiped furiously at her eyes, desperate not to give in to the weak heartache threatening to break her in two. They were wrong. Sinna was wrong. She did care about them. Hadn't she spent every possible moment with them? Hadn't she talked to them, listened to them, laughed with them? It was their fault. They betrayed her, just like Ssanek.

Of course, the Fire agreed. *After all you did for them, now, when you need them most, they desert you?*

Now she had no one.

You don't need them. All you need is right here.

Well, that was fine. She'd been alone before. She was used to it.

I would never betray you. I'll always be here for you.

She didn't need anyone.

Christa reached into her skirt pocket and took out the journal she wrote to Mama in. She didn't need this anymore. Mama was gone. More lost to her than even Sinna and Westrel. If only she could burn it right here. For a moment she wished she could talk to Silvana. Surely she would understand. Surely *she* would forgive her.

She barely noticed as she exited into the yard and barely registered her name being called. It wasn't until Marellel was nearly on top of her that her voice broke through Christa's misery.

"Christabel. I've been wanting to talk to you."

Christa nodded, finding it hard to meet Marellel's eyes. Sinna's words kept repeating in her mind. *First Lisilan, then Marellel, and now Westrel have paid for your impulsiveness.* She'd never even tried to apologize to Marellel.

"Would you walk with me a bit? I will make sure Seneschal Faradan knows you were with me."

"Sure," Christa agreed. She really didn't have a reason not to.

They walked in silence through the yard, then out through the main palace doors and into a cleansing spring storm. The sky was heavy, leaving the surrounding park in dull shadow made hazy by the falling rain. Yet Christa only felt a few drops, and Marellel didn't seem any more wet. It was probably her doing. Christa sighed. It would have been nice to feel the rain on her face, let it soak through her. But Marellel probably thought she was doing her a favor.

"Lovely weather," Marellel commented with a smile as a peal of thunder rumbled across the hill.

Christa just watched her for several steps.

"I wanted to tell you, Christabel, that I am sorry. I should have talked to you sooner. I imagine you must think I am terribly mad at you. And I was. But I couldn't stay that way."

Christa shook her head. "I'm the one who should be apologizing. I let you down. I told you I would try my best."

Marellel chuckled. "I put too much pressure on you. Rested too many of my own problems on you. You weren't ready. I just saw so much of Chrysolbel in you. That same determination. And I couldn't bear to let her down. I couldn't bear to let him win."

"Who?"

"Director Dalan, of course." She stopped to regard Christa. "You must know by now that he used you to get to me." She shook her head. "He always was better at games."

Christa nodded. She knew.

Whispers at the Altar

"At any rate, I am sorry you had to get mixed up in all of it." She started walking again, looking out over the hill as she ambled toward a nearby gazebo.

"So what is that?" she asked after a moment, motioning to the journal Christa had forgotten she still held.

Christa was suddenly hot despite the cool rain. "It's just a journal." She tried to sound nonchalant. "Silvana suggested I write in it, like I was talking to Mama. To help me missing her."

Marellel stopped again and turned abruptly. "Who?"

"Silvana." Christa shrugged. "She's another Elementalist trainee at the Roost. About Sinna's age, I think." Just mentioning her former best friend made her stomach queasy. "Don't you know her?"

Marellel shook her head. "What is her name? Her real name?"

Christa thought. "I don't know. I don't think she ever told me. She just said I could call her Silvana. That everyone did."

"What does she look like?"

"I don't know. Dark blond hair. Blue eyes. A bit taller than me. Always dresses in light, springtime kinds of colors." Christa shrugged. "Honestly I didn't notice much unusual about her. Except her eyes. They always seemed as if they could look right through me . . ."

Christa faded off as she noticed the look on Marellel's face. Like Christa was talking crazy.

"What? What's wrong?"

"And you saw her. Silvana. At the palace?"

"Yes. And outside it. But what's wrong?"

"I need you to meet me in my office, Christabel. I will be there as soon as I can." She turned and started to hustle back, forcing Christa to jog to keep pace.

"Are you going to tell me what it is?"

"No. Not yet. Not until I know for sure. Just meet me there."

Christa gave up, letting Marellel go on ahead, and the rain shield with her. What could possibly have gotten into her? Something about Silvana? It didn't matter. She looked up into the sky, letting

443

the water wash over her face, feeling each tiny impact against her skin. It didn't matter. At least she had someone who didn't hate her. Maybe she wasn't as alone as she thought.

Vaniel watched Christa walk out of the yard with Marellel. She had debated walking up to her. But she couldn't decide what she would do. She didn't even know what she was feeling. All she knew was that Christabel used her. Just like Dalan. Just like Palatan. Just like every person who had ever claimed to be her friend. Vaniel had given up everything for her: family, wealth, *everything*. Only to find that Christabel didn't really care about her at all. Vaniel was just a tool to her. Like she was for everyone else. She wanted to scream at her. She wanted to . . . to do . . . something. Anything. But what could she do? She was nothing now but a friendless, talentless Third Tier Eyas with no family or connections.

She could go to Dalan with the real story, beg his generosity.

She threw the stone she was holding into the pond. No. She would rather take the secret to her grave than give him the satisfaction. She watched her reflection wavering in the ripples of the water. No, she wouldn't go to Dalan. He was as bad as Christabel. But she would find a way to pay them both back. And Palatan, too. She would never be anyone's tool ever again. All she needed was the right power and the right leverage. And they would curse the day they had ever used her. She at least had Christabel to thank for one thing. Now she knew better than to trust anyone.

Illusions

The door to Marellel's new office was smaller and tucked at the end of a row of similar doors in an unremarkable hall of the Essence Tower. It could have been Christa's imagination but the door looked even smaller than the others. She knocked, just in case, and listened to the sound of water dripping from her dress and hair as she waited. She must have stayed out walking in the rain longer than she thought because the door opened and Marellel's bright blue, worried eyes greeted her.

"Christa, thank goodness. Please, come in." She opened the door farther and Christa immediately wondered if it might be better for her to stand outside. The office was barely big enough for the three people already in it, not to mention the desk and two chairs.

"Gracious, Christa," Elirel said from one of the chairs. "You are drenched. You must be freezing."

Christa shrugged as she took the one step in that she needed to reach the other chair. "Not really. I wrung most of the water out in the

Yard." She gave a nod to Director Namarian who was leaning against the wall behind the desk. The room was more like a cell than an office. There wasn't even a window.

Marellel shut the door and edged around to sit behind her desk, nearly knocking over a stack of books as she did so. "Christabel, I know this must seem very strange, but I wanted Director Elirel and your uncle to hear what you were telling me."

"About Silvana?" She noticed Namarian's eyes look up. "What about her?"

"Does she appear in your dreams?" Elirel said. "In your nightmares?"

Christa blinked, taken aback, "Silvana? No. I mean, she's just another trainee."

"No, Christabel," Marellel said. "She is not. That is why I asked. She may . . ."

"What do you mean, 'She's not'?" Christa squinted. "Of course she is. I've *seen* her. Since the first day I arrived. We talk all the time. Or at least we did."

"I am sure you thought you did." Marellel reached out to place a hand on Christa's shoulder.

Christa backed away. "You think I imagined her? For years? That's crazy."

"You didn't have many friends," Elirel said. "You were alone in a new place. Afraid. It is not unreasonable that you would invent a friend to share your troubles with. Someone you could confide in more than anyone else." She cocked her head to one side. "Tell me. Were there secrets you told her you wouldn't tell anyone else? Were there things she did with you or for you that no one else would?"

Christa's expression must have been all the affirmation the director needed.

"And when you talked to her, was anyone else there? Or if they were, did they acknowledge her? Did anyone *else* see her?"

Christa thought. She *had* been lonely. The first time she saw Silvana, in the yard, she had felt achingly lonely. Could she have made up an imaginary friend? But she had imaginary friends as a child. Even then she knew they weren't real. Silvana was as real as Sinna or Westrel.

"The library!" She remembered. "I talked to her once in the library and there was someone else there. They kept shushing me. They *must* have seen her."

Elirel shrugged. "I doubt it. They probably only saw you talking to yourself." She gave a small smile. "I wonder if you ever even touched her. But even if you did, it would be easy enough for your mind to imagine feeling flesh and bone."

Marellel cleared her throat. "It comes down to this, Christa. You said she was an Elementalist trainee. I was the Elementalist director. I know every trainee we have. There aren't that many. I promise you, there is no one going by Silvana training at the Roost."

"Not anymore," Namarian murmured, squinting suspiciously at Christa.

Christa looked to Marellel, "What does he mean?"

"There *was* someone who had that nickname here years ago." Marellel cleared her throat. "Your mother."

Christa blinked. "You think I've been seeing Mama? Silvana doesn't look anything like her?"

"Perhaps not to you," Elirel said, scooting closer. "Perhaps you disguised her, so you wouldn't recognize her. It really is fascinating the lengths some people will go to in order to deceive themselves."

"That's ridiculous. Besides, I never knew Mama had a nickname."

"You may have heard it without remembering. Maybe you—"

"We are getting off track, I think," Marellel said. "The point, Christa, is that you have been seeing, talking to, and interacting with someone who is not here. Someone who, from your own description, appears to be Chrysolbel. There are only two possibilities. Your mind invented someone for you, or . . ." She glanced to Namarian who sighed and turned away.

"Or what?" Christa said. "A ghost?"

Marellel spread her hands. "The real question, either way, is why."

Christa scoffed. "How should I know? Ask her."

"What happened?" Namarian blurted, standing up straight. "All that criminal, Janus, would tell us is that she died in an accident." Marellel made to calm him but he shook his head. "No. I think it is high time we knew. What happened to her, Christabel?"

Christa backed away, as much as the chair would let her. Suddenly the room was like a cage, the walls smothering around her. "I don't know. It was an accident. She fell. I don't know why."

"Then why can't you let her go? Why did you need to bring her back so badly? I remember the desperation in your face that day in the chapel. Something else happened, didn't it?"

Christa stammered, "No. I just . . . I just wanted to say goodbye. That's all."

"No, that isn't what you asked me for. You wanted her back. Permanently. Something happened between you, didn't it?"

"Namarian, please!" Marellel stood, interposing herself between them.

He turned with a growl, leaning back against the wall once more. "She may not even remember."

"Or she is lying to herself as well as us," Elirel said softly, a small smile on her face.

"I'm not . . ." Christa started, but she couldn't finish.

"Christabel," Marellel turned calmly back, "is there anything you are not telling us?"

"I could always find out." Elirel suggested, earning a sharp look from Marellel.

"I brought you here to assess her mental state, not fish around inside her brain."

Christa barely heard them. She was so very cold. She reached for the Fire, but it lay low, uncaring.

She looked past them, to Namarian. Mama's brother. She could see how much he was hurting.

"We had a fight," she whispered.

•*Whispers at the Altar*•

Silence, as all eyes turned to her.

She sniffed and wiped a wet sleeve over her nose.

"I . . . I got mad at some boys . . ."

Christa fell to the ground with a grunt. Her wrists stung where they skidded a few inches through the dirt and needles. She glared back over her shoulder at Gavin and his cronies.

"What are you gonna do, freak? Huh?" He flicked the ring into the air and caught it. His cronies, well used to their role, laughed in perfect time. Gavin leered over her, holding up Mama's ring and giving a dramatic pause to prove his point.

Christa balled her fists in the dirt as air whistled through her clenched teeth in rapid breaths. Her chest tingled. Not like when her foot fell asleep. This was like hot sparks flashing from her father's flint, singeing her lungs.

"That's right. Nothing. Crawl in the dirt where you belong. You and that demon witch you call a mother." He made to pocket the ring, but his hand never made it that far.

Christa screamed, a sound that startled even her. It tore from her gut, where the sparks had caught into something like a hard, bright coal. Bright enough to burn away everything else. A Fire. She didn't think. She just did.

Her foot jerked out and connected with Gavin's knee with a sickening crack. He cried out in pain as the joint bent back and he collapsed to the ground. The other children backed away, then fled as Christa stood, picking up a fallen branch. It was roughly as long as her arm and at least as thick. It took both hands to swing it, but she did. Over, and over. No other thought pierced the hot cloud in her mind but grim satisfaction at each jarring impact.

He would never talk about her mama that way. He would never even think about it. He was the one who should be crawling in the dirt. He was less than dirt. Less than the worms that crawled through it.

Crack.

449

Allan C.R. Cornelius

Snap.

Over and over.

Her throat was dry, hoarse. How long had she been screaming?

Finally, there was nothing left. The coal dimmed. Her vision cleared and, for the first time since she fell, she really saw Gavin. At least, she saw the barely recognizable form lying unconscious at her feet she assumed was Gavin.

She heard shouts coming from the nearest houses. She dropped the club and ran into the woods.

Once the words started, she couldn't stop them. Christa stared at the top of Marellel's desk, her voice barely above a whisper.

She didn't know how long she ran through the forest. But she stopped when she reached the edge of a ravine, unable to go forward and unwilling to go back.

It was their fault, she thought as she stood staring into the chasm. They made her do it. If they hadn't pushed her. If they hadn't called Mama names . . .

She spun around as she heard the brush behind her rustle. Mama walked between two bushes.

"Christabel Anne Sellers. What did you do?" The frown on her face and disappointment in her voice was more painful than anything Gavin had said or done.

"I had to, Mama," Christa pleaded. "You should have heard what he said. About you!"

"Christabel, nothing he could have said could possibly have warranted what you did. It was inexcusable."

The coal glowed.

"He called you a witch! And a demon! He stole your ring!"

"A ring he never would have been able to touch if you hadn't stolen it first!"

Brighter. Hotter.

"No, Mama. You don't understand. He's always—"

•Whispers at the Altar•

"No, Christabel. You don't understand." She walked forward to put her hands on Christa's shoulders. Her voice leveled. "I don't care what he said or what he did, you can't—"

Christa's body felt on fire.

"You never care!" She threw Mama's hands off her shoulders and started walking back into the forest.

"That isn't true, Christabel, and you know it. But this has got to stop. You could have killed him!"

Christa spun, her body drenched in sweat. "I don't care!" She sliced the air with one hand and the ground rumbled. "I hate him!"

She stomped forward another step and cracks of molten rock spread from her foot.

"I hate them all. They won't leave me alone. And they're always there. I hate them!"

The cracks spread, out and down, and the cliff face groaned as if in pain. But still Christa didn't notice. All she saw was her mama. All she knew was the Fire swelling within her once more, burning away everything else until she was ready to explode with it.

"Christa! Stop!"

"No! Listen to me!" she roared, and the cliff face under Mama broke away with a sound as if the very earth had broken. The ground tilted. Christa screamed, scrambling back.

"Christa!" Mama called as she scrambled to climb the rock as it slid away on a sheet of red-hot lava.

She reached out a hand, pleading—Christa could see it in her eyes—begging Christa to save her.

"Mama!" Christa lunged forward.

Their fingers touched.

The cliff face gave way in a tumble of melted rock and crushing boulders.

Christa screamed. A sound she didn't know her lungs could make. She stood there staring down into the ravine as the rocks settled. There was no sign of Mama.

451

Nothing.

She ran home. Barely able to see her way through the tears that wouldn't stop or catch her breath through the sobs that wracked her body.

When she stumbled through her door, every heaving gasp was like someone stabbing her in the side.

Papa jumped up from his worktable and rushed over to cradle her.

"Christa. Christa, what's wrong? What's happened?"

"Mama . . . fell . . . the . . . ravine." Christa managed.

She stopped, sniffling into the dead silence. She couldn't tell them the rest. They wouldn't want to know anyway. But that didn't stop the memories from replaying in her head. Images she fought to forget.

Papa was gone for what seemed an eternity. Leaving Christa to lie on her bed, alone, replaying the argument on the cliff over and over and over. It was Mama's fault. Why couldn't she just listen? Why did she have to say those things?

It was nearly full dark when Papa finally walked through the door. He stopped just inside. She could see his wide shoulders fill the doorway as it swung closed behind him. She hadn't lit the candles, hadn't started the fire. She could feel his eyes looking at her, and she looked back at him. Willing him to talk to her. To tell her he forgave her.

He turned his back and walked to the fireplace.

How could he forgive her?

How could anyone?

She was a monster.

The silence broke with the screech of chairs that made Christa jump as Namarian forced his way out, slamming the door behind him. Leaving her. Just like Papa.

The sudden fright shattered what small barrier she had left. She fell onto Marellel's desk and wept the same bitter tears she had that night. Tears she tried every day to forget. The conversation continued like a fly, buzzing above her.

"We already knew she was dangerous," Elirel commented coldly.

"I am not arguing that. I am asking you what she needs to get better."

"It is hard to say. Hallucinations, uncontrollable outbursts, emotional distress . . . She could be fine for days, years even, but we would never know what would set her off."

"But she doesn't even have magic now."

"She just admitted to beating a boy nearly to death, Marellel. What might she do with a knife?"

There was a long pause. It vaguely occurred to Christa that they were talking about her, but she didn't care. What more could they do to her?

"So . . . can you help her?"

"I could try to go in, it might be a simple thought process problem. Tweak a few of those, and she could be normal again."

Christa's head jerked up. "I *am* normal."

Elirel shrugged. "*More* normal then."

"I am not letting you or anyone else root around in my head," Christa stated, standing up. "I'm fine. You said she could have been a ghost. Then there would be nothing wrong with me."

"No, Christa," Marellel said gently. "It wouldn't. Even if the Silvana you have been seeing is a ghost, you have already tried to kill someone in a loss of temper. That is far from fine."

"So, what? Are you going to lock me up?" Christa yelled as she threw her hands up. First Sinna turned on her, now Marellel.

"No. But if you will not allow Elirel to . . . fix you, then we will have to put in a suggestion that you be monitored."

"Your duties will be adjusted to ensure you cannot be a threat to those around you," Elirel added.

"And you will most likely be made to attend regular meetings with one of the Mentalists." Marellel leaned forward. "Those are your options, Christabel. The choice is up to you."

Christa didn't even have to think about it. "I am *not* letting anyone in my head."

Camping

Christa was relieved when Faradan, the seneschal, told her she would accompany the army on maneuvers as a camp menial. She would be responsible for cooking, laundry, dishes—anything the soldiers couldn't be bothered to do. She gathered it was Marellel's idea. Probably thought that some fresh air and time away from the palace would do her some good. And she was probably right. Christa was even a bit excited. The chance to not just get out of the palace, but out of Ellsabareth entirely, was too good to be true.

She didn't bother to say goodbye to anyone. There weren't many people left who cared if she was gone. Except maybe Kadin. But after the argument with Sinna, and with Vaniel avoiding her like the plague, she couldn't bring herself to face him. What if he thought the same way?

So she threw herself into the maneuver preparations. She took on extra work to keep herself busy and tried to forget about everything else. Then they left. Five days sitting in a wagon with nothing to do but think and stare at the passing fields and hills. Her mind kept going in circles. From Mama, to Silvana, to her friends, to Ssanek, and back again. She didn't know what to think anymore. She was all worn out inside. Tired. And the only relief was when the column stopped for the night. Then she could throw herself back into work hard enough to make her body as tired as her soul.

Things were only a little better now that they encamped. She had envisioned assisting knights with their horses or maybe catching some conversation on what strategies were being employed. Or better yet, observing first-hand how the elves employed their magic in battle. Not that she had any real desire to witness magic being unleashed on anyone, but the chance to learn anything new was something to jump at these days.

Instead she was assigned to a small medical camp far behind the main camp. There she was to cook, clean, and mend for a medico of ten healers and a squadron of guardsmen. She still tried to keep busy enough to avoid the persistent doubt and bitterness, but every day it managed to catch her, pressing its teeth into her until she bled.

The soft thunder of a horse's hooves as it came up the hill broke Christa out of her trance. She had let her arms slide so far into the washtub that water had already crept halfway up her sleeves. Glancing around in embarrassment, she finished washing the plate she held and set it on the pile with the others.

It was probably just another messenger from the main camp. She dried her hands as she walked to the edge of the pavilion. Not just a messenger but an outrider for a dozen new wounded. Christa could see them clearing the trees about a half mile off.

Try as she might, Christa couldn't understand the magic involved in the Divinists' training. Some form of Illusion was involved, but how exactly did it interact with the magic of the Divinist Hawks? All she knew was that patients came in with very real looking injuries, real enough to cause obvious pain, and the Divinists healed them.

•*Whispers at the Altar*•

It made her a little sick to her stomach to think the elves would hurt their own people just for some training.

Christa considered heading to the medical tent to help. Then remembered Namarian yelling at her to stay away after the last attempt to help ended in her third dropped batch of dressings. They were the first words he'd spoken to her since Marellel's office.

She headed for her tent instead. Perhaps she could get some reading in.

A glint from the woods stopped her. She turned back, raising a hand against the sun as she squinted into the darkness of the trees. There it was again. She searched for the sentries, but the three on duty were busy with the outrider. It was probably nothing anyway. Just a trick of the light or something caught in the branches. She'd seen some magpies earlier.

The last soldier in the column of wounded staggered and fell.

Christa took a step forward.

A man in front turned, saw him, and ran back to help. He knelt, then rolled a couple paces, and came to rest with an arrow sticking out of his neck.

Christa ran. The alarm bell was in the center of camp, right next to the pavilion. She shook the cord, and the frantic clanging echoed out over the small hill.

Shouts joined the ringing as guards rushed out of their tent, some still buckling armor, heads swiveling this way and that.

"Over there!" Christa pointed to where the wounded were now running as best they could manage away from the tree line. Other shouts joined the fray of noise, guttural and harsh. No sound an elf would make. Giving up on the bell—the soldiers were all out now anyway—she ran for the wounded. "Come on. We have to help them!"

She didn't bother to look back. Either they would come or they wouldn't. She had no idea what she would do when she got down the hill, just that she couldn't stand by and let defenseless people be slaughtered. Ten steps down, she saw the enemy. They surged from the shadows of the trees in a mob of hoots and shouts of bloodthirsty glee.

Humans.

But not like any she'd ever seen. These were brutes, clothed in furs with wild hair surrounding savage expressions. They lopped forward, leaving behind the broken, bloodied, and torn bodies of the elves first to fall.

Christa stumbled to a stop, and the guards sprinted past her. Swords free and faces set in sneers of hate, they caught the humans as they overtook the bulk of the wounded and the area erupted in screams.

Christa gazed into that maelstrom of death and dying and her heart chilled. What could she do? She was no warrior. Not like Westrel or Kadin. She didn't even have her magic. As hard as the Fire battered at its prison, it couldn't help her now. If she ran in, all she would find is pain and death. And for what? For whom?

But there were so many of the humans. The elves couldn't hold out for long. She couldn't save them all. But she might save one. Wouldn't that be worth it?

But why? The Fire purred. *What have they ever done for you? Leave them. They deserve it.*

Then the echo of Sinna's voice followed on its heels.

When was the last time you really cared about anyone but yourself?

She shoved the Fire down. That wasn't a monster. She may have let it make her into one. But that wasn't her.

And she charged.

She didn't remember yelling, but her throat was hoarse by the time she picked up the spear. She ran at the first human she saw, lunging wildly. The spear's tip sank into his leg, and it buckled. His wild, red eyes glared at her, nothing behind them but madness. An elven blade toppled his head, and the fire winked out.

The ally moved on, and Christa barely had time to register it all before another human was on her, swinging an enormous axe over his immense head. She yanked on the spear, but it was stuck fast in her first target's leg.

The axe swung down, forcing her to jump back. Her feet caught the shaft of the spear, and she fell instead, the axe-head missing her by inches. She struggled to get up but the man was quicker. He leapt into the air. Christa had a brief vision of her body split like a log. She tried to roll to the side.

There was a haze of movement and a sharp grunt as something hit the human from the side. She blinked, and the blur resolved into Kadin shoving the human from his sword. The Anathonian was covered in blood. Christa could only hope most of it was not his. Still, he limped on his right foot, and his left arm was clutched close to his side.

She stood up before he could offer her a hand. She had an overwhelming impulse to hug him, but she fought it back. Instead she yanked the spear with both hands, staggering back when it gave way.

Already the odds were worse. Everywhere humans hacked upon elven bodies. With Kadin's help, they forced their way to the center of the battle where the last five guards stood ground around what was left of the wounded.

Christa ached for her magic. The Fire clamored inside, ready to explode out of every pore. It begged, pleaded, to be released, and that scared her almost as much as the death around her.

There was only a small group of humans that kept them occupied. But it was enough to let the rest busy themselves with those unable to resist. Christa tried not to watch, but the noise was horrifying.

"This is useless," one of the guards yelled as he parried aside a vicious spiked club.

Christa thought his name was Yvannan? Or Yassanan? Something like that. She jabbed her spear between two guards, driving a human back.

"There are enough of us, and they are distracted. We should break for the camp," he continued.

459

Christa balked, "We can't." She gestured to the wounded she was practically stepping on. "They can't walk, let alone run. We'd be leaving them to . . . that." She didn't need to specify what "that" was. They could all hear it.

Yvannan buckled under an axe blow, recovering only when another elf—Yassanan?—thrust his sword through the human's side. "If we stay we are as dead as they are. The human devils won't amuse themselves out there forever."

"Why are we arguing about this?" Yassanan yelled. "Especially with a half-human traitor." He shoved back an attacker, gaining a moment's respite, and looked around. "Come on. We can regroup with the Divinists."

Christa tried to object, tried to call them back, but all five were off with a yell. They ran for the hill's summit, slicing any human close enough. Christa stood, dumbfounded, staring after them. The Divinists. Shouldn't they have come down to help? Unless of course . . . they couldn't.

"A trap."

The humans, recovered from the shock of the charge, turned again to the remaining defenders. Leering grins spread across blood soaked faces that promised more than pain.

She pressed her back against Kadin's as she waved the spear in front of her, taking comfort from the solidity of it. She looked around at the desperate faces of the wounded, each of them gripping their slender swords as best they could, ready to go down fighting.

She smiled.

It might have been a crazy, insane smile, but then it reflected the mad recklessness within. If this was how it was going to be . . .

"Come on then!" she yelled to the human animals around her. "We are elves of Ellsabae! Not cowards. Come and taste our steel before we join our forebears. Because, by the pit, we will send even more of you to the abyss before we go. Come on then!"

Allan C.R. Cornelius

Kadin roared behind her, joined by the wounded around her.

The humans charged.

Her eyes caught on the bright green pennant floating from the tip of her spear. Like the ribbon she wore to the last spring dance back home.

She laughed.

Strange the things you remembered when you were about to die.

FORGIVENESS

Steven swatted away yet another mosquito. He'd lost track of how many had met the same fate mere moments after they made camp. He didn't understand why they insisted on pestering him. There were nine other people in the camp to sate their bloodlust. He sat up and pulled the thin blanket around him as tight as he could, as if the meager barrier would make him any more challenging a meal.

His gaze strayed over the small camp with its little brown mounds, each a Yahad warrior somehow managing to sleep despite the droning insects around them. Without thinking, he sought out and found Honovi's blanket. She was sleeping on the opposite side of the camp from him, next to Hareb. She'd been maintaining that distance since they left the Shona. Between that and Hareb determinedly keeping himself between them, he'd barely managed a glimpse of her.

Not that he wanted to look at her. What did he care if she was here? After all, he was nothing to her. Of course that wasn't the tune she sang in Ssanek's camp. He slapped another bloodsucker, this one finding a chink in his armor around his neck. *Oh please, please take the lying demon's deal and live with me for the rest of your life.* Never mind that neither of them knew why Ssanek was making such an offer. Steven grumbled and forced himself to look off over the rolling hills and into the night.

"Brings back memories, doesn't it?" Brogan grumbled as he eased himself down next to Steven. "Though it has been a while since we were this close to it."

Steven grunted and batted at another mosquito.

"Keeping watch over her despite her wishes? That's very romantic but—"

"I'm not watching over her," Steven snapped as he again wrenched his gaze away from her shifting blanket. She was tossing and turning. He wondered if she was having a nightmare, and if hers were the same as his.

Brogan only shrugged. "Right. Well, that's a shame because after what you two went through I would think you would understand that some watching over is exactly what you need."

"I know," Steven said. "You and Hareb are doing a fine job of it."

"I don't mean by your parents, though I'll admit that I don't plan to let you out of my sight anytime soon. I mean by each other."

Steven scoffed. "She did a fine job of that. She betrayed me. When I needed her most, she let herself be manipulated by our biggest enemy."

Brogan punched him in the arm with surprising strength considering how wiry thin his arms were.

"You don't get it do you, boy? Listen to yourself. She betrayed *you* . . . when *you* needed her . . . Do you love her?"

Steven flinched. "I don't know. I thought I did, I guess."

"You thought? You guess? Boy, you either do or you don't. Either way, maybe you should start thinking about her instead of moping about yourself."

◆Whispers at the Altar◆

"I *was* thinking—"

"Really? Have you stopped to wonder what she went through while in that camp? Did you ask her? Did you think how that strong young woman we know could have been broken?"

"But—"

"Did you even apologize?"

"Yes!" Steven stood up, waving his blanket at the swarm of bugs that wouldn't leave him alone. "I told her. *Multiple* times. She didn't care."

Brogan grunted. "Maybe you need to stop looking at yourself and your wounds, and think about her and her wounds. That's what love does. That's what it *is*. It's putting the other person first and expecting nothing in return."

Steven considered Brogan's words as he watched the lump of brown that was Honovi shift and twist on the ground. What *was* she dreaming about?

"We may not be related, but we're the closest thing to family that either of us has. And no father wants to watch his son make the same mistakes he made."

Steven looked at Brogan curiously. "Is this about the Chisaran king's wife?" Brogan had never talked much about her, beyond the brief mention when they visited the city, but Steven had often wondered.

Brogan shifted uncomfortably. "I lost her, Steven. And I didn't have to. But I was young and stupid. I let my pride get in the way of what I needed to say to her, and I let my selfishness blind me to what really mattered. Don't do the same."

He stood and walked over to grip Steven's arm. "If you love her . . . then *love* her. Whatever she says. Whatever she does. It doesn't matter. What matters is what you decide." He turned to walk away, but Steven reached out to touch his shoulder.

"What if . . . what if I lose her? I can't protect her. I can't protect any of you." He blinked back tears.

465

Brogan looked over his shoulder, a smile crinkling his wrinkled face into a web of chasms. "No. You can't. But you can love her while you have her. Give everything you can to her. And then have faith that all that work will produce some kind of fruit. Have faith that the only one who can protect her, will. And when the time comes, as it must for all of us, let go of her. That's all any of us can do."

He pulled away, walking back to his own bed, and Steven watched him go. He seemed older somehow. His steps less sure and his back more bent. For the hundredth time Steven worried what this trip might do to him. He could die. They all could. What would life be like without him?

Steven swiped absently at a mosquito and turned back to Honovi. Just in time to see her jerk upright.

Her hands clawed frantically up and down her body as if she were attempting to tear her clothes off. After a few seconds she threw the blanket away, and her hands stilled. She sat there breathing hard for a minute before standing and stalking out of the camp without a glance to anyone else.

Steven hesitated, then followed. He moved quickly through the sleeping soldiers, keeping a wary eye on Hareb as he passed. This might be the only chance he would get to talk to her, the last thing he needed was Hareb "protecting" her from him.

Honovi stopped about a hundred paces from the edge of the small camp, along the crest of a hill that looked down into the plains to their south. The same plains where her village had once stood and where, if all went as they hoped, their army would be meeting Ssanek's in battle.

Steven stopped, watching her body silhouetted against the stars. She shivered despite the warm summer breeze and hugged her arms around herself. Brogan's words echoed again in his ears. Did he love her? How would he know? What did he know about love? He knew he cared about her. He knew he didn't want anything to happen to her. Ever. Was that love? Or did he just not want anything to happen to her because he was afraid of being alone? How could he tell the difference?

With a soft grumble, Steven closed the remaining distance. She turned as he came up beside her, but made no move to leave. She simply examined him with a detached gaze before turning back to the south without saying a word.

The silence grew. Not the comfortable, pleasant silence Steven found relaxing, nor the cold icy silence that grew between them as they made their way back to the Shona. It was something in between. Something . . . tired.

"I . . ." Steven started, "I'm sorry I didn't tell you the truth," he tried. "About everything. It was wrong. And I'm sorry you had to go through what you did at the . . . at *his* camp. I mean, I don't know what you went through. I wasn't there. In the tent, I mean."

He took a deep steadying breath. "But whatever it was. I'm sure it was awful. I know it wasn't like you. You're stronger than that. I—"

"Shut up," Honovi whispered.

Her tone was flat, emotionless, and the suddenness of it shocked Steven into silence. Anger began to rise, but he forced a deep breath. Forced himself to remain quiet.

"It wasn't awful," she said in the same emotionless tone. "It was wonderful. At least what I remember. It comes in flashes. Bits and pieces. I remember the food most. How it tasted. As if I had never really tasted food before. And the bath. The smell. The warmth."

She shivered.

"I was weak."

Steven opened his mouth, but couldn't think of anything to say. Part of him was angry, seething at the idea that she had given up so easily. He had been right to be mad. She betrayed him.

"So was I," he answered finally.

She turned to look at him with a mix of anger and incredulity.

"Your friendship was so . . . it felt so good. To have you talking to me. To have you . . ." He sighed, frustrated. "That was why I lied. I wasn't strong enough to tell you the truth." He reached out to take her hand, but she jerked it away.

"Is that supposed to make it right?"

Steven shook his head. "No. Of course not. I'm just saying . . . that you don't have to feel bad about what happened. That I forgive you. I know what it's like to—"

"I don't need your forgiveness," Honovi hissed between clenched teeth. "I'm not here to get it. I'm here to pay him back. That's all."

"That's fine," Steven said, nodding slowly. "I understand. I have a few scores to settle as well. I just . . . I wanted you to know that if you want to talk. About anything." He took a step back and shrugged. "I'm here."

"I don't need to talk." She faced back to the south.

Steven wondered if she was trying to see home, or at least where home used to be. "Are you sure? Not even about the nightmares?"

She shook her head, but Steven caught the subtle movement of her fingers clutching at her clothes.

"I'm sorry, Honovi, for all of this. I never wanted to hurt you or anyone else. But I promise I'll do everything I can to make it right. For everyone. But especially for you."

He walked away but had only taken three steps when her voice made him stop.

"He's stronger now."

Steven turned back, confused. "Who?"

She scoffed and shook her head. "You *know* who. Something's happened. He . . . he was taunting me. He said we should have taken his offer."

"You know why we couldn't do that."

"He said you gave him something." She turned to glare at him. "He said his 'little servant' gave him more than he could have hoped for."

Steven held his hands up, "I'm his *son* remember? And I haven't given him anything. I swear."

She shook her head again, and Steven caught the glint of a tear in one eye that betrayed the look of stone she gave him. "We won't be able to beat him."

"Perhaps not. But we're still going to try."

Recovery

"Christabel."

Her eyes snapped open as the sound pierced through the thick fog coiled around her brain.

"Where am I?" She tried to sit up but some invisible force held her. She shifted, squinted, trying to take in as much of her surroundings as the bond would allow. A tent slowly came into focus above her, cloth flapping in a slight breeze, and soft cots lay to either side of her, each with another occupant. White robed Divinists walked among them whispering prayers and stopping now and then to touch a nearby patient.

"The main field hospital."

"I can see tha—" She stopped as she saw Director Namarian, sitting on a stool by the bed. "Sorry, I . . ."

"No apology necessary, Christabel. Waking from a healing is disconcerting even when you are used to it." He gave a small smile.

"Do you still feel any of the pain? Sometimes the Illusion can leave phantom—"

"Why are you here?" Christa didn't feel in the mood to be polite. "Where's Kadin?"

The corner of Namarian's mouth twitched up as though he might laugh. Something Christa was fairly certain by now that he was incapable of. "Kadin is giving a report to the Medico commander. It seems Anathonians recover quite quickly. He was up hours ago." Namarian leaned back. "As for why I am here . . . I thought you would prefer to wake to a face you knew. As I said, healing's can be very—"

"You've barely said a word to me in four years. I don't know you. You're just the man who bought me from my father in the marketplace." She rolled over, though it took every ounce of strength to do. What did those humans do to her? And how did she survive it?

She thought she would enjoy the silence her verbal barb might bring. But instead it left her hollow. Virtually no friends left and here she was shooting arrows at someone who, just maybe, wanted to help.

"I know I have not been a friend to you in the past, Christabel," he said at last. "That I have not been family to you, even when you most needed it. But I would like, when you are feeling better, if I could speak with you. If you care to."

Christa willed herself not to turn over, not until after she heard him stand and walk away. The nerve of him wanting to talk after what he did. After years of ignoring her. What could he have to say now that she would want to hear?

There was one silver lining to all of this. At least she wouldn't have to work.

•*Whispers at the Altar*•

For one day. That was how long it took the Divinists to pronounce her fit for duty. The shortest vacation ever, but at least the exhaustion made it hard to think about anything and easy to sleep away the hours. Sleep with no nightmares. It had been so long she forgot what it felt like not to worry about whether she would wake screaming and covered in sweat every time she closed her eyes. It was the best sleep in years.

Sure, there were dreams of humans hacking apart elven bodies. But they were somehow more distant, less personal. As if they happened to someone else, not her. For that day, at least, she rested.

When she stumbled out of the hospital tent, blinking back the sunlight, it was with orders to report to the Quartermaster for reassignment. But the camp was vast, and she was sure no one would miss her for a few hours. Instead, she wandered around, letting her feet take her wherever they wanted while her mind meandered down the many trails of thought she avoided while lying on the cot.

All of them led back to Namarian. Would it hurt her to listen to him? He seemed different. Less formal. Or was that her imagination? Was she just so desperate for a friend she was inventing them where none existed?

She had only taken a handful of steps when a tap on the shoulder brought her spinning around.

"Kadin!" Without thinking, she reached out to wrap him in a hug, then stopped awkwardly halfway as she realized what she was about to do.

It didn't matter. Kadin wrapped his strong arms around her regardless, nearly crushing her to his chest before he let her go.

I thought it was you! How are you? His clothes were dusted with dirt, but his face shone with excitement.

Christa shrugged. "Well enough, I suppose. At least the Divinists say so."

You look . . . tired.

Christa barked a laugh. "I've slept an entire day, not to mention being unconscious for another. I don't see how I could be tired."

Not all fatigue is physical. You seem tired inside.

Christa found his gaze both comforting and uncomfortable and started walking again to give herself an excuse to look elsewhere. "Before the other day, I didn't know you'd come."

I've been attached to an infantry unit near the edge of the fighting. I'd heard you were out in one of the auxiliary clinics.

"Head cook and laundry maid. That's me." She chuckled. "How did your meeting with the Medico commander go?"

Well. By now I don't think he's the only one who knows what you did. Guards talk, and nothing stays a secret long in a military camp.

Christa glanced around, sure everyone was staring at her even if no one was.

He frowned. *Some are saying you ruined the scenario. They think the guards would have protected the Divinists instead if you hadn't interfered.*

"Scenario?" Christa stiffened. "What do you mean, scenario?"

Kadin blinked, *You mean . . . did no one explain that to you?*

He stopped, scribbling frantically, and Christa was forced to wait. She had to force her foot to stop tapping in impatience. Twice.

It was all part of the exercise. The Illusionists create the enemy army and the sounds and effects of the battle. The humans, the wounds the soldiers suffered, none of it was real. The wounds feel real enough, enough to cause shock, but I don't think anyone has ever died.

"But I saw the bodies! I saw what the humans did to them. I felt the spear . . ." She gestured vaguely to her stomach. "I felt their . . ." Her gut turned as she remembered the last moments of the battle. The feeling of bones breaking as their axes struck her flesh.

Kadin placed a hand on her shoulder. *I'm sorry.*

·*Whispers at the Altar*·

She looked up, eyes rimmed with tears. "I killed them, Kadin. I wanted to, and I did it. I can still remember what it felt like." Christa stepped forward and wrapped her arms around him, her knees too weak to hold her as the memories came flooding back.

He held her, and Christa was glad for the silence.

She'd killed them. Never mind that they weren't real. She could still hear their cries as the plunged the tip of the spear into them. After all the times she had thought she wanted to kill . . .

After several minutes, Kadin pushed her gently back to arms' length as she sniffed and blinked back tears.

They weren't real, Christa. You didn't kill anyone. They were never alive.

"It doesn't matter. Can't you see that? I would have."

He paused, his dark brown eyes locked on hers. *Yes, I believe you would. Because you're a good person, and you wouldn't sit by and watch people be slaughtered. Not to mention, if it was real, they would have killed you the same as the wounded.*

"What makes my life so much more valuable than those humans?"

Kadin shook his head. *I can't answer that for you, Christa. I just know you made a hard choice. And if it had been real I would be glad you chose as you did.*

She didn't know if it made her feel much better, but something in his certainty was comforting. "Thank you, Kadin." She took a deep breath to steady herself. "I'm sorry I haven't talked to you since . . ."

You've had a lot to deal with. I understand.

"Aren't you going to ask about . . . you know. About what happened?"

He shrugged. *I assume you'll talk about it when you're ready.*

She narrowed her eyes suspiciously. "You fought some kind of dragon demon. And you nearly died. And you're not even going to ask why?"

Do you want me to?

Christa laughed. "No. I don't guess I do."

He smiled. *Just remember you always have friends in the palace.*

"Fewer now, I think," she said.

More than you think. He gave her hands a quick squeeze then stepped back. *I need to get back to my duties. But I'll try to find you again later.*

Christa nodded, they waved, and then he walked away. But as he left, Christa realized she knew exactly where she needed to go next.

She was ten paces from Namarian's tent when he walked out. They both stopped, staring, waiting for the other to move first. Finally, they met in the middle.

"You said you wanted to talk to me," Christa said.

"Yes . . . would you like to go for a walk?" He motioned toward the edge of the camp.

Christa looked back out over the camp. "I guess." She reminded herself of Kadin's words, that she had more friends than she thought. Perhaps Namarian was one after all. The least she could do was give him a chance.

They walked in silence. Namarian's tent sat toward the edge of camp, but it still took a quarter of an hour before the tents thinned and gave way to a string of sentry pickets, and then to the rolling hills of eastern Ellsabae. Christa knew from her lessons that if she were to follow these hills east, they would become higher and rockier until they rose to form the Erradine Mountains, ancestral home of the Dwarf nation of Kibarak. But here, many leagues away, the hills were content to ripple lazily under their blanket of green, sheep-trimmed grass.

"I should have talked to you sooner." Namarian broke the silence.

Whispers at the Altar

"Why didn't you?" Christa tried not to make it sound like an accusation, even if it was.

He shook his head. "You are so much like your mother. And I was still so angry."

"Why? What did I do to you?"

He chuckled. "You misunderstand. I was never angry with you. At least, not when you first got here."

Christa thought about this for a moment. "What did she do? Is it because she left?"

Namarian nodded. "She promised, when we came to the Roost, that we would always be together. But then your father came."

"And she left with him."

Namarian nodded, stopping to lower himself down onto a log half submerged into the ground. "Of course she told me what she planned, and I advised against it." His gaze wandered over the hills. "I reminded her of the future she had in the Hawks. Of all the good she could accomplish. To throw all of it away . . . on a human. I mean, he would die within the century, but her reputation would be tarnished forever." He sat there, lost in memory for a moment before shaking himself back to the present.

"She insisted, of course. Said she loved him. I am afraid I lost my temper. Not only was she wasting her potential, her career, for a human, but she was breaking her promise." His face became drawn, pained.

"You could have gone with her."

Namarian chuckled. "Yes. And perhaps I should have. After all, I made a promise, too. But I did not see it that way at the time. She left that same day. She wrote several times. About her time there and about you. But each letter brought back the anger, so I stopped reading them. Until I got one from your father."

"When she died." Christa dropped onto a rock outcropping, and started plucking blades of grass from it.

Silence crept around them like a slow fog as each drifted back into their own memories.

"I'm sorry," she said at last, barely more than a whisper.

Namarian nodded sadly. "I know you are, Christabel. It was an accident. No one blames you."

Christa shook her head and wiped her eyes. "You don't know. I *wanted* to. In that moment, when it happened. I was so . . . angry. Just like with Sinna. And Silvana. I . . . I *wanted* to." She looked up through the hair that had fallen in front of her bowed head. "What's wrong with me?"

Uncle Namarian walked over to sit next to her, draping an arm around her shoulders. She leaned into him.

"There is nothing wrong with you, Christabel. You are exactly as the Creator intended."

"So He gets some kind of enjoyment out of making broken people?"

"We are *all* broken people." He turned her to face him, lifting her chin with one hand. "I held a grudge against my own sister for over a decade. Then took the grudge out on her only child. Does that sound like a perfect person to you? No, what you are is unique. Yes, you have made mistakes. We all have. But—"

"No, you don't understand." Christa shook her head. "I've done other things. Horrible things. I—"

"It doesn't matter." His gaze was firm. Kind. "I forgive you, Christabel. Your mother forgives you. You need to forgive yourself."

"How? How could anyone forgive that?"

Namarian smiled. "Because the Creator already has. And if He can . . . who are we not to?"

"It can't be that easy," she protested. "I have to pay for what I've done. For what I am."

Namarian frowned. "You have paid. And you will continue to pay. The hurt will always be there, the emptiness. But that doesn't mean you can't be forgiven."

•Whispers at the Altar•

"Papa won't," Christa whispered.

Namarian paused, considering. "You can't control other people. I won't lie. Maybe he will never be able to forgive. Can you forgive him that?

Christa thought about that. What if he never did forgive her? What if he hated her? Forever. It hurt to even consider. But she had hurt Uncle Namarian, and he had forgiven her. Could she forgive Papa?

Her thoughts were broken by Namarian's hurried rise. She turned, but somehow knew what she would see before she ever made it around. Something in the way the sun shone a little brighter, and the air felt a little warner. Perhaps the grass even glimmered a shade greener.

"And here I find you, Christabel," Queen Elisidel scolded. "Evading your work as usual."

Christa leapt to her feet then dropped back down into a deep curtsy. "Your Highness, I was just—"

"You were just taking a much-needed rest I am sure." She regarded the bowing director. "And catching up with your family. Another excellent idea."

Christa stood as the queen waved her up. "Yes, Your Highness." She wished she could think of something to say, anything, but all that came to mind as the queen walked closer was a cold worm sliding down her throat.

"If you will excuse us, Director Namarian, I need to speak to Attendant Christabel alone."

Namarian bowed again. "Of course." He gave Christa's shoulder a squeeze, smiled, then walked in the direction of the camp but paused after two steps. "I am sorry, Christabel. For . . . everything." He stood there for a moment, cleared his throat, and headed off.

The queen waited, and Christa shifted from foot to foot until the director passed out of sight on the other side of the hill. "Well, Christabel," she paced over to the log Namarian had sat on and lowered herself onto it. The moss reached up, becoming thicker and greener even before her violet dress touched it. "You have been busy, haven't you?"

Christa froze. Did she know about the Observatory?

"Please, sit," she motioned to the stone Christa bounded from earlier. "And stop looking at me as though I am going to eat you."

Christa eased herself back down.

"I am sure you have heard your little adventure is the talk of the camp. You have caused quite a bit of debate."

"I'm sorry." She relaxed just a smidgen.

"Oh, don't be. Debate is good. Like all the debate I have had over what to do with you."

She shook her head, "What do you mean, Your Highness? I thought that was decided already?"

Queen Elisidel leaned back, sinking her long thin fingers into the now lush moss. "Why did you try to save those wounded? They weren't your kind. They weren't your responsibility. For all you knew they were as good as dead already. Why add yourself to the pile?"

Christa's mouth moved for a moment but nothing came out. "I guess . . . I guess I thought that was where I could be the most useful?"

The queen's face was impassive. "So you ran into certain death because you thought the Divinists could look after themselves."

"No." She flung away another handful of plucked grass and balled her fists into her lap to still them. "I mean, I couldn't stand there and watch them die." She took a deep breath, then bowled forward. "I've been very selfish since I came here. I saw a chance to help someone. Someone besides myself."

"So you did it to ease your own conscience."

"No!" Christa planted her feet and leaned forward. "I did it because it was right. It was the right thing to do. They were defenseless. Yes, they died even after I tried to save them, and me along with them. But if I didn't do anything . . . at least by trying there was a chance!"

Whispers at the Altar

Queen Elisidel smiled. "Ah. So now the truth comes out. It is shocking how often we do things and do not stop to consider the real reason." She stood, holding out a hand to Christa. "Walk with me a moment, Christabel. I have something to offer you."

Christa starred at the hand.

"Oh come, girl. I don't bite. And there is no law saying you can't touch me. Goodness, am I so intimidating?"

"No, ma'am. I just . . ." Christa took her hand, afraid to grip the delicate fingers too tightly.

But the queen lifted her up as Christa would pluck a flower. "Now," she led Christa off, keeping the camp at an even distance to their right, "before I begin, you must promise to be completely honest with me, Christabel. I may not have the magic of a Mentalist to tell if you are lying, but I assure you I am very practiced at it. Agreed?"

Christa nodded.

"Good. So how do you like being an attendant?"

The question took Christa aback. "I . . ." She glanced at the queen who stared at her as if to remind her of the promise she just made. "I hate it. I mean, I don't mind the work, but I feel like a slave."

"A slave?" The queen laughed. "At least you are being honest. What makes you feel like a slave?"

Christa glared. "The fact that I can't go where I want? Or do what I want. That I work every day until I'm exhausted just to collapse into bed, wake up, and do it all again. Or how about that I'm not even paid for it?"

She just grinned. "Christabel, my dear, much of that is simply life. Do you think your father can go wherever he wants whenever he wants? I am sure his duties, wherever he works, keep him very busy. He has responsibilities not easily left behind or severed. Do you think I can up and leave Ellsabareth whenever the mood strikes me?"

"At least it's an option," Christa mumbled.

Queen Elisidel patted Christa's hand. "I know what you are saying. But let us not forget you chose this."

"When I was a child!" Christa gestured to the sky. "I didn't know what I was doing. I'd just been abandoned by my father in a strange and magical place. Told I could use magic, that I could do the impossible, if only I stayed. What child wouldn't say yes? I wasn't thinking about a *year* down the road, let alone ten or thirty."

"And if you were given the same choice now?" The queen stopped walking and faced her, one eyebrow raised. "Remember your promise, Christabel."

Christa started to answer, to tell her just where she could put her lifelong obligation of obedience to the crown, but found she couldn't. "It doesn't matter now. I can't use magic. I wouldn't even get the chance."

"But what if you could? What if you could use magic and you were given the chance to join the Hawks again?"

"What do you mean?"

"Exactly what I am saying. You have proven to me where your loyalties lie and how much you can be trusted. You laid down your life for my people, for your people, and that is not something I take lightly."

"It wasn't even real."

"You thought it was. That makes a significant difference."

"But . . . I'm crazy, haven't you heard?"

"Christabel if you want to say no, say it. Otherwise, let me worry about the details."

"So," Christa narrowed her eyes, "you're saying you want to try to fix me, and then make me a Hawk again?"

"That is exactly the choice I am giving you. Attempt to become a Hawk again, with all the responsibility and opportunities that entails, or stay an attendant. This is the only time I will make the offer, but consider carefully. For one, I do not know what removing the Arkius will do to you. It might kill you."

Christa considered for a moment. "So . . . how would this work? Exactly?"

"The first step would be to remove the Arkius. If you survive, you would need to pass a test."

Christa chuckled dryly. "Of course. But as a Hawk I serve the crown. Couldn't you just . . . wave your hand and—"

"And undo my own decree? Certainly. But what then? You have regained *my* trust, yes. But without a test, a public test, questions about your loyalty will plague you the rest of your life. Director Dalan will continue to have ammunition to use against you. Against Marellel. Even against me."

Christa shook her head. "Politics."

"Yes, and if you mean to be successful as a Hawk you better learn them. Nothing in the palace is ever as simple as it seems."

"So then, what kind of test would this be?"

"An excellent question." Queen Elisidel squeezed her hand in both of hers. "For starters, let us say you will either come out a Hawk or you will not come out at all."

The remainder of the exercise flew past for Christabel.

Her thoughts, day and night, were consumed by what the queen told her. A second chance. True, it might kill her. But if not, she would get her magic back. During the day, with the sun shining down on her, she often felt it would be worth dying if only she could use the Essence again for even a short time. The Fire leapt at the news of course. It licked against the walls of its stone prison in eager anticipation of the walls crumbling. At last it would have victory. At last it would course through her again.

But it was at night that the sober part of her rose, bringing images of all the ways she might die. The queen told her the test would be spawned from the depths of her own mind. Whatever the Stone of

Trials decided would most test her loyalty. She was grateful to Marellel and Elirel for helping her overcome her greatest demon. She could only hope there were not greater ones lying just under the surface.

Of course the Fire reassured her everything would be fine. Whatever the challenge, there was nothing it could not face, nothing it could not destroy for her. She had only to trust it, believe in it, and, most of all, free it.

THE SWAMP

"Is it always this hot here?" Honovi struggled to pull her foot out of the sucking mud without losing the boot.

Steven grunted a vague affirmative as he trundled on ahead of her, not bothering to offer a hand or even wait long enough to be sure she made it out of the sludge and onto the patch of relatively dry land.

Of course, neither did her father who walked next to him. Honovi sighed in frustration, braced the butt of her spear against the cold ground, and crawled up onto the bank. Her fingers raked furrows in the dark, weed-covered clay.

It was three days since they had entered the swamp. Three days of increasing bickering, arguments, and even the occasional scuffle. She couldn't blame them entirely, despite the fact that she seemed to be the only one able to keep her head. If the mud and stench weren't enough, the constant droning assault of insects far larger than any had a right to be was enough to unnerve anyone.

Then there was the oppressive humidity. It crept through cloaks—which they had long ago abandoned—clothes, and flesh to settle in the bones. Combined with the brutal heat, it was enough to make anyone miserable. Honovi felt like the frogs she used to watch her mother boil over the fire.

"I think you've led us the wrong way again, Brogan," Steven yelled ahead to where the old man walked in the lead. Steven clutched his spear in a white-knuckled grip as he peered at the sky. Which was ridiculous. The chances of him seeing the sun through the constant clouds was remote. The only way they even knew it was up was the vague lightening of the haze above them. It reminded Honovi of Ssanek's camp, and the memory brought with it a shiver that crawled up her body like a snake.

"This from the only one of us to get himself lost and nearly killed in these swamps," Brogan responded over his shoulder.

"I'm not the one who led us in circles for an entire day," Steven called after him.

"No. You're the one who dragged us into this dung heap to begin with."

Hareb shook his head. "The child is right. You said we would travel west for three days. It has been five. Obviously you do not know where we are."

"I am not a child," Steven said, turning on Hareb.

Honovi flicked mud from her fingers as she walked between them. "He didn't mean—"

Brogan stopped and turned around. "And I suppose you would have better luck weaving your way through these bogs with no stars or even the sun to tell you one way from another." Brogan glared at Steven and Hareb as they faced one another. "Are we stopping?"

Hareb regarded him flatly. "I see no reason to continue following a man who has no idea where he is going."

Honovi shook her head. "Father, he is—"

"Exactly," Steven said, as if he had been doing so for days.

Whispers at the Altar

"Nor do I see why I should follow a boy whose arrogance and ignorance placed us in this place to begin with."

"And I suppose you think we should all follow an ignorant savage like you who couldn't find his way back out let alone forward to the altar." Steven strode around Honovi, straightened his spine, and stared up at Hareb.

Honovi tried to put herself between them. "Stop, both of you!"

"I think children should listen to their elders, and lack of respect should be driven out of them!" Hareb swung one massive fist in a backhand aimed at Steven's head, but the Chisaran ducked. Honovi barely had time to register the incoming blow before it caught her across the jaw.

Honovi nearly fell to the ground under the weight of the blow, stunned. She had known her father was strong, but it had always been the kind of comforting reserved strength she could rely on to drive away nightmares or provide solace from another's unkind words. Never had it struck her so directly.

She was still forcing back the tears and clearing her vision when Steven launched himself at Hareb. He was an idiot, but she had to stop him before Hareb killed him. She stood, a hammer beating in her head, and tried to make sense of the chaos.

Steven and Hareb rolled and twisted on the ground, Hareb's giant hands unable to find a grip on Steven's sweat soaked body. Spears lay forgotten in the sickly yellow grass as both combatants beat at each other with fists, knees, and even teeth. All while Brogan stood over both, his face twisted into something unrecognizable and his eyes wide, as he beat them both with his walking stick. A weak, high-pitched keen whistled from his clenched teeth and faded into the mist like the cry of some wild animal.

She had to act quickly, already the hunters were reacting, some running to help Hareb, others drawing bows. She rushed forward just as Hareb pinned Steven beneath him, his hands around the boy's throat.

"Stop! Everyone! This is madness." She tucked her shoulder and flung herself at Hareb, toppling him to the side just as Brogan's staff swung across where her father's head had been. Her father grunted beneath her as they hit the ground. She rolled away immediately, knowing full well now what one swipe of his arm could do to her. She sprang to her feet a short distance away, and twisted in time to see Brogan fall, one of the hunter's arrows in his back.

Honovi didn't know what to do. Steven screamed wordlessly as he crawled to Brogan's body. Hunters ran toward him, spears raised. And Hareb stood, his back to her, gripping his own wide-bladed spear over Steven's quaking mud slick body.

It was madness, all of it. But no one would listen to her.

She ran back to Steven, determined to put herself between him and her father. Maybe then Hareb would listen to her. But then she saw it.

It looked like a snake writhing through the grass, its pale white body glistening in the dull light as it made its way from the murky water toward her father's ankles.

"Look out!" She yelled. "In the grass!"

She barely registered something—else—something wrong, before she brought the blade of her spear down on the body of the snake. It sliced cleanly through the slimy body and sank into the soft earth beneath. Half of the snake recoiled into the air, streaming black ichor as its severed portion thrashed in the grass in front of her.

There was just enough time to realize this was no snake before the water and mud she climbed out of only moments ago exploded into the air. A shrill wail pierced her ears. The sound reverberated into her skull and down through her bones, carrying nausea with it.

Honovi braced herself against her spear, looked up, and saw something through her pain-clouded vision that her darkest nightmares could not have conjured.

It rose from out of the mire, three times the height of any man. Its sinuous, sickly pale body covered in plates of black chitin that shimmered green with slime. A dozen short, powerful legs waved

•Whispers at the Altar•

in the air, from the middle of its body to its distended mandibles. Each one terminated in a scythe-like blade of chitin. From around the gaping maw, long, barbed tentacles, like the one Honovi severed, dripped the same ooze that covered the rest of its body as they lashed out at anything that came close. And beneath the long plate of chitin that swept back to form the nightmare's head, Honovi saw rows of dull red eyes. Eyes filled with malice, hunger, and—Honovi knew—intelligence.

She saw her father charge, and his battle cry broke though whatever spell the creature's scream had placed on her own limbs. His madness was forgotten, or at least redirected. She spared a look down to Steven. His face was paler than she had ever seen it, whether from the beast's sound or his father's injury she couldn't tell, but he was focused entirely on attending to him. She wished she could help, but she knew his knowledge of medicine was greater than hers. If any of them could save the old man, it was Steven.

So she followed her father, screaming the same wordless cry to banish the fear that threatened to seize her will. Hesitation would only kill her that much faster. Instead, she called on her anger. She tapped into all the seething hate she carried since that night in Ssanek's camp. It rose within her, giving her strength, speed, and burning away any trace of dread. It overflowed into her scream until her throat was hoarse with the effort.

Father reached the monster first, his heavy spear, its nearly three span head like a wide double-edged sword, whirled in front of him as if it weighed no more than a willow branch. Ichor flew through the air as its blade sliced through the horror's reaching tentacles, easily keeping them at bay. Arrows from the seven remaining hunters sang through the air, clattering and ricocheting off armored plates.

Honovi barely heard the monster's screams as she ducked around her father's right side to drive all her spear's slender, two-span blade into the flesh below the joint of one of its dozen clacking legs.

The leg went limp, and the monster jerked to one side dragging Honovi along with it.

Allan C.R. Cornelius

Then it dropped to the ground, a mass of severed tentacles, rattling chitin, and stabbing legs.

Honovi was forced to leap to the side but her spear, caught between two of the plates, was wrenched from her grasp. She reached for her bow as she came back to her feet, but it had fallen off when she caught her father's backhand. Not that it mattered. Her bowstring was safely stored in her pack, lying next to it.

She cursed.

Hareb squared off alone against the monster. The thing writhed and darting in front of him like some enormous centipede with a mouth three times what it should be.

His spear darted in and out as he danced just outside the reach of the closest pincers and the gaping maw, but he had yet to find the opportunity to take the offensive. The hunters, their arrows useless against the beast's entirely armored back, charged forward in a half-circle around it, spears raised.

"Surround it!" Hareb called. "Don't give it a target. Attack its flanks. Get under it. Kill it!"

Honovi searched for a weapon, any weapon, that might be useful. Her eyes fell on Steven's forgotten spear—one of her own spares— and she smiled.

She snatched up the weapon and ran around to the beast's side. By now the hunters had arrived and the thing was thrashing wildly back and forth, its sheer weight as much a danger as its bladed legs as it threw itself into the hunters around it.

Honovi waited patiently, her spear up and ready for any flash of soft flesh beneath the plates of chitin.

A hunter screamed from the other side as the monster's body jerked in that direction, crushing him even before its legs sliced effortlessly through leather and skin.

But the shift exposed a gap and Honovi took it. Her spear jerked forward, piercing through pale flesh.

The beast screamed, but she didn't stop.

She pressed forward, letting every ounce of anger burn through the muscles of her arms, legs, and back as she forced the spear deeper.

She was lifted from the ground as the monster twisted away.

There was another scream, this one human, a moment of blinding pain, then nothing.

Steven barely registered the end of the battle as he finished bandaging Brogan's wound. He didn't dare try to remove the arrow. Not here, covered in who knew what kind of filth. But it would have to be done soon.

He looked up to see Hareb bending down over Honovi. The nightmare lay on its side, no fewer than three spears protruding from its corpse like giant needles. One, Hareb's by the size, jutted from the thing's mouth, still quivering with its death spasms.

"What was all that about?" Brogan said, his voice a harsh rasp.

Steven looked back down to see Brogan's eyelids fluttering as much as his breath. "Nothing. Just some of the local wildlife."

Brogan grunted. "Be sure to . . . get a sample."

"Of course." Steven chuckled. "And a drawing. Like always."

"How bad?" He pointed feebly at the small piece of arrow still protruding from his back.

"It missed your lung. Too low. But it might have hit something else. I won't know until I try to take it out."

"Not . . . easy."

Steven tried to sound nonchalant. "I know. But you've taught me how. And you're strong. You'll be back on your feet again in no time."

Brogan chuckled, the sound accompanied by a grimace of pain. "I'm old. Living on . . . borrowed time."

Steven looked up as Hareb crouched down nearby.

"It was a mistake." The big man gestured to the arrow with a frown. "Some magic of this place?"

Steven shook his head slightly. "I think we all knew what we were doing. Something here might have egged us on, but I don't think it used anything we weren't already feeling." He shrugged. "Just a theory, though. It doesn't matter now."

"It was my kinsman who shot him. I would offer justice . . . but . . ." he motioned with one hand to where two dead Yahad were being laid out by the other hunters. Honovi sat nearby, her eyes fixed on the beast.

"It doesn't matter," Brogan said. "It's done. We need to be going."

"No," Steven stated flatly. "You aren't in any condition to travel." He looked up to Hareb.

"Yes. Honovi is injured as well. We will stay here tonight."

"But—"

"No, Father." Steven said. "We're staying. No arguments. Hareb, how many of the hunters do you need to bury the fallen?"

He considered. "We should burn them, send their spirits up to the Great Watcher."

"I know. But a fire that large here is sure to attract attention. Attention we don't need. If we don't make it to the altar, there will be a lot more spirits that don't ascend."

Hareb frowned. "It is a terrible thing you ask, Steven. To bind their spirits here."

Steven reached out to place a hand on Hareb's shoulder. "It is the greatest sacrifice they can make. Do you believe they would make it?"

"I do. They were brave."

"How many will you need?"

"Two."

"Good. Send the other four to scout a circuit. Make sure nothing else is hiding out nearby waiting to pounce on us while we're sleeping. I'll get a small fire going and set up a spot to work on Brogan."

"I'll help."

Whispers at the Altar

Steven turned to find Honovi standing over them, her own blood seeping down the right side of her face from a gash in her skull and every other part of her covered in mud and black gore. He stood, trying to wipe the mud from his face but only managing to smear it around. "All right. But first I'm going to take a look at that knock on your head."

Fifteen minutes later the graves were under way. Hareb even added his own back to the labor despite the fact he could obviously barely stand himself. Steven pulled the first pot of boiling water off the fire and replaced it with another; he had three more lined up waiting.

He poured some into a bowl then turned to where Honovi sat upon a stone. "Now then . . ."

"I don't need any help." She waved a hand at him irritably.

Steven set the bowl down and picked up a clean rag, luckily the swamp had yet to find a way into the watertight bag he kept in his pack. "Stop. Just stop. We both know you do."

Honovi glared at him. "You should be helping Brogan."

"I will. But first I need to help you if you're going to be any use at all during the operation. Now hold still, and let me look at that wound." He walked up behind her, tilted her head back against him, and began to clean the wound. It wasn't deep. In fact, he was more worried about the impact itself than any external damage. Brogan had taught him head wounds could be very tricky.

"I'm sorry, you know," He spoke softly as he worked, glancing from the wound to her eyes. "For anything I might have said before."

"Do you really think those were all things we really wanted to do?"

"Maybe. But not really." He smiled, amazed at how much like Brogan he sounded. "What I mean is . . . there are a lot of things that pop into our heads, all kinds of things. It doesn't mean we do them. We realize it isn't who we really are and decide not to."

"So you think something took that away? The ability to decide. The creature?"

493

"I don't know. Ssanek has shown us he can manipulate people, make them do things they ordinarily wouldn't. Maybe it's this place." He dropped the rag into the water and grabbed a dressing.

"Do you . . . do you think that's what happened at the camp?"

"Absolutely." He wanted to say more, how he didn't blame her, but he still wasn't sure it was true. Had it only been Ssanek? Or had there been more?

Honovi turned to face him, her eyes damp. "He visits me, Steven. He tells me I will always be his. That he *knows* me. He reminds me, every night, that I failed. That I was weak . . ."

Steven pulled her to him. "Why didn't you tell me? You're not *his*. And he definitely doesn't know you." He wanted to say more, but the words jumbled up inside his head, and he found he couldn't place them into any kind of logical order.

So he held her.

And he tried with all his might to project into her the feelings behind all those words. It was stupid. But it was all he could think to do.

Someone cleared a throat.

Steven turned, still holding Honovi close. Hareb stood by the fire, his hands and arms slick with dirt.

"It is done. We have said what prayers we can. They are out of our hands now." He glanced to Honovi, then back to Steven and gave the barest of nods before turning to go.

"Hareb," Steven called, taking a step forward. "I could use your help with Brogan. It will be a difficult process, and we've little to dull the pain."

Hareb turned and gave another nod. "I will help."

•*Whispers at the Altar*•

Though Brogan had explained the process of using a knife to remove foreign objects from a body, the discussion had been theoretical and entirely unpracticed. Steven checked the table for the fourth time to make sure everything he needed was within reach.

"What if I can't see what kind of damage there is through the blood?"

"That's what the cloths are for," Brogan whispered from the table. "You'll need to clear away enough blood to see."

"But what if I'm not fast enough? What if you lose too much blood? Couldn't we just cauterize the wound after we take it out?"

"That won't help any internal bleeding. That's the real danger."

Steven picked up the knife and looked across at Honovi who already held one of the few cloths ready.

"You can do it," she whispered.

He took a deep breath, nodded to Hareb who placed his enormous hands on Brogan's frail shoulders, then bent over the shaft of the arrow. He muttered a prayer to the maker and watcher of old men and orphans alike, then made the first incision.

The first feeling was that of shock. The knife had slid through so easily. He had expected it to take more effort, but only the slightest pressure was required. It was so easy.

The second was sheer terror as, by Steven's own hand, his father's blood began to drain from his body. For an instant he was a boy again, watching Mother's blood flow over the altar.

His hand shook, and he pulled back.

"It's fine, Steven." Honovi placed a hand on his shoulder. "Do what you know to do."

Steven wiped his forehead with one arm, leaned back over, and cut again.

The premise of the operation was simple enough. Cut enough to remove the arrowhead without further damaging the tissue around it, search for any damage to internal tissues, repair as needed, then close the wound. But never had Steven been made aware just how far premise and practice were from each other.

He prayed with each incision, his mouth moving in a constant muted litany. The arrowhead was removed, and still he prayed, though now he was barely aware he did it. He was barely aware of anything. It was as Honovi had said, he simply did what he already knew to do. And prayed it was enough.

It didn't take long before he suspected it might not be.

"Clear out the blood. I can't see!"

"I'm trying to," Honovi said with forced patience. "But we are running out of cloth."

Brogan had fallen unconscious somewhere in the midst of the pain, and for that Steven was grateful, but the rest of his body just wouldn't cooperate.

"I can't get it," he pleaded. "I can't see it well enough." He glanced to Hareb who stood staring, his strength no longer needed. "Get something hot to seer it closed with."

"But you said that—"

"Get it! I can't do it. We have to take the chance." Steven focused on the wound with renewed intensity.

Please . . . please, Maker. Watch over him. Don't let him die. I need him.

He whispered the prayer over and over. *I'll do anything. I'll give anything. Just don't let him die.*

There. A hole in the stomach. He could barely make it out, but he slipped the needle through tissue, sewing as fast as he could, hoping he was doing it right.

If Ssanek can do all of this, surely You can do more. Brogan believed you could . . . and so do I.

A soft glow covered his fingers. It was working. The stitches were holding. Even the blood was slowing. Steven could see again.

•Whispers at the Altar•

"I've got it! Just clean this out for me." He glanced up to see Honovi staring at him, eyes wide. "Honovi!"

She jerked herself back, nodding as she applied the cloth again.

It was working. Steven didn't know how. It was like the tissues had wanted to be repaired, like they had knit themselves back together. It didn't make sense, but it didn't matter. What mattered was that Brogan would live. He was sure of it.

Freedom

The announcement was made the day after Christa returned to the Palace. She'd hoped for something grand, a loud voice echoing through the halls saying Christabel Sellers was not a traitor and proof would be provided at high noon. It was a shock to hear of it only in a succinct note delivered by a young page.

The test would take place that very afternoon in the throne room. She was to report to the east antechamber at the first afternoon bell. She hoped, given the circumstances, she might be allowed to leave her duties in the stable early, but the seneschal showed no such sympathy.

As a result, it was five minutes until the bell before Christa came rushing into the antechamber, dung still clinging to the soles of her boots and stands of straw stabbing out in every direction from her tangled hair.

She stopped short.

"It's about t-time you got here," Sinna muttered, pacing up and plucking a piece of straw from Christa's hair. "You know they aren't going to wait for you."

Christa pushed the hand away. "What are you doing here? How did you know? I thought you—"

"Everyone knows, Christa." Sinna let out an exasperated sigh and reached out to hold Christa's shoulders. "Tell me you're done. With S-Ssanek, with trying to bring your mother back. All of it. Promise me things will be different."

Christa swallowed. "I promise." Christa wrapped her arms around her friend and squeezed. "I swear. I'm done with all of it. It was a horrible mistake. And I'm sorry. For everything. You were right. I wasn't thinking about you, or Westrel, or . . . anyone."

"You can tell me how r-right I was after you beat this test." Sinna hurried her over to the throne room door, plucking more straw out on the way. "It'll be nice not to have to walk clear over to the attendant's quarters to see you anymore."

"I'm looking forward to having a real desk again." Christa brushed hopelessly at her dress to rid it of even a little of the dirt and dust a day's work in the stables deposited on it.

"Just remember everything you learned. You can do this." Sinna paused her fussing. "You're the s-smartest and bravest Eyas I know."

"But I'm not an—"

Sinna pished. "You will be again. I know it. Now go in there and p-prove to them what we already know. Christabel Sellers is the most loyal and capable Eyas in the Roost. Westrel and I'll be watching."

Christa gave her hand a quick squeeze, took a deep breath, and pushed open the throne room doors.

The room hummed with conversation. Two guards took up position on either side and led her toward the massive gold and silver trunks dominating the center of the glade. She had thought the attendance at the trial was a crowd, but this made that seem an intimate gathering.

◆Whispers at the Altar◆

With no seats provided, elves stood across the expanse of grass like bright spring flowers. Every head turned as she was announced and each followed her slow progress to the foot of the throne of Ellsabae.

It surprised her how few she recognized. What interest did these people have in her? Who was she to them? She saw Vaniel, her face an emotionless mask, and wondered if Vaniel would ever forgive her. Other faces were open in their disdain and contempt. Had they all come to watch her fail? To watch her die.

Then she approached a group of soldiers whose faces were familiar. The wounded she fought to protect at the "battle." They snapped to attention as she approached and offered silent salutes as she passed. She smiled in return, started to salute back, then wondered if that would be presumptuous. In the end she settled for a small wave before clasping her hands behind her to ensure they remained still.

She was now thirty paces from the roots of the great thrones, and the only spectators here were those whose business kept them close to those thrones. She saw all six directors, standing to one side, wolfish grins plastered across Dalan and Ophidian's faces. Elirel was there as well, impossible to read. There was one encouraging look among them, Uncle Namarian. She waved to him then looked away and saw Marellel. Beside her stood Darian, Westrel, and Kadin. And Sinna, who was just now squeezing into position between Westrel and Darian. Christa tried to wave to them as well, but the guard's firm hand on her shoulder pulled her back a step to a stop.

"Christabel, daughter of Chrysolbel," Queen Elisidel spoke in a clear voice that echoed off the ceiling of twined branches above them, "you have been found guilty of attempting to slay one of my servants."

Christa faced the thrones and belatedly dropped into the deepest curtsy she could manage, holding it as the queen spoke.

"As such, you have been blocked from using magic of any kind and consigned to the seneschal to be used in the crown's service as best you might."

There was a long pause as Christa waited, then realized she should speak. "Yes, Your Highness," she said in a voice which sounded, to her ears, like a mouse squeaking at the lion.

"Rise."

Christa did so, grateful for the relief to her shaking legs.

The queen's gaze rose, roaming over those assembled. "Due to courageous actions on the field, I have decided to give my servant this *one* chance to fulfill the potential I see within her. She will be given the Stone of Trials." This was news to none in the room, and the words echoed with no response. "Before this can be done, the Arkius Stone within her must be stripped away." This produced a ripple of murmurs among those who had not heard the entire story. "Christabel, do you accept the risks of this procedure, knowing full well it has never before been attempted?"

Christa wished her heart would stop hammering in her chest. "I do," she managed on the second try.

"Director Namarian." He stepped forward as she called his name. "You have agreed to perform this ritual."

"Yes, Your Highness."

"Very well," Queen Elisidel said, turning back to her throne. "You may—"

"Your Highness, if I may?" All eyes turned to Director Dalan who had already taken three steps closer to the throne.

The queen stopped and turned slowly to face him. "You have something to add to my decision, Director?" she asked coldly.

"Only this, Highness." He turned back to the crowd.

Christa tried to catch Marellel's eyes, or Elirel's, or even the queen's to get some idea of what was going on, but everyone's gaze was fixed on Dalan.

"I have new evidence to present that I am sure Your Highness is not aware of." He spoke loud and clearly, as much or more toward those assembled as the queen. "Else I am certain you would not even consider the possibility of providing this," he sneered at Christa, "animal, with such power again."

"If you have something of value to add, Director, then speak. But you will heed your words. It is *my* servant you speak of."

Christa watched the queen take a step forward, her gaze focused on the director. From here the anger in her eyes was unmistakable, though few others would have seen it save Dalan had he bothered to look.

Instead he swept his arm out over the crowd. "I have discovered that this child has admitted to the slaying of her own mother, Hawk Chrysolbel."

Christa tried to protest, but her words were lost amid the clamor of voices filling the hall. She looked to Marellel, but her eyes were focused past Christa on Elirel.

"And I know," Dalan continued, his voice magnified by his proximity to the throne, "that she admitted this before no less than three reliable sources who I can produce this very instant."

"Enough!"

Queen Elisidel voice echoed, deafening, around the chamber. The room stilled at once and as the last echo died she looked down at Christa. Try as she might, Christa could find nothing of emotion in those dark eyes.

"I will hear it from her own mouth."

Christa cleared her throat and took a small step forward, gripping her hands tight behind her. Now was not the time for fidgeting. Now was the time for honesty. If she was truly to put the past behind her, this was her first step.

"The Director is correct."

A chorus of murmurs broke out, cut short by the raised hand of the queen.

"I was angry. I didn't know what I was doing, and I didn't even know I could use magic. I was a child. I wish every day that I could

503

take it back, that I could have her back. It's something I will have to live with the rest of my life."

Christa took another step forward, drawing level with Dalan and turning to face him.

"But there is more. Since I arrived here I have lied, manipulated my friends for my own purpose, and betrayed the crown. I admit to all of this."

The smile on Dalan's face was sickening, and for the first time Christa truly saw him for what he was: a pathetic snake, his vision focused completely on himself and his ambitions.

She turned back to the queen and knelt before her.

"I admit to all of this. I have been weak and selfish. But I promise you, that no matter what your decision today, I will always serve you, in whatever capacity you would have me."

Dalan snorted, "High words from a traitor."

Queen Elisidel glared at him.

"She admits it!" he continued. "Return her magic and she will use it against us. As she already has." His voice quieted to a whisper heard only by Christa and the queen. "Returning her magic is aiding treason against the Crown."

"I *am* the Crown," Queen Elisidel whispered, taking a threatening step toward him.

Dalan shook his head. "No. You are the queen. And the Crown is bigger than either of us."

She stopped, fuming, then turned to pace back to her throne. She sat, and a heavy quiet fell over the room.

"Please, Your Highness. Just send me back," Christa whispered. "I—"

The queen locked her gaze on Christa, her expression once more unreadable. "Do you wish to serve the Crown of Ellsabae, Christabel Sellers?" she asked, her voice ringing once more through the silence.

"I do."

"And do you swear to abide by all of our laws and obey the orders of the Crown?"

Allan C.R. Cornelius

"Of course, but—"

"My sentence for your crimes is to endure the removal of the Arkius Stone. A process that may kill you. You will then complete the Stone of Trials, which may also slay you. If the Creator brings you through these tasks, I and all those assembled will know He has forgiven you your crimes. And so shall we. You will be pardoned and your former position restored."

She waved one hand. "Proceed, Director Namarian." She spared a glance to Dalan who wore a self-satisfied smile. "You may return to your appointed spot, Director."

He gave a low bow. "You will regret this decision . . . Your Highness," he whispered, then turned and strode away.

Christa looked between them, but both were unreadable. Politics. She was sure it was something she would never understand.

Namarian approached Christa. He spoke softly enough that only Christa would hear. "This will be painful, Christabel. I will need to reach inside you, find the pieces of Arkius Stone, and draw it out. However, since I cannot affect it directly, I will need to cut through what it has attached itself to, your self.

"How long will it take?" Christa asked, no louder than Namarian.

"I cannot say. There are many pieces and each must be drawn out. I will not know more until I begin."

Christa nodded and turned to face her friends. She wanted this. She needed this. If she ever wanted to use magic again, to really help people, this was the only way.

Namarian said nothing, raised his hands, and began to mutter something Christa could not quite catch.

Christa locked her gaze on Kadin as something moved in her stomach. At first it was only like a bit of gas, a churning in her gut. Uncomfortable, but not painful. There was a pause, and the churning became a sudden and vicious wrench. Her hand drifted to her stomach and she ground her teeth as something coiled around her intestines, squeezing them mercilessly.

506

•*Whispers at the Altar*•

She bent double as the thing slid around inside, tightening. It would crush her from within. She would collapse here on the soft grass of the throne room, liquefied organs sloshing about within a flask of human skin.

She retched, heaving up everything she ever ate, and still she couldn't stop.

Dropping to her knees she dug her fingers into the ground as her vision blurred. She needed something, anything, to keep her head from spinning into unconsciousness. And there, in the darkness behind her lids, she saw it. The Fire leaped and clawed at the crumbling walls of its cell. It could sense the weakness, could feel the chains breaking, and she saw what would happen when it broke free. She knew what it wanted, and she threw her will against it. But it had been too long. And the heaving in her stomach, the convulsive spasms that cramped her sides as her gut tried to expel what it no longer contained, would not let her focus.

Then the real pain started.

Pinpricks of fire exploded around her chest like barbed needles jabbing from the inside out. They spread, multiplied, until her entire body lived as a constellation of pain, each star a diamond point of agony burning its way through her flesh.

She screamed, alternately arching and curling her back. She lost any other feeling but those tiny suns burning away at her. And still the Fire rose to an inferno as its prison crumbled around it. It laughed at her efforts to contain it, searing them to ash as it bounded forth to claim what they stole from it.

Freedom.

They will pay. All of them. We will make them pay. They thought to contain us. They don't trust us. And they shouldn't. They should fear us.

"No. He was wrong," Christa screamed wordlessly back. "They care about me."

But they don't know you. Not the real you.

Then, through the pain, through the Fire, she saw her friends. She saw the hundreds of innocents around her who would be the first to suffer for the freedom the Fire craved. And a different anger kindled. The same she felt as she watched the humans butchering her people. She would not stand by, a prisoner in her own body, while the Fire wrecked misplaced vengeance upon these people. She was not a vessel. She was Christabel Sellers, and the Fire was *hers*!

Groaning with the effort, she slammed her own barriers into place to supplant those now missing. Barriers of will. Walls of conviction. The Fire roared against them like a cornered animal, but she pressed forward. She would not be used. Never again.

When she opened her eyes the pain was gone. Only aftershocks and echoes remained, twitching muscles as they coursed down her arms and legs. Her vision cleared, and she saw Kadin smiling, a wide, proud smile that sent warmth coursing through her and into the walls she built. Each of her friends wore the same expression, and each strengthened the cage holding back the Fire, but none so much as his.

She stood, unable to remember when she'd curled into a ball, and faced Uncle Namarian who was even now presenting something to the queen. A small lump of stone.

"Christabel Sellers."

The queen's voice grabbed her attention. She tried to drop into another curtsy but the muscles in her legs wouldn't allow it. "Your Highness." Her voice cracked in her dry throat, coming out as a hoarse whisper.

Queen Elisidel gave the smallest of smiles, one Christa was sure only she could see. "You will now be given the Stone of Trials. Through its magic all those assembled will see what you see. We will witness your choices. And we will perceive your loyalties. Make your choices wisely, for you will either exit the other side a Hawk or perish."

Whispers at the Altar

She motioned to one side and an Attendant came forward carrying a slim pedestal of silver before him. At first Christa thought that must be the stone, but then she saw it. A small, faceted, brown gem nearly identical to the Dueling Stone rested atop the riser, dull and cold. To Christa it seemed to be brooding, waiting for someone fool enough to touch it. Her gaze never left it as the Attendant placed the pedestal before her.

The queen motioned again and a guard unsheathed his sword before moving to stand next to Christa, weapon ready.

"Christabel. Take up the stone, and may the Creator watch over you."

She looked back to the stone. It drew her forward, need flowing off it like ripples in a dark pond. She inched a hand out, hovered over it, and drew a single deep breath.

She seized it, and her world washed away in a flash of light.

TRIALS

"You know you don't have to go."

Christa blinked and the daydream, something about the throne room and the Stone of Trials, shredded into tiny fragments impossible to catch again. She shook her head, then focused back on her packing.

"You know I do, Mama." She folded another white dress and placed it into her bag. "I'm a Hawk."

Mama scoffed. "I am sure I could convince Queen Elisidel you were more needed here."

Christa turned. The sharp retort on her lips died as soon as she saw her mother. Something about her tore at Christa's heart. It wasn't the way her hands fussed with her immaculate green skirt. It wasn't the pleading look in her blue eyes or even the way the first signs of tears glistened in them. Something else, some other point, somehow broke through the ordinary and the familiar to stab at her.

"Mama," she said, walking over to take her hands, "please don't. I need to do this."

"But why?" she implored. "There are plenty of Hawks. Plenty of Elementalists to destroy the humans. Why do *you* need to go? You could stay here, with me. Study. Learn. Grow up and grow old." The threatening tears began to drip down. "Creator's light, Christa. They are *your* people. Doesn't that mean anything to you?"

Christa sighed, pushing her bag over to sit on the bed. "Of course it does, Mama. It isn't like I want to go."

"Then don't." Her mother seized on the foothold. "Stay here. With me."

Temptation bit into Christa's soul. She could do it. Mama could convince the queen. Christa didn't want to go fight her own people. And no matter how much time she spent with her mother, it was never enough. As though she were always making up for lost time somehow. But if she didn't go, another would have to. What about that person? And did she have the right to pick and choose what orders to follow? She was a Hawk. She had duties. Responsibilities.

"No, Mama," she whispered. "I can't. I have to go." She walked back to the closet, removing another dress. She couldn't bear to turn around, couldn't stand to see the look on Mama's face. She waited for an admonition or the next argument, but none came. Only silence followed by a soft click as the door closed.

Christa wiped the moisture from her eyes and threw the dress into her bag.

It exploded in a flash of yellow.

"Commander."

The single word snapped Christa out of her reverie so abruptly her head hurt. She glanced around the command tent blinking back tears. Had she drifted off? She'd dreamed of Mama . . . She faced the sergeant, rubbing her eyes to hide the fact she was actually wiping them. "Yes, Sergeant Atan."

"An emissary from the humans to see you, Ma'am."

Whispers at the Altar

"Oh? Chief Ithmar again? I already told him his terms were unacceptable." She crossed the tent, working her way around the large map table that dominated the center, and her Sub-Commanders surrounding it.

"No, Ma'am," the guard said. "King Ethron himself."

Christa stopped short, feeling everyone staring. Ethron was not just one of the six kings of the humans. He was the most powerful of them. Her mouth went dry. This kind of negotiation was beyond her. He should have gone to General Osellman. What was he doing here?

"Show him in," she whispered, trying her best to appear confident. She would not be intimidated. She opened the gate an inch for the Fire, feeding off its supreme certainty.

The guard opened the tent flap and a broad-shouldered and tightly muscled man strode in. His face was covered in hair, as was the custom of his tribe, hiding the tanned skin that showed on his bare arms. Christa inspected his rough, bone-studded armor for weapons, but of course found none. The picket guards would have checked him already.

Christa put on her most diplomatic face, the one she learned from Marellel. "Good afternoon, King Ethron. Forgive me for not being prepared for your visit, I was not told you were coming." She spoke in her father's language, not much different from Ethron's dialect.

The man frowned, a lowering of certain parts of his facial hair. "I'm not here to do some elven dance of diplomacy." He sneered the words back in his own tongue. The way he said "diplomacy" and "elven" were not much different than the way most of her own officers said the words "human" and "savage." "I have a deal for you, Christabel. For *just* you." He peered past her to the Sub-Commanders.

"I understand." She did not. This was highly unusual. But she was confident she could kill the man before he could move a foot, and equally confident he knew it. She motioned for her staff to leave, never taking her gaze from the king. She drew a little more of the Fire out, careful to keep its hunger at bay, but needing a bit more of its strength.

513

When everyone filed out, save Kadin standing silently in one corner, she motioned to a pair of slender camp chairs. "Will you sit?"

Ethron seemed to consider this for a moment, his small bright blue eyes flashing between the chairs and her, then shook his head. "Christabel, I have taken your mother captive. She is held now in Aeringsdale."

Christa took a step forward, but pushed back the overeager Fire. Instead, she watched the man, looking for any sign of deception. "That's not possible. Hawk Chrysolbel is in Ellsabareth."

He shrugged. "My men found her traveling across the river with a small group, easily overcome. She carried this . . ." He held out a ring, the exact twin of the one Christa wore.

The Fire purred within her. *He deserves to die. He is weak, and now he threatens you?*

"And what do you want?" Christa said, trying to maintain the appearance of calm.

"You will come with me to Aeringsdale. There you may live with her, in comfort, as you teach my wise men the use of your 'magic.'"

Christa scoffed. "How do I know you haven't already killed her?" The Fire surged, flooding through the small gap in its prison door. She imagined burning the man where he stood. A pile of ashes, that's all he was.

He gave another massive shrug. "You don't. But if you do not come, I will be forced to try to convince her to teach us. She has not proved willing so far. It may take considerable 'convincing.'"

She took a step forward. "So you come here, threatening to torture or kill my mother and demanding I commit treason?" She could barely see now, the Fire crowded everything else out. "I should kill you here and now and lay waste to your precious Aeringsdale."

The king crossed his arms before his barrel chest. "You may. But you will never see your mother again if you do. And what would your elven friends think? Violating truce . . . slaying an emissary . . . and a king. Is your anger ready for the wrath of my people? How many more would die?"

"It is treason," she hissed. "I cannot teach you. I don't even know if you could learn."

"You learned. You are half-human. I will trust you to do your best."

Christa spun away, pushing the Fire back. She needed to think rationally, and the Fire would never let her. All it wanted was death and destruction. Even as it retreated she could feel it begging, pleading to be allowed to kill this upstart human. To set loose the wheels of war and death once again.

She couldn't give in to his demand, could she? The only thing holding the line for the elves now was their magic. If the humans had that . . . But wouldn't she just be leveling the playing field? And wouldn't it be nice to live somewhere in peace with her mother? Besides, who knew if the humans could even learn to use magic? It was her elven blood that let her do it, wasn't it? For a moment she could picture it, walking with Mama, no responsibilities to separate them, no war to endanger them. And all she needed to do was teach her *own* people the knowledge she had been given.

But what about her friends? And weren't the elves more her people than the humans? They were all she'd known for decades. How many elves would the humans kill with the magic she taught them? How far would King Ethron go? To the gates of Ellsabareth itself? Could she sacrifice all those people for her own happiness?

"No," she whispered, surprising herself by saying it aloud. She turned back to Ethron, firm determination set in her stomach. "I will not. You will not extort my people's secrets from me. And what is more, I will make sure your fellow kings hear of this. They will all know you hid behind a woman like a coward as you tried to peddle your way to greater power over them."

The world flickered.

King Ethron frowned again, and for the first time Christa saw real anger there. And part of her was glad.

"Now get out of my camp."

He spun on his heels.

The world stuttered.

He spun on his heels.

Christa frowned, nausea striking her as the earth shifted left while the tent lurched right.

The world tore itself apart in front of her.

When she could finally see again, she saw only death. The charred, bloody, and broken remains of a battlefield. Bodies lay strewn about as far as the eye could see and the drone of flies was nearly deafening.

Where was she?

She had been in the test. She remembered it, the human king, her mother, all of it had seemed so real, but this . . .

You are home. The words echoed, not in her ears, but in her mind, scraping across her barely recovered nerves.

She spun, then stumbled back, tripping over a corpse and landing on it. Still, the viper, twice as long as she was tall, held her full attention. "What are you?"

A soft chuckle pattered over her mind. "Why Christabel, I'm hurt. And after we did so much for each other." It slid closer as it spoke, a smile, if such a thing could exist on a reptilian face, inched wide enough to swallow her down in one bite.

Realization dawned on her. "Ssanek?" She shook her head and tried to stand on the uneven corpses. "You betrayed me. You didn't do anything for me."

"That is who I am, little morsel. And in turn I showed you who *you* really are. And isn't that the great lesson here? We all must be what we truly are."

"That wasn't who I am."

"Isn't it?" The snake hissed then lunged forward, jaws snapping. They found Christa's leg and seized upon it, teeth sinking into her calf.

Christa cried out, the pain not just coursing through her leg, but searing her mind.

•Whispers at the Altar•

It pulled, dragging her with impossible strength over the corpses. She tried desperately to catch hold of one, hands grabbing at anything she passed. She screamed for it to stop. She screamed that it could not be real. And she screamed for help. But every name she called out to was only the next body she passed. Their eyes vacant or already plucked by vultures. The screams stopped by the fourth body, but still her thoughts cried out each name. Their corpses all passed in a horrible parade. Father, Marellel, Sinna, Westrel . . . Kadin. The pain in her leg paled next to the cries in her heart and all she could do was whisper over and over, "It isn't real."

Eventually, the snake stopped, and Christa lay still, in too much pain to move and too grieved to care.

"Do you believe now?" the snake whispered in her mind. "This is your future. Now look upon your past."

She tried to turn away, tried to ignore the agony of her leg.

"*Look!*"

The force of the command opened her eyes. She sat up and choked back a sob. Her mother lay there, burned and broken, her limbs twisted at impossible angles, bones crushed and crumpled. Christa wept, her tears falling to splatter on blackened skin.

"It wasn't my fault. It wasn't. It was an accident. I didn't know."

That low chuckled echoed again. "Accident? Not your fault? *All* of this is your fault. This is your future. Pain, death, destruction. Do you think the Fire will settle for anything less? You are nothing but chaos. And you will never be anything more. You are a catastrophe, Christabel Sellers. And everyone you ever loved has and will pay the price for it."

Christa shook her head violently as if she could loose the mocking voice from her head. "No. I've made mistakes but—"

"Mistakes?" It laughed now, an unnatural spitting sound, as it circled around her, it's scarlet orbs never leaving her. "Forgetting to bring an umbrella is a mistake. Kissing your best friend's sweetheart is a mistake. You are a disaster. A cataclysm who brings destruction to

517

everyone around her. Your mother, your friends, your mentors . . . their lives would all be better without you. Look around you!"

"No! That isn't who I am." The Fire surged within her, contradicting her words. It leaped and kindled at every word the snake said. Still, she fought on. "My friends believe in me. Marellel believes in me." A memory floated through her mind of Kadin sitting with her by the fountain. *It doesn't matter if other people think you don't belong. What matters is if you are determined to finish.* She struggled to her feet, fighting against the throbbing pain.

"I may have been who you say. But not anymore. I will finish what I started. I beat you once, and I can do it again. I know who you are. You're nothing but lies and smoke, and I'm not afraid of you."

She reached out, and the earth responded, jutting a spear of rock up from the ground and into the viper's mottled body. The snake made a high-pitched sound of shock, writhed like a stuck worm, then, with a shudder, went limp.

She watched it die, feeling no joy at the sight. When the light went out from its eyes she let out a shaky breath. It was over. Pressing her lids closed she willed herself back to the throne room. She pictured it in her mind, just as she would in the Observatory. She imprinted it, knowing when she opened her eyes she would be there.

Her lids crept up.

Nothing changed.

Except the snake. The grotesque thing, impaled on a spike of stone two paces away, decayed. What did she do wrong? She took a step forward, watching the beast, careful to keep her gaze from the corpse of her mother in front of her. The beast's eyes were vacant, staring, but as she watched them she could swear she saw them move.

They twitched toward her.

Christa jumped back, a small, strangled scream escaping. Instinct brought the Fire, and it swept out toward the serpent in a torrent, washing over it. Once released it would not be denied. It called on her frustration, her anger, and her fear, pouring the emotions into a stream of flames that grew more intense with each bundle of fuel.

And then, through the roar of the flames, came a frighteningly familiar chuckle. Not the snake's animalistic parody of the human act, but the deep, rock-crumbling rumble Christa had tried so hard to forget.

Vaniel watched Christabel take the stone. She hated the entire farce. Christabel had lied to all of them. She admitted it, owned it proudly in front of the queen herself, and still she was given another chance. She was handed everything. Power, prestige, position—all while she laughed in their faces. Meanwhile Vaniel had watched all the same things ripped from her, no matter how loyal she tried to prove herself.

She watched as Christabel lied her way through the first two tests, the images displayed above the stone for the entire throne room to see. Of course the people believed her. She was the sweet and innocent Christabel. The tragic martyr of the Roost. Vaniel ground her teeth and was about to walk out—she could already see how this was going to end—when the test jittered and shuddered, replaced by something . . . else.

Gasps filled the throne room and a few shouts as people closer to the liar tried to help her, but once the stone was taken, it could not be pried away. Then the snake bit her, and Vaniel could hear Christabel's cry of pain from where she stood. That was when the concern around the thrones turned to panic.

Vaniel didn't care. Christabel deserved whatever pain she received. Vaniel watched the snake show Christabel who she really was. It didn't speak aloud, but her words and the images it showed were more

Allan C.R. Cornelius

than enough. The snake knew. And Vaniel smiled at the tortured look on Christabel's face.

Then another laugh came from the stone. It echoed around the throne room, and Vaniel's satisfaction turned to fear. She knew that laugh. She had looked into the eyes of that horrible face and seen her own death a hundred ways. She wanted to run, to hide, but her feet wouldn't let her. She couldn't look away as the snake began to change.

The Altar

"Stop fretting like an old woman." Honovi nudged Steven in the side with her elbow.

Steven grunted. He appreciated her trying to cheer him up. He appreciated her just sitting next to him after the weeks of separation and silence, but comparing him to an old woman wasn't helping.

"I should have gone with them."

"You are many things, but two things you are not: a trained hunter or an idiot." She smiled and Steven couldn't help doing so, too. "Well, not usually an idiot anyway."

"It was my idea to come out here—"

"And it was their idea to accompany you. As it was theirs." She motioned to where Brogan and Hareb sat in a small patch of dry in this world of wet, their backs against an enormous cypress tree. Brogan seemed well enough now, especially for someone who had been shot with an arrow only days before. Steven couldn't help being proud of his work, but he wasn't sure he could take all the credit. Brogan was hard at work on something now, it was hard to tell what. Steven suspected it had something to do with the upcoming fight.

Steven recognized the tree they leaned against. It might be more twisted, more vile—like the rest of the land around them—but it was as imprinted on his mind as everything else from that day nearly five years ago. The reminders had come more and more frequently the past two days. Everything he saw knocked about in his head like a bean in a rattle, shaking loose all the memories he had tried so hard to forget.

"Tell me what is really bothering you," Honovi said, reaching out to place one hand on his knee.

"You mean besides being terrified? Or knowing that all of this is my fault in the first place?" He shifted on the damp rotting log they were using for a bench and faced her. "I walked with Mother all the way here. I should have known something was wrong. I should have stopped her. But I tagged along like some stupid puppy. And now . . ."

"You were a child. If what your father says is true, you were even less than that. It is not your fault. It is hers. She started this." Honovi looked into his eyes, her gaze firm and broking no argument.

"But I'm the one who—"

"Who what? Refused to be sacrificed? If you had been, then Ssanek would still have returned, and he undoubtedly would have given her power. At the least you denied him another servant."

Steven shook his head. "Did I? Remember what he told you? That his servant had given him more than he hoped for? I know he wasn't talking about either of us."

Honovi thought for a moment. "The Seer?"

"That's possible I suppose, but somehow it feels wrong." He sighed, picked up a stone and threw it into the bog as hard as he could. "I wish I knew who it was. I wish I could talk to them. Reason with them."

Honovi scoffed. "I would as soon just kill them before they could do anything worse."

Steven shook his head. "No. Even Mother wasn't always bad. Maybe they could be convinced to stop."

"I think you are overly optimistic. Next you will be asking to reason with the Seer instead of killing him." Honovi grinned, and Steven relished the twinkle in her eye.

"No. I just can't stand the thought of someone else so broken. Just like Mother."

They sat in silence for several minutes, and Steven found his thoughts constantly returning to that day. What had she been thinking? She had been hurt, that much was obvious, but what could have bored such a hole in her heart that Ssanek could fill it with so much hate?

The brighter spot in the clouded sky was sinking low to the horizon by the time the hunters returned. Steven didn't even notice them until they were practically standing in the midst of the makeshift camp. Everyone jumped up, crowding around them as they in turn took the vacated seats.

"It is ahead, as you said," the leader, Atah, said. He shook his head and took a long drink from the waterskin Hareb offered him. "A clearing," he continued. "But filled with water, not just the pools you spoke of. In the middle is a . . ." He shook his head, the disbelief plain on his face.

"What of numbers?" Hareb asked. "How many?"

"Twenty of the lizard soldiers," provided another hunter. "Another ten of the mutated Chosen."

Hareb shook his head.

"And . . . the Seer?" Steven asked, trying to sound as unafraid as possible.

The hunter nodded.

Steven let out a long breath. The weak point of his plan had always been in assuming the Seer would be here. It had seemed logical, but the idea of trekking all this way for nothing had tormented him from the start.

"Perhaps we should all have a seat," Brogan said. "Let you start from the beginning."

They all sat down in the driest spots they could find, and Atah began sketching out a map in the damp earth.

He started with a large circle. "While the number of the Soldiers is distressing, they are spread out and appear to want nothing more than to soak in the fetid water." He placed a large number of dots randomly through the circle. "I assume that you have some plan for getting past such ordinary defenses. What worries me more is the altar itself." He drew a smaller circle in the middle.

"We observed four of the Chosen, crab-legged monstrosities, scuttling up and down the altar. The Seer lay curled at the base. Even with a distraction, I do not believe you will be able to approach without engaging all five."

"Could you see what they were doing?" Brogan asked.

"No. They appeared to be very focused on the altar itself, though we did not get close enough to see why."

Brogan frowned but motioned for Atah to continue.

"The only active defenses we found were a patrol of six more Chosen encircling the lake. These were different from those on the altar island and from each other. But all six were large and powerful, built for battle and with eyes all about."

"Perfect guards," Hareb muttered. "When do they rest?"

Atah shook his head. "They do not appear to require rest. Or food. We saw them stop for neither."

Steven sighed. "We knew this wasn't going to be easy. I see you've saved the biggest for last. What about Ssanek?"

"He floats above the altar, turning circles like a lazy cat. I do not know what to make of it. He did nothing else."

"Perhaps his attention is elsewhere as we hoped," Honovi said.

Hareb nodded. "Perhaps, but that could change."

"It could," Brogan agreed, "But if we strike quickly we should have enough time. The target is the Seer. Nothing else matters."

"And how do you propose to reach him?" Hareb asked, his tone heavy with skepticism.

"Simple." Brogan held out his hand for the stick with a smile.

Steven crouched in the rancid water doing what he could not to keep looking up and over the low hill they were hiding behind. He hated this plan. Not just because it involved him sitting in water up to his neck, though that didn't help, but because Brogan had insisted on creating the distraction on the opposite side of the lake. There was no way for Steven to know if he got into trouble or needed help.

It didn't make matters any better that this was by far the best plan they could have come up with.

"How long has it been?" Steven whispered to Honovi who waded close beside him.

"About two minutes since the last time you asked," she said with a sigh. "Be patient."

Steven gripped his spear tighter and tried to think about anything else, but this close to the altar, with Ssanek's shadow circling around them, it was nearly impossible. He tried reviewing over his part in the plan, but doing so only made him more nervous.

He focused on his spear. He had sharpened the long, double-bladed head that morning. They all had. But now his eyes seemed to invent nicks and burs that he should have cleaned off. He watched the blade dance as his arm shook. It was possible the shaking was because he was cold, but the water was nearly as warm as the air.

The Chosen sentries should be another twenty paces in according to the hunters, but Steven felt sure their eyes were on him. He jumped when Honovi touched his arm, swinging the spear around in a loud splash.

She ducked easily, the soft smile not leaving her face as she slid up to him, wrapping one arm around him. "Stop worrying," she whispered in his ear. "Everything will be all right."

"But Brogan—"

"I get the feeling Brogan has done this kind of thing before. And he has two of our best hunters with him."

"But his wound—"

"Is healed. You made sure of that. Which is why I know we'll be fine."

Steven turned his head to look at her curiously, only to find her face nearly touching his. "What do you mean?"

She laughed so softly it could barely be heard over the lapping of the water. "Of course you did not see it. You are far too worried about the future to see anything in the moment."

Steven furrowed his brows. "What?"

"Your father's wound. I watched you heal it. I saw the light around you. I saw the holes in his body close at your touch."

Steven scoffed and shook his head. "You saw me stitch them together. There was nothing magical about it, Honovi. Just real medicine."

Her grin only widened. "You may think that, but you know it is only the flowers. You know, underneath, that something else happened. You have been touched by some power. Marked by it. And it is not Ssanek. That is how I know you will succeed. That and . . ." She looked down at the water. "And because I love you."

Steven stared. "I . . . I love you, too, Honovi." And as he said the words, he knew they were true. Any doubt he might have had before was carried away like smoke. "I—"

A guttural roar of defiance echoed through the mist to be answered by another and another. The swamp seemed to explode with them.

"Brogan," Steven whispered. He looked to Hareb who waited behind the next island. "Was that the signal?" he asked in a loud whisper.

Hareb looked over, his already wide eyes going wider at their embrace. "No. But this is neither the time not the place for *that*." He gestured at them. "His signal will come—"

Whispers at the Altar

A deafening sound ripped through the afternoon, blowing shreds of the low cloud past their faces and shaking the ground under them.

"*That* was the signal," Honovi said with a wild smile. She kissed Steven deeply, then with an animal growl turned and waded up and onto the hillock.

Steven crouched there for two seconds, stunned, then gripped his spear and trudged after her.

He had tried to imagine in the quiet times as they traveled through the swamp, what this moment would be like. But nothing came close. Smoke rose in great billowing clouds from across the lake. Even as Steven came up to the shore, another concussive roar issued from slightly further south throwing the trunks of trees, boulders, and hopefully some Chosen into the air.

A handful of Soldiers scrambled up the far eastern shore while still more swam after them, their huge claws and tails propelling them through the shallow water at an incredible pace.

Steven counted only five left on their side of the lake.

And past them, the altar.

He nearly stumbled as he saw it. It stood taller than a tree, the base as wide as a house. Its surface writhed and shifted with the movement of snakes as thick as logs. It towered over them all, and at its summit Ssanek flew in slow circles. Steven stared at him, entranced by the power inherent in his sheer size, until another explosion shattered the spell and all the noise of the battle surged back in.

Honovi and Hareb were already five paces ahead, wading through the water that rose to Honovi's thighs. The remaining soldiers had already seen them and were closing in, only to be assaulted by a stream of arrows from either side as the six remaining hunters joined the battle.

One went down under a rain of hawk fletching that peppered its chest while another was forced to turn aside to present its more armored back to the deadly hail.

Allan C.R. Cornelius

Honovi was forced to stop as a soldier burst from the water. It swept a claw across, drawing a line of red over her chest. She stumbled back but caught her footing just as Hareb lunged forward, his own wide-bladed spear tearing into the beast's belly and back out, spilling organs and blood into the foul water.

The soldier fell back into the lake, but another was already there to take its place. With one claw it drew a long, jagged sword of black stone, while with the other it snatched Honovi's throat.

But the exchange had given Steven time, and before the lizard could bring the blade to bear Steven punched the head of his spear up into the pit of the soldier's arm until it ground against bone.

The soldier roared in pain, dropped Honovi, and Hareb's spear sliced through its throat.

Then they were off running again, the entire exchange having taken less than a score of Steven's frantic heartbeats.

Steven looked back and forth for the two remaining Soldiers as he ran, but couldn't find them. For all he knew they were under the water sneaking up behind him. His gaze came back to the altar island, and he realized it didn't matter. He couldn't spare any attention for them.

What had appeared to be an island was a pile of broken skeletons barely larger than the altar that stood upon it. Chosen, the arms of their gray, emaciated bodies replaced by clusters of short tentacles, scuttled up and down the altar. As they reached the bottom, they bent down to suck dark liquid from its base into the long proboscis dominating their face, before hurrying back up the side.

The Seer stood on the shore facing them, one claw casually waving away the occasional arrow with screens of solid shadow. His eyes were focused on Steven, and Steven could swear he was smiling.

There was a crack of thunder above them, and Steven dared to glance up. Ssanek, his body as much a swirling cloud of shadow as it was flesh and scales, curled above them. His eyes were closed except for one that cracked open to look down at them.

528

•Whispers at the Altar•

"We have to hurry!" he yelled over the splashing of their running. But his companions needed no urging. They were already pushing ahead, leaving Steven struggling to keep up.

He watched them surge out of the water onto the island and close with the Seer. Its claws flashed as it deflected one blow after another, but the intensity of the Yahad's assault left it unable to retaliate. Two of the Chosen ceased their tasks at the altar and turned, called without words to their priest's defense.

Steven was nearly there. He scrambled up the slope of mud-slick bones, his hands slipping over human skulls and his feet crunching through ribcages. The Chosen were almost down the side of the altar. He slid back, got his feet under him, then sprang forward just in time to shove his spear before the face of one of the Chosen.

It wheeled toward him, distracted, as another rumble came from above, this one more like a growl than thunder. He didn't have time for this. Ssanek was waking. Steven had to keep his attention away from the Seer.

The Chosen took advantage of the distraction to wrap one set of tentacles around Steven's spear and nearly yank it out of his hands. Steven jerked the spear back, but the thing's grip was too strong. So instead he swung it toward the Chosen and lunged forward. The slender blade bit into the creature's chest then thrust clean through its back and into the wall of snakes behind it.

Steven didn't lose a second. Already Ssanek's eyes were open, peering about the clearing blearily.

He side-stepped around the Chosen he had pinned to the side of the altar, slipped under the wild swing of its other "arm," and used its shoulder to heave himself up. Steven's outstretched hand grabbed one of the twisting snakes, and he began to climb. Razor-sharp ridges sliced into his hands and legs but he kept moving.

The closer he got to the top, the smaller the snakes making up the altar became. Until, moments later, he reached the top where the serpents were barely bigger than his arms. He grabbed the edge of the altar, heaved himself up over its lip, and froze as he looked across its undulating surface.

"Mother?"

Honovi saw the path to the Seer clear, and a smile curled across her face as she ran. She had never expected them to survive—it was only a matter of time before the rest of the Soldiers returned—but at least they would kill the shadow cursed Seer.

She pushed any remaining doubt aside and charged beside her father. They reached the Seer at the same time. Father's spear flashed in a high sweep while Honovi thrust low where the creature's feet would be—if it had any.

The snake arched back, avoiding the sweep, then brought one claw forward to block Honovi's spear dead with a shield of midnight.

She pulled back, reset her footing, and slid two steps right even as Father went left. They had never fought together before this trip. But already they knew each other's movements.

She had a brief glimpse of Steven struggling up the slope of the island, but she couldn't spare any attention let alone assist him. Two Soldiers were unaccounted for, and the arrows from the hunters had slowed, but she didn't have time or attention for that either.

The Seer flicked one hand at each of them, and shards of shadow shot out. Honovi somersaulted to one side, her spear held firmly against her stomach, gained her footing, and thrust out again.

Only he wasn't there. He had moved forward, pressing against Father, raking at him with claws gauntleted in darkness. She ran forward to assist him, but then her arm jerked back as something wet and slimy wrapped around it.

She had just enough time to turn and see one of the Chosen, its tentacles wrapped firmly around her forearm, before it pulled her backward off her feet and threw her to the ground. She screamed as her shoulder blade slammed into a skull. Then the scream turned to a cry of frustration as her spear rattled away toward the water—and the Seer.

Steven stared.

"I watched you die."

But then, was she really alive? She lay naked upon the altar, the snakes twisting and coiling around her body. Two of the Chosen ministered to her, sibilating softly as their oily tentacles closed the gashes in her pale skin that the snakes opened with their razor-edged frills, over and over.

Blood poured out from these wounds and from the gaping hole in her stomach. The hole Steven had placed there. The blood ran down and over the altar and the snakes drank it greedily, while the Chosen sucked up the remnants and the waste from the altar's base to feed her.

She stared up at Steven with vacant unseeing eyes, her face twisted in an endless alternation of pleasure and agony, and Steven knew she was beyond communication. Beyond thinking.

He looked up at Ssanek. *He* did this.

Steven yanked the knife out of his belt and thrust it into the face of the Chosen bending over his mother. It fell back, gurgling around the hole in its throat as Steven climbed to stand atop the roiling altar. The last Chosen reached out to grab him. Its tentacles wrapped

Allan C.R. Cornelius

around one of Steven's legs, but he kicked out with the other. His boot caught the Chosen in one of its eyes and it slid back down the side.

Steven knew it would return, but it gave him enough time. He stood over his mother, her face a rictus of pain as her body tore to shreds without the attentions of the Chosen, and looked up at Ssanek.

Its eyes were open and fixed on Steven. Steven smiled. With one hand he grabbed the tip of Ssanek's tail that spun lazily over him, while with the other he thrust his knife through it.

His arm vibrated with agony, but he refused to let go.

And then the world exploded in an eruption of shadow.

Desolation

Christa's fire sputtered out and fear clenched her innards into knots nothing could penetrate. As the smoke and steam cleared she saw the serpent shift its head and stare at her. But these eyes were pits of black streaked with cracks of burning lava. It shook its body, and the scales and decaying flesh stretched. The head lengthened. Christa heard the cracking of bones and the snapping of sinew as its form grew. She backpedaled, nearly fell, spun, and ran.

She didn't dare glance over her shoulder. She didn't need to. She could hear whatever burst from the snake growing. But she couldn't run fast enough. The bodies plotted against her, reaching out to trip her up at every opportunity. And as the voice echoed out from behind, she knew she could not escape.

"Why do you run, little snack? Are we not friends? Haven't I given you all you asked for?"

She stopped. Whether from courage or hopelessness she could not say. But once she stumbled to a halt, her breath coming in ragged gasps, she knew running was not the answer. So she turned.

The battlefield was gone. Ssanek crouched in front of her. The white claws at the apex of each webbed wing gripped the tops of towering boulders as black as his own scales. The blasted rocky landscape rose to merge with the slopes of the craggy mountains around her that shed dust and soot with each blast of wind that whistled through their peaks.

She was alone under a rolling thundercloud, but she stood firm.

"You aren't here," she yelled. "This is only part of the test."

There was a moment of silence after her words flew off, like sparrows in a gale.

Then Ssanek laughed. The sound cracked boulders and dropped slopes of scree down into bottomless chasms with a roar of breaking rock. Christa fought to keep her footing, but was forced down to one knee.

"Do not mock, little morsel, what you do not understand and cannot comprehend. It is *you* who do not belong here. This is *my* home, and I will come and go as I please. I have brought you here to present an offer. An accord, if you will."

Christa stood, her back straight as she stared up at the face she had once worshiped. "I've seen what you give in return for favors. I'm not interested."

"But it is most impolite to refuse without hearing what the offer is, little morsel." He slid closer, claws raking furrows in the rock deep enough to bury her.

"It doesn't matter. Your offers only end one way," a foreign voice called out.

Christa spun to face a boy sliding down the slope in a half-controlled fall to crouch less than ten paces away. A human boy—and a filthy one at that—dressed in mud and sweat stained wool and animal skins. He stared at Ssanek with a defiance that mirrored her own.

"Ahh, son. So nice of you to join us." Ssanek showed none of the surprise Christa felt at this new addition. "I've been wanting to introduce you for so long. After all, you have so much in common. Christabel, meet Steven, my son. Son, this is Christabel, my most devoted servant."

"I'm *not* your son!" the boy yelled, walking to stand beside her.

"I'm not your servant!" Christa yelled at the same time.

She took an unconscious step away from the boy, but the fire in his azure eyes resonated with her somehow, as if there were something familiar about him that went beyond acquaintanceship. "And it doesn't matter. There's nothing you can give me."

"On the contrary, my pet, I can give you *everything*!" The word nearly knocked her to her knees. "I offer what you have always wanted. Power!"

Christa shook her head. "I've never wanted that. I've only wanted to help people."

The stones rumbled again as Ssanek laughed. "Truly? Is that why you scoured books for knowledge? Is that why you risked your friends lives to summon me? So you could help people? I can smell the magic in you, delectable treat, and it is strong. You could be powerful indeed. A ruler over those around you. I offer you dominion over everything you see!"

The air around her shimmered, and in a second she stood atop the Observatory, gazing down at the city around her, Ellsabae beyond, and still farther to the human lands in the west, to the mountains of the dwarves in the east. Even the kingdom of Anathonia fell under her gaze, and she knew it was all hers. Every soul under her command to live or die. Every decision, every judgment under her purview. She could change it all. She could punish those who deserved it and protect those who needed it. She could watch over them, guide them, help them.

"All of this can be yours, morsel," the gravelly voice whispered by her ear. "You have the power within you. They cannot stop you. They know it. They have already tried to lock you away once. They will try again. They call you *monster*. But I know what you really are. Beautiful. All you need to do is give yourself to the Fire. It knows what to do. It knows what it wants, what you want. Stop fighting and accept who you truly are."

Christa could see it all. Could see the justice she would bring. The wrongs she would right. The lives she would save. The Fire surged inside, begging, pleading, promising.

Steven shifted closer. "You don't know me," he whispered. "But I know him. I know what he does to people. What he did to my mother. His words are poison and they will destroy you. Please, listen to me."

Christa looked from Steven to Ssanek. "They wouldn't let me rule them."

"Perhaps some will not understand the good you do," Ssanek hissed softly. "But they are the ones inflicting the most harm. If they weren't, they would want what was best, too. They would realize *you* are what is best."

He was right. She could help them all. And if there were those, like Dalan, who could not see that . . .

"He's twisting the truth," Steven insisted. "No person could possibly know what was right for everyone. You're a better person than that, Christabel. You must be."

Ssanek barked a stone-splitting laugh. "You don't know her at all, son. She killed *her* mother when she was even younger than you. She's tasted power, reveled in it. Which is far more than I can say for your disappointing decisions."

"It doesn't matter what she's done, what matters is who she is."

Christa heard the argument faintly as the world below her wheeled and flashed. Of course she was a good person. That was why she would do what was best for everyone, wasn't it?

Of course, the Fire agreed. *That is why you tried to help Mama. When everyone else gave up on her, you kept trying.*

• *Whispers at the Altar* •

But had that ever been about Mama? Or was it her own guilt she had worked so hard to relieve?

No. It—

But she already knew the answer.

"No!" she screamed, silencing the argument around her. "I will not sit by and watch others suffer. And I *won't* be the cause of that suffering."

"Your world *is* suffering," Ssanek purred, his attention focused once more. "It only needs someone powerful enough to seize it. Control it. Direct it to the right ends."

Yes! Exactly!

But Christa had seen the Fire's lies. And Ssanek's. She shoved the Fire back, clamping it into the prison she made for it. The vision around her faded, replaced once again by the desolate landscape of Ssanek's domain.

"I don't want any of that." She turned to face Ssanek once more, barely registering the smile on Steven's face. "I don't need it."

There was a low rumble, whether a growl or a chuckle Christa could not tell.

"Then I do not need you." His eyes turned to Steven and thin lips pulled back over long fangs. "And thanks to my little servant here, I no longer need you, either."

There was barely a warning, hardly a hint of movement, before a roar of writhing shadow and bitter cold shot from Ssanek's mouth like a tidal wave. Christa only had time to flinch away and try to surround herself with a bubble of air.

Ssanek's attack shred through her meager shield like paper. Yet still it did not strike her.

Lowering her arm, she saw the shadow boil around her, beating itself against a barrier that flashed opalescent with each impact. She turned to see Steven standing upright, eyes closed, his hands raised in defiance of the serpent as white light spread from his open fingers.

Christa gaped but only for a moment. It wasn't possible. Humans couldn't use magic. Everything she had been taught by the elves con-

537

firmed it. But whether they could or not, this stranger had bought them precious time she could not allow to be wasted.

She uncaged the Fire and unleashed it in a burst up into what she hoped was Ssanek's open mouth. There was a high shriek of pain as the torrent of darkness ended, replaced only by the searing line of flame spewing from her own hands. She had a glimpse of Ssanek's head whipping back and forth to avoid her fire. She tried to track it and managed several sweeping passes over his neck and wings before Steven's shout alerted her to the real danger.

All about them, wherever Ssanek's dark breath had touched, the ground twisted and writhed with umbral snakes. They pressed against Steven's shield on all sides, and already it was buckling.

Christa's attack faltered, and Ssanek seized his advantage, bringing both claws down in crushing sweeps upon her.

With a grunt, Christa seized the Essence of the rocks around them, throwing them up and over them both in a dome and tossing shadow snakes like weeds in the wind.

Steven's shield fell, and blackness came with it.

Then the first blow struck the dome, and cracks the size of Christa's arm splintered through it. The second blow shattered the dome completely, sending it crashing down upon them. Christa fell into Steven and they both lost their footing. She twisted to avoid one slab but didn't even see the boulder that crushed her left ankle and pinned her in place as the shadow snakes renewed their attack.

Christa screamed in pain. After the Arkius Stone she wouldn't have thought she had any screams left.

Desperate, she groped through the pain to the Essence, seized the earth with both hands, and shoved against it with all the strength she could muster. The rock she and Steven lay on, and everything immediately surrounding it, shot away from Ssanek, just as another claw came whistling down to gouge where they had been only a breath before.

Whispers at the Altar

As rubble flew into the air, a lance of blinding light shot from Steven's hands. The light arced across the space they covered, tearing through Ssanek's wing to carve into the body beyond it.

They came to rest an arrow's flight away as Ssanek roared once more, the high-pitched cry filled with pain and frustration. The enormous wings beat, and he took to the sky, disappearing into the heavy clouds above.

"Are you all right?" Steven whispered hoarsely.

Christa stared at him.

"Oh, of course not," he said as he saw the rock crushing her. "Here, let me help. I'm sure he'll be back soon." He knelt and tried to get his fingers under the rock to lift it off.

Christa shook her head. Whoever he was, he had determination. "Stop. Just stop. And keep an eye out for him." She pushed his hands away then reached into the Essence of the boulder and, with a grunt of pain, lifted it off. A flick of one hand sent it flying across the valley, then she leaned over to examine the ankle as best she could without moving it.

"Oh." Steven alternated between looking at her, her ankle, and the sky.

"I should have smelled the magic in you, boy." Ssanek's rumbling hiss came out of the clouds, echoing around the valley and making it impossible to tell where it came from. "He is breaking the rules. Humans were to be left untouched. Mine."

"We aren't yours," Steven shouted at the sky. "We never will be. We'd rather die."

Definitely a possible outcome, Christa thought. She looked across the valley to see the snakes slowly dissipating. Even so, she couldn't move, and Steven obviously had little idea what he was doing with his apparently newfound powers.

Still . . . they fared better than Christa would have thought. Steven had actually injured him, and she had seen the scorch marks her own attack had left on Ssanek's body. If they could keep him still, they might be able to win. As long as they did it before fatigue made her useless.

They had to end this fast.

"Then you will die, boy. An eternal death bleeding atop my altar, the same as your mother. The magic in your blood will be the catalyst to make me even stronger."

Honovi scrabbled against the skeletal ground, trying to find something to grab hold of as her eyes searched wildly for some help. She saw her father pressed back into the water step by step by the Seer's assault. She saw another explosion of fire and shattered trees, this time much closer to the shoreline. And she saw Steven, standing atop the altar.

She barely had time to even question this before he reached up and touched Ssanek, and fell.

Like a cast off waterskin, he dropped and rolled over the side, colliding with one of the Chosen as it climbed up. They both hit the ground with a sickening crunch, and neither moved.

Honovi's heart tore apart, and she screamed with the pain of it. Grabbing the nearest bone, some poor victim's leg, she channeled all that pain and rage as she swung down at the tentacles holding her. When those let go, she beat the body they were attached to. Again and again, she swung. When the bone broke, she stabbed its splintered end into the Chosen's pallid flesh. Over and over.

When she finally stood, the body was limp and lifeless.

She tossed the bare stub of bone away, and ran to snatch up her spear. She turned, only to see her father fall back into the water, his chest and arms torn and bleeding in half a dozen places. The Seer stood over him, one arm nearly severed, though it didn't bleed, and the other umbral sheathed claw raised. Three hunters ran through the lake to help them, but it would all be over before they arrived. One way or the other.

A whistle of air was all the warning Christa and Steven had before Ssanek dropped out of the clouds, his wings folded as he streaked toward the ground.

A small cry of surprise escaped Christa's mouth before she threw her hands up focusing enough to throw the air around her at him, anything to slow Ssanek's descent.

Steven's hands rose as well, the same light radiating out until it nearly blinded her.

Ssanek's wings snapped open at the last minute, arresting his fall just as his massive tail swung forward.

The crash of its impact was deafening.

Steven dropped to his knees as cracks formed in the shield he had made.

Christa pushed as hard as she could but couldn't make the air coalesce fast enough. Her shield collapsed around her, the air just slipping through her fingers.

Ssanek's bulk fell to the ground like an earthquake, his long claws once again hammering onto them. His jaw snapped forward to grind long white fangs against Steven's shield, sending flashes of golden light down his wide winding gullet.

Impact after impact echoed across the shield as Steven screamed with the effort of maintaining the shattering barrier.

Christa laid one hand on his back, anything to show him she was still there, as she used the other to send stream after stream of fire at Ssanek. Each time he twisted out of the way, only to coil back, a claw flashing forward, or teeth snapping at them.

"Would. You. Hold. Still!" With a cry Christa let the Fire loose. It poured out of her, eager to be free. Eager to burn. It spread in a wave that charred rock and seared scales as it roared past and over Ssanek.

A monstrous scream echoed off the mountains as Ssanek's wings disintegrated, and his scales blistered and broke. Then, with a final swing of its now naked arms, it tore Steven's weakened shield apart. The shining barrier shattered like glass and the shards flew to the far edges of the valley.

Honovi had no battle cry to scream as she charged. Her heart was too pained, her mind too worn. But she screamed anyway. A wordless voicing of every hurt and pain she had ever suffered by Ssanek or his servants. She was still screaming as the Seer's claws ripped across her father's belly.

And then it turned to face her.

She moved the spear through every routine she knew, every one Father taught her. The slender haft whistled and flexed as it spun and thrust, but the Seer was faster. And now, without the arrows of the hunters as a distraction, it could focus entirely on her.

Honovi ducked under the swipe of a claw, swept her spear across, rolled right, feinted a thrust then brought the head down, only to be met by another ebony shield that sent waves of cold shooting through her arm as her blade struck it.

She sped up her attacks, the spear a blur in front of her that even she could barely track and barely control. The Seer hissed and spat as it struggled to keep pace with her, but even she knew she could not maintain this pace for long.

She slipped on an arrow and nearly lost her footing entirely. There was barely time to roll to the side before the shadow shards sizzled into the ground where her feet had been. She immediately launched back into her attack, slower now as fatigue and the biting cold of the Seer's barriers took hold. The Seer barely attacked at all now. Most likely content to wait her out, confident she was nearly spent.

He wasn't wrong, but now she had an idea.

She shifted her attacks into a routine favoring her right hand. He batted them aside easily, but she kept at it, thrusting across at his limp right arm while she stepped slowly toward her target. Slowly she pulled the haft of the spear back, her grip shifting further and further forward.

Then, when she reached the discarded bow, she brought the spear back with a smooth twist and let it fly, straight for the Seer's chest.

It tossed the weapon casually aside, sensing her weakness and eager to finish. But she was already kneeling, bow in hand and its quiver at her side. It didn't see the arrow flying behind the spear. Or the one behind that.

The first took it in the chest, staggering it backward. It batted aside the second, but the third slipped through its claw, while the fourth pierced its shoulder. Another through its chest. Another through its throat.

Honovi didn't stop firing until the quiver was empty.

Christa gasped for breath and leaned against Steven who panted beside her. Ssanek stood over them, smoke rising from the burns in his flesh, but still very much alive.

"Did you really think you could win, little morsel? You gave me the rift-blood that made me strong. You severed my ties to this empty world. And now I will devour you both. Your blood will make me even more powerful. In the end you will understand that all you have done is hastened the deaths of those you love. Your people, all of them, will be mine."

"You will *not* kill anyone else," Steven panted, his voice rising with each word. His hand rose and a blinding flash of light tore out, striking Ssanek full in the chest and throwing him back with the impact.

"And you will not lay a finger on my people," Christa said, rising to her knees despite the pain shooting through her leg. "*Either* of them!" With a slash of one hand the floor of the valley broke, tearing free from itself to tilt down into a chasm of nothingness. Rocks of all sizes slid down in a growing avalanche that pummeled Ssanek.

The monster clawed frantically at the shifting ground, fell, caught himself with one claw, and began dragging itself back up.

"Steven, pin him down. Use that shield, but on him. *Now*."

He screamed with the effort, but the shield materialized. Not as a dome, but a cage of prismatic light flashing with color reflected in Ssanek's few undamaged scales.

"I can't hold it!" he cried. And even as it formed, Christa could see parts of it flicker uncertainly.

Christa looked into the sky and the thunderclouds above. She would have to work quickly. With both hands raised, she reached into the cloud's Essence and pulled the little drops together. Slowly at first, then faster and faster until she couldn't hold the ball of water together any longer. Then she let it go, and as it fell she pressed against it, crushing the slick beads together until they couldn't move at all. Until they were no longer water. Until they froze.

The shard of ice hurtled down to Ssanek's prison like a spearhead thrown by the Creator himself.

It shot through the bars of light, pierced Ssanek's body, and sank into the rock before shattering into a million slivers that sliced into skin left bare by charred scales.

Whispers at the Altar

Another followed, and another, as Christa reached into the fertile fields of water above her. Until Steven collapsed in exhaustion and his cage faded into nothing,

The last spear of ice shattered across Ssanek's horned head, pounding his jaw into the rock, and Christa fell with it. She crouched there at the edge of the cliff, looking down at Ssanek as he lay pinned to its face by the spears impaled through his body.

Their eyes met, and Christa could feel him pleading.

You could be so powerful. I could give it to you. Everything you've always wanted. I could give you your mother. Think of her. Imagine her walking beside you again. Your whole family . . . together again.

"I *am* thinking of Mama," she whispered, then reached into the spears of ice and set the water free. The ice melted, setting Ssanek's broken body free to tumble down the slide.

You will wish your decision had been different, little traitor. He said as he fell. *One day soon, you will weep as you wish it, and all you will find is death.* Smoke swirled around him, wrapping around his form like a cloak.

I did not lie, Christabel Sellers. I showed you your future. I gave you a chance to change it. That chance will not come again. Take your choice! And rot with it!

The edge she crouched on broke. Steven reached for her hand, then they both tumbled through darkness. Boulders crashed against her and she screamed at every impact, every breaking bone. The rocks shattered every part of her, grinding her down to nothing. All that remained was the pain, constant and unbearable. It filled the blackness.

She came to an agonizing rest after what seemed an eternity of falling. There was something else. She felt it through the pain. Something in her hand, if she still had a hand. But she must. She could feel it there, biting into her clenched fist.

A ring.

545

She clutched it in front of her face. She couldn't move, couldn't breathe. The rock pressed down on her, suffocating her. Straining, tears squeezed out with the effort, she inched one finger open.

Light poured out, illuminating the blackness of her tomb and a face pressed inches from her own.

Calm and serene, Mama's face gazed at her through the light her ring poured out between them. She smiled, and Christa *felt* something from her. Love, pride, encouragement. And through them all, like the harmony in her favorite song, forgiveness. It filled Christa up, washing away the pain and worry until the whole world was just the two of them.

Slowly, Mama reached out to place her hand on Christa's, and slowly the light faded. Until Christa could barely make out her sapphire eyes. And as they too vanished, the world lurched around her once again.

A Hawk

Honovi dropped the bow as Ssanek began to scream above them. The keening wail pierced into her mind and sent images of ruined towns, blackened fields and charnel cities careening before her eyes in waves she couldn't stop. She pressed her hands to her eyes and bent double as the sound and nightmarish images invaded her.

Then, with a blast that knocked her sideways, the altar exploded. And as suddenly as the sound began, it stopped. Or rather, all sound stopped. When she finally opened her eyes, there was no scream of the dying, no hiss of snakes, only a high painful ringing.

She struggled back to her knees, remembering her father. She searched frantically around the clearing, now filled with the smoking remains of enormous snakes, and saw Hareb's body not far away. She stumbled to it and fell to her knees beside it. She thanked the Great Watcher his head had not fallen into the water. She put her ear to his chest and, after a moment of panic, heard his heart beating weakly.

A hunter ran up beside her, yelling something she couldn't hear. She shook her head, then gestured to Hareb's body, and together they lifted the man up. Another hunter ran out of the swamp, Brogan close behind, and Honovi gave a weak smile. They had not all died. But the sight of Brogan's frantic eyes as he surveyed the devastation reminded her of what Ssanek's death had driven from her mind.

Steven.

Christa gasped for air. For a second she saw the throne room and people crowded around her. She even felt the Stone of Trials fall from her hand. Then she was buried again. She fought, pushing back arms she could swear were cadaverous, but as the realization of where she was began to sink in she gladly collapsed into her friends.

Every part of her hurt. Every inch was exhausted. She let her friends hold her, half-listened to their congratulations and their sympathy, and gave in to the fatigue consuming her. Over Sinna's shoulder, she could just make out Silvana's beaming face, her smile breaking into a small laugh before she waved and turned away.

Honovi jerked awake as Steven stirred on the makeshift bed of moss and branches. She leaned forward and watched his eyes flutter open for the first time in days.

"Welcome back," she whispered.

He smiled faintly. "It's good to *be* back. How . . . how long?"

"Two days. Ever since Ssanek's defeat."

He sighed deeply and his gaze strayed up to the sky.

Honovi inched closer and took his hand gently in hers.

"Did everyone..." Steven looked over at her, the question obvious in his eyes.

"Six of the hunters fell. My father was severely wounded."

Steven's eyes widened, and Honovi placed a calming hand on his chest. "Brogan has been attending him as he has you. He will live and have impressive scars to tell stories about to his grandchildren." Honovi winked, but the joke fell flat as Steven barely smiled.

"Something happened," Honovi guessed. "On the altar. I saw you touch him."

He nodded. "I went... somewhere. I met her. The servant he spoke of. He was... testing her. Tempting her."

"What happened?"

He shrugged. "She refused. He tried to kill us. It's strange. She didn't even look human. I mean she was, and she wasn't. And her hair was all white." He chuckled dryly, "And she could do the most incredible things. Magic."

Honovi scowled. "Perhaps it is good that you only see this mystery woman in your dreams."

Steven started to laugh, then winced in pain.

"Serves you right. Leaving me in the mud worrying over your broken body while you go off to slay a god with some magical, white-haired woman."

Steven nearly doubled over in pain as he tried to stop laughing. Which in itself was very inconsiderate. Couldn't he tell how perfectly serious she was?

Christa spent the next week in the infirmary. Marellel wanted to make sure there was no lasting damage from the Arkius removal. Not to mention the numerous other mysterious wounds that had sprouted upon her body during her confrontation with Ssanek.

Christa didn't mind a bit. There were no chores, no demands, and though her dreams sometimes returned to that desolate battlefield, nothing hid there to torment her. She refused to believe what Ssanek said. Her future was hers. There was no way it could know.

She was an Eyas again. It seemed her choices during the test, and refusal of Ssanek's offer, were proof enough of her loyalty. Though there *was* some debate as to whether that was actually part of the test. Christa let them believe whatever they wanted.

There was no grand ceremony of reinstatement. No visit from the queen. Instead Sinna told her. She came most days, sometimes with Westrel, and sometimes alone. But Kadin was always there. At least as often as the Healers would allow it. He brought her books and sat with her as she read. He even managed to find a book on how to communicate with your hands, and they both practiced in silence punctuated by muffled laughter.

By the end of the week, Christa had to force herself to get out of bed.

"Come on lazy bones," Westrel called, yanking the sheets off her. "I can't believe you would rather sleep than go to graduation."

"I've never gone to graduation," Christa groaned, pulling the pillow over her head.

"Maybe so, but you have never had a friend graduating."

Christa threw the pillow off. "Sinna!" How could she have forgotten?

"Exactly. Now hurry up and get dressed. I will meet you in the throne room by the east entrance."

Christa practically threw her clothes on. As it was she had to stop at the fountain to run her hands through her hair and make sure she didn't look a complete mess before running into the throne room.

" . . . know your duty," the queen was saying from in front of her throne.

Whispers at the Altar

Christa slipped just inside with Westrel and watched from the back. She could see Sinna standing along with four others directly before the throne. The same spot Christa had occupied a week before.

"You have shown both the Secretary of Intelligence and myself, that you process the ability, the discipline, and the principles to be entrusted with this duty. And so I name you the eyes, ears, and hands of the Crown's will. Welcome, Hawks."

There was a thunder of applause as each received their cloaks, and then the ceremony was over. Christa fought through the crowd that pressed around the graduates, jumping up and down as she waved for Sinna.

"Christa! You came."

"Of course I did," she said, wrapping Sinna in a hug.

"She wouldn't have missed it," Westrel said and gave Christa a wink.

"I'm glad you could make it. I was—"

"It is good to see you all together again."

They turned to see Queen Elisidel standing beside them with a wide smile on her face, and they immediately dropped into curtsies.

"Please . . ." she waved them up. "Congratulations, Sinnasarel. I understand you will be staying with us for a time."

"Yes, your M-M-Majesty. As an instructor."

"That is good to hear. But I wouldn't get too comfortable. I may have some business of my own for you soon."

Sinna's face reddened.

"T-thank you. Anything you n-n-need me for . . . I'd be happy to . . ."

The queen placed a hand on Sinna's shoulder. "We will discuss it later in more privacy. Do you think I could borrow Christabel for a moment?"

Sinna blinked, looking at Christa in surprise. "Well . . . yes."

"Thank you. I won't keep her long. I am sure you three have a lot of celebrating planned." She walked away, and Christa hurried to catch up.

"I wanted to tell you how proud I am of you for what you accomplished last week," Queen Elisidel said as they walked to the edges of the crowd.

Christa shrugged. "I just did my best."

"And proved some powerful people wrong in the process."

Christa said nothing. She hadn't seen Dalan since that day and was perfectly happy keeping it that way.

"I also wanted to ask you if you wanted to talk about what happened during the final . . . test."

Christa bit her lip and looked away. "It was just a test."

The queen smiled, her black eyes sparkling. "Indeed? You know, I have always been a student of history. The beast who tempted you, the one you fought, it looked rather familiar."

Christa considered. "I honestly don't know what happened, Your Majesty. Perhaps the stone picked an image from my own mind to use against me. That is what the Stone of Trials is said to do, isn't it? Perhaps I was simply slaying my own demons."

"Perhaps." The queen did not appear convinced. "And you won?"

Christa walked in silence for a moment as she thought about that. Ssanek's offer *had* been tempting, and she couldn't deny that a part of her still wanted what he offered. To have Mama here with her, to walk with her. To dance with her again. Christa knew that would never happen, but for the first time the thought didn't feel like a knife stabbing through her heart. It still hurt, as Uncle said it would, but the ache was covered by something else.

Peace?

"Yes," she said at last. "I think I did."

Vaniel...

She walked through dark corridors filled with flitting shadows. It was night, and she was dreaming. She'd had this dream a hundred times since Christabel's test.

Vaniel...

Every time she could hear someone calling her name, but she could never find them.

I know what you want, Vaniel...

She paced through empty hallways, opened every door. Whoever it was, she had to find him. He had something she needed. She knew it. Something to help her teach Christabel a lesson. But the sound was always so faint.

And I can give it to you...

So soft.

Like a snake hissing in the dark.

Steven tipped the last shovel of earth over the grave, then planted it into the ground.

"Do you want some time alone?" Honovi asked, taking his hand and squeezing it tightly.

Something had changed since the altar. She rarely let go of him anymore. Sometimes he would even catch her with tears in her eyes after she hugged him, though she would never have admitted it.

"No. Thank you."

Of course he'd be lying if he said he hadn't changed as well. Nearly dying would do that, he supposed. But it was all over. Honovi had told him Ssanek had vanished in the altar's explosion. Of course Steven had seen him suffer another fate, but the point was that he was gone.

There had been no trace of Soldiers or Chosen as they made their way out of the swamp, and by the end of the week the clouds had even cleared enough for them to see the sun—a fact that made even Hareb cheerful.

"Steven!"

He turned to see Brogan limping up the hill from his half-rebuilt shack.

"Hareb's back with the lumber," Brogan yelled. "Make yourself useful, and help him unload it. I'd like to actually have four walls by tonight if it isn't too much trouble."

Steven chuckled and swung the shovel up onto his shoulder. "You go down, Honovi. I'll be right there."

She nodded and ran down the hill.

He watched her go, enjoying the way the sun flashed off her wild hair. He reached out a hand to pat the tree. "I'm going to marry her, Mother. And I'm going to be good to her. Like someone should have been to you." He sighed. "I think you would have liked her. But at least, here, you can watch your family grow. And maybe, one day, you can be happy, too."

Acknowledgements

Jason Jack Miller, a mentor and friend, once said of this book that, "One does not create a story like this casually, or by accident..." I couldn't agree more. Its creation depended on too many other people. In fact, more people than I can count have contributed to this achievement, but I would like to take a moment to thank as many as I can.

The story of Christabel Sellers goes back over two decades, to a text based, online role-playing game or MUSH. That was where Christa took her first steps, where she met her friends, Sinna, Weste, and Kayne, and where I first started to believe that some version of her adventures might make a good story. And so, to all the players and staff of the Cuendillar and Heroes of the Wheel MUSHes, but especially those closest friends, thank you. I hope this book finds its way into your hands and that you enjoy all the little references I've hidden inside.

But the bulk of this story was formed many years afterward in the halls of Seton Hill University, and among the numerous talented writers of its Writing Popular Fiction Masters program. From my mentors, Jason Jack Miller and Paul Goat Allen, who taught me so much about writing and were so generous with their time, to all the writers who ever critiqued a chapter in a workshop. This book wouldn't be what it is without your help. And, of course the other founders of "Team Avatar": Mary, Deb, and Vanessa. The value of your insight and hours spent listening to me rambling about things like the intricacies of elven culture cannot be underestimated.

Of course, the production of this book may never have happened without the support of a brave few who supported an unknown author with their own hard earned money. To my Patreon and Kickstarter supporters (in no particular order)… Brant Finstad, Jason Nelson, Jonathan Zysett, Angela, Lee Habig, James Butcher, Amanda M. Ecret, Chris Basler, Mike Maroon, Bryan McCausland, Chris Phillips, Chad Bowden, Susan Jessen, Jeff Cornelius, J. D. Cook, John Kitsteiner, Denise Bradley, Shane Warren, and Carrie Gesner. A heart-felt thank you. I owe you more than whatever reward you got.

Lastly, and perhaps most importantly, I would like to thank my family. All of whom have sacrificed something to help me reach this dream. I will never be able to thank you enough. I love you all!

About the Author

Allan Cornelius has been creating Fantasy and Science Fiction worlds to play in since he started his first gaming group in high school. Along the way he has accumulated four degrees, including an Associates in Space Systems Technology and a Master of Fine Arts in Writing Popular Fiction from Seton Hill University. He currently lives in Colorado Springs with his wife and family and can often be found at the annual Pikes Peak Writers Conference. Whispers at the Altar is his first novel.

CPSIA information can be obtained
at www.ICGtesting.com
Printed in the USA
FSOW01n1535250717
36583FS